MARILYN'S
LAST SESSIONS

MARILYN'S LAST SESSIONS

a novel

MICHEL SCHNEIDER

**Translated from the French
by Will Hobson**

CANONGATE

Edinburgh · London · New York · Melbourne

First published in Great Britain in 2011 by
Canongate Books Ltd, 14 High Street,
Edinburgh EH1 1TE

1

Copyright © Michel Schneider, 2006
English translation copyright © Will Hobson, 2011

First published as *Marilyn dernières séances* in France in 2006
by Editions Grasset, 61 rue des Saints-Pères, 75006 Paris

www.canongate.tv

*The publisher acknowledges subsidy from the Scottish Arts Council
towards the publication of this volume.*

*This book is supported by the French Ministry of Foreign Affairs,
as part of the Burgess programme run by the Cultural Department of the
French Embassy in London (www.frenchbooknews.com).*

For text permissions, please see page 403

British Library Cataloguing-in-Publication Data
A catalogue record for this book is available on
request from the British Library

ISBN 978 1 84767 036 6

Typeset by Palimpsest Book Production Ltd,
Falkirk, Stirlingshire

Printed and bound by CPI Group (UK) Ltd, Croydon, CR0 4YY

To Marilyn

'There's always two sides to a story.'
Marilyn Monroe

New York, April 1955. The writer Truman Capote is at a funeral with Marilyn Monroe.

MARILYN: 'Seriously, though. It's my hair. I need colour. And I didn't have time to get any. It was all so unexpected, Miss Collier dying and all. See?'

She lifts her kerchief slightly to display a fringe of darkness where her hair is parted.

TC: 'Poor innocent me. And all this time I thought you were a bona-fide blonde.'

MARILYN: 'I am. But nobody's that natural. And, incidentally, fuck you.'

Like Marilyn's hair, this novel is a phoney of the bona-fide kind. It is inspired by actual events and, except where changes have been made to respect the privacy of the living, its characters appear under their real names. Locations are accurate, dates verified, and quotations from accounts, notes, letters, articles, conversations, books and films are the protagonists' own.

But it is a work of fiction. The forger in me hasn't hesitated to impute to one person what another has said, seen or experienced, to ascribe to them a diary that hasn't been found, articles or notes that have been invented, and dreams and thoughts for which there is no source.

In telling this story, a loveless love story of two characters who became fatally embroiled in each other's lives, my aim is not to find the truth, or probable truth, about Marilyn Monroe and her last analyst Ralph Greenson, but to observe a couple in the act of being themselves, and register their uncanniness as if it spoke to me of my own.

Los Angeles, Downtown, West 1st Street
August 2005

REWIND

Rewind the tape. Rerun the story. Replay Marilyn's last session. The end: that's always where a story starts. I love movies that open with a voiceover. There's almost nothing on screen – a pool with a body floating in it, the tops of some palm trees stirring in the wind, a naked woman under a blue sheet, splinters of glass in a half-light – and someone's talking to himself so as not to feel utterly alone. A man on the run, a private detective, a doctor – a psychoanalyst, why not? – looking back, telling the story of his life. He says what's killing him so you'll know what he lived for. 'Listen to me because I'm you,' his voice seems to say. It's always the voice that makes the story, not what it says.

I'm going to try to tell this story. Our story. My story. It would be an ugly little tale even if you could get rid of the ending. A woman, already half dead, drags along a sad little girl by the hand. She takes her to see the head doctor, the words doctor. He gives her his time, tells her her time is up, then listens to her with a sort of abject love for two and half years. He doesn't understand a word she says and ends up losing her. Such a sad, grim story. Nothing could lighten its weight of melancholy, not even the smile that seemed to be Marilyn's way of apologising for being so beautiful.

The title of this unfinished piece of writing was underlined three times. Handwritten and undated, it was found on his death among the papers of Dr Ralph Greenson, Marilyn Monroe's last psycho-analyst. His was the voice that Sergeant Jack Clemmons, watch commander at West Los Angeles Police Department, had heard on the night of 4–5 August 1962 when a call had come in from Brentwood at four twenty-five a.m.

'Marilyn Monroe has died of an overdose,' a man's voice had said dully. And when the stunned policeman had asked, 'What?' the same voice had struggled to repeat, virtually spelling it out syllable by syllable, 'Marilyn Monroe has died. She has committed suicide.'

REWIND

The city seems to John Miner to sweat even more in August than it used to in spring. Pollution casts a pink veil wherever he looks and, even in the glare of the midday sun, the streets have a fuzziness to them, like the sepia haze of an old movie. Los Angeles strikes him as even more unreal than it had done forty years earlier. More metallic. More naked. More null and void. His eyes still smarting from downtown's murky, oppressive reek, he enters the journalist Forger W. Backwright's office in the *Los Angeles Times* building at 202 West 1st Street. Tall and stooped, he looks around constantly, as though he were lost. An old man of eighty-six come to tell an old story.

As head of the medical-legal section at the District Attorney's Office, Miner had attended the autopsy on Marilyn Monroe's body conducted by Dr Thomas Noguchi, the coroner who, six years afterwards, would perform the same procedure for Robert Kennedy, one of the people suspected, by those who believed such things, of organising Monroe's murder. Miner had observed smears being taken from the actress's mouth, genitals and anus. The autopsy's principal discovery was the mysterious presence in her blood of 4.5 milligrams of a barbiturate, Nembutal, for which no sign of injection or oral ingestion could be found. It returned a verdict of 'probable suicide', an expression Miner has turned over in his mind ever since. They used that wording in the final report; initial accounts spoke merely of 'suicide' or 'possible suicide'. Of course, you'd say it was probable if you looked at the case from a purely psychological point of view, Miner has always thought, but that doesn't mean the star hadn't spent thirty-six years committing this probable suicide, or that a criminal hadn't been employed to do the actual deed. He thinks of other expressions to describe what had happened: 'foul play' or, as Dr Litman of the Suicide Prevention Team had put it, 'a gamble with death'.

REWIND

Given the choice, the long-since-retired Miner would simply play the journalist one of the tapes Marilyn had recorded for her analyst at the end of July or the start of August 1962. Ralph Greenson had labelled them 'MARILYN: LAST SESSIONS', and Miner had listened to them and transcribed them forty-three years previously, but never seen or heard of them since. They had vanished during the analyst's lifetime – or after his death, who could tell? The only trace left of them is the summaries Miner has made in his meticulous lawyer's handwriting, and so, after greeting the journalist, he shakily holds out a sheaf of crumpled pages from a yellow legal pad. Backwright tells him to sit down, and gives him a glass of iced water.

'What makes you want to speak to the press after all these years?' the journalist asks.

'Ralph Greenson was a good man,' says Miner. 'I knew him well, before his patient died. When I studied medicine before taking up criminal law, I attended his psychiatry lectures and seminars at UCLA. I respected him – I still do. He fascinated me.

'Two days after Marilyn Monroe's death, he asked me to interview him because he wanted to go back over his initial statements to the police. He was very worried at being portrayed in the papers as "the weird psychiatrist" and "the last man to have seen Marilyn alive and the first to have seen her dead". He insisted I listen to two tapes she had given him on the last day of her life, Saturday, August fourth 1962. He left them with me to transcribe on condition that I never revealed the contents to anyone, even the district attorney or the coroner. I had too many unanswered questions after the autopsy not to want to examine any new evidence, however difficult I might find his request to respect its confidentiality.'

'Where and when did you meet him?'

'I spent several hours with the psychiatrist on Wednesday, August eighth, after he had attended the actress's funeral.'

'And you've never discussed your conversation with anyone?'

'I remember what he said when the rumours started,' Miner says, his voice trembling. '"I can't explain or defend myself without speaking about things that I don't want to reveal. It's a terrible position to be in, to say I can't talk about it. I just can't tell the whole story." That's why I didn't reveal the content of the tapes, out of respect. It was only when biographers began rehashing old accusations of violence, or even murder, that I decided to speak out. But I didn't disclose everything, as I would have liked to. I decided to get his widow Hildi Greenson's permission before I went back to my notes and showed them to you.'

Forger Backwright reminds him that Hildegarde Greenson had assured the *Los Angeles Times* she'd never heard her husband talk of any tapes and knew nothing of their existence. Miner replies that Greenson was very strict about medical confidentiality.

'I have kept this secret for Greenson's sake. I'm breaking my promise only now because he has been dead for over twenty-five years and because I pledged his widow not to leave unanswered all those people who have tried to implicate Marilyn Monroe's last analyst in her death. Some have spoken of criminal negligence. I have decided to make these tapes public to respond to all the accusations that have sullied the reputation of a man I respected.'

REWIND

In the muggy, sweltering heat of another Californian August, in front of another tape recorder, Miner, with a mixture of hesitancy and vehemence in his voice, tells the journalist about his visit to Dr Greenson in August 1962. He had found a grief-stricken, unshaven figure in the ground-floor consulting room of his villa overlooking the Pacific. Greenson had spoken freely, as if he were a trusted confidant. He had asked Miner to sit down and, without preamble, played him a tape lasting forty minutes. Marilyn was talking. It was her voice on the tape. Nothing else. No hint of anyone listening or any conversation. Just her, alone. Her voice seemed to hover on the edge of her words – out of discretion, rather than fragility, as if she were leaving them to fend for themselves, to be heard or not, as the case might be. A voice from beyond the grave that entered into one with the incalculable immediacy of voices heard in dreams.

It couldn't be a therapy session, Miner explains, because the psychiatrist didn't record his patients. He says Marilyn purchased a tape recorder a few weeks earlier to record herself free-associating outside her sessions and share the results with her analyst.

Miner had taken very detailed verbatim notes that day. He had come away from Greenson's office convinced it was highly improbable Marilyn had committed suicide. 'Among other things,' he says, 'it was clear that she had plans and expectations for her immediate future.'

'What about Dr Greenson?' Backwright asks. 'Did he think she had committed suicide or been murdered?'

'That is something on which I cannot respond. All I can say is that in the report I subsequently had to make to my superior, I maintained that the doctor did not believe his patient had killed herself. As far as I remember, I wrote something like: "As requested by you I have been to see Dr Greenson to discuss the death of his late patient Marilyn Monroe. We discussed this matter for a period of hours, and as a result of what Dr Greenson told me, and from what I heard on tape recordings, I believe I can say definitely that it was not suicide." Then I sent it in. It was never acknowledged, and the case was closed ten days later, on August seventeenth. My memorandum disappeared.'

REWIND

After another glass of iced water, Miner goes on.

'There was one question Dr Greenson didn't give me a clear answer to the day I saw him: why did he call it suicide at first if he was convinced it wasn't one? There's a simple answer to that, but it's taken me years to work out: he called it suicide *on the telephone* in the dead woman's house, because he knew the whole place was bugged—'

'Okay, so Greenson probably wasn't a murderer,' Backwright interrupts, 'but couldn't he have played a part in covering up a murder by making it look like suicide for reasons we don't know?'

Miner says nothing.

'Who killed Marilyn if she didn't herself?' persists the journalist.

'That's not the question I ask. Not *who* but *what* killed

8

Marilyn. The movies, mental illness, psychoanalysis, money, politics?' Miner stands up. As he leaves, he puts two faded, battered manila envelopes on Backwright's desk.

'I can't give you proof of anything. I heard what she said. The voice she said it in has . . . how can I put it? . . . has been lost. Every trace a person leaves erases another trace or, if they're lying, covers one up. There is something I can leave you, though. Something that doesn't prove anything either. Some images.'

Backwright waits until he is alone in front of his computer to open the envelopes. He has to write an article that night about the circumstances in which the tapes have come into his possession: they are going to run the contents in tomorrow's edition. The first envelope contains a single photograph of a body on a table in a morgue. A vision of white on white: a naked, bruised blonde, her face unrecognisable. The second contains six pictures taken a few days before the first photograph, at the Cal-Neva Lodge, a luxurious motel on the border between California and Nevada. They show Marilyn on all-fours having sex with a man who laughs into the camera as he lifts up the shock of hair covering the left side of her face.

REWIND
Hunched with age, Miner walks down the stairs of the *Los Angeles Times* building and, confused about the way out, finds himself lost in a basement smelling of musty ink. Forty-three years have passed since Marilyn's death, and twenty-three since the Los Angeles County District Attorney's Office reopened the archives, combed through the evidence all over again, and then confirmed the verdict of the original investigation. Miner can't bear to leave the actress's memory to a cult, to the fans from all over the world who gather every day at her crypt in Westwood Village Memorial Park. He's never believed that Marilyn took her own life, but neither has he come out and said the contrary. Years have passed, and he doesn't want to die without putting

something right, without showing the world the image that the tapes reveal of a woman full of life, of humour, of desire – anything but depressive or suicidal. Miner knows from experience that people who are full of drive and hope one minute can kill themselves in an efficient, resolute manner the next; that one can want to stop living without wanting to die; and that a longing for death is sometimes just a desire to put an end to the pain of living rather than life itself. But he refuses to believe these contradictions applied to Marilyn. Something in the tapes tells him she couldn't have killed herself.

But there is something he cares about even more. The endless profusion of theories has convinced him that no one will ever know for sure who killed her or why. What he knows *can* be cleared up, what has made him go public with the recordings, is Greenson's role on the night of the murder. Miner remains haunted by the psychiatrist's silence, by his expression of utter dismay as he stared out of the picture window of his Santa Monica villa at the swimming-pool bathed in the fluorescent purple evening light. He had felt compelled to ask, 'Forgive me, but what was she to you? Just a patient? What were you to her?'

'She had become my child, my pain, my sister, my madness,' Greenson had replied in a murmur, as if he were quoting something.

REWIND

Miner hasn't come to see Forger Backwright to provide him with a key to the conspiracy, an answer to the question that torments FBI Special Agent Dale Cooper in David Lynch's *Twin Peaks*: 'Who killed Marilyn Monroe?' He has come to lay another question to rest: what happened in those thirty months when Greenson and Marilyn were swept up by the insane passion of an analysis that overstepped all its boundaries?

Los Angeles, West Sunset Boulevard
January 1960

At the end of his life, Dr Greenson still vividly remembered the first time he was summoned to Marilyn Monroe's bedside.

'We looked at each other like creatures from different species, who are so alien to one another, who so obviously have no business being together, their first instinct is just to turn and walk away. Her so beautiful, me nothing to write home about. The diaphanous blonde and Freud's doctor of darkness – what a couple! But now I can see all that was just on the surface. I was crazy about acting and used psychoanalysis to satisfy my need to please, while she was an intellectual who shielded herself from the pain of thinking by talking in a little girl's voice and putting on a show of being dumb.'

Marilyn turned to the man who would prove to be her last psychoanalyst when she was supposed to be starting filming on *Let's Make Love*, a George Cukor picture in which she co-starred with Yves Montand – with whom she later had an affair. Her anxieties about her performance marked another unhappy chapter in the trials she faced as a Hollywood actress, and by this stage in her career, it had become second nature to her to take to the analyst's couch whenever she was suffering a crisis on a film. In an attempt to overcome the turmoil of inhibitions and self-doubt that paralysed her every move on set, she had first gone into analysis five years previously in New York. She had already seen two psychoanalysts, Margaret Hohenberg and Marianne Kris, and in the autumn of 1956, while filming *The Princess and the Showgirl* with Laurence Olivier in London, she had even had several sessions with Anna Freud, the daughter of Freud himself.

Now, at the start of 1960, she was in acute distress again, in front of the cameras of 20th Century Fox, who had treated her as badly as they were paying her. She still owed them a film under the terms of an old contract, but *Let's Make Love* was beset with problems. Marilyn couldn't get to grips with her character, Amanda Dell, a dancer and singer oblivious to wealth and fame, who unwittingly falls in love with a millionaire. While the crew waited for her to wake up, after she'd knocked herself out with barbiturates, and eventually appear on set hours late, her stand-in, Evelyn Moriarty, would walk through scenes, testing and confirming lighting cues and camera angles and rehearsing with other actors. On the first day of filming, Montand had confided to Marilyn that he was as terrified of failure as she was, and this shared anxiety immediately established a bond between them. To make matters worse, the movie was mired in rewrites and producers' second thoughts. Hamstrung by the director's elegant, casually *distrait* approach, an air of disaster enveloped the studio. Although she wasn't by any means solely responsible for the delays, the producers told Marilyn she had to straighten up or she'd jeopardise the film's chances of being completed on time.

Without a regular analyst in Los Angeles, she turned for advice to Dr Kris, who had been treating her for three years in New York. Kris gave her the name of Ralph R. Greenson, one of

Hollywood's most prominent therapists, but only after asking Greenson if he'd be prepared to take on a difficult case. A woman in utter disarray, Kris explained, whose abuse of drugs and medication showed markedly self-destructive tendencies. Her immediate problem was severe anxiety stress, but her fragile personality was a source of more fundamental concern. Dr Greenson agreed to become Marilyn Monroe's fourth psychoanalyst.

For reasons of discretion and the actress's poor health, their first session took place not, as the psychoanalyst would have wished, in his office, but at the Beverly Hills Hotel, in Marilyn's apple green, wall-to-wall carpeted bungalow. It was brief. After a few questions regarding her medical condition, as opposed to her psychological history, Greenson suggested he see her from then on at his practice, not far from the hotel. For the rest of filming, virtually the next six months, Marilyn would leave the set every afternoon to go to her analyst in Beverly Hills, on North Roxbury Drive, halfway between Fox Studios on Pico Boulevard and her hotel on Sunset.

The architecture of the Beverly Hills Hotel gives a fair indication of its clientele. Pretty pink façade; sprawling, schizoid, neo-something design; rooms in the garish hues of Technicolor films. Fox installed Marilyn and her husband, Arthur Miller, in Bungalow Twenty-one, and Yves Montand and his wife, Simone Signoret, in Twenty – Mediterranean-revival-style affairs reminiscent of pre-war movies. 'Revival': Marilyn used to laugh at that word. As if anything could revive. As if one could re-create what had never existed. Not that that stopped her regularly flying-in an old woman from San Diego who, thirty years previously, had dyed the hair of many stars of the silent era, notably Mae West's soft white wavy locks, and the platinum curls of the diva of Hollywood's heady years, Jean Harlow. Marilyn used to send a limousine for Pearl Porterfield and lay on champagne and caviar. The colourist used the old technique for peroxiding hair

– Marilyn would accept no substitute – but what she liked best was hearing stories about Jean Harlow, her burning life and icy death. The stories may have been as fanciful a creation as the platinum of her hair, but this was the movie business, and Marilyn was watching herself up there on a screen full of memories.

Hollywood, Sunset Boulevard
1960

Los Angeles, the city of angels, had become the dream factory in more ways than one. The meeting of Ralph Greenson and Marilyn Monroe would have been inconceivable anywhere but Hollywood. Two people with such disparate histories could only have found one another in Tinseltown, the city of spotlights, sequins and glitter, among the limitless cast of characters orbiting the studios – all those blindingly bright sets on which actors exposed the half-light of their souls.

This was where psychoanalysis and the movies acted out their fatal romance. They were like two strangers who turn out to share compulsions rather than, as they had first thought, affinities, and only remain together through a misunderstanding. The analysts threw themselves into interpreting the movies, occasionally successfully, while their film equivalents grappled with the unconscious. Rich, vulnerable, neurotic and insecure, both professions prescribed themselves heavy doses of the 'talking cure'. Ben Hecht, the scriptwriter of Alfred Hitchcock's *Spellbound* and, ten years later, the ghostwriter of Marilyn's autobiography, published a novel in 1944 called *I Hate Actors*, in which he portrayed the Golden Age of Hollywood as an object study in mental pathology, riddled with psychoses, neuroses and perversions of every kind: 'There's something everybody in Hollywood has got coming to them at some stage or another, and that's a headlong plummet into nervous depression. I've known film producers who haven't had a single idea in ten years and then, *boom*, one fine morning or evening, what do you know, they've fallen to pieces like regular overworked geniuses. The number of actors laid low by depression is something truly spectacular.'

Hollywood had reached its apogee in the 1930s, when Marilyn was born in one of its Nowheresville suburbs, and it was entering its decline by the time she met Ralph in early 1960. Nowadays the major film studios have become echoing deserts haunted by the ghosts of actors whose names mean little to the coachloads of tourists spilling out onto their plywood streets. On Sunset Boulevard, Hispanic prostitutes stand outside Korean convenience stores with cracked windows – one starburst for every break-in attempt – and psychoanalysis is no more than 'an option' for anyone wishing to tune the spiritual receiver of his or her being into the vibrations of the New Age. The search for a meaning to one's life comes some way down people's list of priorities. So, it's hard to imagine the relationship between psychoanalysis and the movie business in Hollywood's heyday. A marriage of intellect and artifice, it was invariably sealed with money, often with glory, and occasionally with blood. For better and for worse, the people of the image and the people of the word tied the knot. Psychoanalysis took it upon itself not only to heal the souls of Hollywood's denizens but also to build the city of dreams on celluloid.

Ralph and Marilyn's relationship replayed that between psychoanalysis and the movie business, each succumbing to the other's madness. Like all *coups de foudre* and lasting unions, the two professions' encounter was based on confusion: the psychoanalysts were straining to hear the invisible, while the filmmakers sought to put on screen what couldn't be articulated in words, and, slowly but surely, the film industry drove psychoanalysis out of its mind. The entire episode lasted for twenty years or so, and came to an end when Hollywood itself did. But the spectres endured and, like patients in analysis, the movies suffered from involuntary flashbacks for a long time afterwards.

Hollywood, Beverly Hills, Roxbury Drive
January 1960

Norma Jeane and Ralph. A world of difference separated the poor, uneducated LA girl and the prosperous East Coast intellectual – he, a son of the bourgeoisie raised in a bookish environment, she, a daughter of blue-collar parents, who'd grown up surrounded by images – and yet immediately they seemed to feel that deep down they knew one another. Each came to think of the other as a long-lost friend, who would recognise the entreaty where others would see only a smile. But something cast a shadow, something each refused to see in the other. A message from Fate: here is your death making its entrance.

After an exhausting day's filming, Marilyn was half an hour late for her first session at her last psychoanalyst's office. She was wearing a pair of loose slacks, Dr Greenson noticed, and he was struck by how upright she sat in the chair he showed her to, as though waiting for someone in a hotel lobby.

'You're late,' he began. An avid chess player, he was fond of opening moves that threw the other player off balance.

'I'm late because I'm late for everybody, for all my meetings,'

Marilyn retorted, deeply hurt. 'You're not the only person I keep waiting.'

Later, remembering these words, Greenson thought one should always treat the first session as if it were the last. Everything that would subsequently prove of importance came out then, even if merely by implication.

With a mixture of anger and sadness, Marilyn continued, 'Since the production began, Cukor has been unable to shoot for a total of thirty-nine hours on account of the fact that I am always late. I guess people think that why I'm late is some kind of arrogance and I think it's the opposite of arrogance . . . A lot of people can be there on time and do nothing, which I have seen them do, and, you know, all sit around and sort of chit-chatting and talking trivia about their social life. Do you want me to do that?'

The analyst had treated troubled actresses before, but he was alarmed at her condition. She must have taken a lot of sedatives, since she barely reacted when Greenson tried to draw her into conversation, and she painlessly said painful things. She wanted to lie on the couch for the kind of Freudian therapy she'd been used to in New York, but Greenson suggested face-to-face supportive therapy instead.

'Fine, whatever you want,' she said. 'I'll tell you all I can. What can you say when you feel you're being swallowed up?'

He asked her about the facts of her day-to-day life. She complained about the part she had to play in a film she detested; about her acting coach Paula Strasberg, the wife of her drama teacher in New York; and about Cukor, who had made his dislike for her obvious and constantly put her down.

'"We all think we're original," he told me in that syrupy voice of his. "We think everything about us is unique and different. But it's incredible how much we echo other people, our families, how our childhood shapes our every curve and contour." Curves and contours, are you kidding? That old fairy. What does he know about this body I have to live in?'

After a long silence, Marilyn told him about the cocktail of drugs she took for her chronic insomnia, and about how she secretly went from doctor to doctor for the prescriptions. She showed a staggering knowledge of psychopharmacology, and recited the litany of drugs she took, often intravenously: Demerol, Sodium Pentothal, phenobarbital, Amytal. Greenson was furious with her doctors and immediately advised her to use only one physician, Hyman Engelberg, to whom he would entrust every aspect of her physical well-being. He told her to leave everything up to him: he would decide what medication she needed.

He definitely disconcerted her, this doctor: he listened but resisted her demand to be soothed, cherished, made whole.

And then her hour was up and they parted company.

When she got home that evening, Marilyn thought of the calm, gentle figure she had met and the cool, slightly brisk way he had questioned her. The challenge in his eyes when he had looked at her seemed to conceal worrying reserves of tenderness. When she had asked him if she could lie on the couch, as she did with Dr Kris, he had advised against it. 'Let us be modest about what we want to achieve here. We don't have to make a deep change since you'll soon return to New York and your analyst there.' The word 'modest' had wounded her; tears had welled in her eyes. The analyst had been quick to reassure her it wasn't meant as a criticism but as a goal for himself, a benchmark for what they could achieve in their time together.

It's strange all the same, thought Marilyn, strange he didn't ask me to lie down. I'm always surprised when a man doesn't want to see me on my back. See my ass when I turn away from him. Glass in hand, looking at her bungalow's white walls and black drapes, she continued replaying the session in her mind. Dr Greenson doesn't have ulterior motives, I don't think. It's lucky he didn't ask me to lie down. Perhaps he's afraid. Of me?

Of himself? It's better this way, I think. I was afraid – not of him, though. It was nothing to do with sex.

If she was truthful, she didn't like being asked to sleep with someone. She was afraid of the night: afraid of it starting, afraid of it never ending. She often made love standing up, in the day.

Brooklyn, Brownsville, Miller Avenue
September 1911

Ralph Greenson wasn't yet fifty when he began analysing Marilyn Monroe. He was born Romeo Greenschpoon in 1911, in the Brownsville neighbourhood of Brooklyn, the twin brother of a sister called Juliet, who became a brilliant concert pianist. Their parents were Russian-Jewish immigrants who had become relatively prosperous, thanks to the drive of the twins' intelligent, ambitious mother. Katherine Greenschpoon had pulled off the unlikely feat of acquiring a job and a husband all at once when she was hired as the dispensary assistant at Joel Greenschpoon's pharmacy. Impressed by his ability to diagnose his customers' ailments, she had convinced her husband to go to medical school. Romeo's father had therefore qualified as a doctor comparatively late, when his first two children were three years old.

An accomplished pianist, Katherine encouraged all four of her children to play music. She had cultural aspirations of her own and eventually swapped the pills and prescriptions for the art world and became an artists' manager. Surrounded by New York's divas and impresarios, Romeo's head was filled with the romance of the stage, but often he'd escape to the misty, black and white silhouettes up on the screen at Brooklyn's grand movie house, and lose himself in the romantic travails of the actresses, with their translucent complexions.

'Wherefore art youse, Romeo?'

The taunts of the kids in his neighbourhood echoed those he heard every day in the classroom, where he and his sister were taught to say, in unison, 'We're Romeo and Juliet, and we're twins.' When he was twelve, he decided to change his first name, but it took him until 1937, during his internship at the Cedars of Lebanon Hospital in Los Angeles, to change his last name. He once said they were like scars on his face. Yet his friends continued to call him Romeo or, more often, Romi, and he kept an extra R on his brass plate, after his new first name, Ralph. Marilyn called him 'Doctor', but when he wasn't there, she toyed with his nickname, pronouncing it plaintively, almost like a question.

At the end of his studies at medical school in Berne in Switzerland, where he enrolled in 1931, he met Hildegarde Troesch, whom he married shortly before returning to America. She was won over by his intelligence and adaptability – among other achievements, he learned German in two months so he could read Freud in the original. With his medical degree in his pocket, Ralph travelled to Vienna at the start of 1933, where he was analysed by Wilhelm Stekel, one of Freud's earliest adherents and a founding member of the Vienna Psychoanalytic Society, the man Freud would later refer to as a 'pig' and 'treacherous liar'. Greenson also worked directly with Freud, and it was through talking to him about tragedy and pathological characters in theatre that he understood Shakespeare's depiction of Romeo and Juliet as accursed lovers who could only be together in death. Throughout his life, his feelings for Freud would remain less those of a devout disciple than a loyal comrade in arms. Privately, he called him 'the man who listened to women'.

At the age of twenty-six, Greenson set up in Los Angeles as a psychiatrist and psychoanalyst – American psychoanalytic practice didn't distinguish between the two. He immediately set his sights on becoming a key figure in the local psychoanalytic community. Its leader, Ernst Simmel, was suspicious of the over-tures of a student of the renegade Stekel, but Greenson was bright – or opportunistic – enough to erase the taint of his origins by undergoing another analysis. He spent four years on the couch with Otto Fenichel, an unimpeachable Freudian grandee who had emigrated from Berlin to Los Angeles in 1938.

After the war, Greenson felt the need for another analysis. For his third therapist, he chose neither a doctor nor a man, but Frances Deri, who sported a crew-cut and a long cigarette holder *à la* Marlene Dietrich, which she kept permanently clamped between her teeth. Before emigrating to Los Angeles in 1936, she had been a midwife in Germany and then trained as an analyst in the team of Freudian Marxists created by Ernst Simmel at the Schloss Tegel clinic near Berlin. She had been analysed twice, by Hanns Sachs and Karl Abraham, pillars of Freud's inner circle and members of the 'Wednesday Committee'. Both had disagreed violently with Freud in 1925, when they had collaborated on the first film to attempt to depict psychoanalysis, *Secrets of a Soul* by G. W. Pabst. Like her mentors, Deri had an all-consuming passion for cinema. Known as *Madame* Deri by her colleagues in the Los Angeles Psychoanalytic Society and Institute (LAPSI), she specialised in analysing actors and remained a guiding light for Greenson when he set about establishing his own client base. Crucially, though, she provided him with a fresh imaginative link to Freud, one that would problematically revive the conflict between words and images that had been a feature of his analysis. Privately, he wanted to be known to posterity as 'the man who listened to images'.

In the Californian Babylon of the studios, among the sound-stages, lots and banks of spotlights, Greenson avidly pursued the glittering contradictions between image and identity, seeking in the magical word 'Action' that launched every shot a salve to the inaction he was confined to by his analyst's chair. Acting and the performing arts would remain integral parts of his work and life. Fascinated by actors, he constantly returned to performers' psychology: 'The movie actor or actress is not a star until he is instantly recognisable not only by his peers but by the world at large . . . I have found the . . . budding star and the fading film stars to be the most difficult with whom I have tried to work,' he wrote in August 1978, a year before his death. While Marilyn was still his patient, Greenson began a textbook that has been used in psychoanalytic training all over the world for the past fifty years: *The Technique and Practice of Psychoanalysis*. In it, he compares the analytic session to a scene of a play or film: 'In a strange way the analyst becomes a silent actor in a play the patient is creating. The analyst does not act in this drama; he tries to remain the shadowy figure the patient needs for his fantasies. Yet the analyst helps in the creation of the character, working out the details by his insight, empathy and intuition. In a sense he becomes a kind of stage director in the situation – a vital part of the play, but not an actor.'

Psychoanalytic conferences across the length and breadth of California gave him the opportunity to fulfil his ambitions as a performer. Word reached Europe that he was the most actorly of orators, the most brilliant of speakers. He never showed any nerves at the lectern, which he approached with quick, bouncy steps: 'Just think,' he seemed to be saying, 'these lucky people get to hear *me*!' At glittery Bel Air or Beverly Hills parties, he would launch into veritable one-man shows, describing in detail the cases of a happy few whose identities he'd veil sufficiently thinly for them to be obvious.

Greenson shared a thriving practice with his colleague Milton

Wexler at 436 North Roxbury Drive in Beverly Hills, not far from Bedford Drive, otherwise known as Couch Canyon. He lived in Santa Monica, on Franklin Street, near the Brentwood Country Club. From the back of his house, one could see Pacific Palisades and the ocean to the west. At the start of 1960 he was a slender, elegant figure known for his judicious pronouncements. By the time he started analysing Marilyn Monroe, he had become the acknowledged star of the Hollywood branch of the Freudian unconscious, 'the backbone of psychoanalysis in the western United States', as one colleague put it. He had long been clinical professor of psychiatry at the University of California at Los Angeles, and was president and dean of the training school at the Los Angeles Psychoanalytic Institute affiliated to LAPSI. He was very involved in his analyses and showed a passionate interest in his patients. Many of them, such as Peter Lorre, Vivien Leigh, Inger Stevens, Tony Curtis and Frank Sinatra – then Marilyn's lover – were actors, while others were in the business, like director Vincente Minnelli or producer Dore Schary.

Quietly confident of his saturnine looks, he liked encountering his patients face to face. His large, heavily shadowed brown eyes lent his face a tender, craggy quality, further accentuated by a bushy moustache. Seductive in so far as he didn't consider himself a seducer, Greenson displayed in his analysis the mannerisms that characterised his lectures and private relations, 'an unpredictable interplay between the wry, the weary, the impatient, the disenchanted', as Leo Rosten wrote – and the self-absorbed: when Marilyn once mentioned a previous analyst, he couldn't help saying, 'Let's not talk about her! What about me? What do you think about me?' before bursting out laughing.

Wanting it with a passion yet hardly realising it, Ralph Greenson entered into one of those fatal attractions to which intellectuals succumb with all the more abandon because they think they're in control. His greatest enemy was boredom, and when Marilyn suddenly appeared in his wearily familiar sky, shining with her incredible white brilliance, she represented an escape from the monotony of his practice he could never have dared hoped for. Surprise, after all, is one of the subtlest of pleasures, just as ruination is the most dandified of misfortunes.

Hollywood, Beverly Hills Hotel, West Sunset Boulevard
January 1960

For a time, sessions reverted to Marilyn's bungalow at the Beverly Hills Hotel, since she was too depressed and weak to make it to her analyst's office. Greenson began the next session with the usual questions about the first years of her life and her childhood. Marilyn didn't say anything for a long time, then only a name: Grace.

'What relation was she to you?'

'None. She was a friend of my mother ... my so-called mother, I mean. Grace was my real mother; she wanted to make me a film star. I don't know what the other one wanted. Me to be dead, maybe. It's strange, you're the only person I can say this to, but I always tell journalists my mother is dead. She's not, but I'm still telling the truth really. When they put me in the orphanage on El Centro Avenue, I screamed, "I'm not an orphan. I have a mother. She's got red hair and soft hands." That was true too, even if she never touched me.'

Greenson took this at face value. Marilyn's mother might still have been alive, but she was right to think of her as dead to her.

Rather than interpret, he asked, 'What did you study before becoming an actress?'

'I didn't finish high school. I sat for people, did some modelling, looked at myself in the mirror or in other people's eyes to see who I was.'

'Do you need to be seen by other people for that? Men?'

'Why just men? Marilyn doesn't exist. I come out of my dressing room Norma Jeane. I'm still her even when the camera's rolling. Marilyn Monroe only exists on screen.'

'Is that why you're so anxious about having to shoot? You're scared of your image being stolen by the picture? That the woman on screen isn't you? That your image is not only giving you life but also taking it away? Do you feel the same when people look at you in real life?'

'Too many questions, Doctor. I don't know. Men don't look at me, anyway. They run their eyes over me. It's different. You don't, though. The first time we met, it felt as if you were looking at me with all your heart, as if you were about to introduce me to someone inside myself. That made me feel good.'

It took the psychoanalyst a while to notice a strange and unsettling thing. When she wasn't being looked at, when nobody was paying attention to her, her face would go utterly slack and come apart, as if it had died.

Greenson knew she was intelligent, but was still surprised by her faultless taste in poetry, theatre and classical music. Arthur Miller, her third husband, whom she had married four years earlier, had undertaken to educate her. But while she was grateful for the education, she expressed at the same time a venomous resentment towards him. She claimed he was cold and unresponsive, attracted to other women and dominated by his mother. But by this stage their marriage was faltering. Yves Montand had been a catalyst; the real reasons for their estrangement lay elsewhere.

The first time Greenson met Marilyn, he sensed her body was something she possessed rather than who she was. After her death, Miller confirmed this when, staring off into space, he told Greenson, 'In the end, something of the order of the divine resulted from her feelings of disembodiment. She was utterly incapable of condemning or judging anyone, even if they'd hurt her. To be with her was to be accepted, to pass from a world where suspicion reigned into a luminous, sanctifying realm. She was part queen, part waif, sometimes on her knees before her own body and sometimes despairing because of it.'

The analyst confided his first impressions to his colleague, Wexler, soon after he started treating Marilyn: 'As she becomes more anxious, she begins to act like an orphan, and masochistically provokes people to mistreat her and to take advantage of her. As fragments of her past history come out, she begins to talk more and more about the traumatic experiences of an orphan child. She feels at times that she is unimportant and insignificant. At the same time, although sexually dissatisfied, she glories and revels in her personal appearance, feeling that she is an extremely beautiful woman, perhaps the most beautiful woman in the world. She always takes great pains to be attractive and to give a very good appearance when she is out in public, although when she is at home and nobody can see her she might not be able to put herself together very well. The main mechanism she uses to bring some feeling of stability and significance to her life is the attractiveness of her body. I tried to tell her that in my experience truly beautiful women are not beautiful all the time. They look plain, or even ugly, at certain moments and from certain angles. And that's what beauty is, a temporary quality rather than a state. But she didn't seem to understand what I was saying.' Greenson didn't give his colleague the chance to respond, but that didn't surprise Wexler. He knew it was questions Ralph Greenson was short of rather than answers.

Los Angeles, Downtown
1948

The first photographer in the life of the woman still known as Norma Jeane Baker, André de Dienes, was a good-looking thirty-three-year-old, who had been brought over from Europe in the early 1940s by the producer David O. Selznick. He had hired Norma Jeane for her first modelling job, a five-week road trip through California, Nevada and New Mexico in 1945. She was nineteen.

At the end of the 1950s, *Life* magazine commissioned him to do a photo shoot of Marilyn and her drama coach, Natasha Lytess, a failed Hollywood actress of Russian extraction who had emigrated from Berlin. The set-up was straightforward enough, an acting lesson at Lytess's Beverly Hills house, but things went badly from the start. Lytess and de Dienes argued. De Dienes didn't like what Marilyn was wearing: a voluminous blouse that covered her completely, and a long, unattractive skirt almost down to her ankles. He hated her formal hairstyle and wanted to show her as glamorous, provocative, desirable. He suggested to Marilyn that she take off her clothes and stand there, facing Natasha, wearing only her short, black slip with her hair messed up. 'Make real dramatic movements,' he told her. 'I want action going on for the pictures.' Natasha had other thoughts. She started shouting that Marilyn was going to be a dramatic actress, not a 'sex-bobble'. De Dienes pointed out that Marilyn's sex appeal was the reason she was becoming famous, then packed up his equipment and stormed out, yelling he didn't work with hypocrites.

Throughout her life, photography would represent a haven Marilyn could retreat to whenever she was suffering. The greater her anguish at the prospect of shooting, the more acute her terror at having to repeat a scene twenty times in front of a hundred people, the more the ballet of a man dancing round her armed with a camera seemed to shelter her from her fears.

Look bad, dirty, not just sexy. Such, no doubt, were the dismal instructions the unknown cameraman gave Marilyn before he started rolling his camera in some squalid Willowbrook apartment in downtown Los Angeles. The resulting film lasts three minutes forty-one seconds and is in black and white. Originally silent, it has since been soundtracked with an extract from a Monroe song, 'My Heart Belongs To Daddy'.

Provided it's not a fake, this short film is the first trace of Marilyn on celluloid. To survive in Hollywood, as a twenty-two-year-old, she sold what she had to whoever wanted it: her body to producers and its image to the anonymous spectators who watched the pornographic shorts with titles like *Apples, Knockers and Cokes* that were shot on the fringes of the studios. This one, *Porn,* is particularly horrific. The actress enters in a black dress, which she takes off to reveal a black négligée and suspenders. She seems large somehow, her stomach, her thighs, even her head, her russet-brown hair hanging limply over the left side of her face. Her leaden movements and vague gestures as she takes a tawdrily wrapped box from a man exude something irredeemably crude and exhausted. If it weren't for the glimpse of her face in the last shot, when she smokes a cigarette as she looks down at the man she has just had sex with, one might doubt it was Marilyn Monroe. Only the smile is hers.

This sequence of undressing and desolate intercourse seems like some primeval form of pornography, mesmerisingly ugly in its evocation of how cruel sex can be. The fact it is silent makes it seem even more like the visual representation of a moan or cry of pain. But its black candour about sex shows the truth about cinema as well: worn and unrestorable, the surviving prints reveal how images eat away at themselves, how, as the shadows rise to the surface of the celluloid, the canker of oblivion corrodes even the most studied pose and tells the voyeur, *Nothing to see here*.

One day in January 1951 in Hollywood, a black Lincoln convertible containing the director Elia Kazan and the playwright Arthur Miller eased through the Fox lot, searching for the soundstage on which *As Young As You Feel* was being shot. They heard Marilyn's name being shouted by a hoarse-voiced production assistant before they saw her. The director was cursing the twenty-four-year-old actress, who kept wandering off set and returning dejected and in tears. She had only a small role, but every scene she was in was taking hours. Eventually she appeared in a close-fitting black dress. Kazan was speechless. He had come to offer her a part.

He became her lover, then her friend, then her enemy under McCarthyism, and then her friend again. 'When I met her,' he said later, 'she was a simple, decent-hearted kid whom Hollywood brought down, legs parted.' She was thin-skinned and had a hunger to be accepted by people she could respect. Like many other girls who'd had her sort of life, she measured her self-esteem by the number of men she was able to attract.

Santa Monica, Franklin Street
February 1960

Marilyn continued to arrive late at her psychoanalyst's.

'Why such hostility towards people who want to help and understand you?' Greenson asked. 'We're allies, you and I, not enemies.'

'That's how it's always been. On *A Ticket To Tomahawk*, in the early days, the assistant director threatened, "You know, you can be replaced." "You can too," I said. The idiot! He didn't understand that being late guarantees you can't be replaced and that everyone else is waiting for you, only you and no one else . . . Anyway, when I'm late, it's not as if I'm not doing anything, you know. I check my clothes and make-up, I work on my image, I take notes on what I'm going to say, topics of conversation—'

'You're not on set or at some fancy party here,' the analyst interrupted. 'Do you know what it means to me when you come late? It means "I don't like you, Dr Greenson. I don't want to come and see you."'

'Oh, no, I do like to come and see you. I do,' Marilyn exclaimed.

34

'I like talking to you, even if I have to look away so as not to feel your eyes on me.'

'Your words say that. Your actions say: "I don't like you."'

Marilyn was silent. She'd thought her being late meant only one thing: 'You are waiting for me. You love me. You are waiting just for me. Love me, Doctor. You know it's always the one who loves who waits.' But she stopped coming late after that – started coming early, too early. In the end she still couldn't be on time.

'You see, you don't know what you want,' the analyst told her. 'You don't know what time it is.' He thought her coming early now meant: 'He's there. Who knows about time, but he's there for me. He's there.'

The following summer, during a very emotional session, she told her analyst about filming a scene in *The Misfits* in which she'd rejected her screen husband's attempts at reconciliation.

'I kept getting stuck on the little sentence, "You're not there." Huston got mad, but Clark Gable stood up for me. "When she's there, she's there. All of her is there! She's there to work." Ever since then that's been my favourite expression when I talk about my experiences with men: mostly they're never *there*.'

The first time she sat in the leather chair in the consulting room at her analyst's house, she noticed there were no papers on his large wooden desk. He must write his articles upstairs, she supposed. It was odd not seeing any pictures of Freud on the walls; there had been several in Greenson's Beverly Hills office, as there had in her previous analysts' offices. She was particularly taken by a large picture of a woman sitting with her back to the viewer, gazing at a garden. Her face was obscured, but the gentle light and her clothes suggested it bore a serene expression. She immediately liked the calm, quiet beauty of this huge room, which was shielded from the setting sun by linen drapes with a green and brown geometric pattern.

After a few sessions at his office in Beverly Hills, Greenson had suggested to Marilyn he see her regularly at his home so as not to attract public attention. His children, Joan and Daniel, knew their father had famous clients, but it came as a complete surprise to them when he changed his usual routine and started cancelling appointments at his office to be able to see Marilyn Monroe at their home. Joan immediately wanted to become friends with his new, famous patient and soon her father was telling her to look after Marilyn if he was late and suggesting they go out for walks together. Joan couldn't help feeling awkward, though, when he sent her to pick up medication from the pharmacy and take it to Marilyn at the Beverly Hills Hotel.

In addition to five or six weekly meetings, the analyst encouraged Marilyn to telephone each day. 'Mainly she was lonely and had no one to see her, nothing to do if I didn't see her,' Greenson explained apologetically, in a letter to Marianne Kris. One evening, she took a taxi home from Santa Monica after a session, invited the driver in and then spent the night with him. Greenson was furious at this 'pathological' behaviour; his wife advised her to stay with them if her sessions ran on late, which she did after that from time to time.

Greenson justified his approach to Wexler by saying it was a deliberate emergency strategy to ensure her physical health and enable her to appear on set for *Let's Make Love*. 'Although she may seem a hard-core drug addict, she isn't in any usual sense of the word,' he explained. It was true that Marilyn could stop taking drugs without showing any of the customary symptoms of withdrawal, but it wasn't by any means a rare occurrence for her to ring, begging him to come to the Beverly Hills Hotel to give her an intravenous injection of Pentothal or Amytal. Distraught after one such summons, he said to Wexler, 'I told her that she'd already received so much medication that it would put five other people to sleep, but the reason she wasn't sleeping was because she was afraid of sleeping. I promised she would sleep with less medication if she would recognise she's fighting sleep as well as searching for some oblivion, which is not sleep.'

Fort Logan, Colorado, Army Air Force
Convalescent Hospital
1944

Enrolling in the US Army in 1942, Ralph Greenson was assigned
to a psychiatric ward where he specialised in traumatic neuroses.
In addition to treating combat casualties, he also started giving
regular seminars to medical personnel, military chaplains and
social workers trying to help soldiers readapt to civilian life. His
experiences as an army psychiatrist inspired a hugely popular
novel by Leo Rosten, *Captain Newman, M.D.*, whose heroic
protagonist was based on him. The book came out in 1963, and
was made into a movie that year.

Greenson used to tell one story in particular from that time.
He had had to give an intravenous injection of Sodium Pentothal
to a waist gunner of a B-17 bomber on his return from a mission.
The man was displaying symptoms of extreme shock: insomnia,
nightmares, trembling, sweats. He had flown fifty combat missions
but, although he was noticeably reluctant to talk about his sorties,
he insisted he wasn't aware of any particular source of anxiety.

He had agreed to take Pentothal partly because he'd heard it got you high, 'swacked', so he wanted to see what that was like, but mainly because it meant he wouldn't have to report to his superiors. As soon as Greenson had injected the hypnotic drug, the man sat bolt upright in his bed, tore the needle out of his arm and started screaming, 'Four o'clock! Oh, Jeez, coming at us from four! Get a bead on them or they'll get us, those bastards! Omigod! Oh, Jeez – three more – one o'clock, one o'clock! Get a bead on them, get a bead on them! Omigod, I'm hurt! I can't move! Get a bead on those bastards!'

The patient carried on screaming and yelling like this for more than twenty minutes, his eyes filled with terror, sweat pouring down his face, his whole body trembling as he gripped his right arm, which hung limply by his side. Greenson finally said to him, 'OK, boy, we got them.' Hearing this, the patient collapsed back onto the bed and fell into a deep sleep. The next morning the doctor asked him if he remembered the effects of the Pentothal. He gave a timid smile and said he remembered yelling but it was all very confused. When Greenson told him he'd talked about a mission on which he'd been wounded in his right hand, and hadn't stopped yelling 'Get a bead on them', the patient said, 'Oh, yes, I remember. We were coming back from Schweinfurt and they jumped us. They came in at four o'clock, then one o'clock, and then we were hit . . .' Under the effects of Pentothal, the patient had managed to bypass all his resistances and defences and recall without difficulty what had happened to him.

For some time after this, Greenson continued to search for the secret of forgotten experiences with 'the truth serum', as Pentothal was called in the movies of the day. It wasn't until his analysis with Frances Deri that the injection of memories lost its fascination for him and he turned to another method for excavating his patients' buried truths: transference, the psychoanalytic procedure whereby love is the only medication, and words are what allow repressed experiences to emerge. But his use of drugs left him with the sense that the therapist must always play an active part in treatment, offering aspects of his psychological and physical self for the patient to draw on.

Beverly Hills, Roxbury Drive
November 1979

'Hello, Mr Wexler?' the voice on the phone said. 'I was wonder-ing if there's any chance we could meet. I'm a journalist and I'm writing a book about Marilyn – well, mainly about Greenson, actually, and the part he may have played in her death. You knew them both intimately, so I was hoping you could talk to me about what they were like and your relationship with them.'

Wexler declined this request, one of an infinite number he had been bombarded with over the years. He put off the journalist, just as he had all the other conspiracy- and scandal-seekers, and tried to forget the whole thing. But memories kept welling up, so he called the journalist back the next day and suggested instead that he help him write his memoirs. A psychoanalyst in the Golden Age of the studios . . . he already had the title: *A Look Through the Rear-view Mirror.*

'Where to begin? It's all such a long time ago, all this,' Wexler said. 'It goes back to the year after Marilyn died, but you'd have to start with the Greenson I knew just after the war. I can't resist telling you about that. *Captain Newman, M.D.* was the story of a heroic army medical officer in the Second World War. A joke, really . . . not Romi, or Gregory Peck, he was no worse than usual. No, the film. I remember it coming out in 1963. It was a big hit, unlike John Huston's *Freud*, which was put out at the same time with that ridiculous subtitle, *The Secret Passion*. You know, the picture Marilyn was meant to be in until Ralph Greenson did everything he could to stop her.'

'No – what happened?' the journalist asked.

'Don't you know about that? I'll tell you another day . . . Oh, well, what the heck? I haven't got time to stand on ceremony with the dead any more. Get this: while he was doing his utmost to make it impossible for a film to be made about Freud, Greenson was busy casting himself as the saviour psychiatrist. He had no problem with being portrayed as a courageous analyst himself, but he did with his patient playing one of Freud's hysterics. I'm not saying Newman the shock psychiatrist wasn't an accurate portrait of Romi's time in the army when he treated soldiers who'd fought in the Pacific, mind you. Ever dynamic, ever the handsome lead, that was Romi. Wherever he went, something larger than life would happen, like in the movies. Ralph was a dramatic guy, but light with it, very humorous. The movie portrayed a valiant psychiatrist struggling to repair the shattered psyches of three battle-weary soldiers. His sidekick, the orderly Jake Leibowitz, played by one of Greenson's patients, Tony Curtis, provided some light relief, but basically it was about the tragic dilemma faced by a conscientious doctor in wartime: why should he help traumatised soldiers back on their feet if it was just so they could go off and fight? Is curing someone effectively sending him out to get killed or live a miserable life? Sometimes in our humbler endeavours we ask ourselves the same thing.

'Greenson wrote the *Captain Newman* script but his friend, the writer Leo Rosten, advised him he'd better not put his name on the credits in case his former patients tried to sue. He agreed, not that he was exactly thrilled about keeping a low profile. He'd met Rosten when they were both at the beginning of their careers, and the two of them immediately hit it off: Romi took the writer to meetings of the psychoanalytic study group and Leo reciprocated by taking him to Hollywood dinner parties. A remarkable storyteller, Romi would launch into vivid descriptions of his sessions. Rosten once said, "As an analyst he had to keep quiet all day, and that frustrated him. Soon he was telling his stories all over Hollywood." I think he always regretted not having been an actor. He didn't give his lectures, he acted them out. He put on a real show.

'Romi loved power or, rather, he loved playing with the idea of it. "If I wanted, I could dominate all this, everyone would be in my debt" – that sort of thing. He craved the limelight . . . But I'll stop there. You're going to think I didn't like my colleague. And, anyway, all this is tiring. Will you leave now?'

Moments later, Milton Wexler caught up with the journalist on the doorstep.

'The kicker, you know, is that, without telling him, Romi's patient was living her life as if she were in a movie just when Romi was making his into one. Everyone's got one in them, I guess.'

Santa Monica, Franklin Street
March 1960

The filming of *Let's Make Love* was chaotic from start to finish. On 26 January, Marilyn broke off a take of 'My Heart Belongs To Daddy'. She arrived on set at seven in the morning and had her make-up done, then left the studio and disappeared for three days.

'You're going to see what it means to shoot with the worst actress in the world,' she told Montand, when they finally had to do their first scene together. 'I want to vanish. Into the picture or out of it, I don't care, just vanish.'

'So you're scared,' Montand replied. 'Think of me a little bit. I'm lost.'

His compassion struck a chord.

In March, Marilyn caught a chill. She shut herself away in her bungalow. One evening Montand pushed open the door, sat next to her on the bed, took her hand. She drew him down and kissed him with a sort of despairing gaiety. She quickly realised that the Frenchman was just another extra in the love story she had been telling herself since childhood. 'It's always the same,' she told her analyst. 'The man goes to sleep with Marilyn Monroe and wakes up with me. But I want Montand to love me. Play it again, Yves. Cue the record.' Greenson immediately advised her to break off her relationship with Montand.

Santa Monica, Franklin Street
Spring 1960

The Greensons hosted glittering parties for celebrities and analysts at their beautiful, sprawling, Mexican-style house. Attendance was compulsory for members of the Los Angeles élite, who'd gather to listen to chamber music and nibble canapés off paper plates. Greenson spent money freely to show he didn't think of it as a means to acquire power or recognition. One of his patients, the painter Tony Berlant, who was penniless at the time, related that Greenson didn't charge him. Berlant spoke of a schism in his former analyst's personality: there was the arrogant, seductive, brutally candid talker at the Santa Monica parties and then there was the person underneath, who was generous and open in the therapeutic situation.

Everything was simple and extremely chic at Romi's. Conversation was the main attraction at his parties. As one guest later said, 'It was the only analytic salon where you could have fun. You knew you'd always meet a cross-section of people – Anna Freud, Margaret Mead, Masters and Johnson, plus lots of Hollywood people.' If you lived in Los Angeles, a visit to the

Greensons' in Santa Monica was like chancing upon an intellectual and artistic oasis in a desert of money.

A regular at the musical soirées in the picturesque hacienda, Marilyn would run into people from the film business: the scriptwriters Lillian Hellman and Leo Rosten, patients and former patients of Greenson, such as the producer Dore Schary, and Celeste Holm. Analysts would be there in numbers: Hanna Fenichel, Otto Fenichel's widow, Lewis Fielding, Milton Wexler. The host's mother, Katherine Greenschpoon, would have the place of honour in the middle of the room. Everyone would be surprised to see Marilyn sitting off in a corner, curled up in a blue velvet chair, gracefully swinging her hand to the music. 'If you want to get closer to the music, you need to move further away from the musicians,' she once told Hildi. 'That's the thing about music: there's nothing to see.'

Marilyn was very much among family at these events. She heard her analyst's twin sister, Juliet, and his younger sister, Elisabeth, play. Elisabeth, the wife of Milton 'Mickey' Rudin – Marilyn and Frank Sinatra's lawyer – was another concert pianist, who wasn't averse to sitting in with jazz bands. On Sunday afternoons, she would accompany her brother's hesitant violin in chamber pieces. An unrequited aesthete, Romi didn't work hard at his instrument, not that that prevented him launching self-importantly into erratic solos from the Brandenburg Concertos.

On these evenings, Romi would see a childlike sadness in his patient's eyes, the loneliness children can feel when grown-ups are playing music and they feel more excluded than if they were hearing them talking or even making love. Everyone is so bent on conveying the emptiness inside themselves, their terror, that they become invisible to one another and communicate through sound in a way they could never touch each other with their words or hands.

*   *   *

The first time Marilyn entered the Greensons' spacious living room she was struck by their piano, a Bechstein concert grand. She thought of her mother's white piano, a Franklin baby grand. According to family legend, it had once belonged to the actor Frederic March, and her mother Gladys Baker had bought it when she and Marilyn had briefly lived together in Los Angeles in a house on Arbol Street, near Mount Washington, Then, when Marilyn was living with one of her foster mothers, Ida Bollender, her mother had paid a woman called Marion Miller to give her lessons on it for a year. Gladys could pick out a few light classics and was always secretly proud of her ability to play 'Für Elise'. But Marilyn's chaotic life, shunted from home to home, soon put an end to her playing. *Baby grand* – she always laughed when she said the name. That was her: grand, in a way, and yet so little, really. The old white piano had been sold when her mother was committed to a mental hospital. Marilyn had never really known how to extract music from it and she regretted her repertoire didn't extend beyond the plonky, vaguely comical polka she and Tom Ewell play four-handed in Billy Wilder's *The Seven Year Itch*. But, at the first chance she got, she bought it back and would return to it like a lost friend, running her fingers over the keyboard whenever people became deaf and life unlivable.

Perhaps the side of Greenson's character Marilyn loved most was that of the pathetic, ridiculous musician. Like his voice, there was something that captivated her about his violin playing. Music seemed even more important to him than words or ideas. It afforded him respite from the incessant need to see or be seen. Once, after playing a Mozart trio, he put a hand on her shoulder and led her to the bay window looking out to sea. 'This is one of those skies, like that piece of music, that makes you want to die,' he said, 'that fills you with the desperate pleasure aroused by anything perfect.' She wondered if he was quoting something and, without understanding it completely, felt it play on her mind.

Hollywood, Santa Monica Boulevard
1946

Marilyn was twenty years old with an emptiness in her heart that she tried to staunch with men and women. She'd go out walking until dawn. She roamed all over Los Angeles and hung around the studios, her eyes full of hazy images, her blonde hair framed against the white sky like the halos that gild actresses on the over-exposed screens of old movies. A thought kept running through her mind, like a chant: she was going to become somebody strong, a great, enigmatic figure whom people could avoid as little as they could avoid their destiny.

Out on a drive one afternoon, André de Dienes and Marilyn stopped at the Hollywood Memorial Cemetery on Santa Monica Boulevard, where they wandered through the grand marble halls of the mausoleum in search of Rudolph Valentino's grave.

André remarked to Marilyn that she was born the same year, 1926, that Valentino had died – maybe she had been born to replace him and continue his legendary career! And maybe she, too, would become famous!

'It's not worth it if you die so young,' Marilyn answered.

'What more can you ask?' André said. 'He became immortal!'

She responded that she would prefer a long, happy life. Then she lifted a rose out from one of the urns on both sides of his bronze plaque.

'You don't steal flowers from the dead!' exclaimed André.

'I'm sure he would be very pleased to know that a lonesome girl took the flower home to keep it next to her bed. What about Jean Harlow? Do you know where she's buried?'

'No. I don't care either.'

'I do. I go to Forest Lawn Memorial Park a lot, where she's laid to rest in a private chapel. She died when she was twenty-six because her mother was a member of a sect and wouldn't let doctors treat her.'

When they left the mausoleum, he asked her to forget her appointment at the studio and stay with him so he could read to her from a large quotation book that was always with him in the trunk of his car. They sat on the lawn and read about life, love, happiness, fame, vanity, women, death and other things, but it was the word 'fame' that caught her attention the most . . . Then she suddenly decided she'd had enough poetry and philosophy and should go to her appointment, even if she was already very late. A pang of jealousy gripped him.

'Are you going to lay that producer?' he shouted.

'Yes! Why not?' she angrily answered.

He dropped her on the corner of Melrose Avenue and Gower Street.

A few days later, André read her a poem entitled 'Lines on the Death of Mary'. She said it was written for her, but the lady who wrote it forgot to put the 'lyn' after 'Mary'. He remarked that in the cemetery she'd told him she preferred a long, happy life and now she was saying she wouldn't live long—

'OK, that's enough, pose for me,' André interrupted himself. 'Let your face do the talking.'

The reading ended and he began taking pictures of her, one

by one, depicting the moods she interpreted for him. An entire spectrum of life, happiness, pensiveness, introspection, serenity, sadness, torment, distress – he even asked her to show him what 'death' looked like in her imagination. She threw a blanket over her head; that was how she interpreted it.

The photo that followed was her own idea. She told André to get ready with his camera because she was going to show him what her own death would look like – some day. She looked down with a very sordid expression, pointing out to him that the photo's meaning would be 'THE END OF EVERYTHING'.

'André, do not publish these photos now. Wait until I die!'

'How do you know you're going to die before me? After all, I am twelve years older than you.'

'I just know,' she said, in a sad, low-toned voice.

But the mood passed: soon she was gay and cheerful again, looking forward to her dinner date, and she urged him to hurry, hurry, pack everything into the car and leave.

De Dienes often went to Marilyn's grave during the twenty-three years he outlived her, and always visited on 1 June, her birthday, and 4 August, the anniversary of her death. Each time he'd steal some flowers and put them in a glass next to his bed. He'd think about her when he went to the Westwood Village movie theatre, knowing her coffin was behind the screen, only fifty feet away. She had said to him one day, 'You want me to become a cloud? Take pictures of it. That way I'll never completely die.'

Each time he pictured her on the phone, he remembered how she had put a false number on the dial of her home phone to protect her privacy and throw the prurient off the scent. If they called the number, they got through to the Los Angeles morgue.

Los Angeles–New York
March 1960

Angeleno by birth, Marilyn became passionately attached to
New York the moment she went there in late 1954. Even as a
young starlet, studying at LA's Actors Laboratory, she had
pictured the metropolis to the east as a magical place, 'where
actors and directors would do very different things with their
time than stand around all day arguing about a close-up or a
camera angle'. She dreamed of becoming part of that life, a more
thoughtful, articulate world, less in thrall to images.

With its unchanging skies and temperature, Los Angeles
seemed to her permanently to be sunk in a tepid stupor. She left
her home town the way, in bed, you move away from a body
that's too close and hot, and suddenly feel you can only be yourself by being alone. Cities are like bodies: some are skin, some
bone, and Marilyn wanted to feel part of a skeleton. After her
first visit, she always loved going back to New York, the upright
city. Its verticality, its buildings straining towards the sky were
an exhilarating break from her home town, with its supine, virtually flat expanses punctuated solely by the Hollywood Hills to

the north and the skyscrapers of the port district to the south. Los Angeles remained the city where you shone, you blazed, where the sun overwhelmed everything with its terrible perpendicular glare, reducing the streets and houses to a flat, shimmering mirage. Just as the idea of eternity, once it takes hold of someone's mind, makes sleep impossible, so the Californian skies always seemed to her to afford its streetscapes too much light, and the souls wandering them too little shade.

The moment she landed in Manhattan, it became her city. *The* city. The place where she could think. She never felt disoriented in New York. If anything, it gave her her bearings, the chance to find herself among its shadows and greys. Surrendering to the dizzying but lucid feeling that she was falling into herself, that she was yielding to an indefinable impulse, she immersed herself in its beauty. The changing seasons, the force of the elements – everything in New York made her feel vital. She found herself thinking about the city, through it. She thought the best photographs of her were in black and white, like New York, or like a chessboard.

Marilyn went back to New York for the first time after going into analysis with Greenson in March 1960, just after she'd won the Golden Globe for Best Actress in *Some Like It Hot*. She returned for a longer stay after an extended period of analysis with him culminated in the completion of *Let's Make Love*. At her last session before leaving, she told him about a recurring dream: 'I am buried in sand and I'm lying there, waiting for someone to come and dig me out. I can't do it on my own.'

She associated it with a memory. 'Ana . . . I called her Aunt Ana, but she wasn't really my aunt, just the best of all my foster mothers, who I lived with for four or five years . . . Ana died when I was twenty-two. I went and lay down in her bed the day after she died . . . just lay there for a couple of hours on her pillow. Then I went to the cemetery and these men were digging a grave and they had a ladder into it, and I asked if I could get down there and they said, "Sure," and I went down and lay on the ground and looked up at the sky from there. It's quite a view, and the ground is cold under your back.'

'Did you love her?' asked Greenson, troubled by certain aspects of the story that seemed too gruesome to be true.

'Sure. If that word means anything, it's not what happens between a man and a woman. I never found love before or after Ana, the love that picks out other children when they're growing up like the mysterious light on an actor's face in a movie. I compromised by dreaming of attracting someone's attention, of having people look at me and say my name. That's what love is for me now.'

In the burning heat of a New York July, on Greenson's advice, Marilyn returned to her husband Arthur Miller and her analyst Marianne Kris. But she would soon part company with both more or less simultaneously. She had been seeing Kris for three years and Margaret Hohenberg for two years before that, but now there was Romi, whom she rang every day. In a state of wild elation, she told her maid, Lena Pepitone, 'Lena, Lena, I've finally found him. He's my saviour. He's called Romeo. Can you believe that? I call him Jesus. My saviour. He's doing wonderful things for me. He listens to me. He's a doctor and a genius. He gives me courage. He makes me feel smart, makes me think. I can face anything with him. I'm not scared any more.'

Then she rang Greenson: 'I've fallen in love with Brooklyn. I'm going to buy a little house in Brooklyn and live there. I'll go to the coast only when I have to make a picture.'

The next day, on the C Train to Broadway, she sat opposite an ageless woman wearing a frilly pink doll's dress, pink pumps, white lace socks and a paste tiara, and sucking a dummy. Terrified, she called her saviour that night.

Vienna, 19 Berggasse
1933

Greenson was close to finishing his analysis with Wilhelm Stekel in Vienna when he was invited with several other aspiring young analysts to attend one of Freud's monthly talks on psychoanalytic technique. He was trying to make sense of the stage he'd reached in his analysis. What did finishing mean? He had discussed it at length with Stekel, but hoped the Master would be able to elucidate it fully before he started treating patients himself.

Freud's office was entered by the right-hand door on the first-floor landing of 19 Berggasse. There was a simple foyer with bars on the inside of the door as protection against burglary, not an unusual feature in middle-class Viennese homes, and two doors opening off it: one to the waiting room on the right, its walls hung with pictures and awards that Greenson did not recognise (he later found out that only one was of a colleague of Freud's, Sándor Ferenczi), and another, covered with the same dark wallpaper as the foyer's walls, for those who wanted to leave discreetly without having to walk past the patients waiting their turn. Ill-lit and thick with cigar smoke, with an armless sofa and a small

55

table with chairs around it as its only furniture, the waiting room was where the Master held his gatherings. He would greet the faithful coldly, without a smile. Only a dozen practising analysts were invited, with a permanent core of six, while a constantly changing selection of débutants, Freud's 'disciples from afar', made up the numbers. That evening the subject was the handling of transference – 'transference-love', as Freud termed it, the sort of euphemistic name one might give an illness to rob it of its terror.

'I have no great fondness for the expression "handling of transference",' Freud began. 'Transference is not a tool we manipulate. If it resembles anything, it is a hand that seizes hold of us and either caresses us or spins us round.' He spoke of the force of this attachment, its similarity to actual love, its duration, the extreme difficulty of unravelling it, and the dangers of revoking it, like a contract, by reminding the patient that neither of them was the real object of the other's feelings. He quoted Montaigne's line, 'I loved him because it was he, because it was I.'

'You see,' Freud said, 'it serves no purpose telling a patient, "You love me because it is not you, because it is not I." No purpose whatsoever.'

Beverly Hills Hotel
Late April 1960

A pink cloud draws across the evening sky around the bungalow. Georges Belmont, a French journalist, has come to interview Marilyn, who is back in Los Angeles for a few days. Their conversation ranges widely before eventually turning to death. Lapsing into long silences, Marilyn seems at once constrained and impulsive, as she says in her tired young girl's voice, 'Of course I think about it . . . quite a lot, actually. Sometimes I find myself thinking I'd rather think about death than life. It's so much simpler in a way. You push open a door and you know there most likely won't be anyone on the other side. Whereas in life, there always is. At least one other person's always in the room. In you go, and it's never your fault. As for getting out . . . Do you know how to get out of people?'

'Tell me about your childhood,' Belmont asks, avoiding the question.

'I never lived with my mother. That's the truth, no matter what some people have said. As far back as I can remember I've always lived with other people. My mother was mentally ill. She's dead now.'

That made two untruths in as many sentences, not that the interviewer was to know. Norma Jeane had lived with her mother for several months when she was about eight years old, in a little apartment on Afton Place near the studios, before her mother was admitted to a mental hospital for a long period. Then she had her to stay for a few weeks in a small place she had on Nebraska Avenue when she was twenty and starting out in the film business. Gladys Baker was also still alive at the time of the interview. Mentally ill, but in good health, she would outlive her daughter by twenty-two years. In 1951, when the studios put out the story of Marilyn being an orphan for publicity purposes, she received a letter from Gladys: 'Please dear child, I'd like to receive a letter from you. Things are very annoying around here and I'd like to move away as soon as possible. I'd like to have my child's love instead of hatred.' The letter was signed, 'Love, Mother'. Not 'Your Mother' or 'Mom', just 'Mother', which Gladys had not been able to be, and which Marilyn in her turn wouldn't be either.

Marilyn thanked Belmont after the interview and said she'd been glad to be able to talk. Answering journalists' questions still terrified her, so she'd appreciated being treated as a human being rather than as a star. That evening she went to a party in Beverly Hills given by the influential Hollywood literary agent Irving Lazar. She ran into Greenson and his wife, who greeted her affectionately, spotted the familiar faces of John Huston and David O. Selznick, then spent a long time talking to a sixty-year-old man she had never met who had just moved to Brentwood Heights in Hollywood. He told her his favourite Californian pastimes – going walking in the north-east, past San Fernando, in the green and blue jacaranda-covered hills bordering the Mojave Desert, where he hunted rare butterflies for his book on Californian Lepidoptera, driving around the Los Angeles freeways in his Ford Impala, and visiting supermarkets, 'especially at night, for the neon'. He said he'd written a novel called *Lolita* that

Stanley Kubrick was making into a film for Universal. Vladimir Nabokov was trying to adapt to screenwriting as a form.

'What about you? What do you do?' he asked the blonde, who was drinking constantly to get up her courage to talk or remain silent or whatever was needed to make it through the party.

'I'm in pictures,' she replied.

Amused by the expression, he joked, 'Me too, but I'm just a double.'

A few weeks later, in *Let's Make Love*, Marilyn persuaded Cukor to let her preface her rendition of 'My Heart Belongs To Daddy' with the words, 'My name is Lolita and I'm not supposed to play with boys!'

New York, Manhattan
Late 1954

After divorcing her second husband, Joe DiMaggio, Marilyn moved to New York to study with Lee Strasberg at the Actors Studio. She lived at the Gladstone Hotel on East 52nd Street before decamping to the Waldorf Astoria in April 1955. She never had many belongings at her various Manhattan addresses – just her library of four hundred books and, her prize possession, the white piano from when she was seven, which she kept among some imitation French furniture in the tiny space she used as a living room. After years of searching, she had found the piano at an auction in West Los Angeles in 1951. She'd bought it on instalments and moved it into the minuscule studio flat she was living in at the time in the Beverly Carlton Hotel. Two years later it had followed her to a three-room apartment on Doheny Drive. She kept it through all her moves, and, in either 1956 or 1957, she installed it in the thirtieth-floor apartment she shared with Arthur Miller on East 57th Street.

Landing at Idlewild airport, she posed for a barrage of photographers on the steps of the plane for forty minutes. The crew cheered and whistled, but all she could think of was the prospect of meeting up with Joseph L. Mankiewicz, the most intellectual of directors, who used to say of himself, 'I am an author who makes films, not a director. I make films to stop people ruining what I've written.' He had cast her in one of her first Hollywood movies, *All About Eve*, and now she wanted him to pick her for his musical comedy, *Guys and Dolls*, so she could prove to him how much she had changed in the intervening four years. But by the time she had driven into Manhattan, Mankiewicz had set off in the opposite direction to Los Angeles. She called him instead: 'Guess what? I've become a star. Now I'm making a picture with Billy Wilder. It's called *The Seven Year Itch*.'

Mankiewicz was coldly dismissive of the project. She didn't know whether it was because he simply didn't like Wilder (among other things, because Wilder never missed the chance to mock psychoanalysis in his films), or was actually afraid of him. Wilder's masterpiece *Sunset Boulevard*, a bitter portrait of a washed-up actress that served as a brilliant exposé of Hollywood mores, had come out at the same time as Mankiewicz's depiction of an actress's decline, *All About Eve*. Admittedly, Mankiewicz had won the Oscar for best film that year, but he still bore Wilder an inexplicable grudge, and perhaps feared that this time his rival's comedy might be better than his.

Either way, Mankiewicz was very tough on Marilyn: 'No, no. You're too Hollywood. Put on some more clothes,' he said, as if she was worthless, 'stop shaking your ass so much and we'll see.' It felt like a brutal reminder of her early days in Hollywood, of everything she most hated, as if she was still making pornographic films.

The next day, she asked her old lover Milton Greene to take her picture. In his darkened studio on Lexington Avenue, as the Dom Pérignon flowed, he photographed her in a ballerina's dress. A dancer without a dance in the glare of the flashbulbs, sitting in a broken-down armchair against a large black curtain, she was sad and innocent and carnal as she hugged herself in a snow-white dress several sizes too big, her lipstick and nail polish a matching shade of blood red.

New York, Actors Studio, West 44th Street
January 1955

Los Angeles would always be the movie capital, where even psychoanalysts were gripped by studio fever and infected by the prevailing mania for images. So when she moved east, Marilyn set up an independent production company with Milton Greene and resolved to make New York the place where she'd search for the meaning of people and things, the city of psychoanalysis. Lee Strasberg urged her to 'free her unconscious' in analysis, and she asked Greene for the name of a therapist. He recommended Margaret Herz Hohenberg, a psychoanalyst of Hungarian extraction, a large, austere woman who wore her white hair bound in tight braids. She had studied medicine in Vienna, Budapest and Prague, then moved to New York just before the war. She was already treating Greene and analysed them both until Marilyn severed her ties with her analyst and her business partner in February 1957.

Apart from Strasberg's prompting – he thought every actor should face the truth of his or her unconscious on the analyst's couch – Marilyn hoped Hohenberg would help with a range of problems: childhood traumas, lack of self-esteem, inability to sustain relationships, friendships or love affairs, and fear of abandonment. She saw her five times a week, twice in the morning and three times in the afternoon, and was unfailingly punctual for every session. She had a sort of exorcism ritual, which she'd perform when she left the practice on East 93rd Street. Emerging from the building, she'd immediately stop, raise her hand to her mouth and cough until it hurt. Then she'd look up and calmly survey the street, as if all the emotions that had been brought up in the session had been expelled or safely buried. Marilyn instantly became a passionate admirer of psychoanalysis. When she was asked at a press conference what she hoped to get from it, she replied, 'I won't talk about it, except to say that I believe in the Freudian interpretation. I hope at some future time to make a glowing report on the wonders that psychiatrists can do for you.'

Establishing what would become a precedent, Hohenberg became considerably more than a therapist before the year was out: she settled a legal wrangle between Marilyn and her hairdresser, stopped her seeing certain people, and advised her on movie roles. When she wasn't seeing her analyst, Marilyn would attend morning courses at Strasberg's workshop in the Malin Studios, or have private lessons in the evenings at his apartment on 86th Street. Strasberg, who had invented an acting technique he modestly called the Method, wanted, as he put it, to bring to light everything she'd marginalised, everything she'd repressed about her past and to tap all her explosive energy. Marilyn was fascinated by his theories of human nature. Strasberg and Hohenberg decided to work together to convert what they saw as Marilyn's dark core of depression into an ability to sustain viable personal and professional relationships. 'I had teachers and people I could look up to,' Marilyn would later say about this partnership, 'but nobody I could look over at. I always felt I was a nobody, and the only way for me to be a somebody was to be – well, somebody else. Which is probably why I wanted to act.'

'I'm trying to become an artist,' she said, at one of her first sessions with Hohenberg, 'and to be true, but sometimes a window opens and I see how empty I am. I sometimes feel I'm on the verge of craziness, I'm just trying to get the truest part of myself out, and it's very hard. There are times when I think, All I have to be is true. But sometimes it doesn't come so easily. I always have this secret feeling that I'm really a fake or something, a phoney. My one desire is to do my best, the best that I can from the moment the camera starts until it stops. That moment I want to be perfect, as perfect as I can make it . . . Lee says I have to start with myself, and I say "With *me*?" Well, I'm not so important! Who does he think I am? Marilyn Monroe or something?'

New York, West 93rd Street
February 1955

Following a pattern that would repeat itself with subsequent analysts, Marilyn wasn't content simply to pay for her sessions, but instead set about involving money in her analytic treatment in a variety of increasingly intimate ways. She asked her analyst for advice on her business affairs. Then, in February 1956, she drew up a will bequeathing twenty thousand dollars, a tenth of her estimated estate, to Dr Margaret Herz Hohenberg. Among the other legatees, Lee and Paula Strasberg were to receive twenty-five thousand, the Actors Studio ten thousand, and she left enough money to cover hospitalisation costs for Gladys Baker for the rest of her life (but not more than a total of twenty-five thousand dollars). The lawyer who drew up the will jokingly asked Marilyn if she had an idea for her epitaph. 'Marilyn Monroe, Blonde,' she said, tracing lines in the air with a gloved finger.

This symbiotic relationship between talking, love and money evolved. In July 1956, Lee Strasberg negotiated Marilyn's drama coach Paula Strasberg's contract with the producers of

The Prince and the Showgirl. Then in October, Margaret Hohenberg went to London at great personal expense to Marilyn to provide support during filming, as she had first done on *Bus Stop.*

Margaret Hohenberg urged Marilyn to keep a diary, but she never did, although she bought notebooks with beautiful marbled covers. There was something about the bound notebooks, an imperative to write systematically, that was too much for her. She did copy out lists of words from dictionaries, though, either difficult words, like *abasia, abate, abject, abstruse, acronym, adjure, adulate, adulterate* or simple but obscure words, such as *cold, parent* or *I.* Some notes scrawled on scraps of paper were also found among the personal papers and possessions that were left after the police searched the house where she died. It was a meagre haul. Most of her things had disappeared before the police even arrived, which, to some people, gave substance to the thesis that she had been murdered.

The oldest notes date from 1955, when she was studying at the Actors Studio.

My problem of desperation in my work and life – I must begin to face it continually, making my work routine more continuous and of more importance than my desperation.

Doing a scene is like opening a bottle. If it doesn't open one way, try another – perhaps even give it up for another bottle? Lee wouldn't like that . . .

How or why I can act – and I'm not sure I can – is the thing for me to understand. The torture, let alone the day to day happenings – the pain one cannot explain to another.

How can I sleep? How does this girl fall asleep? What does she think about?

What is it there I'm afraid of? Hiding in case of punishment? Libido? Ask Dr H.

How can I speak naturally on stage? Don't let the actress worry, let the character worry.

Learn to believe in contradictory impulses.

Hollywood, Century City, Pico Boulevard
June 1960

Marilyn celebrated her thirty-fourth birthday with Rupert Allan, her PR agent and friend, at his apartment on Seabright Place. She spent the whole evening talking to Tennessee Williams and his formidable mother Edwina. Anxious at the passing of another year, she had resumed seeing her saviour. 'It's starting again. It never stops,' she told Greenson. 'It feels like I'm always going backwards.'

Sometimes it seemed to her as if she was singing her life in playback, struggling to fit lyrics to a pre-recorded tune. 'What am I afraid of?' she had written on a piece of paper, while she was waiting to be called on Fox's set for one of the last scenes of *Let's Make Love*. 'Do I think I can't act? I know I can act but I am afraid. I am afraid and I should not be and I must not be.'

On her previous film, Billy Wilder's *Some Like It Hot*, she had panicked twice when she felt her body, the rampart protecting her vulnerable inner self, was under threat. The first time was when she had refused to come out of her dressing room to do the scene where she sings 'Running Wild'. Wilder had asked

Sandra Warner, who was playing Emily, one of the musicians in the orchestra, to sing the number in playback: 'Marilyn will come out when she hears your voice instead of hers, take my word for it.' And sure enough, Marilyn appeared as soon as she heard the singing backstage. She shot Wilder a filthy look as he coldly announced, in his Viennese accent, 'Let's do it over', flourished her ukulele, then launched into the song with furious panache. Then, at the end of filming, she was too pregnant to appear in publicity stills, so they suggested Sandra wear her costumes and pose between Jack Lemmon and Tony Curtis; they superimposed her face on the photos afterwards. Marilyn had no choice in the matter but that didn't stop it hurting, and she begrudged Sandra Warner the theft of her body for a long time.

On the same film, after a fitting with the two male leads, who were in drag for most of the film, the costume designer Orry-Kelly measured up Marilyn. He was rash enough to say, 'Tony's got a nicer ass than you.'

She turned round in a fury, pulled down her blouse and shouted, 'Yeah, but he hasn't got tits like these!'

But there was another Marilyn. Wilder always remembered the day when an assistant director was sent to get her from her dressing room and found her reading Thomas Paine's *The Rights of Man*. 'Go fuck yourself,' was her pithy response to the interruption.

After that, whenever anyone talked about her lateness on set, Billy Wilder would say, 'I've never had any problems with Monroe. Marilyn has problems with Monroe. She's got something inside that bites and gnaws away at her. She's an out-of-kilter soul, searching for some part of her she's lost. Like in that scene in *Some Like It Hot* when, drunk and half-asleep, she had to open the drawers of a chest-of-drawers and say, "Where's that bourbon?" We put a sticker in each drawer to remind her of the line. But she couldn't get it. That was eighty takes or something. I took her to one side after about take fifty, and said, "Don't worry about it." "Worry about what?" she goes. But it was worth it in the end. She is a truly great actress. Better Marilyn late than any other actress on time. I've got an old aunt in Vienna who acts. Her name, I think, is Mildred Lachenfarber. She always comes to the set on time. She says her lines perfectly. She never gives anyone the slightest trouble. At the box office she is worth fourteen cents. Do you get my point?'

One evening when Wilder went home, he kissed his wife, the tall, beautiful Audrey Young, and announced, 'Marilyn was sensational. If I had to cheat on you with anyone, it'd be her.'

'Me too,' Young answered.

Billy Wilder saw Marilyn Monroe for the last time in the spring of 1960 while she was shooting *Let's Make Love*. It was at a party at Romanoff's in Beverly Hills after a screening of *The Seven Year Itch*. He offered her the female lead in his next film, *Irma la Douce*. It was Oscar time and Wilder had been awarded the Oscar for Best Director for *Some Like It Hot*. I. A. L. Diamond had won Best Screenwriter, Jack Lemmon Best Actor, Orry-Kelly Best Costume Designer. Marilyn, who played the unforgettable Sugar Kane, wasn't even nominated. When she heard Simone Signoret had been nominated for Best Actress for *A Room at the Top*, a low-budget British film, she seemed unaffected, almost happy.

The following day, Wilder asked, 'How's it going? You're not finding it too hard, are you?'

'No. I learned from Freud that sometimes our unconscious wants us to fail. And, anyway, let's face it, when it comes to women, a lot of people don't like it so hot.'

New York, Gladstone Hotel, East 52nd Street
March 1955

In Manhattan, Marilyn could dissolve into anonymity. She was nobody. She could hide from herself. She would wear a baggy sweater, an old coat and no make-up, knot a scarf under her chin, slip on dark glasses and go strolling through the crowded streets to the Actors Studio, where she attended group classes, always sitting in the same place in the back row, or to Margaret Hohenberg's practice. Her time in Manhattan was intellectually exhilarating: she was absorbed by 'the mysteries of the unconscious', as she laughingly told her friend, the writer Truman Capote.

They had met in 1950 while she was filming *Asphalt Jungle* with John Huston. Superficially different, the gay writer and the symbol of heterosexual desire were nonetheless profoundly similar. They shared a sense of something poorly articulated, a secret suffering in the depths of their being. The same abandonment as a child, the same destructive way with drugs and sex, the same traumas over their art, the same panic about success, the same physical decline and, eventually, the same death from an overdose of prescription drugs. They'd drink cocktails in bars on Lexington Avenue, one half vodka, one half gin, no vermouth, which they called White Angels. Marilyn would arrive in a cheap black wig, which she'd whisk off with a flourish, and Capote would call out 'Bye-bye, blackbird. Hi, Marilyn.'

He opened his heart the first time they met. 'Have you any idea what it's like to be me?' he asked. 'An ugly dwarf in love with beauty, a nasty, luckless kid from nowhere who spends his time ferrying words from people to the page, from one book to another, a homo who only gets on with women—'

'I can guess,' she cut in, downing her vodka in one. 'Do you know what it's like to be me? The same, except without the words to express it.'

After Marilyn's death, Capote would say, slightly falsely, 'There was something exceptional about Marilyn Monroe. Sometimes she could be ethereal and sometimes like a waitress in a coffee shop. She'd been a call girl, off and on, to make ends meet, but in her mind money was always associated with love rather than sex. She gave her body to whomever she thought she loved and money to whomever she really did love. She loved being in love; she loved thinking she loved someone. One day I introduced her to Bill Paley, a tycoon who fancied her like crazy. I tried telling Marilyn he loved her. "Don't shit me," she said. "You love someone after you sleep with them – and even then that's kind of rare – never before. At least, that's how it's been with me and men. Sex and love always go together for me, just like these." And she pointed at her tits. "I wish I could turn sex into love and forget about bodies. I wish I could *make* love, as they say. I love that expression."

'"I don't," I said. "What two people make isn't love. You never make love. You never have it. You're just in it or you're not. That's all."

'She stared at me with a bitter smile. I didn't make a big thing of it. Everyone's entitled to their illusions. But later I had my character in *Breakfast at Tiffany's*, Holly Golightly, say, "I mean, you can't bang the guy and cash his cheques and at least not *try* to believe you love him."'

In 1955, Truman and Marilyn met up again. She was living in a suite on the sixth floor of the Gladstone Hotel, and in February had taken her first lesson at the Actors Studio. Meeting Lee Strasberg had changed her life. The drama teacher said he wanted 'to open up her unconscious'. 'Rather than my legs,' Marilyn told Truman. 'That's what's known as a godsend.'

One day Truman took her to see Constance Collier in her dark studio on West 57th Street. The old English actress, whose sight was failing and who was losing sensation in her limbs, gave her diction lessons and voice coaching. 'Oh, yes,' Miss Collier said afterwards, 'there is something there. She's a beautiful child. I don't mean that in the obvious way – the perhaps too obvious way. I don't think she's an actress at all, not in any traditional sense. What she has – this presence, this luminosity, this flickering intelligence – could never surface on the stage. It's so fragile and subtle, it can only be found by the camera. It's like a hummingbird in flight: only a camera can freeze the poetry of it.'

After that Marilyn went back to Los Angeles and Truman didn't see her again until Constance Collier's funeral. She was staying on the twenty-seventh floor of the Waldorf-Astoria. She liked looking down on Park Avenue from her suite at night, the way one looks at the face of someone asleep. Her favourite thing about the hotel, though, was the revolving doors at the entrance, always spinning. She was fascinated by them, by the name. Truman once said to her, 'They're like life. You think you're moving forward, but in fact you're going backwards. You never know if you're going in or coming out.'

'I guess,' she said. 'It makes me think of love more, though. We're all alone in our plate-glass compartments, chasing round and round after someone but never catching them. We think we're right next to the other person but really we're far away, deep inside ourselves. No one knows who's leading and who's following. Like children, we wonder where it all started. Who fell in love first, who fell out of love first.'

Marilyn arrived late at the funerary chapel, all apologies and nervous indecision about her make-up and her dress.

He understood her profound anxiety. If she was never less than an hour late wherever she went, it wasn't vanity: it was because she was too uncertain and anxious to set off on time. It was anxiety, the tension of constantly having to please, that was responsible for her recurrent sore throats that were so severe she couldn't speak, her chewed fingernails, damp palms and fits of giggling like a geisha; the terrible raw nerves that aroused passionate sympathy in whoever witnessed them and, if anything, only made her more radiant in their eyes. Marilyn was always late, like everyone who has appeared at the wrong moment in their parents' lives, all the unexpected souls.

They fell out of touch. The White Angels grew further and further apart until eventually they vanished into the white blur of oblivion. She had given him the character of Holly Golightly – or, rather, he had taken it from her, from her words, her hands, her hopes, the chaos of her soul – and now she wasn't of any use to him except to make him sad, like a worn car tyre left lying on the tarmac of a parking lot, or a lost key. He saw her for the last time in Hollywood a few weeks before her death, and said afterwards, 'She had never looked better. She had lost a lot of weight for the picture she was going to do with George Cukor, and there was a new maturity about her eyes. She wasn't so giggly any more. If she had lived and kept her figure, I think she would still look terrific today. The Kennedys didn't kill her, the way some people think. She committed suicide. But they paid one of her best friends, her press attaché Pat Newcomb, to keep quiet about her relationship with them. That friend knew where all the skeletons were, and after Marilyn died, they sent her on a year-long cruise round the world. For a whole year no one knew where she was.'

Four years later, Truman Capote threw his famous black and white ball in New York's grandest ballroom at the Plaza Hotel. He spent months drawing up lists, covering page after page with names, underlining some, crossing out others. People thought he was working on his next novel, but it was his last party, his immolation on the funeral pyre of celebrity. He invited five hundred people: hardly any writers, lots of Hollywood types, including Sinatra, a few ghosts, such as the old diva Tallulah Bankhead, but neither John Huston, for whom he had written *Beat the Devil* and who had introduced him to Marilyn, nor Blake Edwards, who had massacred *Breakfast at Tiffany's*. He wanted people to hide their faces and wear black or white, like pieces in a chess game. After his death, a note from 1970 was found in his papers. 'A white bishop. That's how she saw me. Marilyn and I were destined to find each other but not touch. It can be that way sometimes, like Holly and the narrator in *Breakfast at Tiffany's*.' Truman also noted in his diary, 'Strange. After my parents' divorce, I was brought up in Monroeville, Alabama.'

Phoenix, Arizona
March 1956

After fourteen months in New York, Marilyn returned to Los Angeles to film *Bus Stop*. On 12 March 1956, Norma Jeane Mortenson, as she still signed herself, became Marilyn Monroe. 'I am an actress and I found my name a handicap,' she said. 'I have been using the name I wish to assume, Marilyn Monroe, for many years and I am now known professionally by that name.'

On set, director Joshua Logan discovered just how much of a Freudian devotee the actress had become. In one scene Don Murray, who was playing a cowboy, was supposed to wake Marilyn with the words, 'No wonder you're so pale and white. That's the sun out there.' Instead he said 'so pale and scaly'.

Logan called, 'Cut.'

'Don,' Marilyn said gleefully, 'do you realise what you just did? You made a *Freudian* slip . . . It's a sexual scene and you gave a sexual symbol. You see, you said "scaly", which means to say you were thinking of a snake. And a snake is a phallic symbol. You know what a phallic symbol is?'

'Know what that is?' Murray retorted. 'I've got one! Do you think I'm a fairy or something?'

'What do I know? Let me tell you a story. You know Errol Flynn? Well, when I was about ten, I saw *The Prince and the Pauper* three times. And then ten years later I met him in the flesh in Hollywood. Next thing I knew, my prince had whipped out his dick and was playing the piano with it. Errol Flynn! My childhood hero! I'd just got into modelling, and I went to this half-ass party, and Errol Flynn, so pleased with himself, he was there and he took out his prick and played the piano with it. Thumped the keys. He played "You Are My Sunshine". Christ! Everyone says Milton Berle has the biggest schlong in Hollywood. I wouldn't know about that. But I've seen Errol's . . . So you'll have to do better than that!'

During the filming of *Bus Stop* in Sun Valley, Marilyn tried out the psychoanalytic methods of Strasberg, who was a close friend of Logan's. She replaced the sumptuous costumes that had been designed for her with a shabby black dress and a trashy blue silk and fishnet basque, reminders, perhaps, of the porn shoots when she was starting out. She wanted her clothes to be as tattered and patched-together as she felt. She gave her character a stutter like her own, even a tendency to forget her lines that wasn't in the script.

Reno, Nevada
Summer 1960

Her problems with filming didn't let up after *Let's Make Love*. Her next picture, based on a short story by Arthur Miller, was *The Misfits*, co-starring Clark Gable and Montgomery Clift, directed by John Huston and shot on location in Reno, Nevada. Filming began behind schedule, without her. The crew took over the Mapes Hotel and used a nearby movie-house, the Crest Theater, to watch the daily rushes. Two days later, Jim Haspiel, the most devoted of Marilyn's admirers, went to New York's LaGuardia airport to see her off. She looked terrible, with 'bags under the eyes and a period stain across the back of her skirt'. He couldn't bear to see her that way.

On the tarmac at Reno, Marilyn kept everyone waiting while she changed in the lavatory of the aircraft. The sun set, the photographers readied their flashes, and finally the star emerged from the plane, like a white dream blossoming out of the darkness.

The next day the desert heat reached at least 100 degrees in the shade, and Marilyn began filming. She was like nothing human anyone had ever seen or dreamed. She was like a ghost, so pale that the people around her were like shadows picked out by the moon. As a journalist described her, 'Disdaining all lingerie and dressed in tight, white silk emblazoned with countless red cherries, she became at once the symbol of impartial and eternal availability, who yet remained forever pure – and a potentially terrible goddess whose instinct could also deal death and whose smile, when she directed it clearly at you, was exquisitely, heartbreakingly sweet.'

When Huston had offered her the part of Roslyn a few months earlier, Marilyn hadn't been particularly enamoured by the prospect of playing a woman torn between her need for love and her abhorrence of suffering. It all felt too close to home. 'She's my double,' she told Greenson. 'The same anxieties, the same sense of abandonment, the same problems living. I don't want to play a woman who's had an awful childhood and a crazed relationship with her mother and whose only refuge is innocence, you know, the wonder she feels when she looks at children and animals. *Roslyn*: that's Rose, as in the Rose I played in *Niagara*, the cheap whore who killed her husband, and -lyn, as in Marilyn. Me basically.'

She had only taken the role in the end because she was tired of doing comedies and because Huston had assured her he would write the final version of the script, which her husband had tailored to fit her like a lethal glove. 'Even Marilyn's pain expressed life,' Miller said later, 'the struggle against the angel of death.'

'Why do you want to film in black and white?' Marilyn asked Huston, after agreeing to play Roslyn.

'You're on so many drugs,' Huston shot back in his tough-guy way. 'With those bloodshot eyes and veins of yours we couldn't film in Technicolor even if we wanted to and could afford it . . . Now, don't take that badly and go and jam down another handful of pills. I wouldn't want you to be any deader than you are already. Suicidal neurotics get on my nerves. I mean, kill yourself if you must, be my guest, but, honey, why do you have to make everybody else's life hell while you're at it? . . . Why else do I want to shoot in black and white? Well, if I'm doing a psychological study, like my Freud picture's going to be, I'm more interested in showing what's going on behind people's eyes than the colour of them. And nothing's black and white in life and I only want to film what exists in the movies.'

'Why do you want me?' Marilyn wondered.

'Because you're more like a hooker than an actress. Like real hookers, the good ones, you don't pretend to an emotion, you give your whole self, body and soul. But you do know she's not you, this woman, don't you? I can't stand that whole Actors Studio Method – thank God Strasberg hasn't managed to ruin you with it yet. That fucking technique where you have to go deep into yourself to find an emotion from your past and then smear it all over the screen. I've got a lot of respect for psychoanalysis and a lot of respect for the job of an actor, but put the two of them together and you've got a recipe for disaster. The great thing about you, Marilyn, even if you don't realise it, is that you've broken free from Strasberg's Method. You won't *act* Roslyn. You'll give the viewer what he wants to feel and see and love, like a hooker who wants the customer to get his money's worth. If you do the exact opposite of what Strasberg has taught you, I'm telling you, everything'll be fine. Forget all that "go inside yourself" crap. Go outside – that's where you are, that's where the audience is. And as for your anxieties, hang on to them. They're a precious resource for an actor. Don't think your analyst is going to free you from them. No one can and, anyway, they shouldn't. If you don't feel anxiety in this business, you might as well give up.'

'So why are you making a film about Freud?' Marilyn asked. 'Is it instead of going into analysis yourself?'

Huston didn't reply straight away. At fifty-four, he found

himself confronted by the same anxieties, conflicts and deep-seated problems that had plagued him throughout his childhood and adolescence. Fascinated and terrified in equal measure by the unconscious, his investigations into 'depth psychology' – they didn't call it 'psychoanalysis' in Hollywood in those days – dated from his first film.

'It's true, I'm very interested in psychoanalysis,' Huston said, after a while. 'Traumas and buried memories were the subject of a documentary I made about soldiers returning from the front, *Let There Be Light*. Is that how you think of analysis, as something that will let the light into your darkened soul so you can bear the sun coming up, the glare of a new day? I know it'll never do that for me. I'll make do without it. I'm going to set my anxieties in motion, put everything I've repressed up on screen, and then face my demons twenty-four frames a second. I'll get them out in a movie, not on the couch – a movie about Freud, why not? Play it again, Sigmund.'

'I don't understand why you're so hard on Monty,' she said.

'I'm a man's director. I loathe passivity. Initiative, action: that's what I like. Filming should hurt. Hurt my actors, my crew, my producers. I'll tell you a secret: the movies are made to hurt the spectator. Monty and I have a relationship he likes. He gets off on it. I treat him like the alcoholic, masochistic, drug-addicted fairy he is. Devastated and lost. That's why I'm thinking of getting him to play Freud. I'd like my Freud to be like Perce in *The Misfits* in lots of ways. One of those men who's out of true, a bit cracked deep down.'

One evening in Reno at the crap tables, Huston asked Marilyn to throw the dice.

'What should I ask the dice for, John?'

'Don't think, honey, just throw,' Huston told her. 'That's the story of your life. Don't think, do it.'

But she needed to think about her role as much as ever. Once on set, Marilyn stopped talking to her husband and the director. If they wanted to communicate with her, they had to go through Paula Strasberg, a perennial presence in her black dress and little black veil. Marilyn secretly called her 'the witch' or 'the vulture', but she made sure Paula was on a higher salary than she was. The crew nicknamed her 'the Black Baroness'. 'How many directors are there on this film?' Huston occasionally yelled, to no one in particular.

Progress was painfully slow and, in his version of grinning and bearing it, Huston took to losing chunks of the budget in Reno's casinos. Marilyn started refusing to come out of her trailer, retreating further and further inside herself. The Method was her sole article of faith. Fox decided to call on Greenson.

Los Angeles, Bel Air
August 1960

On the second to last weekend in August, Marilyn took advantage of a break in filming to fly to Los Angeles. She saw her analyst repeatedly, their sessions sometimes running on for hours, but also found time to go to Joe Schenck's bedside. Schenck, a movie mogul and producer, one of the founders of 20th Century Fox, was seriously ill and would die shortly afterwards.

They had met in 1948 at a party at his lavish mansion on South Carolwood Drive. An extravagant medley of Spanish-Italian renaissance and Moorish architecture, it was an appropriate backdrop for the gargantuan poker evenings Schenck liked to throw. His friends would roll up with an attractive woman on each arm – models and starlets, hoping for advancement in their careers, and if that meant providing something a little more personal, well, who were they to refuse an executive's wishes? Schenck was a well-established producer, and Marilyn, by her own admission, a willing lamb to the slaughter – but she wasn't to succumb that first evening.

As she looked at the wretched octogenarian hooked up to

every sort of machine on his hospital bed, she could no longer remember when it was she had finally submitted to him. At the time she had wanted desperately to work, to be a star, and afterwards she spoke openly of her affair with Schenck, who had immediately given her what she was looking for. He had put her in touch with his poker buddy Harry Cohn, then head of Columbia Studios and the man who had transformed a dancer named Margarita Consino into Rita Hayworth.

Cohn's offer of a contract came with one condition: after a week of electrolysis, hydrogen peroxide and ammonia treatments, the mirror reflected her new image – like her beloved Jean Harlow, her dirty-blonde hair had vanished under a haze of platinum.

After approving her new look, Cohn sent her to take classes from Natasha Lytess, who would later say, 'I made Marilyn. I made everything about her: how she read, her voice, her acting, her pronunciation of her *t*s and *d*s, her walk, heel to toe, the way she swung those hips like no one had done before.'

Gazing at Los Angeles' leaden sky through the window of the hospital waiting room, Marilyn thought about coincidences; about the distance between the hospital block where Schenck now lay, fighting for breath, and his mansion, where they'd first met; about the way his hair looked almost blond against his pillow, as if it had been bleached. She caught sight of her reflection in a mirror and was startled by her excessive, almost unbearable blondeness, the magnet for *The Misfits'* spots that were intended to bathe every shot in a sphere of ethereal light. She'd wanted to be a different shade of blonde in every film she appeared in: ash, unbleached dark, golden, silver, amber, honey, smoky, topaz, platinum – anything except natural blonde. Seven years earlier, she remembered, Howard Hawks had given her a part in his movie opposite Jane Russell, who was playing the brunette and, try as she might, Marilyn hadn't been able to get a dressing room. She'd finally had to descend to their level by saying, 'Look, after all, I am the blonde, and it is *Gentlemen Prefer Blondes*.'

'Remember, you're not a star!' the production team repeated.
'Well, whatever I am, I'm the blonde!'

Dyeing hair, dying hair, Marilyn thought, as she turned away from the mirror. How many hours have I spent in waiting rooms, front offices and foyers since starting out? Maybe it's not men I've been trying to keep waiting by showing up late, maybe it's Death. OK, mister, you can have the last dance, but not this very moment. She stifled a laugh. I'll talk about it to the words doctor. As she went back into Schenck's room, tears welled at the memory of a Chihuahua he had given her, which she'd called Josepha, after him. She'd been very fond of Schenck. He had really cared about her in the early, hard days; she had always been able to go to him if she'd needed a meal or a shoulder to cry on. Schenck heard someone approaching his bedside but couldn't make out who it was.

Santa Monica, Franklin Street
August 1960

During an afternoon session on her break from *The Misfits*, Greenson commented on how rarely she talked about her sex life.

'You know, Doctor,' she said, 'I think of my sex life – my life, period, in fact – as a series of jump cuts. A man comes in, gets all excited, has me, loses me . . . And then in the next shot you see the same man – or maybe another one – come in again, but this time his smile's different, he's got a new set of mannerisms, the lighting's changed. He was holding an empty glass a minute ago and now it's half full. We look at each other through different eyes. Time's passed but we're still caught up in an image we have of ourselves, we still think we're meeting for the first time. Does that make any sense to you? I don't know if it does me either, but I wonder whether that's what relationships between men and women are really like. We try to touch as we pass each other but we're not separated just by space, time is against us too.'

By this stage in her analysis, Greenson was starting to think Marilyn's problems lay not so much in her sexuality as in a confusion in her self-image. He had coined a collective term, 'screen character patients', for people who, for defensive reasons, represent their desires as a screen. They may project 'screen hunger', for instance, or 'screen affect', but, in general, they manifest a 'screen identity'. For them, the twin acts of showing oneself and being seen by others constitute a uniquely exciting or terrifying experience, most often both. 'In ordinary language,' he wrote, 'the word "screen" may mean to conceal, to filter, or to camouflage.' In Marilyn's case, he thought, the word 'screen' also referred quite literally to a cinema screen, but it had plenty of other associations. He believed that, in the psychoanalytic sense, it specifically denoted a process whereby an individual uses a viable self-image – not necessarily wholly invented or false – to mask the pain of existence, some unbearable truth about him- or herself. He thought of the image that had shown on every TV channel five years before: the still from *The Seven Year Itch*, fifty feet high, covering most of Loew's State Theater in New York. Her body and windblown dress had floated over Broadway like a huge white flower for a fortnight in the run-up to the première.

Greenson still knew Marilyn primarily through her film roles, in which she incarnated desirability in its most unattainable form, but he found himself wondering whether icons of desire such as her actually felt desire themselves. Years later, he would read something Vladimir Nabokov had written about the movie star: 'It is possible this great comedy actress saw sex purely as comedy.'

After several months, the psychoanalyst was inclined to think of Marilyn's various personae – the diligent Actors Studio pupil, Marianne Kris's diligent patient, the diligent reader of the writers of her age – as 'screen images'. She construed herself as an apprentice New York intellectual in order to blank out the fear of being stupid that had haunted the little girl from Nebraska Avenue, who'd dreamed of shining like a fantastical constellation in Hollywood's firmament.

*   *   *

At their second session that day, Marilyn looked across at her analyst and said, 'I think that when you're famous every weakness is exaggerated. This industry should behave like a mother whose child has just run out in front of a car. But instead of clasping the child to them, they start punishing the child. All this industry does is take. All those shots you have to do a hundred times over, all those takes . . . but who's giving, who's receiving, who's loving? If you've noticed, in Hollywood, where millions and billions of dollars have been made, there aren't really any kind of monuments or museums . . . Gee, nobody left anything behind. They took it, they grabbed it and they ran, the ones who made the billions of dollars, never the workers. I'm not in this big American rush, you know, you got to go and you got to go fast but for no good reason, and I'm never going to be.'

'Fine,' said Greenson. 'I think that's a good place to stop for today.'

'Oh, you're the same as all the rest. Cut! Next take! One last one, Marilyn!'

In April 1952 Marilyn had to have an appendectomy at the Cedars of Lebanon Hospital. When Dr Marcus Rabwin lifted the sheet covering her in order to start the operation, he found a little handwritten note taped to her stomach:

Dear Doctor,
   Cut as little as possible I know it seems vain but that doesn't really enter into it – the fact that I'm a woman is important and means much to me . . . - for Gods sakes Dear Doctor No ovaries removed – please again do whatever you can to prevent large scars. Thanking you with all my heart.
   Marilyn Monroe

Outskirts of London, Englefield Green
July 1956

Her current drama teacher, Michael Chekhov, taught Marilyn a number of things about her acting and the way men looked at her on screen. One day, in the middle of a scene she was doing from *The Cherry Orchard*, Michael suddenly stopped, put his hands over her eyes for a moment, then looked at her with a gentle grin.

'May I ask you a personal question?' he asked.

'Anything,' she said.

'Will you tell me truthfully?' Michael asked. 'Were you thinking of sex while we played that scene?'

'No,' she said, 'there's no sex in this scene. I wasn't thinking of it at all.'

'You had no half-thoughts of embraces and kisses in your mind?' Michael persisted.

'None,' she said. 'I was completely concentrated on the scene.'

'I believe you,' said Michael. 'You always speak the truth.'

'To you,' she said.

He walked up and down for a few minutes, then said, 'It's

very strange. All through our playing of that scene I kept receiving sex vibrations from you. As if you were a woman in the grip of passion. I stopped because I thought you must be too sexually preoccupied to continue.'

She started to cry. He paid no attention to her tears but went on intently: 'You are a young woman who gives off sex vibrations – no matter what you are doing or thinking. The whole world has already responded to those vibrations. They come off the movie screens when you are on them. You can make a fortune just standing still or moving in front of the cameras and doing almost no acting whatsoever.'

'I don't want that,' she said.

'Why not?' he asked gently.

'Because I want to be an artist,' she answered, 'not an erotic freak. I don't want to be sold to the public as a celluloid aphrodisiac. Look at me and start shaking. It was all right for the first few years. But now it's different.'

'All you have to do is be sexy, dear Marilyn.' This was the bitterly condescending note Laurence Olivier, resplendent in his Grand Duke of Carpathia's uniform, gave Marilyn Monroe when they started filming *The Prince and the Showgirl* at Pinewood Studios in the summer of 1956. A disenchanting fairy tale, with only a terrified prince awaiting discovery by the showgirl, the film contains a number of scenes that bear out low expectations, not least the one when, as she is preparing to curtsey on first meeting the monocled grand duke, a strap of her dress snaps, baring her shoulder and almost her entire breast. Marilyn found this scene coming to her mind at a première at the Empire Theatre in London towards the end of the shoot, when she was presented to the Queen, with Joan Crawford, Brigitte Bardot and Anita Ekberg.

Marilyn had chosen Olivier, the great Shakespearean actor,

not only to star in, but also to direct this period comedy, the first and only film produced by Marilyn Monroe Productions (*Something's Got to Give*, which she co-produced in 1962 with Fox, never saw the light of day). Olivier had returned the compliment by thinking of her as an uneducated, self-obsessed idiot. She immediately resorted to her usual displacements and evasions: arriving late on set, taking drugs, going missing.

'Olivier hated me, I think,' she said, when it was finally all over. 'Even when he smiled, he had a poisonous look in his eyes. I don't know, I was sick half the time, but he didn't believe me or else he didn't give a damn. He always looked at me as if he'd smelt rotten fish, as if I had leprosy or something. He tiptoed up to me at the start as if he was walking into some sleazy dive and told me in his patronising voice just to be *sexy*. That killed me. I felt terrible around him. I was constantly late and he hated my guts for it.'

Newly wed to Arthur Miller and pregnant with a child she would lose in August, Marilyn arrived in London on a rainy afternoon in mid-July. The subsequent three weeks of shooting brought her to the verge of a nervous collapse. Nothing was working: the film, her marriage, her exhausted body, which was constantly failing her.

One day she found her husband's notebook lying open on the dining table. She read, 'I shouldn't have got married, not to her. She is an unpredictable, forlorn child-woman, abandoned and selfish. My creative life will be threatened if I give in to her relentless emotional blackmail.'

Devastated, Marilyn rang Margaret Hohenberg in New York and talked for hours. Her analyst flew over and gave her therapy on set. 'He thought I was some kind of an angel,' Marilyn told her, 'and now he guesses he was wrong to marry me. His first wife had let him down, but I've done something worse. Olivier is beginning to think I'm a troublesome bitch, and Arthur says he no longer has a decent answer to that one.'

Overwhelmed by her patient's depression and anxieties, the tyrannical demands for love she had been making for more than a year, Hohenberg decided she couldn't leave her New York practice unattended any longer, and sought a solution *in situ* that would help Marilyn fulfil her professional commitments.

London, Maresfield Gardens
August 1956

Under the virtually white sky of a boiling August day, a black
Rolls-Royce stops outside 20 Maresfield Gardens. Silhouetted
against the light, a heavily built chauffeur opens the car door,
then pivots to allow a young blonde to slip past and hurry towards
the house. Paula Fichtl, the Freud family's housekeeper for the
past twenty-seven years, opens the door and shows the stranger
into the hall. Dressed in a plain blue raincoat with the collar
turned up, no make-up, her platinum hair hidden under a floppy
felt hat, her face behind a pair of big sunglasses, Marilyn Monroe
has arrived for her first analytic session with Sigmund Freud's
daughter.

The appointment has been arranged with the utmost discretion
and speed. Despite her dread of publicity, Anna has overcome
whatever initial hesitation she might have felt, and for the
following week, Marilyn doesn't appear on set. No one knows
where she is or what she's doing. Every day her car stops in
Maresfield Gardens and every day she disappears into Anna
Freud's study. 'She wasn't remarkable, I wouldn't say,' Paula later

recalled. 'She was a pretty girl, of course, but not especially elegant. Miss Monroe was very natural and unpretentious and slightly anxious, but you could see she could be attractive when she smiled.'

One day Anna shows her patient around the clinic's kindergarten. Marilyn immediately becomes animated and, completely at ease, starts joking and playing with the children. Afterwards, very impressed by the work Anna is doing, she tells her about reading *The Interpretation of Dreams* when she was twenty-one. She was particularly fascinated by its description of dreams about nudity. Compulsive nudity, the need to undress in public, is something she had talked about at length with her first therapist. Anna makes her diagnosis, which she writes up on a card that can still be found in the file index at the Anna Freud Centre. A coded summary of 'the Marilyn case', it reads: 'Adult patient. Emotional instability, exaggerated impulsiveness, constant need for external approval, inability to be alone, tendency to depression in case of rejection, paranoia with schizophrenic elements.'

Employing a technique borrowed from child psychotherapy, Anna Freud gets Marilyn Monroe to play a game. They sit facing one another at a table with a handful of glass marbles in the middle. The analyst waits to see what she will do with them. After a while, Marilyn starts flicking the marbles towards her, one by one, which, from a psychoanalytic point of view, means a desire for sexual contact. Anna's accelerated course of treatment proves, as far as she can tell, a complete success. At the end of the week, Marilyn resumes filming, the picture is completed and, on 20 November, she takes a plane back to New York.

Miss Anna and Miss Monroe parted on good terms, according to Paula Fichtl, so much so that a few months later a cheque for a considerable sum drawn on Marilyn Monroe's account arrives at Maresfield Gardens.

Colombo, Ceylon
February 1953

Laurence Olivier's wife, Vivien Leigh, became a patient of Dr Greenson for a spell in 1953, after panic attacks and fits of depersonalisation had forced her to pull out of location shooting in Ceylon on William Dieterle's *Elephant Walk*. Leigh was embroiled in an affair with her co-star Peter Finch, her husband in the film, when she suffered a recurrence of her manic-depressive psychosis. Suddenly the bluish heat of Ceylon's jungles seemed to saturate her summer dresses, and invade every pore of her skin. She was seized by persecution mania whenever she saw too many brown Sinhalese faces; their looks filled her with something more acute than terror. On camera, she took to striking vampy poses, flirting with Dieterle and stumbling uncharacteristically over her lines. Olivier sent her back to Hollywood.

Greenson was urgently sent for and he saw her for six days running – fifty hours in total, which he billed at $1,500 – but was unable to prevent her foundering before his eyes, although he continued to reassure Paramount that she would be able to return to Ceylon. There was no question of Leigh resuming

96

filming, however, and she ended up going to England to be admitted to a hospital in Surrey.

Seven years later, when he was in the thick of analysing the star of *Let's Make Love*, Greenson returned home one summer evening feeling bitterly discouraged. He told his wife how struck he was by the parallels between Vivien and Marilyn's situations. Both had come to him after breaking down on a film in which their co-star was their lover. He had given Fox exactly the same assurances about Marilyn as he had Paramount about Vivien: that she would be working again in a week. He hadn't cured either of them.

'Marilyn isn't mad, though, is she?' he asked Hildi.

'No. Nor are you. But the potential's there.'

'What – we could go *crazy* about each other?' he joked.

'I was thinking you could drive each other out of your minds.'

Los Angeles, Beverly Hills
Late August 1960

At one point during the filming of *The Misfits*, Clark Gable found Marilyn sitting in tears in the make-up trailer. They'd just shot the devastating scene in which Roslyn tries to stop the mustang hunt, which ends with a very brutal shot of her and Gable with the sun at their backs, their bodies bisected by the horizon, as she turns and screams, 'I hate you' at him. As she'd said her line, it wasn't the animal's suffering she was feeling any more, it was hers. She was in physical pain; she couldn't tell herself this was just a movie any more, a series of images. Despair had reduced her to a body flayed by the lights. Her image on film, something that once would have done her good, felt like a wound now, as if her skin was being torn off strip by strip. From then on, whenever swarms of photographers would shout at her to turn their way and she'd tilt her head back to keep her face in shadow, she'd feel like that horse, hobbled and cowed by the men's shouting.

"'Honey,'" Gable said to her, quoting their script, "'we all got to go some time, reason or no reason. Dying is as natural as living;

man who's afraid to die is too afraid to live, far as I've ever seen. So there's nothing to do but forget it, that's all. Seems to me.'"

Soon the question on everyone's mind was 'Is Marilyn working today?' Her last film had exhausted her and the wreckage of her love life was piling up. Her affair with Yves Montand was over. Miller, who had written the short story that was the basis for *The Misfits* in Nevada when he was waiting for his first divorce to come through, now found himself back in the same place as his second marriage was drawing its last breath. Seeing Marilyn in the divorce court in the opening scenes of the movie was agonising for him, like an excruciating dream he couldn't wake up from. But despite the tension between them, she still often turned to him for help.

Meanwhile Lee Strasberg was flown out for moral support and showed up in the desert dressed as a cowboy in plaid shirt, chaps, boots and spurs. The sight of him in those clothes, as opposed to his usual Marxist priest's uniform, made Marilyn cry with laughter. But he had no more luck than anyone else in weaning her off the twenty Nembutals she took each day, sometimes pricking the capsules with a pin to speed up the effect. On Saturday, 20 August, the day before *Let's Make Love*'s world première at the Crest Theater in Reno, to which Montand and Signoret had been invited, no one could find Marilyn. In the afternoon the Sierras went up in flames. Clouds of black smoke blotted out the sky. Fire-fighting planes flew back and forth, dumping chemicals in a vain attempt to contain the brush fires. The following day the power lines were cut. Reno was plunged into darkness. The première was cancelled. As darkness fell, with only the eerie white glow of the generator-powered hotel sign for illumination, Marilyn sat on the terrace of the deserted Mapes Hotel drinking champagne with the crew and watching the conflagrations far off in the night.

Filming resumed three days later without her. Cameraman Russ Metty told the producer, Frank Taylor, 'That's it . . . the pills. She can't be photographed. If this is going to go on day after day, we're finished here.' On 26 August, Marilyn had to leave the set, not to return until 6 September. The rumour going around was that she had been saved from death only by having her stomach pumped. In the broiling heat, she was evacuated to Los Angeles. She was carried onto the plane wrapped in a wet sheet. Predicting (or hoping) that she would collapse for good this time so that she could be replaced, Huston returned from the airport a relieved man, and headed straight for his usual table at the casino. The producers decided to close down the film for an unspecified period of time.

Marilyn didn't collapse immediately, however. Instead she checked into the Beverly Hills Hotel and attended a smart dinner party at the home of the director Charles Vidor's widow. The following evening, Greenson and her physician Hyman Engelberg jointly decided she should be hospitalised. Since United Artists would cover the costs of a private hospital, Marilyn was admitted to a comfortable room in the Westside Hospital on La Cienega Boulevard, and spent ten days there under the name of Mrs Miller. Marlon Brando and Frank Sinatra visited. Greenson was at her bedside, day and – at least in part – night.

During this crisis, the psychoanalyst struck his patients as hopelessly distracted and confused. His colleagues heard him talk about the fatefulness of birth, the irreparability of destiny. Then he seemed to snap out of it. He organised follow-up treatment for Marilyn and rang Huston to assure him she'd be back at work in a week. 'If I can't finish *The Misfits*, I'm ruined as a director,' Huston stormed. 'No one's going to want to produce or insure anything I do.' Gossip columnists ran stories saying Marilyn was a very sick girl, much sicker than had at first been thought and that she was under psychiatric care. Engelberg spoke his piece to the press: 'Miss Monroe is suffering from acute exhaustion and needs rest and more rest.' Frank Taylor talked about cardiac problems and the strain of a location shoot so soon after *Let's Make Love*. Neither of them, however, saw fit to mention the huge amounts of narcotics – Librium, Placidyl and chloral hydrate – that Greenson had discovered she was taking.

She couldn't resist calling Yves Montand from the clinic. The receptionist at the Beverly Hills Hotel put her on hold, then came back on the line to say that Mr Montand couldn't take her call. She felt herself falling through empty space. When her analyst saw her after this call, she seemed lost and kept saying, 'Did you see what he said, the bastard, in his interview with that bitch Hedda Hopper? He said I was a simple girl without any guile, who had a high-school crush on him. A hopped-up little teenager. He's sorry he gave in. It was a moment of weakness because I was like a hurt child. He even said the only reason he screwed me was to make the film's love scenes more realistic.'

Greenson tried to convince her to resume filming, come what may. 'You've reached a dead end. Love's dead end. When that happens, the only way you can hurt the other person is by hurting yourself.' Shortly afterwards, Huston came to see him in Santa Monica to check on Marilyn's condition. 'All we can do is wait and expect everyone else to do the same,' Greenson told him. 'Movie stars forfeit their status as men and women, you know. They become children whose time is spent waiting – between movies, between scenes, between takes. They have no control over anything, their role is entirely passive, which is why actors often become directors or producers, to escape. But actresses are more used to it. Waiting is a woman's fate in many ways. This is something you have to understand about her, but I can assure you she'll be able to start filming again within a few days.' Huston was about to interrupt Greenson's clinical disquisitions when Marilyn suddenly appeared, as if in confirmation of everything he was saying. She was bright-eyed, vibrant, full of winning charm. She greeted the director, then turned to her analyst with the chastened smile of a child. 'I know what the barbiturates did to me, but that's over now.' Then she said to Huston, 'I'm so embarrassed by how I behaved and I want to thank you for making me stop filming this week. I'd like to come back, though, if you'll have me.' The director didn't say anything. Greenson broke the silence, saying she'd be ready, without the barbiturates this time.

Marilyn returned to Reno on 5 September. As the plane landed in the hot night, a marching band played, fans cheered and chanted her name, placards blared: WELCOME BACK MARILYN. 'Those fucking producers sure know how to milk publicity from a situation,' Huston exploded. 'For God's sake, spare me the outbreak of mass euphoria.' Marilyn was on set at the crack of dawn the next morning. But when she stepped in front of the lights again, she felt something unreal inside her and wherever she looked.

Shooting in Nevada finished on 18 October. By the end, Arthur Miller was rewriting constantly and Marilyn would find out about the changes so late she would have to stay up all night learning her new lines. Clark Gable finally ran out of patience. Enlisting Marilyn's help, he flatly refused to take on any more pages of new dialogue. At the start of November, the last of the interior scenes were completed at Paramount's studios in Hollywood. Ernst Haas, a Magnum photographer who had flown out to cover the final stages of filming, later described the atmosphere: 'Everyone involved in that picture was a misfit – Marilyn, Monty, John Huston. All of them had a sense of impending disaster.' Gable, as ever, hardly said a word throughout. On the last day of filming, when Huston's assistant director,

Tom Shaw, yelled 'It's in the can!', Marilyn burst out laughing. 'If only we all were! I bet it feels good in there. A bit cramped maybe, but at least you'd get some peace.'

Everyone who heard this realised that some actors are like stars whose visibility belies the fact they've stopped shining. Their light may still reach us, but only because it has so far to travel. Acting in a fictional reflection of their own lives, it's as if they're attending their own funerals.

At the start of December, Marilyn went to see Frank Sinatra perform at the Sands Hotel in Las Vegas. Two of President Kennedy's sisters, Pat Lawford and Jean Kennedy Smith, were in the audience with her. On her return, Greenson found her terribly lonely, and told Marianne Kris she expressed 'a feeling of mistreatment, which had paranoid undertones'. He felt Marilyn was reacting to her current involvement with 'people who only hurt her', but didn't mention any names, even by initials.

Soon afterwards Henry Hathaway, who had directed her in *Niagara*, saw Marilyn in Hollywood. She was standing alone in a darkened soundstage, crying. When he asked her what the matter was, she sobbed, 'I've played Marilyn Monroe, Marilyn Monroe, Marilyn Monroe. I've tried to do a little better and find myself doing an imitation of myself. I so want to do something different. That was one of the things that attracted me to Arthur when he said he was attracted to me. When I married him, one of the fantasies in my mind was that I could get away from Marilyn Monroe through him, and here I find myself back doing the same thing, and I just couldn't take it, I had to get out of there. I just couldn't face having to do another scene with Marilyn Monroe!'

One weekend during the filming of *The Misfits*, Marilyn had gone to San Francisco – presumably to meet somebody, but it is not known who. What is documented is that she went to a nightclub, Finocchio's, to watch a transvestite impersonator 'do' her. Also documented is that she walked out before the end of the act.

Santa Monica, Franklin Street
Early September 1960

When John Huston flew to Los Angeles to see Greenson, his aim was not simply to check on Marilyn's mental state, but also to discuss *Freud*, which he was having trouble getting off the ground. He was only too aware of the psychoanalyst's aversion towards the project and his influence over Marilyn, and wanted to make a final effort to win him over.

'I flew all the way from Reno to LA just to see Greenson,' the director told Arthur Miller afterwards. 'Not her. She'll sort herself out with her pills . . . let's hope, anyway . . . but he's been holding up my *Freud* for two years, that bastard. The only trouble was Marilyn came out right in the middle of our conversation, so I couldn't convince him she had to do the picture.'

That was when Huston realised all hope of Marilyn's appearing in his film was lost. He had been working on the project for years and, several months before, had offered Marilyn the role of Cecily, the female lead who, in the script he'd written with Sartre, conflated several of Freud's early patients, from whose wombs psychoanalysis had sprung. Through Freud's analysis of Cecily's sexual pathology, the film would tell the story of the invention of psychoanalysis. As Huston was fond of pointing out, cinema was born in the same year as Freud's discovery of the unconscious, 1895.

When Huston told Marilyn he wanted her to play Cecily, with Montgomery Clift as Freud, she was delighted. 'I'm good at being a patient, though not of a very patient kind . . .' she joked. She knew Huston couldn't stand her, but she was fascinated by the part and had no regrets about working with him on her first major film, *Asphalt Jungle*, or even *The Misfits*. Perhaps she had a slightly superstitious feeling that she was destined never to make more than two films with the same director, but still . . . A few days later, however, everything had changed. 'I can't do it,' she told the director. 'Anna Freud doesn't want a picture made about her father. My analyst told me. Poor old Freud: he would have enjoyed waiting for me, playing with his antiques.'

Greenson was trying to reconcile the interests of his profession with those of his patient, whose artistic and financial manager he had become. When Huston talked to him about the film, he was adamant: 'Freudian imagery is fine. Images of Freud himself, though, are out of the question.'

'I don't understand,' Huston said. 'Psychoanalysis deals with sex and love and forgotten images, all the things Freud wanted people to put into words.'

'Freud was visual, of course, but he couldn't stand having his picture taken. A film about him would be a complete misrepresentation of his work.'

'I don't agree at all. He invented that strange arrangement of the couch and chair, which means that, instead of looking at one another, the patient and analyst look at the images projected by their words. That's what I want to show in my *Freud*. The basic truth about cinema, that people's gazes are fixed on a secret behind the screen, something they can't see. The spectator tries to hear what images are saying. Anyway, it all started with hypnosis for you analysts, didn't it? A gaze that makes someone say something they've forgotten. So tell me: is this ban on films about psychoanalysis because they're fundamentally opposed to each other, as you say, or because they're too alike?'

'Neither,' said Greenson. 'It is because Anna is still alive and extremely solicitous of her father's memory.'

London, Maresfield Gardens
Spring 1956

Ralph Greenson and Anna Freud maintained a formal relationship, conducted mainly by letters, for a long time. But gradually
a more personal note crept into their exchanges. In 1953, he sent
her some photos he had taken of her when he was staying in
London. She sent a strange reply. 'Usually,' she told him, 'I look
like some sort of sick animal, but I find myself very human in
yours.' In 1959, when Anna visited Los Angeles for the first and
only time, she stayed with the Greensons. Ralph took her on
long walks, encouraged her to swim in the pool and gave her a
guided tour of Palm Springs once she'd finished her course of
lectures at LAPSI. At the party he gave in her honour, none
of the guests dared to sit on the sofa next to Freud's daughter.
Afterwards Anna wrote to thank him and said, 'I find it very
difficult to imagine Los Angeles without me.'

A year later, Ralph and Hildegarde Greenson went to see her
in London and stayed for several weeks at Maresfield Gardens.
'The Greensons had my room,' reported Paula Fichtl, the Freud
family's housekeeper. 'The Herr Doctor even slept in my bed.

Miss Freud spent several hours with Herr Doctor and Dr Kris conferring about Miss Monroe.' The Greensons gave Anna an Indian-maiden doll in buckskins. 'I play with the doll sometimes,' Anna wrote, thanking them, 'but at other times I only look at her and imagine she is my heathen goddess.'

In 1956, the year Anna Freud briefly treated the most famous actress in the world, Greenson was devoting all his energies to protecting the interests of the Freudian establishment. The psychoanalytic community was caught up in preparations for Freud's centenary. Some hoped to get their hands on various films made of Freud by Mark Brunswick, a former patient who had decided that he would finance his current psychoanalysis by selling them, ideally to the Sigmund Freud archives. Anna and Ernst Freud, the Master's children, wouldn't hear of it, even though they found Brunswick's situation pathetic, and they enlisted the community of Viennese analysts in America to back their stance.

The professionals in Hollywood had their plans as well, which it became more and more urgent to stop. John Huston recruited two of his collaborators on *Let There Be Light*, the producer Julian Blaustein and the screenwriter Charles Kaufmann, to work on *Freud*. 'Making this film,' the director announced, 'is like having a religious experience. I am realising an obsession based on the firm conviction that very few of man's great adventures, not even his travels beyond the earth's horizon, can dwarf Freud's journey into the uncharted depths of the human soul.' But Anna Freud's resolute opposition was to delay the project for five years. Deeply though he admired Freud and his discoveries throughout his life, Huston developed a visceral hatred for psychoanalysts, the officiants of his cult.

The daughter of the father of psychoanalysis flew into a fury when she first heard of his project. As the years passed, her sources of frustration varied, but the most galling detail of all was that Marilyn was being considered for a role. The thought of her father being turned into a matinée idol, listening to Marilyn Monroe stretched out on his couch and speaking dialogue written by Sartre, was too much for the temple guardian, who chose to be buried in her father's overcoat and always signed her letters with 'ANNAFREUD' as one word.

By the time Huston offered Marilyn the part, Marianne Kris was seeing her only occasionally, when she was in New York, so she was in no position to prevent the calamity of her accepting the role. Anna couldn't ban the film outright, so she turned to Greenson to exercise his influence on her former patient. Cecily's part was given to Susannah York. Filming lasted five months. *Freud, The Secret Passion* came out in 1962 and was a commercial failure, which Huston attributed to the fact that Marilyn wasn't playing the sexually troubled lead. At the première, he declared, 'We have attempted to accomplish something new in storytelling on the screen – to penetrate through to the unconscious of the audience, to shock and move the spectator into at least a subliminal recognition or awareness of his own hidden psychic motivations.'

Huston invited Greenson to a screening of the film in Hollywood, but he didn't go. A few weeks later, however, he called the director to talk about Marilyn. 'I've got nothing to say to you,' Huston barked. 'You're a coward. In fact, it was a good thing in the end we couldn't get her to play Freud's hysteric. No one would have understood why the old man didn't just push her back on the couch after a few seconds of the talking cure.'

New York, Central Park West
1957

Marilyn stopped seeing Margaret Hohenberg in early 1957 and, on Anna Freud's recommendation, went into analysis with Marianne Kris instead. As the daughter of the Freud family's paediatrician, Kris was more than simply one of Anna's American colleagues. They had been childhood friends in Vienna, and went travelling together until Kris went into exile in America in 1938. Like Anna, she had been analysed by the Master himself, so Marilyn thought that seeing her would take her right to the heart of Freudian analysis.

Kris was fifty-seven years old, a dark-haired, handsome woman who had just lost her husband, an analyst and art historian. Marilyn's third analysis (counting the one with Anna herself) lasted four years. In the spring, she began seeing Kris five times a week at her office, 135 Central Park West, in the same building as the Strasbergs' apartment. Every day, after her session, she'd take the elevator to the Strasbergs', where the business of remembering would continue in theatrical mode. Strasberg would set her sense-memory exercises revolving around childhood and youth: don't play it, give it a voice, Strasberg said, or, rather, let it speak through you – a lonely waif, a confused schoolgirl, a jilted fiancée.

Marilyn's psychoanalysis had become a source of conflict in her marriage. Miller thought that, in most cases, psychiatrists couldn't help people, and he deemed Marilyn's analysis a failure, although he acknowledged Kris's integrity and devotion to her patient.

Lee Strasberg evidently did not agree with Miller. He thought analysis would begin to liberate Marilyn, and treated their work in class at the Actors Studio as 'an analysis of her analysis'. When a scene proved difficult because an actor or actress was blocked and unable to get in touch with a past experience, he thought remembering it in analysis could help them get past it. One day Marilyn, who was slightly scared of Kris, confessed to Susan Strasberg that she often couldn't remember details from her childhood in sessions. When her psychoanalyst asked her a question she couldn't answer, she'd just make up something interesting. She felt she was going round in circles with Kris, as she had with Hohenberg, trying to grasp an inaccessible past. 'It was always how did I feel about this, and why did I think my mother did that – not where was I going, but where I had been? But I *knew* where I had been. I wanted to know if I could use it wherever I was *going*!'

To blot out the suffering caused by this double course of analysis, she upped her intake of barbiturates, which had a more immediate effect, until finally she took an overdose. Miller found her in time, and afterwards said that it was pointless trying to trace her suicide attempt to anything anyone had said or done. 'Death, the longing to die, always comes out of nowhere.' Nowhere: the space inside, her inner life doomed to oblivion, her suffering waiting for an object.

Pyramid Lake, near Reno, Nevada
19 September 1960

After John Huston had secured an advance of twenty-five thousand dollars from Universal for his film about Freud, *The Misfits* resumed with a five-minute dialogue scene between Marilyn and Montgomery Clift. Behind a run-down saloon, the Dayton Bar, in a back-yard littered with beer cans and junk automobiles, Roslyn and Perce were meant to tear into one another. But no matter how many takes they did in front of the ten-thousand-watt lights, the air under the black tarpaulin thick with flies, they couldn't say their lines the way Huston wanted, clipped and vicious. They came out like the caresses a wounded animal might give its mate.

Three days later they shot a scene in which a fully clothed Clark Gable had to wake Marilyn, who was naked under a sheet. It didn't go any better. On the seventh take, Marilyn seemed to remember Laurence Olivier's injunction, 'Be sexy.' Be your image, in other words; that's all you know how to be. Departing from the script, she sat up, allowed the sheet to drop and exposed her right breast. It was a sad moment, the Magnum photographer

Eve Arnold recalled, as if the actress felt that was all she had to offer; as though she were sacrificing her craft to justify Olivier's contempt and in the misguided hope of pleasing Huston.

'Cut!' Huston called impatiently.

When Marilyn flashed him a look, he drawled, 'I've seen 'em before.'

A few days later, they reshot Roslyn and Perce's scene, and this time Marilyn gave the director the performance he was looking for. It was the high point of the film, Huston enthused. But when he came to collect her that evening at the Holiday Inn, where she was staying with Paula Strasberg, he found her in a terrible state. Her hair was a tangle, her hands and feet were filthy and she was wearing just a short nightgown, which wasn't any cleaner than the rest of her. She greeted him euphorically, then went into a kind of trance. 'You see, Marilyn, that's what drugs do,' he said sadly. 'They make you mistake your terror for ecstasy.' As he walked out, a doctor was looking for a vein in the back of her hand to give her an injection of Amytal.

'When I had to stop filming,' Huston said later, 'I knew something terrible was going to happen to her. I had a sort of premonition. She couldn't save herself and no one could do it for her. Seeing her sleepwalking into the abyss, I thought, If she carries on at the rate she's going, she'll be in an institution in two or three years or dead. But the thing I remember most from that time was her innocence. I like the corruption of Hollywood; I like people who know they're rotten, who know they've gone off, like meat. But that never happened to her. There was something about her that could never spoil. One day, I was talking about her to her masseur, Ralph Roberts, the "masseur to the stars", who'd been an actor as well, and he told me he'd never known anyone else with skin like Marilyn's. Her flesh was incredibly soft and deep. A miracle, really. You see that on screen . . . it's all you see, in fact. As a director, you don't film a body, you're blinded by the light that streams from it, even in *The Misfits* when she was a bit puffy. Or as Sartre said one day, "It's not just light that comes off her, it's heat. She burns through the screen."'

New York, Manhattan
1959

Towards the end of 1959, Marilyn struck up closer friendships with writers she admired in New York. Carson McCullers invited her to stay at her house in Nayack, where they were joined by the novelist Isak Dinesen, and had long talks about poetry and literature. The poet Carl Sandburg, whom she met while making *Some Like It Hot*, often came over to her apartment in Manhattan for extended tête-à-têtes, and she would read out poetry and do impersonations of actors. She and Truman Capote also met up again.

'I want to tell you about something I'm working on,' he told her one day. 'Last year I wrote a novel called *Breakfast at Tiffany's*. The girl in it – she's called Holly Golightly – is me. That's something I learned from my master Flaubert, my secret friend. But she's you too. I like to think of my novels as memories of memories – I'd like people to remember my characters the way they remember a dream, with that same mixture of vagueness and precision. Shall I tell you the first line? "I am always drawn back to the places where I have lived, the houses and their neighbourhoods." The narrator is remembering a girl he used to know: a good-time party girl, who drank a bit too much and was a bit crazy, and used to hang out in a bar on Lexington Avenue. She's one of those girls who don't belong anywhere or to anyone, least of all to herself. A displaced person, always searching, moving, running away, someone who never feels at home. If anyone asks her what she does, she says, "I go away." In the novel, she has a card with her name on it and underneath just "Travelling". Anyway, now it's going to be made into a movie. Do you like the sound of it?'

'If it was me,' said Marilyn, 'I'd say, "I come back." My travels have always been of the same kind. No matter where I've gone or why I've gone there, it ends up that I never see anything. Becoming a movie star is like living on a merry-go-round. When you travel you take the merry-go-round with you. You don't see natives or new scenery. You see chiefly the same press agent, the same sort of interviewers, and the same picture layouts of yourself. The days, the conversations, the faces – they all go by just so they can come back again. Like in those dreams when you think, I've already dreamed this. That must be why I wanted to be an actress, so I could travel without going anywhere, and always end up in the same place. Movies are like merry-go-rounds for grown-ups.'

Marilyn was very keen to play Holly Golightly. She worked up two complete scenes by herself and acted them for Truman, who thought them terrifically good. They spent whole nights rehearsing, drinking White Angels and breaking into 'Diamonds Are A Girl's Best Friend', her song in *Gentlemen Prefer Blondes*. But Hollywood had different plans for the novel's heroine and ended up choosing the brown-haired, utterly unsensual Audrey Hepburn instead. 'Marilyn would have been absolutely marvellous in the role,' Capote said afterwards, 'but Paramount double-crossed me in every conceivable way.' He was disgusted by the studio's adaptation, which changed the whole point of his novel.

Instead of reminiscing about a girl he's lost, the film's narrator convinces Holly to stay in New York 'because that town and her belonged together for ever'. In the novel, Holly says the opposite, 'I love New York, even though it isn't mine, the way something has to be, a tree or a street or a house, something, anyway, that belongs to me because I belong to it' – the feeling Capote had heard his double, his white angel, express.

Los Angeles, Sunset Strip
Late September 1960

In analysis with Greenson for eight months, Marilyn had been left by Yves Montand. She wanted to love, but didn't know *whom* to love. She phoned André de Dienes, and poured out a litany of complaint. Teasingly, he suggested that she come over to his place in the Hills, where he had a 'cure for all ills'. 'Leave all your cares behind and come to hear about my cure,' he told her. She did not come that day, but a few weeks later a mysterious lady got out from a taxicab at the bottom of his driveway. Marilyn was so bundled up in a scarf, dark sunglasses, jeans and a coat that André didn't recognise her until she walked up to the garage, where he was doing some gardening. She took off her sunglasses when she was ten feet away and he finally recognised her. What on earth had happened to his lovely, laughing-all-the-time Norma Jeane? How could she look so unglamorous, so unhappy? She said she had come to find out what his 'cure for all ills' was.

'What's bothering you?'

'I didn't sleep all night.'

'Did you drink much coffee yesterday?'

'No.'

'Are you broke?'

'No.'

'Are you worried about many things?'

'Yes, quite a few things! I'm being swindled.'

'Well, that's cause number one for sleeplessness. You're angry because you feel used. Are you lonesome? Tell me the truth, Marilyn, the absolute truth.'

She didn't answer.

'When did you last make love? When did you have your last orgasm?'

'It's been weeks and weeks. I don't care.'

André offered to fix her a cocktail. She was about to accept when they were interrupted by another visitor. As de Dienes later wrote, 'A young beautiful model came to see me, sent by the model agent. In great contrast to Marilyn's disguise that did not show any of her sex appeal, the model wore a skin-tight pink silk dress to emphasise her sexy contour and dainty high-heeled shoes, her long hair flowing down on her shoulders splendidly. The young lady put on her best smile and all her charms as she entered my house, and as she was walking through the long corridor, I could see she was imitating the famous Marilyn Monroe walk! For a few seconds the entire event became like an incredibly ironical confrontation with Fate's trickery! The model, who was willing to pose nude for fifty dollars, was sexier than Marilyn!'

Marilyn called a cab, and disappeared into the bathroom until it arrived. As André helped her into the cab she turned to him, and asked what the 'cure for all ills' was. Too embarrassed to talk about it in front of the driver, he asked her to wait for a few seconds, dashed into his office and scribbled something on a bit of paper, then gave it to her as the cab set off. 'Sex. With me,' Marilyn read.

'The idiot,' she said. 'The real cure is death.'

Then she crumpled up the bit of paper and threw it out of the window into the evening dust blowing across the steep hill leading down to the Sunset Strip.

Los Angeles, Westwood Village
November 1960

The last evening in Reno had been thick with pathos. Drunk on bourbon, Marilyn had said, 'I am trying to find myself as a person. Millions of people live their entire lives without finding themselves. The best way for me to find myself as a person is to prove to myself I am an actress.' On 4 November, in Hollywood, Huston shot a final retake of *The Misfits*' happy ending, in which Marilyn and Gable's characters head off for a life together, and with that the film was finally finished, forty days behind schedule. The following weekend Marilyn and Arthur Miller left for New York on separate flights. She kept the apartment on East 57th Street while he moved into the Adams Hotel on East 86th.

She resumed her daily sessions with Marianne Kris and spent the rest of her time going over the black and white contact sheets of the photographs Henri Cartier-Bresson, Inge Morath and Eve Arnold had taken during the filming of *The Misfits*. She scratched out, with a red cross, all the photos that included Arthur. Twelve days later, when she heard Clark Gable had died, Marilyn said nothing to Kris about it. It was only a few weeks later when she got back to Los Angeles that she rushed to Greenson's office in Beverly Hills and said: 'You can't believe how shattered I've been since Gable died. In the kissing scenes on *The Misfits*, I kissed him with real affection. I loved his lips, the way his moustache tickled when he turned away from the camera. I didn't want to go to bed with him, but I wanted him to know how much I liked and appreciated him. When I came back from a day off the set, he patted my ass and told me if I didn't behave myself he would give me a good spanking. I looked him in the eye and said, "Don't tempt me." He burst out laughing so hard he was tearing up. Those bastards at the Academy of Motion Picture Arts and Sciences,' she stressed the words ironically, 'didn't even give him an Oscar for *Gone with the Wind*. I saw that first when I was about thirteen. I have never seen a man who was as romantic as he was in that picture. It was different when I got to know him. Then I wanted him to be my father. I wouldn't care if he spanked me as long as he made up for it by hugging me and telling me I was Daddy's little girl and he loved me. Of course you're going to say that's a classic Oedipal fantasy.' Greenson said nothing, merely stroked his moustache.

'The weirdest thing,' Marilyn continued, 'is that I dreamed about him a few days ago. I was sitting on Clark Gable's lap with his arms around me. He said, "They want me to do a *Gone with the Wind* sequel. Maybe I will if you will be my Scarlett." I woke up crying. They called him "King" on set. What respect and deference he had from the actors and crew, even Huston. Some day I hope I'll be treated like that. He was Mr Gable to everybody on the set, but he made me call him Clark. One day he told me that we had something very important and secret in common. His mother had died when he was six months old.'

Shortly afterwards, during a very troubled session, Marilyn gazed off into the distance with dilated pupils and said in the sort of light, almost playful, voice you'd use to tell a fairy tale to a child, 'When I was a little girl I would pretend I was Alice in Wonderland looking into a mirror, wondering what I could see. Was that really me? Who was that staring back at me? Could it be someone pretending to be me? I would dance around, make faces, just to see if that little girl in the mirror would do the same. I suppose every kid's imagination takes over. The looking glass can be magical, like acting, in a strange way. Especially when you're pretending to be someone other than yourself. This did happen when I put on my mom's clothes, tried to fix my hair as she did and powder my face with her big powder puff, and, oh, yes, her red rouge and lipstick and eye shadow. I'm sure I looked like a clown, not sexy, because people couldn't stop laughing. I started crying.

'I always had to be dragged out of my seat when I went to the pictures. I wondered, Are the movies a make-believe land, just an illusion? Those huge images up there on the screen in the dark theatre were bliss – they put me in a trance. But the screen was always a mirror. Who is that looking back at me? I'd think. Which is really me? The little girl in the darkness, or the woman up there in the silver light? Am I her reflection?'

Hollywood, Doheny Drive
Autumn 1960

Images are a skin, hard and cold. Under hers, Marilyn was coming to pieces again. When she didn't know who to be any more, she tried to find the answer in a man's eyes. It was a trade: with your eyes, hands, penis, tell me I exist, tell me I've got a soul, and I'll let you have my body, in the flesh or in a photograph.

One day in the autumn she again showed up at the house of her on-off lover André de Dienes, dressed in a simple, elegant black suit. André thought she seemed calm, even sad. She kissed him, and said, 'André, take pictures of me again! Tonight, and tomorrow too . . . I'll stay with you.'

Not tempted by the offer, he walked her home, a few blocks away. Her apartment was full of partly packed suitcases and empty movers' boxes, with two large wardrobe trunks in a corner. She was using the boxes as tables, one for vodka cocktails, another for a lamp, portable record-player, telephone and a vase of yellow roses. Rough wooden cases with a jumble of books on top of them lined one wall. André liked the room, its air of a moonlight flit. Holly Golightly's flat, he thought.

But Marilyn was unhappy – she felt she didn't belong anywhere any more. As the photographer later remembered, there was 'the world's most publicised, most glamorous, most adulated beauty, in that musty-smelling old lousy apartment; she was alone and had no place to go'. He asked her about the farm she had bought in Connecticut, where she'd lived with Arthur Miller. 'Wasn't that your home?' he asked.

She answered that she had given it to Arthur.

'Are you crazy?' he shouted. 'Are you crazy? You gave away the only home you ever owned! Having a home is the most important thing in life, and you let yourself be out in nowhere, due to your stupidity, to your damned kind heart! Oh, Norma Jeane, what are you doing to yourself?'

She looked at him, then poured champagne from a half-empty bottle into two glasses.

The telephone rang, and she let it go for a long time before picking up. As she listened, and answered in a low, monotonous voice, her expression turned sad, and she wiped away tears. De Dienes went into the bathroom, and when he returned he heard Marilyn's last few words: 'Yes, I'm coming! I'll be there tomorrow.' Then she hung up the receiver and turned to him, saying, 'André, please go home, I have to go back to New York tomorrow.'

Halfway down the street, overcome with regret, he turned round and ran back to her. She was on the phone again, sitting in the same place, crying. He knelt down in front of her. 'Come back. Let's go to my house right now. I'll take photos like nothing you've ever seen. Please, Norma Jeane, don't go to New York.'

'No, they're waiting for me out east.'

When he rang next morning, Marilyn had left.

New York, YMCA, West 34th Street
Winter 1960

Marilyn flew to New York, where she met up with W. J. Weatherby, an English journalist she had got to know in Reno while making *The Misfits*. They had arranged to meet in a bar on Eighth Avenue. It was an icy winter's day, and Weatherby wasn't sure she'd come. She was the one who'd wanted to see him, but why should she stick to the plan if she was in a hole? It wasn't as though he were a close friend or psychiatrist. He waited for an hour. She didn't appear. He returned to the YMCA on West 34th Street and had just reached his room when the phone rang. 'Apologies, apologies, apologies. I was sleeping. I took some pills. Too many. Will you forgive me?'

The journalist had forgotten he'd told her where he was staying.

'Can we still meet?' she asked anxiously. 'Or are you too tired?'
'No. Not really.'

During the year they'd known each other, the journalist had come to understand that, for all her love of show, there was only one thing Marilyn really wanted: to hide. She had a unique ability to disappear even when she was with you, to be whoever people wanted her to be while keeping her real self profoundly hidden.

A quarter of an hour later they met. She had made herself up and was very lively at first. He figured she was putting on a performance to hide her real feelings. He wished she trusted him enough not to bother, but thought perhaps she was afraid of breaking down.

Somehow Yves Montand and Simone Signoret's names came up.

'They certainly seem to have an understanding,' she said. 'He can flirt and then go back. When I was interested in my husband, I wasn't interested in anyone else.'

The journalist remembered Miller telling him about her affair with Montand, but he still felt she was speaking the truth. Perhaps the marriage was over by then, and she hadn't felt like his wife any more.

'Is it the same with a movie?'

'The movies are like love, you know. When you're not looking for it, all kinds of opportunities come your way. If you run after it, you get nothing. That's the story of my life. Being an actress has never been as much fun as dreaming of being one, and I've never been offered so many star roles as when I was on the verge of giving up. You've got a choice: be a slave of the studios or an untouchable celebrity. I can't just give up being a screen idol.'

The conversation turned to the Kennedys, whom she vehemently defended against all criticism. The tone grew heated. Weatherby thought it better to return to a calmer subject: books.

'Have you ever read Scott Fitzgerald's great novel *Tender Is the Night*?' he asked.

'No. I know Fox is working on an adaptation.'

'There's something of you in it. A film actress who goes . . .' Weatherby checked himself, remembering Marilyn's mother and her own fears.

'What – crazy?'

'Yes. Nicole Warren, the female lead, is a vulnerable actress. She marries her analyst but becomes more and more disturbed until she has a breakdown. She only recovers when she leaves her husband. That's the proof she's recovered, he realises, that she's strong enough to extricate herself from their mutual madness. In the end, he's the one who cracks up.'

Weatherby immediately realised he had it wrong. Nicole and the actress were two different characters. But did it matter? He hadn't read the novel for a long time, but in his memory the actress in *Tender Is the Night* had a golden Monroe quality. It was as though Fitzgerald had anticipated Marilyn, or at least aspects of her. If you combined the two characters, he thought, you'd have a portrait of the woman sitting opposite him. Marilyn had left her husband as well, but it hadn't cured her. She was still seeing her analyst every day.

'That's a nice title,' she said, to say something. 'The night *is* tender. Sometimes. At any rate, that's how you'd like it to be.'

'The doctor drops from sight into the night of obscurity. The wife, for a time, escapes her mental night.'

She didn't know if that was a quote from the novel or a prediction. 'That sounds familiar,' she said jokingly. 'There are times when it's been so hard falling asleep that I hate having to wake up and go through it all again. But that sounds gloomy, I guess.'

The book seemed to have become a dangerous topic. Weatherby steered the conversation to the movie adaptation. 'I can see you playing Nicole. You know, I suggested to Laurence Olivier that he should play the doctor's part.'

'Fantastic! He's an expert on madwomen. But I won't be in it with him; I wouldn't be treated by him for anything in the world, not even on screen.'

'How about Montgomery Clift?'

'Two crazy people together. Great. Besides, Fox haven't offered me the part.'

When they said goodbye, the journalist noticed how pale she

was. She must be tired, he thought. They promised to meet up again. His last view of her was of her back, walking away. She didn't have the greatest legs, he decided.

Marilyn bought Fitzgerald's novel right away. She was fascinated by the story of the rich, famous psychoanalyst Dick Diver, who marries his former patient, a schizophrenic who has been abused by her father as a child. She'd read other novels of Fitzgerald's, but none that seemed to speak to her so directly. In a biography of the novelist, she found out that Nicole was partly based on Fitzgerald's wife Zelda, whom she knew a lot about. When she had flown to New York in December 1954 to embark, as it were, on her new career as an analytic patient, she had bought a one-way ticket in the name of Zelda Zonk.

Now she was struck by a metaphor in the novel, 'Hollywood, "the city of thin partitions"'. That was what she was fleeing by coming to New York. The imperceptible gulf between people, the futility of everything. She was tired of everything always being reversible; she wanted time to mean something; she wanted there to be a difference between insanity and what she could only call desire. The opposite of madness is not simply reason.

In September, John Huston had run into Robert Goldstein, the new head of Fox, at the Scala Theater in Hollywood.

'Where have you got to with your adaptation of *Tender Is the Night*?' the director asked.

'Selznick backed out two months ago,' the producer answered. 'Henry Weinstein's in charge now. He's keeping Jennifer Jones, David's wife, and Dr Greenson's the technical consultant—'

'What?' Huston cut in. 'Greenson? The guy who wanted to stop me making my picture about Freud is giving technical advice on a movie about a psychoanalyst? And it's starring Jennifer, who's a patient of his colleague Wexler's? What a bastard that guy is.'

Henry King shot *Tender Is the Night*, his last film, for 20th Century Fox in Switzerland and on the Côte d'Azur in the spring of 1961. Greenson didn't feature on the screen credits but he played a big part not only in his friend Weinstein's choice of screenwriter, but also in shaping the script. He was very keen to lighten Diver's character and make his attraction for Nicole less fatal, the game they play less deadly, as if the fact that they lose it would deprive his life of the meaning he had tried to give it. He never spoke to Marilyn about the book or the film.

New York, Payne Whitney Psychiatric Clinic
February 1961

Marilyn returned to New York once again. This time, as she got on the plane, she didn't know whether she was travelling into the past or the future. As Billy Wilder had said, when her divorce from Arthur Miller had come through in January, 'Marilyn's marriage to Joe DiMaggio failed because the woman he married was Marilyn Monroe, and the one to Arthur Miller because she wasn't.' After the panning her last film had received, Marilyn thought her career was at a dead end. She retreated to her darkened bedroom on East 57th, listening to sentimental songs, dosing herself on sleeping pills, not eating or talking, seeing no one except W. J. Weatherby and her analyst.

After forty-seven sessions in two months, overwhelmed and terrified by Marilyn's deteriorating condition, Marianne Kris finally decided to have her hospitalised. Under the name of Faye Miller, she was placed in the Payne Whitney Psychiatric Clinic. She was not asked for her consent, but simply given admission papers to sign. She had taken so many pills she was confused and had no idea what she was signing. Marilyn was thirty-four, the age of her mother, Gladys, when she was sectioned.

Marilyn immediately writes to Paula and Lee Strasberg, her closest friends in New York.

Dear Lee and Paula,
 Dr Kris has had me put into the New York hospital – pstikiatric [sic] division under the care of two idiot doctors, they *both should not be my doctors.*
 You haven't heard from me because I'm locked up with all these poor nutty people. I'm sure to end up a nut if I stay in this nightmare. Please help me Lee, this is the *last* place I should be – maybe if you called Dr Kris and assure her of my sensitivity and that I must get back to class . . . Lee, I try to remember what you said once in class, that 'art goes far beyond science'.
 And the science memories around here I'd like to forget – like screaming women etc.
 Please help me – if Dr Kris assured you I am all right I can assure you *I am not.* I do not belong here!
 I love you both
 Marilyn

She was allowed to make only one phone call. She called Joe DiMaggio, in Florida, whom she hadn't spoken to for six years. He caught a flight to New York that night and insisted she be let out of the clinic. After just four days she was discharged, and went to convalesce in a hospital on the Hudson River, on the other side of Manhattan, where she stayed from 10 February to 5 March 1961. While she was there she decided to make Greenson her sole analyst and wrote him a letter, which for a long time was thought to be lost until it was found in 20th Century Fox's archives in 1992.

Dear Dr Greenson,

Just now when I looked out the hospital window where the snow had covered everything, suddenly everything is kind of a muted green. There are grass and shabby evergreen bushes, though the trees give me a little hope – and the desolate bare branches promise maybe there will be spring and maybe they promise hope.

Did you see The Misfits yet? In one sequence you can perhaps see how bare and strange a tree can be for me. I don't know if it comes across that way for sure on the screen – I don't like some of the selections in the takes they used. As I started to write this letter about four quiet tears had fallen. I don't quite know why.

Last night I was awake all night again. Sometimes I wonder what the night time is for. It almost doesn't exist for me – it all seems like one long, long, horrible day. Anyway, I thought I'd try to be constructive about it and started to read the letters of Sigmund Freud. When I first opened the book I saw the picture of Freud inside, opposite the title page and I burst into tears – he looked very depressed (the picture must have been taken near the end of his life), as if he died a disappointed man. But Dr Kris said he had much physical pain which I had known from the Jones book. I know this, too, to be so, but still I trust my instincts because I see a sad disappointment in his gentle face. The book reveals (though I am not sure anyone's love letters should be published) that he wasn't a stiff! I mean his gentle, sad humour and even a striving was eternal in him. I haven't gotten very far yet because at the same time I'm reading Sean O'Casey's first autobiography. This book disturbs me very much, and in a way one should be disturbed for these things, after all.

There was no empathy at Payne Whitney – it had a very bad effect on me. They put me in a cell (I mean

134

cement blocks and all) for very disturbed, depressed patients, except I felt I was in some kind of prison for a crime I hadn't committed. The inhumanity there I found archaic. They asked me why I wasn't happy there (everything was under lock and key, things like electric lights, dresser drawers, bathrooms, closets, bars concealed on the windows – and the doors have windows so patients can be visible all the time. Also, the violence and markings still remain on the walls from former patients). I answered: 'Well, I'd have to be nuts if I like it here!' Then there were screaming women in their cells – I mean, they screamed out when life was unbearable for them, I guess – and at times like this I felt an available psychiatrist should have talked to them, perhaps to alleviate even temporarily their misery and pain. I think they (the doctors) might learn something, even – but they are interested only in something they studied in books. Maybe from some life-suffering human being they could discover more – I had the feeling they looked more for discipline and that they let their patients go after the patients had 'given up'. They asked me to mingle with the patients, to go out to O.T. (Occupational Therapy). I said, 'And do what?' They said: 'You could sew or play checkers, even cards, and maybe knit.' I tried to explain that the day I did that they would have a nut on their hands. These things were the farthest from my mind. They asked me why I felt I was 'different' from the other patients, so I decided if they were really that stupid I must give them a very simple answer, so I said, 'I just am.'

The first day I did mingle with a patient. She asked me why I looked so sad and suggested I could call a friend and perhaps not be so lonely. I told her that they had told me that there wasn't a phone on that floor. Speaking of floors, they are all locked – no one could go in and no one could go out. She looked shocked and shaken and said, 'I'll take you to the phone' – and while I waited in line for my turn for the use of the phone, I observed a guard (since he had on a grey knit uniform), and as I approached the phone he straight-armed the phone and said very sternly, 'You can't use the phone.' By the way, they pride themselves in having a home-like atmosphere there. I asked them (the doctors) how they figured that. They answered, 'Well, on the sixth floor we have wall-to-wall carpeting and modern furniture,' to which I replied, 'Well, that any good interior decorator could provide – providing there are funds for it,' but since they are dealing with human beings, I asked, why couldn't they perceive the interior of a human being?

The girl that told me about the phone seemed such a pathetic and vague creature. She told me after the straight-arming, 'I didn't know they would do that.' Then she said, 'I'm here because of my mental condition – I have cut my throat several times and slashed my wrists,' she said either three or four times.

Oh, well, men are climbing to the moon but they don't seem interested in the beating human heart. Still, one can change them but won't – by the way, that was the original them of *The Misfits* – no one even caught that part of it. Partly because, I guess, the changes in the script and some of the distortions in the direction.

Later:

I know I will never be happy but I know I can be gay! Remember I told you Kazan said I was the gayest girl he ever knew and, believe me, he has known many. But he loved me for one year and once rocked me to sleep one night when I was in great anguish. He also

136

suggested that I go into analysis and later wanted me to work with Lee Strasberg. Was it Milton who wrote: 'The happy ones were never born'? I know at least two psychiatrists who are looking for a more positive approach.

This morning, 2 March:
I didn't sleep again last night. I forgot to tell you something yesterday. When they put me into the first room on the sixth floor I was not told it was a psychiatric floor. Dr Kris said she was coming the next day. The nurse came in after the doctor, a psychiatrist, had given me a physical examination including examining the breast for lumps. I took exception to this but not violently, only explaining that the medical doctor who had put me there, a stupid man name Dr Lipkin, had already done a complete physical less than thirty days before. But when the nurse came in, I noticed there was no way of buzzing or reaching for a light to call the nurse. I asked why this was and some other things, and she said this is a psychiatric floor. After she went out I got dressed and then was when the girl in the hall told me about the phone. I was waiting at the elevator door which looks like all other doors with a doorknob except it doesn't have any numbers (you see, they left them all out). After the girl spoke with me and told me what she had done to herself, I went back into my room knowing they had lied to me about the telephone and I sat on the bed trying to figure that if I was given this situation in an acting improvisation, what would I do? So I figured, it's a squeaky wheel that gets the grease. I admit it was a loud squeak, but I got the idea from a movie I made once called *Don't Bother to Knock*. I picked up a lightweight chair and slammed it against the glass, intentionally – and it was hard to do because I had never

broken anything in my life. I took a lot of banging to get even a small piece of glass, so I went over with the glass concealed in my hand and sat quietly on the bed waiting for them to come in. They did, and I said to them, 'If you are going to treat me like a nut, I'll act like a nut.' I admit the next thing is corny, but I really did it in the movie except it was with a razor blade. I indicated if they didn't let me out I would harm myself – the farthest thing from my mind at the moment, since you know, Dr Greenson, I'm an actress and I would never intentionally mark or mar myself, I'm just that vain. I didn't cooperate with them in any way because I couldn't believe in what they were doing. They asked me to go quietly and I refused to move, staying on the bed so they picked me up by all fours, two hefty men and two hefty women, and carried me up to the seventh floor in the elevator. I must say at least they had the decency to carry me face down. I just wept quietly all the way there and then was put in the cell I told you about and that ox of a woman, one of those hefty ones, said, 'Take a bath.' I told her I had just taken one on the sixth floor. She said very sternly, 'As soon as you change floors, you have to take another bath.' The man who runs that place, a high school principal type, although Dr Kris refers to him as an 'administrator', he was actually permitted to talk to me, questioning me somewhat like an analyst. He told me I was a very, very sick girl and had been a very, very sick girl for many years. He looks down on his patients. He wondered if that interfered with my work. He was being very firm and definite in the way he said it. He actually stated it more than he questioned me, so I replied, 'Don't you think that perhaps Greta Garbo and Charlie Chaplin and Ingrid Bergman had been depressed when they worked sometimes?' It's like saying a ball player like DiMaggio couldn't hit a ball when he was depressed. Pretty silly.

By the way, I have some good news, sort of, since I guess I helped. He claims I did: Joe said I saved his life by sending him to a psychotherapist. Dr Kris said that he is a very brilliant man, the doctor. Joe said he pulled himself up by his own bootstraps after the divorce but he told me also that if he had been me he would have divorced him, too. Christmas night he sent a forest-full of poinsettias. I asked who they were from since it was such a surprise – my friend Pat Newcomb was there and they had just arrived then. She said, 'I don't know, the card just says, "Best, Joe".' Then I replied, 'Well, there's only one Joe.' Because it was Christmas night I called him up and asked him why he had sent me the flowers. He said, 'First of all, because I thought you would call me to thank me,' and then he said, 'Besides, who in the hell else do you have in the world?' He asked me to have a drink sometime with him. I said I knew he didn't drink, but he said occasionally now he takes a drink, to which I replied then it would have to be a very, very dark place! He asked me what I was doing Christmas night. I said nothing, I'm here with a friend. Then he asked me to come over and I was glad he was coming, though I must say I was bleary and depressed, but somehow still glad he was coming over.

I think I had better stop because you have other things to do, but thanks for listening for a while.

Marilyn M.

Marilyn added a handwritten message to the letter, which her secretary May Reis had typed:

There is someone, a very dear friend, who, whenever I say his name, you always raise your eyes and stroke your moustache. He has been a loving friend to me. Very loving. I know you don't believe me but I trust my instincts. It has no future but still, I've never had that before. I have no regrets. He is very attentive in bed. No news from Yves but I don't care. The memory of it is very clear and tender and wonderful. I am almost in tears.

Greenson started a reply but didn't send it, thinking it better to persuade Kris to get her out of the clinic first and interpret later. This note was found in his archives.

> Dear Marilyn,
>   You mustn't expect me to criticise or condemn the people treating you or trying to do so, and certainly not my colleague and friend Marianne Kris. You are not mentally ill but there's every chance you might become so if you stay in hospital. Hospital is the place where you lose children when you miscarry, the place you're reduced to a child when you're treated for your depressions or suicidal states.

After this trauma, Marilyn wanted never to see Marianne Kris again, but, whether inadvertently or intentionally, she retained her as one the beneficiaries of her last will, which she had drawn up three weeks before going into Payne Whitney. Kris acknowledged afterwards that she had done 'a terrible thing, a terrible, terrible thing. Oh, God, I didn't mean to, but I did.' She continued corresponding with Greenson and Anna Freud about Marilyn for the rest of her former patient's life.

At the start of spring Marilyn, now back in California, begged a very hesitant Greenson to take her on 'full-time'. Their sessions resumed. In May, after she had gone back to New York for a spell, from where she'd called him every day, Greenson described his therapeutic method to Marianne Kris:

> Above all, I try to help her not to be lonely, and therefore to escape into drugs or get involved with very destructive people, who will engage in some sort of sadomasochistic relationship with her . . . This is the kind of planning you do with an adolescent girl who needs guidance, friendliness, and firmness, and she seems to take it very well . . . She said for the first time she looked forward to coming to Los Angeles, because she could speak to me. Of course, this does not prevent her from cancelling several hours to go to Palm Springs with Mr F.S. She is unfaithful to me as one is to a parent . . .

A few days later Marilyn rang from New York to tell her Californian analyst she'd decided to return to Los Angeles for good – Los Angeles, the place of her birth; the last place in the world where she would have wanted to die; the city that would become her final resting place.

Los Angeles, Beverly Hills Hotel
1 June 1961

André de Dienes was working in his garden when he suddenly remembered it was Marilyn's birthday. Without the slightest knowledge of where she was, he went inside his house, picked up the telephone and asked Information to give him the number of the Beverly Hills Hotel. When he asked the hotel operator to put him through to Marilyn Monroe's suite, she connected him immediately. He started singing 'Happy Birthday' into the phone. Marilyn recognised his voice and jubilantly asked him to come over right away. She was alone in Bungalow Ten. He was thrilled, like a child who has been given a present they have been promised for a long time. Hooray, the weekend is coming and maybe I can persuade her to stay with me for a few days! he thought.

Marilyn was very cheerful when he arrived. She took out a small jar of caviar and two bottles of champagne from the small refrigerator. They had a long discussion about many things, but the conversation became sombre. She felt unhappy, exploited by Fox, and wanted to go back to New York.

De Dienes asked, 'Why did you let, so often, a big crew of

hundreds of people wait for you to appear on the set? Didn't you realise that every hour of delay was costing the studio thousands of dollars? When we were travelling together in 1945, you were always up early in the morning, at daybreak, putting on your make-up, doing your hair . . . so why the hell did you let an entire crew wait and wait for you to appear on the set day after day? What the hell got into you, acting difficult when you were never like that before with me?'

'André,' Marilyn replied, in a small, distraught voice, 'many times I could not help it! I was too tired, too exhausted to get up so early in the day. You remember how I used to get car sick during those long rides when we were touring the West? You were driving endlessly, all day and night, and I just slumped over and went to sleep because I felt so tired . . . So during all the filming at Fox, I was feeling the same way, just tired and needing rest! Sometimes I was drinking a little, with men I liked, and the nights were far too short, far too delightful, to go to work so early in the morning. Isn't that all very human? I was simply too exhausted and it became almost impossible to cope with all that hard work. And now the studio is mocking me, saying openly that I am going insane!'

As they were talking, she became more and more downcast, bitter and crushed. She looked so lovely, but so sad also, as she stood near the usual large pile of trunks and suitcases. During the short hours they were conversing, she smiled very little and could not withhold her tears. André saw the bed in the adjoining room, uncovered, so he began hugging her.

'Making love will make you feel better,' he said.

'I've just had an operation. Behave yourself! You want to kill me! I need rest, André, please forgive me!'

She handed him his jacket, walked him to the door of her bungalow, and bade him good night. André walked away a hundred feet, then removed his shoes and tiptoed back to her veranda, about twenty feet from her bedroom window, and sat for a long while in the balmy, deliciously cool dark of the evening. He wanted to see what she was going to do. Would she get up and leave, or would someone come to visit her? Instead, she turned out the lights in the bedroom. Through the open windows, the nylon curtains were blowing in the breeze, looking, in the darkness, like some kind of ghosts. Unnerved, he left the scene.

The next day, he rushed to Beverly Hills and bought her flowers and a beautiful Italian ceramic fruit bowl. He filled it with oranges and wrote a letter to her to apologise for wanting to make love with her. At the hotel, he gave a generous tip to the bellboy and instructed him to be sure to hand the things to Marilyn personally.

He knew she received it, because a day later, he found one of the flowers at the front door of his house, and she had slipped an envelope full of studio stills of herself under his door. She must have passed by before going to the airport.

A year later, de Dienes was looking at a set of unpublished photos of Marilyn without make-up from 1946. One was of her gazing at the sun, with a macabre expression on her face. When he had taken it, she had said, 'André, I'm looking at my own grave.' Another was of her lying on her back, eyes shut, pretending she was dead. While he was preparing this set of photos and finding the negatives dealing with death, André had no idea Marilyn was going through the darkest period in her life. He was so involved in his work that he didn't have time to read any newspapers or follow the vicissitudes of *Something's Got to Give*.

A few weeks later, while still working with the photos, he had a series of nightmares. He saw his mother's coffin underneath his bed; Marilyn often featured. They brought back old memories, of a time when he wasn't André de Dienes – or at least not to her. She had nicknamed him WW, Worry Wart, because he worried about everything. She laughed whenever she called him WW instead of André – same initials as her, MM, but upside down. He called her 'Turkey Foot', because when he photo-graphed her in the mountains, her hands often turned purple from the cold.

After he woke up one July morning from one of these bizarre dreams, he had the strong urge to go to the nearest post office, on Sunset Boulevard. He didn't know where Marilyn was living, so he addressed a telegram to the studio where she was filming. The telegram said: 'TURKEY FOOT, I HAD VERY BAD DREAMS ABOUT YOU LAST NIGHT. PLEASE CALL ME. LOVE WW.' He didn't receive a letter or phone call in response.

On 4 August 1962, in the evening, de Dienes went to the movies. When he came home, he heard the phone ringing while he was trying to find the key at the entrance door. He rushed in but he was too late. For many years he thought she might have called, maybe unwittingly, randomly dialling under the influence of alcohol or drugs. Nobody knows how many telephone calls she might have made during that night, or to whom. The next day, André was shaving when it came on the radio that Marilyn had died during the night. He was in complete shock at first, but after a while, looking at her photos all laid out on his long worktable, he took it quite calmly. He looked at the first photo of Norma Jeane smiling, then at the next photos in which she was more serious, and then at the last series of photos where she was 'dead'. He had worked for several weeks preparing those photos. It was as if he'd known.

Twenty years later, leading a reclusive life in a little house on Boca de Canon Lane, André de Dienes spent much of his time sifting through memories. He remembered once making a scene with Marilyn. She'd ruined his life, he burst out; if he hadn't been stupid enough to fall in love with her, he'd still be a successful photographer. She had lost her temper. 'Who asked you to fall in love with me?' she shouted. 'I wanted to become an actress. Not your maid or whore!' It had degenerated into a terrible fight. She'd got dressed and walked out, and by the time he'd fetched his car and gone to look for her, she had disappeared.

It was thirty-six years since their affair had ended, the length of her entire life; she'd have been fifty-six if she were alive today. *Ended* – in a way, the affair had either never really ended or just been one ending after another. He was thinking about the last time, obviously, but whenever they'd met in the seventeen years during which they had never really lost touch, he had always had a sense they were saying goodbye.

André de Dienes hadn't taken any pictures for almost a decade when he died in 1985 in his house in the hills above Sunset Boulevard. He shut himself away in his darkroom, printing and reprinting old negatives. Very few of his photos of Marilyn were included in the inventory of his possessions after his death. He was buried a few feet from her crypt in Westwood Village Mortuary on Wilshire Boulevard.

Santa Monica, Franklin Street
Summer 1961

In May, Marilyn had moved to another part of Los Angeles, near Rancho Park, not far from Fox Studios. She left her apartment at 882 North Doheny Drive empty, apart from a trunk of books, her clothes and make-up – nothing that recalled the movie business. Hollywood, the city of images, was reclaiming her from New York, the city of words. She just wanted a place to sleep, knocked out on Nembutal, between her daily visit at four to Greenson, for talking and silence, and the weekly one to Hyman Engelberg for pills and injections. She asked Ralph Roberts, her masseur and driver, to install blackout curtains on the apartment's picture windows to kill all the light.

It was Roberts who had picked up Marilyn a few months earlier when she was discharged from Payne Whitney.

One evening she borrowed his beaten-up Pontiac Firebird and went to a fast-food drive-in on Wilshire. She ordered her food, and when it arrived, moments later, she realised they'd given her a children's meal by mistake. She opened the brightly wrapped toy that came with it and found a model of a blonde ballerina tirelessly revolving on a merry-go-round, a prisoner of its perpetual motion. She heard the attendant's voice crackling in the loudspeaker: 'Next customer. Hi, what can I get you?' At two in the morning, lying on her pristine bed searching for sleep, she repeated a chant over and over in her mind, almost as if she could see the words, 'The merry-go-round went round. The merry-go-round went round. I didn't have the words to say anything I wanted. The merry-go-round went round and I lost my chance.'

On 1 June, she sent her analyst a telegram telling him that it's her birthday, the way someone who's afraid of the big day being forgotten might give herself a present: 'DEAR DOCTOR GREENSON IN THIS WORLD OF PEOPLE I AM GLAD THERE'S YOU. I HAVE A FEELING OF HOPE ALTHOUGH TODAY I AM THREE FIVE.'

She rekindled her romance with Frank Sinatra when they saw each other at Dean Martin's birthday party a week later in Las Vegas. Their affair would last until the start of 1962.

At the end of June she returned to New York to have her gall bladder removed, her second hospital admission in as many months. She wrote to Greenson, 'On the balcony of my room, talking to the doctor who operated on me, I looked at the stars and said, "Look at them. They are all up there shining so brightly but each one must be so very alone. It's a make-believe world, isn't it?"'

When she left the clinic on West 50th Street a fortnight later, she was surrounded by a crush of fans and photographers desperate to see the most famous woman in the world. They bombarded her with questions and requests for autographs, trying to touch her, tugging at her sweater. She was terrified: it felt as if they were going to tear her to pieces. Their shouts – 'wolf calls', in photographers' parlance – lacerated her. She was glad when people showed their appreciation, but this time it was different: she felt as if she was being devoured. She instinctively asked to be taken to Dr Kris's but then remembered the madhouse. She would never be able to talk to her again.

Summer passed without Greenson bringing himself to take a vacation. He was seeing Marilyn seven days a week now, charging her a preferential rate of fifty dollars per session. He wrote to Kris:

> I am appalled at the emptiness of her life in terms of
> object relations. Essentially, it is such a narcissistic way of
> life. All in all, there's been some improvement, but I do
> not vouch for how deep it is, or how lasting. On the
> clinical level I have identified two problem areas: her
> obsessive fear of homosexuality and her inability to cope
> with any sort of hurt. She cannot bear the slightest hint
> of anything homosexual. Pat Newcomb dyed her hair
> with a streak roughly the same colour as her hair. She
> instantly jumped to the conclusion that the girl was
> trying to take possession of her and turned with a fury
> against her.

He was terrified by her increasing trend towards random promiscuity. One day she told him she was sleeping with one of the builders working on her house; another day that she had taken a taxi driver home, or that she was caught having sex in a dark hallway at a party. In a letter to Anna Freud, Greenson said she was suffering from 'a fear of men masked by a need to seduce, which makes her literally give herself to the first man who comes along'.

From then on he worried that Marilyn was lost to psycho-analysis, whereas in fact she was lost in it. Like a drowning person who drags their rescuer under, she was increasingly miring her therapist in empty despair. He was one of the idealised figures in her life, and she couldn't abide the notion of any imperfection in him. 'I'm improvising now,' Greenson wrote to Anna Freud. 'She is really very sick. I can't see any solution that will bring her the perfect peace she seeks.'

'Her inability to handle anything she perceived as hurtfulness, along with her abnormal fear of homosexuality' – Greenson would later write – 'were ultimately the decisive factors that led to her death.'

Meanwhile Marilyn's friends – Allan Snyder, Ralph Roberts, Paula Strasberg and Pat Newcomb – were starting to say the psychoanalyst was exerting too great a hold over her life. 'He is not your guardian angel,' Pat told her. 'He has become your shadow, or rather you've become his.'

'I never liked Greenson,' Snyder said years later, 'and never thought he was good for Marilyn. He gave her anything she wanted, just fed her with anything.' There was something unhealthy about Greenson's relationship with his patient, Snyder felt, something to do with money. He was very insistent about that, and his suspicions seemed confirmed when he discovered that Greenson was on Fox's payroll.

Yet each of Marilyn's four analysts had had to intervene on one of her films and give her supportive therapy to get her back on her feet: Margaret Hohenberg on *Bus Stop*, Anna Freud on *The Prince and the Showgirl*, Marianne Kris on *Some Like It Hot*, and Greenson on *Let's Make Love*, *The Misfits* and *Something's Got to Give*. Marilyn told her friends she was happy to obey – to have someone give her guidance, tell her what to do. She said she would even have let her analyst tell her who to be.

Los Angeles, Wilshire Boulevard
Autumn 1961

Cars had lost their thrill: she didn't want to drive one of her own any more. The black Cadillac convertible with the red leather upholstery had been sold, the black Thunderbird passed on to Strasberg; she'd given back the white Cadillac she'd used during location shooting for *The Misfits*.

She told her driver, Ralph Roberts, to head for the sea. On Wilshire she looked out at the scattering of low houses either side of the interminable boulevard. It seemed fake somehow, this transient neighbourhood, these characterless buildings. She remembered the first time she'd gone to Fox's studios for a screen test. She had toured the back lot with its streets and squares from all over the world, representing every historical period. They had seemed so solid; it was hard to remind herself they were just façades held up by wooden struts, a make-believe maze of time and dreams. Here on the boulevard the illusion was the opposite. Marilyn thought you had to have a lot of imagination to think of these pasteboard sets as real houses in which real people were struggling with love and cruelty and money. The sidewalks were empty. No one walks anywhere in this town except me, she thought.

She got Roberts to stop the car and continued on foot, aimlessly. Taking a left towards Pico, she stood for a while on a bridge over the Santa Monica Freeway, looking down at the cars converging in the sunset, like a procession of weary animals. She watched the lines of white headlights, like images in a dream, empty eyes staring at nothing. When it grew dark, she saw a man stopped in front of a garage. She walked past his car. He was very young, and recognised her, despite her black wig. So much about Marilyn Monroe was inconceivable to him: her conversations with the poet and writer Carl Sandburg, her literature course at UCLA. She was insanely beautiful and filled him with desire and terror. All he saw was her body. A body he had to have, and hope he could escape the soul animating it.

The man held the door of his brown Oldsmobile open for her, then drove to a green one-storey house with flaking paint, two blocks from the beach on a street in Venice Beach. Superba Avenue. Or was it Santa Clara? Milkwood? San Juan? Did it matter? She had to remember so she could tell the doctor tomorrow. 'The details,' he always said. 'That's what counts.' Names, names . . . Venice Beach, that's where her grandmother Delia was buried. Her mother's mother, the madwoman who had tried to smother her with a pillow when she was a baby. She had told her saviour about it. He had played on the words 'mother' and 'smother'.

She asked the man to take her from behind. 'You know what I mean,' she added. Caught by surprise, he felt she was giving him a gift, offering up the most intimate, the oldest part of her being. She lay down on her stomach, passed him some lubricant and then he penetrated her, not for very long, but forcefully, almost spitefully. Lifting the hair from her face, he saw she was clasping the rumpled sheet in her right fist like a child's blanket, something tender and warm and familiar-smelling. She was rubbing it gently against her chin.

'Is that good? Can you feel me?' he asked. Then: 'I'm not hurting you, am I? Do you want me to stop?'

She didn't answer his questions, just kept rubbing the sheet against her mouth without saying anything. Saddened by her sadness, he stopped, and they quickly said goodbye, thanking one another awkwardly.

She told Greenson about it the following day.

'I sense something dreamlike about your story,' he said, 'as if you didn't fully experience it. You were present, but not really as yourself any more. In effect, you were trying to free yourself from this man's embrace. The sheet is what we call "a transitional object". We all have our versions of them. The most striking detail is how yours allowed you to form a closed circuit. It's as if you were telling the man, "You won't have my mouth, you won't hear my voice. You can have my anus as much as you want, it isn't part of me any more." You know, unlike the mouth, which is associated with one's voice and identity, the anus is linked to shame, dispossession, waste and vulnerability.'

She didn't say anything. She felt a few tears run down her cheeks, but didn't wipe them away.

Santa Monica, Franklin Street
July 1961

As her analysis progressed and the transference accompanying it grew steadily more chaotic and intense, Marilyn's relations with the Greenson family grew increasingly intimate. She kept a bottle of Dom Pérignon in their fridge and sometimes stayed to supper, cheerfully helping Hildi with the washing-up in their Mexican kitchen. Joan Greenson, who was studying art at the Otis Art Institute, had learned from childhood to keep out of sight of her father's patients, so her role in Marilyn's treatment was thrilling, although she didn't really understand the reasons for it. When the star arrived, Joan would be waiting for her at the door, and they'd often take a turn round the reservoir by the house while they waited for Greenson; sometimes Marilyn would teach her a dance or give her tips on how to make herself up to look glamorous. The Greensons' twenty-four-year-old son Danny, a medical student at UCLA, who was also still living at home, became close to Marilyn as well. Passionately opposed to the Vietnam War, he'd talk politics with their guest. The Greensons' children knew their father's behaviour was strange for a strict

Freudian, but he convinced them that traditional therapy would not be effective in Marilyn's case.

One evening in July, the Greensons threw a birthday party for their daughter. Having helped with the preparations, Marilyn came along too. Once they got over their nervousness, the boys were soon queuing up to dance with her. As Greenson later related, 'It didn't look too promising for the local girls. And no one was dancing any more with an especially attractive black girl who, until Marilyn had arrived, had been the most popular on the floor. Marilyn noticed this, and went over to her. "You know," she said, "you do a step I'd love to do, but don't think I know how. Would you teach it to me?" Then she turned to the others and called out, "Everybody stop for a few minutes! I'm going to learn a new step." Now, the point is, Marilyn knew the step, but she let this girl teach it to her. She understood the loneliness of others.'

Santa Monica, Franklin Street
Late July 1961

After eighteen months of seeing her, Marilyn's analyst felt she was entering a critical phase. He asked her why she had such difficulty saying her lines. She told him she had been troubled by something a critic had said about her, that she was 'really a silent actress who's wandered into the talkies by mistake'. She thought this was true, that her face expressed things that couldn't be put into words.

'Why do you stutter on set but not in the day-to-day . . . not here, for example?' asked Greenson.

'I get afraid.'

'Of what? Of not being heard, or of being heard?'

'You make everything so complicated. I get afraid of words. It's as if my lips didn't want to let them go.'

'Speaking implies separation, absolutely. Once you say a word, it's lost. So you stutter, you clamp your mouth shut over the first syllable. Language is another thing you cannot bear to be separated from.'

'That reminds me of something. When I stuttered as a child,

I'd always get stuck on the letter *m*. I was so shy. After a time I didn't mind being looked at – I even used to dream about people seeing me completely naked – but I always thought it was best if I kept quiet. At least then I couldn't be blamed for saying anything wrong. I remember when I was made class secretary at my school, Emerson Junior High in Van Nuys, when I was about thirteen. I'd stutter like crazy when I had to start meetings, "The m-m-minutes of the last m-m-meeting . . .". So after that I became Miss Mmmm at school. When Ben Lyon chose Marilyn Monroe as my stage name, he hit on the letter I found hardest to say for both my initials. And you know what? The first time I appeared in front of a camera in *Scudda Hoo! Scudda Hay!*, my first line on celluloid was meant to be "Mmmm." But it got cut, so I didn't have a speaking part in that film.' She was silent for a moment, before saying, 'I've always had trouble with words. Learning lines, saying lines. The stuttering lasted for a long time, but now I've worked out how to get over it. I murmur instead. I've turned my nervousness into a weapon, a trap for men.'

'*M* is also the first letter of "mother",' Greenson remarked. 'In most European languages that I know, the word for "mother" begins with the letter *m*. The child psychoanalysts Anna Freud and Dorothy Burlingham have established that children raised apart from their mothers tend to be slower acquiring language—'

'I know Anna Freud,' Marilyn exclaimed. 'She analysed me before you. You knew that, didn't you?'

'The sound "mmm" is autoerotic,' Greenson continued, annoyed at the interruption, 'which is probably why the word "me" also begins with an *m*.'

Marilyn turned away to prevent her analyst seeing her face, and folded her arms across her chest.

In December 1953, seven years before meeting Marilyn, Ralph Greenson had attended the midwinter meeting of the American

Psychoanalytic Association in New York, where he gave a paper entitled, 'About the Sound "Mm" . . .':

> The utterance *Mm* . . ., as produced with a humming or musical intonation derives from the memory or fantasy of being at the mother's breast. The musical quality of this *Mm* . . . sound is probably related to the fact that the contented mother hums cheerfully as she feeds her baby or rocks him to sleep . . . The fact that the sound *Mm* . . . is made with the lips closed and continuously so throughout the utterance seems to indicate that this is the only sound one can make and still keep something safely within the mouth. Apparently it is the sound produced with the nipple in the mouth or with the pleasant memory of expectation of its being in the mouth.

The year before Marilyn's death, Greenson edited an article he wrote in 1949, 'The Mother Tongue and the Mother'. He emphasised that there were particular cases where analysts had to be able to talk to their patients in their first languages, and added in a footnote, 'Whenever stalemated situations occur regularly in psychoanalysis, one should consider the possibility that the patient and the analyst are not communicating on the same wavelength. For example, I would not refer a Brooklyn-bred girl who is now a Hollywood starlet to a prim, cultured, central European analyst. They would not speak the same language.' But was the stalemate in Marilyn's analysis due to the lack of a common language, or to their having in a sense swapped mother tongues? As he drew her increasingly into the language of analysis, she in turn was drowning him in the movies and their inexhaustible sea of images.

As well as going to her sessions, Marilyn made sure Engelberg kept her constantly supplied with sedatives. Greenson had other patients in the business with similar dependencies, but he failed to gauge either how longstanding or how severe the addiction was in this case. Marilyn had started taking drugs when she was eighteen, at the time of her first screen tests, then steadily upped the doses and types of drugs: barbiturates, depressants, amphetamines. Neither Greenson, nor Engelberg, nor Wexler had any success in weaning her off them. 'Marilyn wasn't killed by Hollywood,' John Huston would say when she died. 'It was the goddam doctors who killed her. If she was a pill addict, they made her so.'

Greenson never ventured a final diagnosis in Marilyn's case, which he handled for thirty months. Initially he merely observed symptoms of paranoia and 'depressive reaction'. His colleagues in the Los Angeles Psychoanalytic Society were nonplussed. 'He doesn't seem to understand,' said one, 'that the adoption therapy he's proposing will only remind her of what she's never had – a home – and what she'll never be – a daughter loved by her parents, a sister and a mother in her own right.'

Greenson betrayed his anxiety when he discussed Marilyn with Wexler. 'Aren't I breaking the rules, overstepping the boundaries here?' he asked. 'You should see her, I think. I've found indications of schizophrenia. She had a terrible childhood and, whether fantasy or not, talks of having been sexually abused.' The only thing of which Greenson was entirely certain was that he was dealing with a terribly fragile individual. 'I've taken our line on schizophrenics: put the patient's needs and psychic work first, and one's personal therapeutic aims second. I've tried to let her words and feelings enter into me. But I should be more transparent in my methods, don't you think?'

'No, the opposite if anything,' Wexler replied. 'You should continue down the unorthodox route. To think that the analyst who sits behind the patient is a nonentity on whom everything is projected is ridiculous. I don't think it's very long before the patient knows whether I'm bright or stupid. If the patient says,

"You're a stupid son-of-a-bitch," you can't say, "That's obviously what he thought about his father." Maybe you *are* a stupid son-of-a-bitch. If I write scripts with my patients, if I have dinner with my patients, all they know is that I'm some kind of person. The idea that you can't have any relationship with your patients outside the office seems to me unreasonable, unfair, and just plain silly.'

'And what about a patient's body? Is it crossing a line to touch it?' asked Greenson, running a finger over his moustache.

Soon after the death of their patient, Milton Wexler and Ralph Greenson planned a research project for Beverly Hills's Foundation for Research in Psychoanalysis on 'Failures in Psychoanalysis', which they would then turn into a book. It remained unwritten.

Santa Monica, Franklin Street
October 1961

Greenson often spent his leisure hours sitting in a rowing boat in his swimming pool. He found it restful, gently rocking back and forth. At nearly fifty, he had begun to feel as though he needed to spend more time on his own work, and had therefore decided to resign as dean of the training school and limit his professional activities. He even planned not to attend that year's meeting of the American Psychoanalytic Association.

In truth, he would have liked to put some more distance between himself and Marilyn as well, but he could see how alone she was in the world, and he still hoped he might be able to defeat the forces of death at work in her and learn something from the destructive processes that had her in their grip.

At the start of October, Marilyn was invited to a dinner with the president's younger brother and attorney general, Bobby Kennedy, who was in Los Angeles on government business. She went in a long black sheath dress that set off the whiteness of her skin. The bodice was the strategic component: she wanted to reveal as much of her breasts as possible, which was precisely the sort of self-destructive behaviour Greenson was trying to stop. The dinner was held at Peter Lawford's, the Kennedys' brother-in-law. Marilyn drank heavily, and eventually Bobby Kennedy and his press aide offered to take her home to her little apartment on Doheny Drive.

Ten days later, Fox informed her that she would have to make *Something's Got to Give*. Convinced that Cukor despised her, and that at any moment the side of herself that hated the movie business would resurface and force her to pull out of filming, she threatened to take her own life. Greenson decided she needed to be detoxified again but, in light of the Payne Whitney episode, at home this time. Marilyn's living room, with its heavy blue triple-lined curtains, became her hospital, and her analyst, in return for a substantial retainer from Fox, became the technical consultant and special counsellor to Marilyn Monroe.

'You know,' she told Greenson, when he came to see her one evening, 'I think I've worked out my definition of death. Death is the body you've got to shake off. When people survive an illness or an accident, they feel they've escaped from their body. Sex can be like that too. When a man follows me in the street, I can feel him wanting to escape his body by taking mine. I made a will in New York when I was in analysis for the first time with the Hungarian. For my epitaph, I came up with: "Marilyn Monroe, Blonde, 37–23–36".' Stifling a laugh, she added, 'I think I'll go with that, maybe with a few changes to the measurements.'

When he got back to Santa Monica, the analyst tried to understand the reaction Marilyn's stories and sexual poses provoked in him. He felt vaguely disgusted, sad almost. He could smell her peroxided hair when he sat opposite her, and felt no urge to touch it with his hands or lips – but he couldn't stop smelling that smell. She wasn't his type: he preferred thin women, brunettes, and found Marilyn too childlike, too American.

Looking at her, he would find himself suspended in a state of platonic admiration of her beauty – sexy but not sexual.

He tried to understand why he barely looked at her any more. What gives a word its form are the consonants, not the vowels, he thought. What gives a sentence form and line are the ways it fits together, its syntax, not its words. A body is a little like a sentence. Curves and flesh are not enough to make one want to possess it. One must be able to discern a structure: bones, joints. A form. Marilyn seemed all voluptuous flesh. He saw her bring in her body and set it down in a chair with the implied question, 'Do you like what you see?', and instead of his fear transforming into desire, the abundance somehow repelled him.

Berkeley, California
5 and 27 October 1961

In October, Greenson was asked by KPFA-FM radio station to give a talk in two parts on the 'Varieties of Love'. He described America and Americans as a society that neglected love, that was driven instead by the search for success, money, fame and power. Everyone wanted to be loved, but few people could love, or wanted to love, he argued. 'Love is confused, in many people's minds, with sexual satisfaction, and they equate enjoying somebody sexually, having a pleasant time physically, with love. Or they confuse it with peacefulness. "I live with her and she doesn't bother me and I don't bother her and we love each other." And this is not love. It is a question if this is living!'

Television was a screen that isolated people and prevented them either loving or hating one another. For the most part, they thought of love as a foreign notion, or at least a perverse one, because it was not innate. Babies are not born with the ability to love; they simply survive and breathe and eat. Their life is a polarity between pain, craving and longing, on the one

164

hand, and satisfaction and oblivion on the other, and many adults never progress beyond this state: alcoholics, addicts, bulimics, people hooked on the sensation of danger. No one else exists for them; other people's individuality is utterly unimportant. The only function another person performs is that of provider, giving them something that assuages their pain or satisfies their needs.

Driving home after the second broadcast, he thought of Marilyn and of the phrase that always came into his mind when he tried to review her case: a loveless love.

In the final months of her life Marilyn's relationship with her analyst became more emotional, the professional boundaries fainter. Greenson longed to fulfil Marilyn's fantasy of finding her way back home, to shield her from anything that might hurt her. She spent more and more time at the Greensons' home, and began to telephone him at all hours to talk – about her work, her relationships, everything.

Hollywood insiders had begun to think of Ralph and Marilyn in terms of a script. John Huston burst out laughing when he heard of the tragi-comic set-up. 'We've moved on from *The Prince and the Showgirl*,' he said. 'Now it's *The Analyst and His Double*.' If it weren't for an ingrained lethargy on his part, he would have liked to make a movie about it. Good premise, he thought. They're directing one another without realising it. Each is playing the role they can't have in real life: him the actor, her the intellectual. They've become the other's fantasy. Neither of them was mad before they met, and they still aren't when they're apart, but being together is driving them out of their minds. Years later, in 1983, Huston was able to exact revenge on the Freud family for the way they'd rebuffed his *Freud, the Secret Passion*. To his inordinate pleasure, he was given the part of a seasoned analyst in Marshall Brickman's film *Lovesick*, who not only supervises but also restores to the straight and narrow a colleague who's fallen madly in love with a patient.

One Saturday afternoon in late November, Greenson asked Marilyn to come to his house for her second session of the day. As soon as she arrived, he sent her out to tell Ralph Roberts, who was waiting for her in the car, that he should go back to New York: her analyst had chosen someone else to be her companion. Two Ralphs in her life were one too many. When she'd done what he asked, Greenson congratulated her on her ability in general to get rid of those in her entourage who were taking advantage of her. Freeing herself from hangers-on who were exploiting her was a sure sign of clinical progress.

But Greenson could not free Marilyn from her need to work, and without the alternately desired and loathed compensations of acting, her depression grew. During this sad winter, she sent a short poem to her friend, the poet Norman Rosten:

> Help Help
> Help I feel life coming closer
> When all I want is to die.

At one session, after much intense crying and noisy sobbing, she slowly began to quieten down, consoling herself with the belief that her analysis was helping her pull herself back together into one piece. As she said this, Greenson noticed her gently and rhythmically stroking the burlap wallpaper alongside the couch with her fingertips, her eyes half closed. There was a pause, and then she said, 'You're good to me, you really try to help.' She continued to stroke the wall in silence. Greenson, too, remained silent. After a few minutes, now dry-eyed, she stopped stroking the wall, straightened her somewhat rumpled dress, and said, 'I feel better now. I don't know why, I just do. Maybe it was your silence. I felt it as warm and comforting, not cold as I sometimes do. I did not feel alone.'

At first Greenson did not realise that for her, at that moment, his office was a 'transitional transference object'. The stroking of the wall seemed to have many other meanings. On the one hand, she was stroking the wall as she wanted to stroke and be stroked by her lover and him. The stroking of the wall was also, Greenson eventually discovered, a re-enactment of something of a more infantile nature. The rhythmic movements, the half-closed eyes and the soothing effect of his non-interference should have indicated to him that it might be a transitional transference experience for her.

He began to speak but she quickly interrupted him to say that his words seemed like an intrusion. He waited and then said in a quiet voice that he had the impression that, as she wept, she let herself slip into the past; the stroking of the wall might have brought back an old sense of comfort from childhood?

Marilyn replied, 'I was only dimly aware of the stroking – above all, I loved the tweedy quality of the wallpaper. It has little hairs like fur. Strange, I felt the wallpaper was responding to me in a vague way.'

'So you felt in your misery,' the analyst said, 'that being on the couch, stroking the wallpaper in my silent presence was like being comforted by a kind of mothering person.'

After a pause Marilyn replied, 'You know, I don't quite agree with you. This may sound strange to you, but it was stroking the wallpaper that helped – and also, I suppose, your letting me do it. It reminds me of crying myself to sleep as a child by petting my favourite panda bear. I kept that panda for years; in fact I have baby pictures with it. Of course, then it was quite furry and later it became smooth, but I always felt it as furry.'

Later she had dreams of her analyst with black and white spots, some of which were traceable both to her panda and to Greenson's beard, which she called furry. Recently – almost

unconsciously – he had let it grow, which had provoked considerable hilarity when Wexler saw the results. 'I've never really
understood why men grow beards,' Wexler had said. 'If it's to
make them more virile, forget it. They don't seem to realise the
lower half of their face now resembles their mother's genitalia.'
Greenson had looked at him as if he were mad, and said nothing.

Santa Monica, Franklin Street
Autumn 1961

While collaborating on the screenplay of *Captain Newman, M.D.*, Greenson wrote to Leo Rosten, the book's author: 'Milton Rudin has got me 12.5% of the gross receipts from Universal. It's the least they can do: as you know, the psychiatrist in the film is 100% me, and 90% of the characters are my old patients.' He also took charge of the pre-production of *Something's Got to Give*. In November the producer, David Brown, found out he was being replaced by Henry Weinstein, whose career as a producer only extended to one film, *Tender Is the Night*. Shocked to be sidelined like that, he was told it was a condition of Marilyn's deal. Greenson had given his assurances that, if Brown were replaced by Weinstein, he could guarantee his star would be punctual and the production completed on time. 'Don't worry,' he had said. 'I can get her to do whatever I want.'

Filming was supposed to start in April, and Cukor expected the worst: 'So you think you can get Marilyn to the set on time? Let me tell you something, if you placed Marilyn's bed on set with her in it, and the set was fully lighted, she still wouldn't be on time for the first shot!'

As the end of the year approached, Marilyn's analysis grew increasingly confused. Marilyn, who had entered analysis in character, as 'Marilyn', was becoming less wedded to her image as a way of winning over others. She was beginning to accept that words could keep her warm, covering and enfolding her, like clothing. Whereas Greenson, the highly articulate product of the world of words, who had chosen to go into psychiatry in order to distance himself from other people's bodies, was beginning to lay siege to Hollywood's image factory. Closely connected to a variety of film studios through his patient list of directors and producers, he became particularly associated with Fox, as a note in the studio's archives made clear: 'Although Dr Greenson did not want us to deem his relationship as Svengali-like, he said in fact he could persuade her to do anything reasonable that he wanted. He would determine what scenes she would and wouldn't do, what rushes were favourable and all the other creative decisions that had to be made.'

Beverly Hills, Roxbury Drive
Autumn 1976

Ralph Greenson probably started his unpublished article 'The Screen of Transference: Roles and True Identity' in 1976. This was when he had come across some troubling material in the Freud archives concerning the boundaries between analysis and love, a discovery he couldn't wait to share with Milton Wexler.

'Now I see why Anna Freud didn't want anyone to make a film about her father,' he began. 'Marilyn wasn't the issue. The real issue was love, which is what every movie is about.'

'No kidding,' Wexler replied, with a shrug. 'Has it taken you this long to realise that passion is primarily a matter of representation, of acting?'

'I love the film business,' Greenson said. 'Actors move me; the screen fascinates me. You think I'd like to have been an actor, don't you? In fact it's worse than that: I'd have liked to be a director and do the very thing you must never do in analysis. Write the dialogue, invent the story, run through the scenes.'

'You're too narcissistic for that. The director doesn't appear on screen . . .'

'I'd like to write an article about it,' Greenson continued. 'Something from a historical and theoretical point of view about why Freud, who was so enamoured of images, didn't like the movies—'

'For God's sake!' Wexler snapped. 'All you ever talk about is the movies. What about the passion between lovers? What about love? What movie were you directing Marilyn in? A romance?'

'There was never anything sexual between us, you know that. She took possession of me and, it's true, in a way I did of her too. But the idiots who suspect me of having sexual relations with her will never get it. Her body didn't make any impression on me. I admired it, of course, but I almost didn't see it after a while. I heard a child imprisoned inside it, not even a young girl, a child who had always been afraid of talking because she didn't want to be in the wrong. I don't sleep with children.'

'Lack of desire or lack of love – what enabled you to resist her? Her therapy, and the self-alienation she was looking for it to provide, might have been less destructive if you had slept with her. You probably wouldn't have damaged each other the way you did. And maybe she'd still be alive. I don't get it. What allowed you to escape virtually unscathed from your grand passion – because that's what it was, wasn't it? Your major motion picture.'

'Some other time, if you don't mind. I've got things to do,' Greenson barked, then left the room, slamming the door behind him.

Santa Monica, Franklin Street
December 1961–January 1962

Marilyn cast a circumspect glance around the consulting room before sitting down.

'This'll be the third picture we've worked on together,' Greenson announced cheerfully. 'Now, I don't want any regrets from you about Cecily. I much prefer you as a real patient than one of the Master's in a film. I'm not sure I really understand why you're finding this movie so hard, though.'

'It's not as if it's anything new. I've always had to drag myself on set; the last three pictures I've made have been a nightmare. This one, though ... this one's the limit. *Something's Got to Give* ... it almost makes me want to laugh. So now we know.' She lapsed into a deep silence, her eyes lowered, wringing her hands, until finally she said, 'I didn't tell you what I did in the clinic in New York before I threw the chair at the window. They wouldn't let me out, so I stripped naked and pressed myself against the glass.'

'What did you say?'

'Nothing. I just stood there without saying anything. You know

I have trouble with words, Doctor. Words leave us at the mercy of other people; they strip us far more naked than anyone's hands. Yesterday evening I went to a party at Cecil Beaton's and danced naked in front of fifty people, but I wouldn't have been able to tell any of them the simple thing I find so hard to say now, even to you: my mother . . . Who's that? The woman with the red hair, that's all.'

It was stifling hot when Marilyn left at the end of her hour, and Greenson went to sit by the pool. He unfolded a sheet of yellow paper she had left on the arm of her chair. It was a poem, or rather a sequence of short poems:

> Night of the Nile – soothing –
> darkness – refreshes – Air
> Seems different – Night has
> No eyes nor no one – silence
> except to the Night itself

> Life –
> I am of both your directions
> Somehow remaining,
> Hanging downward the most,
> Strong as a cobweb in the wind,
> Existing more with the cold frost
> than those beaded rays
> I've seen in paintings

> To the Weeping Willow

> I stood beneath your limbs
> And you flowered and finally
> clung to me
> and when the wind struck with the earth
> and sand – you clung to me

On 4 December 1961, Greenson wrote to Anna Freud about Marilyn without mentioning the brief course of therapy she had given her five years earlier.

> I have resumed treating the patient who Marianne Kris saw for several years. She has become a borderline paranoid addict and is very sick. You can imagine how difficult it is treating a Hollywood actress, who has so many serious problems and is completely alone in the world, and yet at the same time is extremely famous. Psychoanalysis is still out of the question and I am improvising constantly, often surprised at where it's leading me. I have no other options. If I succeed, I'll certainly have learned something, but this case is requiring me to expend an impossible amount of time and emotion.

Strangely enough Anna didn't mention her work with the actress either. 'Marianne keeps me informed of your patient's progress, as well as her struggles with her. The question is whether someone can provide her with the impetus to be well that should really come from herself.' Both seemed to have agreed they should gloss over any role Anna might have played in Marilyn's mental state, presumably so that, if anything went wrong, the question of her responsibility wouldn't come up.

That month Greenson wrote to another correspondent about Marilyn: 'She went through a severe depressive and paranoid reaction. She talked about retiring from the movie industry, killing herself, etc. I had to place nurses in her apartment day and night and keep strict control over the medication, since I felt she was potentially suicidal. Marilyn fought with these nurses, so that after a few weeks it was impossible to keep any of them.'

*　　*　　*

Three weeks after J. Edgar Hoover, director of the FBI, informed Robert Kennedy that the Chicago Mafia boss Sam Giancana was planning to use Frank Sinatra to intercede with the Kennedys on his behalf, Marilyn was invited to dinner at the Lawfords' place with Bobby Kennedy. This was going to be her second dinner with the president's brother and she didn't want it to end like the first, with her falling out of her dress, in tears, about to pass out. Over at the Greensons' a few days before the dinner, she and Danny talked politics, while she took notes. Danny – a medical student – was campaigning against American support for the South Vietnamese regime, and they went over all the important issues of the day – the House Un-American Activities Committee, civil rights and so on.

At first she impressed Bobby, but then he saw her studying the list of talking points hidden in her handbag, and gently made fun of her. It wasn't the first time she'd tried to prepare like that – if you think it was a mistake that you were born in the first place, you can't bear being even remotely at fault.

A month later, thinking her intense involvement with the Kennedys was damaging – and hoping to have some time away from her himself – Greenson urged Marilyn to take a holiday in Mexico before starting *Something's Got to Give*. She felt an indefinable change in her analyst, and began to see him as an object of passion rather than as a loving saviour. Imperceptibly the nature of their relationship had changed. Now there was a single self between them, a shared unconscious – love, but not love for each other, only self-love.

Marilyn, like everyone, had her version of true love. Some have more than one version, others an infinite variety. To each their own. 'I love you'; 'I don't love you any more' – those words people say when they're no longer true, or to make them true. But one never says, 'I love you,' without it also meaning 'Love me!' Sometimes that's all it means. As the intimacy between Marilyn and Ralph grew fiercer, a sort of feverish romance developed, fuelled not by love but by passion – passion with its breakdowns and recoveries, its stalemates, its bitter tears and black delights. If love is always reciprocal – each loves to be loved – passion is always asymmetrical.

Brentwood, Fifth Helena Drive
February 1962

The Los Angeles Marilyn returned to from New York was no longer the city of her youth. Under the pressure of six million inhabitants, it had mutated into a flat, amorphous organism, pumping thick clots of traffic round its endless, smog-ridden freeways. Every block glowed with the neon tubes of twenty-four-hour supermarkets. Overshadowed by the Mediterranean-style villas of silent film stars, which had remained secluded behind high stands of palm and eucalyptus for the last thirty years, Marilyn's first address on her return was 882 Doheny Drive, near Greystone Park, north of Beverly Hills – an unprepossessing studio flat with Stengel, her secretary's name, on the bell. She'd lost track of all the houses, hotel rooms, apartments she had lived in: from the YMCA to Chateau Marmont, from hookers' joints like the Biltmore to the Beverly Hills Hotel, from an apartment backing onto the Van Nuys rail track to palatial Manhattan penthouses. She'd stayed in converted garages and the Carlyle's presidential suite, but never once had she felt like she had her own home. 'I seem to have a whole superstructure with no foundation,' she told a journalist.

So Marilyn bought a house in Brentwood, a neighbourhood in West Los Angeles with coastal winds and a village charm, even in the midst of LA's gangrenous, featureless sprawl. She decided to buy a place after Greenson said, as he walked her to his gate at the end of a session, 'Take care of yourself. Do you want us to drive you home?'

It sounded weird, *home*. Instead of answering his question, she had said, 'The other day I was at a reception and they asked me to sign the guest book. I wrote my name after hesitating a little, as I always do, and then in the column for addresses I put, "Nowhere".'

After two psychiatric hospitalisations and two major surgeries, she wanted a house of her own or, more specifically, one of her own like the one of *his* own. That was the ultimate appeal of the place: it was a replica, albeit smaller and less beautiful, of her analyst's house. A faux-hacienda in a nondescript, peaceful neighbourhood at the end of a cul-de-sac. She would live there barely six months.

It had a small swimming pool at the back, a few trees and a lawn rolling down to a deep valley. At first she hardly decorated it: a few ceramic tiles, some masks on the walls, a grandfather clock given her by Carl Sandburg, a few pieces of coloured pottery, an Aztec calendar. She left the rooms sparsely furnished, as if still slightly uncertain, and made a plan to go to Mexico to buy furniture and art so she could re-create her doctor's house in detail.

Marilyn felt she could love that house on Fifth Helena Drive, with its hand-hewn beams and cathedral ceilings. On the terrace, she could feel the strength of the trees, like sturdy arms that hold you without imprisoning you. She liked the roughness of the adobe stucco walls, like the hands of a working mother, the way her feet sank into the bedroom's thick white carpet. 'It will be the child you lost, the husband you divorced,' Greenson had said. 'This house will bring you peace.' She counted all the places she'd lived in: there had been fifty-seven in thirty-five years. This time, she felt, she'd found the right one. The last one. The one where she'd settle, where she wouldn't be afraid any longer.

The last film she was contracted to make for Fox, the last house. It was like turning over a new leaf, but that was good. She could even envisage going to her last session at Greenson's one day.

'I heard you bought a house,' André de Dienes said, when they saw each other soon afterwards.

'Oh, yes. And my analyst congratulated me on my choice. It's a big step towards resolving my transferential attachment, apparently. God knows why. I've moved from three streets away from his office in Beverly Hills to somewhere a stone's throw from his house in Santa Monica. I even felt funny when I found out he lived on Franklin Street. When I was twenty, I lived on Franklin Avenue in Hollywood for a while. I'd left my foster parents who'd put me up when I had no work and was going hungry. They were kind people, but I got sick of their parties in the end and needed somewhere to be on my own.'

'The main thing, though, is you feel good in your home in Brentwood.'

'You're right. It's not big; it's nothing, really. But a nothing with a pool, a nothing I like. You know, deep down what I've always liked about this city is the way it's not really there, it's sort of nothing. A sprawl of shacks in a desert of messed-up emotions, without any life of its own. But LA doesn't pretend to be a city, to be beautiful. It's how I feel when I'm not acting: as if I've unravelled and have no memories – I'm just a body, stretched out. LA's always changing. It's one thing, then that goes, then it's something else . . . on and on like that. So, yes, on my doctor's advice, I've bought a house. It's a start; maybe it'll give me some security. I do feel at home there. But what does that mean? Home is always where the ghosts are.'

Shortly before she died, Marilyn had to fill in an official form that required her to give her father's name. Furiously, she wrote: 'Not Known'.

Santa Monica, Franklin Street
March 1962

Greenson quickly understood that Marilyn hadn't stopped thinking of Manhattan as her real address and intended to return to New York after she'd finished her last film for Fox. She spent a fortnight there in February on her way to Mexico, attending Strasberg's classes every day and talking to Greenson every night. Then she went on to visit her ex-father-in-law, Isadore Miller, in Florida before flying out of Miami. The Mexican trip was a brief respite for Greenson. Chaperoned by her housekeeper, Eunice Murray, Marilyn bought the things she needed for her house, had a dalliance with a left-wing screenwriter, José Bolaños, met some of the Zona Rosa circle of Communist exiles at Fred Vanderbilt Field's: nothing to concern her analyst, who had urged her to take a vacation. Vanderbilt was a long-standing friend of his, which was not something his patient knew but was of great interest to the FBI. A document dated 6 March and headed 'MARILYN MONROE – SECURITY MATTER – C (Communist)' was sent from the Mexico office to J. Edgar Hoover, who was concerned to see the president's mistress talking to reds about subjects relating to national security.

Marilyn had been put under surveillance at the end of 1961: DiMaggio spied on her out of jealousy while Paul 'Skinny' D'Amato, the gangster in charge of the Cal-Neva Lodge Casino on Lake Tahoe, bugged her for Sam Giancana, and the FBI, the final member of the triumvirate, put a tap on her phone after J. Edgar Hoover warned President Kennedy of the Mafia's attempts to undermine him through his relationship with the movie star. Whether in New York or California, Marilyn used public phones wherever possible.

When she returned home from Mexico in early March, along with her Mexican lover, she kept an appointment with Peter G. Levathes, the executive vice president in charge of production at Fox, and swore she was ready to start filming.

'Are you sure?' Levathes said incredulously. He'd heard the story of her recent, very boozy appearance at the Golden Globes. 'You seem completely done in. What's going on?'

She didn't answer, so he told her he had hired Nunnally Johnson, the screenwriter on two of her previous films, to rewrite *Something's Got to Give*.

She went to meet the writer the next day at the Beverly Hills Hotel. 'I'm here to see Mr Johnson,' she told the desk. 'I've got an appointment.'

'Who should I say it is?'

'A prostitute.'

They caught up boisterously on what had been going on since they'd last seen each other, polishing off several bottles of champagne in the process. At one point, she told him to keep his voice down so people wouldn't hear. 'That's a bit paranoid, isn't it?' he said jokingly.

'Just because you're paranoid doesn't mean people aren't out to get you, as the analyst said to the patient,' Marilyn replied. 'No, no, forget I said that: let's talk about the part.'

'Wait, you've given me an idea. You remember *The Three Faces of Eve* I did a while ago? I could see you doing a sort of two faces of Ellen in this. Someone very loving and girlish one moment, who's a brooding, tough bitch the next, back to get her revenge on the man who took her for dead.'

'No. I don't want anything tragic. I've had enough of that. Remember, you've got Marilyn Monroe. You've got to use her. There has to be a scene where I wear a bikini. And, please, forget any alter-ego riffs. Which reminds me: Cyd Charisse wants to be blonde in the film. The studio assured me her hair'd be light brown. But,' she concludes knowingly, 'her *unconscious* wants it blonde.'

Johnson kept his thoughts to himself, but he learned afterwards that Fox had darkened her rival's hair just to be on the safe side. Meanwhile, to Johnson's mounting discouragement, the studio was demanding constant changes to the script. He realised not only that the film would be crucial to Marilyn's career, but also that, as in certain chess moves, she couldn't win, whether she made it or not. Either the film would be finished and a failure, or it would be abandoned and she would be blamed.

Marilyn had booked into the Beverly Hills Hotel with Bolaños for a few days while work was being done to her house. She arrived for her session on the first Saturday in March in a state of extreme agitation.

'Nunnally Johnson's going to tell Fox to screw themselves because they don't know what kind of script they want. No one knows what ending to give the picture, whether to go for comedy or tragedy.'

At the end of her hour, Greenson was adamant she was in no fit state to return to the hotel. He insisted she stay with them until she was feeling better. It wouldn't be the first time she had spent several nights in the Greenson family home, and she accepted his invitation to stay as long as she needed to until she could move back into her house.

The analyst put his patient in a room on the first floor. He dismissed the Mexican lover, and all the other rival lovers and ex-husbands. One evening, a few days later, DiMaggio showed up to take Marilyn back to Fifth Helena Drive. As two trainee doctors looked on, Greenson refused to let her come downstairs.

'She is under sedation,' he told DiMaggio. 'She needs peace and quiet. I'll let you know when to come back.'

Learning that Joe was waiting for her, she wanted to see him, but her analyst forbade it. She protested, screamed. Joe insisted. Turning to one of the doctors under his supervision for psycho-therapeutic training, Greenson said, 'You see, this is a good example of the narcissistic character. See how demanding she is? She has to have things her way. She's nothing but a child, poor thing.'

The student didn't need years of clinical experience to recognise the classic signs of projection. If anyone was the poor thing struggling with his own unanalysed dependency, it was Greenson: he had become his prisoner's prisoner.

Greenson's colleagues, meanwhile, grew increasingly alarmed at his interventionist and authoritarian behaviour. Hollywood's psychoanalytic community, with Milton Wexler taking the lead, found the whole set-up bizarre. Whatever apparent legitimacy it laid claim to, Greenson's approach seemed obviously flawed. Instead of providing the techniques for Marilyn to find within herself new resources for independence and autonomous judge-ment, he made her more dependent, ensuring his own dominance. His severest critics spoke of a *folie à deux*. The more indulgent merely turned a blind eye to a form of treatment that, although unorthodox, did not actually contravene any criminal, moral or professional ethical law. Such was the authority and intellectual influence Greenson exercised over the profession in Los Angeles, both in its practical and educational guises, that a tacit decision seems to have been taken not to go public with any criticisms of his methods, which, in private, had become the subject of much snide comment and rumour.

When Nunnally Johnson left California, the script complete, Marilyn got up uncharacteristically early to see him off. She threw her arms round his neck, then drove him to the airport. Once he was gone, things quickly fell apart.

Santa Monica, Franklin Street
Late March 1962

Greenson told Marilyn he would be leaving for Europe, without mentioning that it was partly so he could see Anna Freud in London. Visibly distressed, Marilyn didn't speak at all during the following sessions. Greenson had anticipated this reaction, and saw her emotional crisis as a manifestation of her terrible fear of abandonment. Marilyn found the idea of his departure devastating. Greenson's wife, on the other hand, tended to think it was a good idea for her husband to have a break from his patient, who now constituted virtually his entire clientele. 'My wife is afraid to leave me alone at home,' Greenson said to a friend. 'I should play it safe and put Marilyn in a sanitarium, but that would only be safe for me and deadly for her.'

But he kept changing his mind about whether he should go, and told Marilyn about his dilemma. One Saturday morning, towards the end of the month, she turned up at his home, far earlier than she normally woke up.

'I'm having a water heater installed and the plumber says I

won't have any water for half an hour,' she told him. 'I'm going to wash my hair here.'

'Fine,' he said. 'But why the rush?'

'Peter Lawford is coming to pick me up to take me to Palm Springs, where I'm spending the weekend with President Kennedy.'

She washed her hair and went home, happy to leave her saviour in a state of acute anxiety – she knew he didn't like her relationship with the Kennedys, and disappearing for a weekend with them was the surest way to make him postpone his trip. Which is exactly what he did.

She spent several hours transforming herself into Marilyn, while Lawford paced up and down her hall. Finally she emerged from her bedroom with a black wig hiding her immaculate coiffure.

A few years later, Greenson would write in his Treatise,

> For many patients, the weekends or the interval between
> analytic hours denotes the loss of a love object. To them,
> the intermission means separation, detachment,
> disengagement, disconnection, or termination. In some
> form or other the patient behaves as though he is feeling
> he is losing a love object. He often reacts to the weekend
> as though it meant a rejection by the analyst . . .
> Sometimes just knowing the analyst's whereabouts makes
> it unnecessary to arrange for some substitute to replace
> him . . . Another problem in technique is the complicating
> circumstance of what the weekend may mean for the
> analyst.

Essentially, he said, the weekend's effect on the analyst was a problem of countertransference, which he would discuss in the Treatise's second volume. Volume II, however, remained unwritten.

Santa Monica, Franklin Street
Early April 1962

Norman Rosten and his wife, Marilyn's friends from New York, came to Hollywood on a film assignment. Marilyn rang them immediately they arrived and said, 'It's Sunday, let's go to my analyst. I want you and Hedda to meet him. I told him and his wife that we're coming.'

Rosten hesitated. 'Is that allowed?'

'He's a great person and has a wonderful family. You'll like them all and vice versa.'

'What'll we do – talk about you?'

'It's OK. As long as I'm not listening. Phone you right back.'

When she rang back, she told them that he'd invited them all over to listen to an impromptu performance. 'Chamber music!' she gaily exclaimed. 'And it's not in a chamber, it's in a living room!'

Introductions at the analyst's were slightly affected. 'My poet friend and his wife, a dear person, and they're happily married.'

Marilyn went off to curl up in an armchair, as though she were at home, and Greenson, with the other musicians who had arrived, played Mozart with passion, if not precision – whatever he lacked in technique he made up for in tone and in the energy of his attack.

After the concert, Norman reminded Marilyn of an evening three or four years previously when they'd gone to hear the Russian pianist Emil Gilels play in New York. In her devastating dress, she had leaned over to her escort. 'Relax, Norman,' she'd whispered, with that little laugh of hers, 'no one knows who you are.'

'Yes, I remember,' she said, in a playful yet melancholy voice. 'It's like that. No one knows who you are when you're listening to music. No one's going to come looking for you.'

Rosten took the psychoanalyst to one side. 'Is she going to be all right?' he asked. 'Is she making any progress?'

'It may seem odd to you the method I'm using to treat her,' Greenson replied, 'but I firmly believe that the treatment has to suit the patient and not vice versa. Marilyn is not an analytic patient, she needs psychotherapy, both supportive and analytical. I have permitted her to become friendly with my family and to visit in my home because I felt she needed actual experiences in her present life to make up for the emotional deprivation she suffered from childhood onward. It may seem to you I have broken rules, but I feel that if I'm fortunate enough, perhaps some years from now, Marilyn may become a psychoanalytic patient. She is not ready for it now. I feel I can tell you these things because she considers you and Hedda her closest friends and there must be somebody with whom I can share some of my responsibilities. By the way, I have spoken to Marilyn and she has given me permission to talk to you in general terms about herself.'

Not long after this, Hedda Rosten left Los Angeles, and came to say goodbye to Marilyn.

'I'll miss you. Please take care of yourself. Promise me you'll rest up before the really hard work begins on the film.'

'I'm in good shape.' Marilyn smiled. 'Well, in body if not in mind. It's all up here, you know. Or so they say.'

Beverly Hills, Rodeo Drive
25 March 1962

She never liked the day to end. As the light began to fade, she became insecure, prey to oppressive thoughts, as hard on herself as she was on everyone else. Dusk triggered a fever of manic anxiety and, recoiling from the coming darkness as if it were a naked flame, she stayed on the phone for hours, more to hear another person's voice than to say anything.

Early one evening in spring, Marilyn called Norman Rosten. 'Can you come over?' she asked. 'I'm going out to dinner, and I want you to meet my date.'

When he got there she whispered through the door, 'I'll be a few minutes. Go on into the back room. You'll recognise him. I told him about you.'

It was Frank Sinatra. The two men sat down, had a drink, talked. A quarter of an hour passed, half an hour, three-quarters of an hour . . . Dressed in a pale green print dress, Marilyn finally appeared. Sinatra was anxious to leave and dragged her away from her friend. She murmured, 'He's a poet. If you need a good writer for a movie, he's great.'

Early next morning, she rang Rosten. 'What'd you think of him?'

Her voice sounded impatient, but he didn't know whether from joy or panic. A few days later, Rosten went back east. They had farewell drinks by the pool at her place.

'Next time you'll swim in it,' she said. 'I'll have a poolside party.'

'I swear I'll stay in the water until they fish me out.'

'A final sip of champagne, a light embrace,' Rosten recalled much later. One of those cursory, stiff embraces people give one another when they have the vague sense they may never see each other again.

'Give everybody a kiss at home,' Marilyn said. 'I'm going now. I'm off to my doctor.'

As it transpired, they did see each other again, on the last Sunday in March. Marilyn had been at a fundraiser for the Kennedys the previous night. She had danced with Bobby and the brothers hadn't left her side all evening. The president had flown back to Washington in the morning and Marilyn woke up at noon in a fragile state. She called Norman and asked him to come to Fifth Helena Drive – 'Down a dead-end street. That's where I am. God, it's going to be a real dull Sunday.'

Rosten drove her to Beverly Hills, figuring that she needed something to distract her. At an art gallery, she found a Rodin statue, a bronze of a man and a woman in an embrace.

She wrote a cheque for it then and there. As she and Rosten drove away, Marilyn held the statue tenderly, and murmured, 'Look at them both. How beautiful. He's hurting her, but he wants to love her, too.' A look of terror and excitement in her eyes. She turned to Rosten, and told him she wanted to show her analyst the bronze.

'Now?' he asked.

'Sure. Why not now?'

Greenson welcomed them in, and Marilyn immediately showed him the Rodin. 'What does it mean?' she demanded. 'Is he just screwing her, or is it a fake? I'd like to know.' Her voice desperate. 'What do you think, Doctor? What's it mean?'

'What? The gift itself or the fact you've given it to me? The gift means that we often use the ties that bind us to someone we're dependent on to try to bind them closer to us.'

'It's not a gift. I'm keeping it!'

Marilyn had once written to Greenson – and told him a hundred times since in person – that she did not know what nights were for. The answer was simple: for waiting. For saying to the other person who has been gone so long, 'Come back!' But that night she wasn't waiting for a person. She was waiting for Nembutal, Librium, Miltown, Demerol, chloral hydrate. When the limousine came for her the next morning, she wasn't answering the door. Two hours later, Greenson discovered Marilyn, overdosed, sprawled under her satiny white sheets.

Santa Monica, Franklin Street
April 1962

Marilyn was to be paid a derisory hundred thousand dollars for *Something's Got to Give*, a third of what Dean Martin was getting for playing her forgetful remarried husband. Dean, who had always had a soft spot for Marilyn, now thought her more lost than ever. Sinatra was leaving her – he had got engaged to Juliet Prowse in January. When Peter Lawford had introduced Marilyn to Bobby Kennedy, Sinatra had enjoyed the prospect of that fearless opponent of the Mafia and upholder of his brother's honour falling under the spell of one of his exes. Marilyn, meanwhile, had fallen hard for the Kennedy mystique. The attorney general and the platinum-blonde goddess had furtive, clumsy sex. Although he was Sinatra's friend, Dean was too fond of Marilyn to leave her on her own to struggle with the Kennedy entourage of politicians and mafiosi. She broke his heart, really – and, besides, he owed it to her to make this film: he was only in it because she'd insisted he be given the part.

*   *   *

'What's the date tomorrow?' Marilyn asked, standing in the doorway to Greenson's consulting room.

'Ninth of April,' answered the analyst.

The first day of filming, like the first day back at school: a grim reckoning you could only escape by playing dead or stupid. Marilyn had to get back into the studio's harness and take direction from Cukor again, Cukor who had loathed her ever since her problems and disappearances had reduced *Let's Make Love* to a virtual fiasco.

'That fucker.' Marilyn was sitting facing Greenson. 'It's not that he doesn't like women . . . anybody can sleep with who they want, I don't care. No, he hates them so much he can't even point his camera at them. He can't even try to understand what they think, what they want. He just waits until they collapse into a heap, until their make-up and tears are all smeared together in a disgusting mush. Did you know he wanted to film *Something's Got to Give* in his house? That says it all. He's too busy looking at himself, his beautiful works of art, his pool, his luxurious mansion. You know what he does with his little boys in the evening round that pool? I do, because I've got a friend who's one of his crowd. He has fake Marilyn competitions. They get dressed up and imitate my walk, my stupid, kinky little girl's voice. Oh, don't worry, Doctor, they don't like you either. When he's asked if I'm up to filming, he says, "I haven't a clue. Ask her psychiatrist."'

Greenson wondered if she was objecting to the film and its director or to the fact she was back playing the ditzy blonde after her tragic role in *The Misfits*.

'I've met Cukor,' Greenson pointed out. 'I didn't get the impression he disliked me. As a matter of fact, he asked me to help him work on your acting. He doesn't hate you either.'

'Are you kidding? A reporter asked him what he thought of me. He said I was so racked with nerves I couldn't even match one take with another and, if the journalist wanted to know why, he should ask my shrink. Well, no, Mr Cukor, I don't know what or who to be in sync with from one shot to the next. No, I'm not the same from one take to another because I never feel in sync with myself. I always feel cut off, always wondering who people want me to be.

'The script's not too bad, though,' she continued, when she got her breath back. 'A woman is shipwrecked with a handsome man on a tropical island. She's reported dead, her husband remarries, and then, after being miraculously rescued, she comes to reclaim him. Her children don't recognise her and she pretends to be a babysitter. Her husband is uneasy about the whole thing, but his second wife keeps him on a tight rein—'

'I know the story,' Greenson interrupted. 'Why can't you play the first wife, Ellen, though? Don't you like the fact your character's unrecognised? Do you feel your image has been taken away from you, that you've been cut out of the picture?'

'You don't get it at all. You were the one who said the men who've made the most impression on me have been photographers – André, Milton Greene and now George Barris, who I've started seeing again. Visual people. That's the point: seeing someone is not the same as knowing them. I want to be seen, constantly, from all angles, by all eyes, men's and women's – and the reason I want that is because then no one will know me.'

'How can you be afraid of filming and yet want to be photographed so much?' Greenson asked.

Marilyn fell silent. When she felt utterly alone, like a little girl on her first day at a new school, and was terrified that this was what her death would be like, she had only one recourse: to have her picture taken, to find herself again in her own image.

'I meant that as a question,' the analyst persisted.

'I'm afraid when I have to talk,' Marilyn declared, her voice suddenly loud. 'When I have to do dialogue, when I have to say words somebody has written for me, in front of the dead eye of the camera. Someone captures me in a photograph, they shoot me – that's the word, isn't it? Shoot. You shoot a story like a gun, you do photo shoots, and it's all wordless, not like the movies. I prefer men who go about their business in silence and don't want a commentary afterwards. Hey, you know what gets me on set and allows me to act? That's a shot too – the injections Fox's doctor with the magic syringe, Lee Siegel, has been giving me since *The Seven Year Itch*. Play it again, Lee. Give me a good youth shot.'

And, with that, Marilyn stood up and left.

Something's Got to Give got off to a nightmarish start. The first day of filming had to be postponed until the end of April and Marilyn took the opportunity to fly to New York, where she attended a dinner for JFK in a penthouse on Park Avenue. She arrived some time after ten looking sublimely pale, like a white ember on the verge of fading out. She strolled nonchalantly over to Kennedy. 'Hi, Prez.'

He turned, smiled at her. 'Hi! Come on, I want you to meet some people.' Then they disappeared.

On the evening of 22 April, a Sunday, Marilyn left her session with Greenson in a state of intense panic and had herself driven to Hermosa Beach, south of Los Angeles. There she got her old hairdresser Pearl Porterfield out of bed to dye her hair so she could face the cameras at dawn the following morning. As always, she had her pubic hair dyed as well. But filming next day had to start without her. For a week, she couldn't get out of bed, and her only contact with the outside world was her analyst, who made daily visits.

One brief appearance on set on 30 April was as much as she could manage – but not even her collapse at the end of ninety minutes of filming could convince the Fox executives that she was really ill. Greenson, who had guaranteed her presence, received increasingly frustrated calls from the studio, and fired off a stream of reassuring memos.

Beverly Hills, Roxbury Drive
May 1962

Marilyn arrived distraught at her next session. 'So this is it. You're really leaving me. Joannie told me.'

'Yes, as I said, I—'

'I know,' Marilyn cut in, 'but I didn't believe you. This is really it, is it?'

'I'm going on a cruise around the Mediterranean with Hildi. She needs to visit her mother, in Switzerland, who had a heart attack recently, then I've got to give a lecture in Jerusalem on transference. On the way back, I have to see my editor in New York to talk about my book on psychoanalytic technique. I'm entitled to a vacation, aren't I?'

'Yes . . .' Marilyn stammered. 'Oh, shit! Yesterday I made a real effort. I arrived at the studio twenty-five minutes early, at six in the morning, just for a make-up call. I worked till four then came here for my session. But today, when I knew Hildi was leaving and that you would be too, that this was it, you were really leaving, I fainted half an hour after getting on set and had to be taken home. I was such a mess when I got out of bed, you've no idea. I had to drag my body to the bathroom like it wasn't even mine. Something's got to give . . . Right. Me.'

'I've had a thought,' her analyst said. 'What if I give you something of mine as a token, which you could give back to me on my return? It could act as a physical bond between us, a talisman. Here, one of these chess pieces, for instance. What do you reckon?'

After walking Marilyn to the door that evening, Greenson returned to his desk and transcribed their conversation. Then he began an article explaining why, with this sort of patient, he had felt compelled to act as well as talk, to give rather than merely wait or receive. He only managed a first draft, dealing with the significance and role of the transitional object as an analyst's substitute, and it wasn't until twelve years after his patient's death that he was finally able to go back and finish it. Writing to forget; writing to obscure the fact he had lost that last game of chess. Even so, he remained hesitant: how could he write about her without naming her? Surely everyone would recognise the anonymous subject of 'On Transitional Objects and Transference', the most neutral title he could think of to avoid any hint of passion. It was Greenson's only published piece of writing in which he mentioned, although not by name, his most famous patient:

> I told an emotionally immature young woman patient, who had developed a very dependent transference on me, that I was going to attend an International Congress in Europe some three months hence. We worked intensively on the multiple determinants of her clinging dependence, but made only insignificant progress. Then the situation changed dramatically when one day she announced that she had discovered something that would tide her over in my absence. It was not some insight, not a new personal relationship, it was a chess piece. The young woman had

recently been given a gift of a carved ivory chess set. The evening before her announcement, as she looked at the set, through the sparkling light of a glass of champagne, it suddenly struck her that I looked like the white knight of her chess set. The realisation immediately evoked in her a feeling of comfort, even triumph. The white knight was a protector, it belonged to her, she could carry it wherever she went, it would look after her, and I would go on my merry way to Europe without having to worry about her.

I must confess that despite my misgivings, I also felt some relief. The patient's major concern about the period of my absence was a public performance of great importance to her professionally. She now felt confident of success because she could conceal her white knight in her handkerchief or scarf; she was certain that he would protect her from nervousness, anxiety or bad luck. I was relieved and delighted to learn, while in Europe, that her performance had indeed been a smashing success. Shortly thereafter, however, I received several panicky transatlantic telephone calls from her. The patient had lost the white knight and was beside herself with terror and gloom, like a child who had lost her security blanket. A colleague of mine who saw her in that interval said that all his interventions were to no avail and he reluctantly suggested that I cut short my trip and return. I hated to interrupt my vacation and I doubted whether my return would be beneficial. Surprisingly, it was. I no sooner saw her than her anxiety and depression lifted. It then became possible to work for many months on how she had used me as a good luck charm rather than an analyst.

The talisman, the chess piece, served her as a magical means of averting bad luck or evil. It protected her against losing something precious.

Beverly Hills, Roxbury Drive
8 May 1962

Marilyn returned home, clutching the chess piece in the palm of her hand. She poured herself a drink and looked through the glass at the distorted golden figure of the knight. She started to cry, remembering a scene in *The Misfits* where Miller and Huston had wanted her to be almost invisible behind a window as a man tried to look in. The next scene they'd had her putting on make-up, anxiously scrutinising her reflection in a mirror. 'Fuck all these windows and mirrors!' she'd shouted at the director. 'Show me straight. Don't put me behind glass!'

She scribbled a few lines in her notebook:

Tuesday 8th. He's given me a present. A knight from a chess set. A game of knights and bishops. All the pieces can take and kill each other. The queen's the strongest. The king's dead before the game even starts. I don't know who I'm playing for, it feels like I'm moving my pieces in the dark.

I don't like writing. I'll have to find some other way of expressing myself. Maybe it's because I like reading too

much. The first time I read books I really love, it feels as
if I'm rereading them. Like when you meet people and
you're sure you've already met before. I came across this
line in Kafka today, 'Capitalism is a condition of the
world and of the soul.' I never finish books though. I
don't like last pages. Last words. Last takes. Last sessions.

Greenson knocked on Wexler's door very late that day.
'Can I talk to you?'
'About her?'
'Of course, who else? I'm entrusting my madwoman to you.
Watch out, though. She's more lovable than you could possibly
imagine. She suffered a terrible childhood, you know, truly terrible
– she was raped, abused by her foster fathers . . . I thought it
was fantasy at first, but now I believe it all happened, I feel
overwhelmed. I'm not going to bring this off. Two things have
been clear since our first session. First: that this wouldn't be a
traditional course of analysis, with well-defined boundaries and
the usual staging of the couch with its back to the chair. Second:
that only death, hers or mine, would us part.'
'No half-measures, then. So what do you want me to do,
baby-sit?'
'I'm going to Europe for five weeks. I can't leave her on her own
and I'm not sure she'll make it even if you take over from me.'
'Well, take her with you, then.'
'Freud used to do that with his favourite patients.'
'He also didn't charge in some cases and invited certain patients
to lunch at home or in his office. He was very talkative in sessions
and analysed his own daughter . . . So what does that prove?
That Freud sometimes wasn't a Freudian and broke his own
rules. That's all.'
'You don't understand. I've been trying to wean Marilyn off
barbiturates for the last two years, and the whole time I've been
getting them for her – even last autumn when she'd stopped

filming and was seeing me seven times a week. Meanwhile Hyman's been giving her Lee Siegel's miracle injections behind my back. Now her analysis has become a drug for her. She and I have become co-dependent unbelievably fast. You ought to know that I have given her permission to call my children if she needs anything when I'm away.'

'Aren't you taking this too far?' Wexler asked. 'Wait a second, I'm going to read you something.' He got up, took some stapled papers from a pile on a shelf and read out,

> 'Psychoanalysis is not the treatment of choice for emergency situations, nor is it suitable for psychiatric first aid. When such instances arise during the course of an analysis, it is usually necessary to do some unanalytic psychotherapy . . . the wish to relieve the patient's misery is fundamentally antagonistic to analysing and understanding his problems. Ralph R. Greenson, MD.'

'Stop! How can you cure someone without intervening, if necessary by force? And love is the only force we have. I am her analyst. I want to be a positive version of the paternal, a father who won't disappoint her, who will awaken her conscious mind, or at least treat her with every possible kindness.'

'But where's it supposed to end, this therapy based on love? Our schizophrenic or borderline patients are not always lacking love, you know that. Love can trigger madness in a person just as much as lack of love.'

'I don't think so. Not in this case, at any rate. It's all a question of degree. I wouldn't describe love as the driving force in my relationship with Marilyn.'

'Who's your Juliet, Romeo?' Wexler asked, as Greenson, staring into space, turned and left his office without a word. 'Read the play again. It ends badly!'

Michigan, Ann Arbor University
1969

Seven years after the actress's death, Ralph Greenson was invited to give a lecture on psychoanalytic technique. Such intellectual high-wire acts had lost their appeal for him, but he accepted anyway, out of friendship for a former colleague who had moved from California to teach in Michigan, and also, he thought, out of loyalty to Marilyn's memory. He began his talk in an unsteady voice: '"Mistakes and Beginnings in Psychoanalysis and Psychotherapy": This was the subject I was going to address for the purposes of your clinical training in this beautiful university of Ann Arbor. I have changed my mind, however. Perhaps because Michigan is a long way from California, perhaps also because Marilyn Monroe is fading from my memory, as I'm sure she is from yours, young as you are, I would now like to talk about her in a way I have not yet had the chance to publicly.

'I was by no means a beginner in 1960 and yet, when the actress was sent to me, I immediately had the feeling that I should forget everything I knew and start again from scratch. After her death, it was awful, but I felt I had to go on. And I went on, and I *was* upset. And my patients saw me upset. Some of them saw no reaction in me, and were furious at me for being so cold and impersonal. They asked how I could come and work the next day, and how I could have taken such a patient anyway. They were angry at me for having decided to shorten or cancel their sessions so I could see her every day. Others felt sorry for me. They'd express their condolences in the usual way, "I'm sorry for your loss", but I'd hear not only, "I'm sorry for the loss you've suffered", but also, "I'm sorry I've lost you. I'm sorry you are not yourself any more."

'Seven years have passed and I am still devastated. I don't know that I will ever get over it really or completely. I still ask myself what I should have done to save her. Perhaps my decision to take on Marilyn Monroe was too much of a gamble, perhaps the stakes were too high. Perhaps I wanted to go down in history as Marilyn Monroe's analyst, and perhaps in the end it was a gamble I lost. I approached it as a game of poker, I think, when really I should have been playing chess, or not playing at all. She was a poor creature whom I tried to help and ended up hurting. Perhaps my own longing for omnipotence had clouded my judgement. Of course I knew it was a difficult case, but what should I have done? Turn it over to a beginner? I knew her love was narcissistic, and that she was bound to feel a hatred commensurate with her dependence on me. But I had forgotten my old rule: a recurrent death wish, fully felt and realised in consciousness, obviates the need for a psychoanalyst.'

Hollywood Heights, Woodrow Wilson Drive
April 1970

Accounts of the actress Inger Stevens's death tend not to mention her psychiatrist's name. The evening before she died, they report, she was dressed in a greyish-beige trouser suit and black blouse, her tall, slender frame emphasised by her blonde hair worn piled characteristically high. Her face was said to be sad, but no sadder than usual, with just the occasional look of cold despair passing through her washed-out blue eyes. During the night of 30 April 1970, a friend, Lola McNally, found her lying unconscious in her house on Woodrow Wilson Drive, close to the corner of Mulholland Drive. She opened her eyes and said something incomprehensible. An ambulance took her to hospital, where she was pronounced dead on arrival.

The autopsy was conducted by Marilyn's coroner, Dr Noguchi, who ruled that Stevens had died of a barbiturate overdose. Three hypotheses circulated as to what might have happened: either she was murdered and the scene was made to look like a suicide, or she suffered a heart attack after consuming too much alcohol and too many pills, or she had wanted to kill herself and had finally succeeded in doing so. Either way, the circumstances of her death remain suspicious. She had just signed a contract to do a TV series – *The Most Deadly Game*, a title that took on strange resonances when her body was found curled up, face down on her kitchen floor – and had seemed very excited about getting down to work, even going out and buying new clothes for her part. Her bedroom carpet had been pulled up. The telephone wasn't in its usual place in the living room, but in the bedroom where there wasn't even a socket. She had bruising on her arm, a cut on her chin and her blood contained traces of asthma medication, which she didn't need to take. She had cooked dinner at home that night for the actor Burt Reynolds, who wasn't questioned by the police and went on to star twelve years later in *The Man Who Loved Women*, which was written by Milton Wexler and directed by Blake Edwards. Wexler, however, was not the only link between the dead actress and Hollywood's psychoanalytic community. Ralph Greenson had been her analyst for many years.

Inger Stevens had had a brief movie career in the 1960s. She was born two years before Marilyn and, like her, had started out as a model and chorus girl before studying at the Actors Studio in the hope of becoming 'a serious actress', as she put it. It's not known if she and Marilyn knew one another in New York, or before that, in Hollywood. She'd left her family home in Kansas and stepped off the Greyhound bus at LA's Union Station alone and without any luggage. No one was waiting for her. Like Marilyn, although she never enjoyed as much of the limelight, she could play comic, dramatic and romantic roles, and when she was offered something sexy, she'd simply say, 'I hope I don't get typecast.' Her most notable role was in an episode of *The Twilight Zone* in 1960, 'The Hitchhiker', where she plays a woman who suffers hallucinations as she drives east across America and thinks she gives her death a lift.

* * *

When he read of Inger Stevens's death in the *Los Angeles Times*, Greenson was working on a book about failures in psychoanalysis, a sequel of sorts to *The Technique and Practice of Psychoanalysis*, which had been published three years earlier. He remembered the other blonde's final hours, then decided the only way to stop thinking about either of them was to write an article about the 'Swinging Chicks of the '60s', actresses without roles, dreamers lost in their glittering self-images. That way he could concentrate on their failures, rather than his own failure to cure them.

He found a letter Inger had written him a few years earlier: 'I live in a constant state of insecurity and crippling anxiety that I try to hide by appearing cold. People think I am aloof, but really I am just scared. I often feel depressed. I come from a broken home, my marriage was a disaster, and I am constantly lonely.'

Greenson closed the file containing his notes on Inger's analysis. He leaned back in his chair, closed his eyes and saw her beautiful, sad face, her childlike eyes. He heard her low, deceptively assured voice. 'A career, no matter how successful, can't put its arms around you,' she had said once. 'You end up being like Grand Central Station with people just coming and going. And there you are – left all alone. The thing I miss most is having someone to share things with. I've always thrown myself into friendships and love affairs where I'm the one doing all the giving. You can't live like that.'

'There's your work as an actress, though. People like seeing you on screen.'

'But that's not me. I'm very proud of what I do. I want to be a success. I don't want to die thinking all I've been doing is passing time, heading on down the road until I crawl off into my grave. I'd like to leave something behind me, to contribute to my generation's legacy, and I'll do that through my work as an actress.'

When he heard of her death, the analyst couldn't help thinking she hadn't been a good actress and, without knowing why, decided not to go to her cremation. He also decided against writing a book about failures in psychoanalysis, or articles about analysts' patients' suicides or Hollywood starlets in the 1960s. Too many old wounds. A friend scattered Inger's ashes over the Pacific from the Santa Monica pier.

Los Angeles, Pico Boulevard
May 1962

On 10 May, Greenson and his wife finally left for Europe for five weeks. His disappearance at this particularly critical time for Marilyn seemed oddly unexplained – he told his associates that he was going on a lecture tour, but he informed Fox that his wife was ill and needed to be treated in a Swiss clinic. And he'd told Marilyn it was his mother-in-law who was sick.

Four days later, having barely worked for the first three weeks of filming, Marilyn was ready long before the studio limousine came to pick her up to take her through the deserted Los Angeles streets to Pico Boulevard. The black Lincoln Continental rolled over Brentwood's low hills, raising a cloud of dust that was visible from Century City. To reach the gleaming new bungalow she had been allocated as a dressing room, Marilyn was driven past the steel and glass administrative buildings that towered over the lot. The studio executives' offices were strategically positioned on the top floor so they could keep tabs on their stars' comings and goings.

*   *   *

Among the brief, truncated jottings Marilyn made during the last two years of her life is this entry in a red notebook:

> This is not a diary. I'm not going to pick it up every day and write, 'Dear Diary'. It's just a notebook, somewhere for my jumbled moods, as messy as the piles of clothes all over my floor . . .
>
> Found out that Fox security, some of them old friends, were filing confidential reports listing the times I arrived and left. It made me so mad. Since then, some mornings I get out of the car by the little service gate and send the limo through the main gate with no one in the back . . . Even on days when I stay at home, my car with its tinted windows still shows up and stops in front of my bungalow for all the world to see. What difference would it make if I was in it anyway? Who's going to care? Why would they? It terrifies me thinking of how short my life is, the eternity before I was born and after I die, and I'm amazed to find I'm here rather than somewhere else. No reason why I should be here rather than there, today rather than any other day. Right: time for a game of chess with those foxes . . .

Marilyn, who had disappeared again after filming had started on *Something's Got to Give*, reported back for work for three and a half days at the start of May. Then, on the seventeenth, she left the studio in mid-filming. She was due to sing two days later at an event at Madison Square Garden celebrating the President of the United States's forty-fifth – and last – birthday. Fox's executive committee had begged her not to leave the set to go to New York. Ignoring the incredible publicity such a performance by one of its top stars would bring the film, the studio sent her lawyer Mickey Rudin a two-page letter threatening her with dismissal: 'In the event that Miss Monroe absents herself, this action will constitute a wilful failure to render services. In the event that Miss Monroe returns and principal photography of the motion picture continues – such re-commencement will not be deemed to constitute a waiver of [Fox's] right to fire Miss Monroe as stated in her contract.'

Henry Weinstein, however, realised that Marilyn was determined to go New York, come what may. 'I mean,' he said, 'here's a girl who really did come from the streets, who had a mother who wasn't there, and a father who had disappeared, a girl who has known all the poverty in the world. And now, she is going to sing "Happy Birthday" to the President of the United States in Madison Square Garden. There's no way for her to resist that.' But no one listened to him.

It was around this time that Norman Rosten sent Marilyn a half-hour tape of him reading his poetry on a local radio station. He knew she'd like the poems, but mainly he wanted her to know he was thinking of her. She was very alone. It was like in chess, she said, it was like what they call *Zeitnot*: the agony of knowing you're running out of time to decide your next move. Any moment now, you won't have any time to think of anything, even your agony. Rosten thought of the poems as his emissaries; perhaps they'd help. When he arrived in Hollywood shortly afterwards, Marilyn's secretary told him she took the tape with her in her bag everywhere she went, like a good-luck charm, and that she had bought a new tape recorder specially.

One evening, she invited Norman over to listen to the poems. She'd get everything ready, she said on the phone. He'd arrive early, Eunice would make coffee, then they'd listen to them together. Lying on the bed, she could use the rewind or fast forward as much as she wanted, skip forward or back and, knowing the recorder would stop automatically, she wouldn't have to worry about falling asleep – but only if he had to leave before the end, of course, she added. When he got there, she was already in her pyjamas. The coffee was made. They drank it and talked about her work and plans, about his projects, his wife and daughter, his work in Hollywood, when he was leaving. She said she hoped her film would go well. She felt nervous but determined. Then she got into bed and Norman sat on the floor by the tape recorder. 'I took a sleeping pill just before you got here,' she said, 'so maybe I'll fall asleep listening to your voice. Is it OK if I slip away before the end?'

New York, Madison Square Garden
May 1962

A deafening whine announced the arrival of an enormous helicopter on the Fox heliport near Soundstage Fourteen. Peter
Lawford leaped from the pride of Howard Hughes's fleet,
hurried to Marilyn's dressing room and escorted her to the royal
blue vision that was going to convey her to Inglewood. Two
hours later Marilyn took off from Los Angeles for what was
still to be named JFK. The presidential gala was going to be
her first appearance on stage in front of a large audience since
her legendary performance before thousands of GIs in Korea.
Full of nervous energy, she sang her contribution, 'Happy
Birthday', on the plane. Like the gala's seventeen thousand
spectators, she'd had to pay a thousand dollars for the privilege
of attending. 'That figures,' she had told Joan Greenson. 'I've
been paying to talk to your father for years. So now I have to
pay to sing.' With Joan's help, she had been rehearsing for
days.

She was going to be reunited with John Kennedy, her occasional
lover. Six days earlier, with oppressive symmetry, it was her

ex-husband, Arthur Miller, who had been placed on Kennedy's wife's right at a banquet for André Malraux. The top table included writers Saul Bellow, Edmund Wilson and Robert Penn Warren, painters Andrew Wyeth and Mark Rothko, the composer Leonard Bernstein, and from the world of the theatre and performing arts, George Balanchine, Tennessee Williams, Elia Kazan and Lee Strasberg. Marilyn was conspicuous by her absence, as if the Kennedys were bent on confirming the split marked out by her destiny that her move to New York and marriage to Miller had been attempts to overcome: words and culture on the one hand, the body and images on the other.

Being back in New York filled Marilyn with the delight of a child let loose in an adult world. She raced all over town in a cab, not asking to go downtown or uptown, just saying, I'm going this way or that way. The city was a carnival and she was its queen, its streets and city blocks a chessboard she could dominate with the strength and beauty of her moves. The white king, the key to the game, was missing. Her mother was the black queen, she the white; Greenson was the white knight – or maybe the black – and the Kennedys were the two black bishops. Manhattan avenged her for everything Hollywood had taken from her.

Some cities are like special languages: no matter how beautiful they seem, you know you'll never learn them. The names in Los Angeles had ceased to mean anything to her. She'd see the signs – 'SUNSET STRIP', 'ANAHEIM', 'EL PUEBLO' – and all they'd evoke would be an indeterminate colour or an ethnic marker, a sense of freeways turning back on themselves *ad infinitum*. They were like names in dreams. She saw them – strange or familiar, beautiful or terrifying – but they made no sense. In Manhattan, it was the opposite. Marilyn became the link between everything she saw, the thread that bound time together. Although she didn't talk to anyone, she felt a part of everything. New York was the city of connections and it made her forget the city of thin partitions with its boundless distances between people, its virtual equivalence between reality and fiction.

She returned to her apartment on East 57th Street late in the evening. When she got up the next morning, she found a letter had arrived from Fox terminating her contract. For a minute she thought it wouldn't have happened if Greenson had been there, but then she was seized by doubt. Wasn't it the other way round? Hadn't her psychiatrist, who was so close to Weinstein and Rudin that the studio called them 'Marilyn's team', left the country because he wanted to send Fox a message that her fate was of as little concern to him as the film itself? Deeply disturbed, she laboured through the final day of rehearsals. In the evening, working together at her apartment, the composer Richard Adler had an uphill struggle getting her to go over the words of 'Happy Birthday' for the thirtieth time. He was afraid of the pain he heard welling up inside her, her breathy whisper, the halting way she sang the lyrics. As the hours passed, her enunciation gradually softened to an exhalation, a sensual caress. Her rendition steadily became more and more sexually charged until, by the time she finally came on stage, after Ella Fitzgerald, Peggy Lee and Maria Callas, Marilyn Monroe had become a parody of herself.

Bobby Kennedy has come to the Democratic Party fundraiser with his wife but Jackie Kennedy has not seen fit to attend, so JFK is on his own. The compère for the evening, JFK's brother-in-law Peter Lawford, introduces Marilyn: 'Mr President, on this occasion of your birthday, this lovely lady is not only pulchritudinous but punctual.' After a long wait in the wings, she emerges unsteadily from the darkness like a flickering blue flame, a vision of skin and rhinestones. Sewn into her dress, she tiptoes on stage with the tiny steps of a geisha, as if the body she's parading before the thousands of spectators is a burden to her. 'The *late* Marilyn Monroe,' Lawford puns – or perhaps it's a Freudian slip – and the audience laughs in the shadows. Marilyn has kept the promise she and Truman Capote had made: to be late for their own funeral. Imprisoned by her dress, which glitters like fallen snow, she teeters a little on her high heels, shrugs the white ermine wrap from her shoulders, brushes the microphone with her fingertips, gestures to the president somewhere out there in the dark, and then closes her eyes, runs her tongue over her lips and starts to sing. Drifting out over the crowd, her husky voice seems to say: 'They've all left me because I was bad, Joe, Frank, Arthur, Romeo. Now forty million other Americans will see how bad I really am.'

At the after-show party at New York theatre magnate Arthur Krim's apartment, Robert Kennedy dodges around Marilyn, like a moth around a flame. The president and Bobby usher her into a quiet corner at one point, where they have an animated conversation for a quarter of an hour. Marilyn is then seen dancing five times with Bobby as his wife Ethel looks on aghast. In the early hours of Sunday morning, the president and Marilyn leave the party and take a private elevator to the basement of Krim's building. From there they walk through the tunnel leading to the Carlyle Hotel and go straight up to Kennedy's suite.

She never saw John Kennedy again. After that night, the president decided to break off all contact between them and deny the rumours that were starting to circulate about their relationship. Even though a number of photographs were taken of Marilyn with the two brothers, there is only one still in existence. Secret Service agents came the next morning to seize the remaining negatives from *Time* magazine's photo lab.

When she'd gone to see Marilyn just before she left for New York, Joan Greenson had found her heavily sedated, as floppy

219

and lifeless as a rag doll. She had given her a children's book, *The Little Engine That Could*, for the trip – 'for your ordeal', as she whispered in her ear. But when the moment had come for the translucent star to go on stage at Madison Square Garden, she had to leave it and the chess piece behind. Fortified by tranquillisers and champagne, she had ventured out into that great black mouth and those blinding lights with a chill in her heart, trailing the shadow of her fear behind her. When she got back to Los Angeles, she described the terrible moment to Joan: 'Everyone talked about my transparent six-thousand-dollar dress that was so tight Jean Louis had to sew me into it. But they didn't understand. My dress wasn't a second skin, it was my skin that was another layer of clothing, my skin that has always kept me from being naked.'

Beverly Hills, Roxbury Drive
21 *May 1962*

Ralph Greenson's papers, archived at UCLA, include the rough drafts for a book he was planning called *Drugs in the Psychotherapeutic Situation*. Chapter 12 contains this passage:

> When I left for a five-week summer vacation, I felt it was indicated to leave her some medication which she might take when she felt depressed and agitated, i.e., rejected and tempted to act out. I prescribed a drug which is a quick-acting anti-depressant in combination with a sedative – Dexamyl. I also hoped she would be benefited by having something from me to depend on. I can condense the situation by saying that, at the time of my vacation, I felt that she would be unable to bear the depressive anxieties of being alone. The administering of the pill was an attempt to give her something of me to swallow, to take in, so that she could overcome the sense of terrible emptiness that would depress and infuriate her.

Her psychoanalyst had left, and so had she. He hadn't come back but she had. Racing on amphetamines, Marilyn reported for work at six-fifteen a.m. on Monday, 21 May, thirty-three hours after the New York gala. She had sent word to Cukor that she was prepared to film all the scenes scheduled for the day except for close-ups. She was obviously ill and Whitey Snyder realised no amount of make-up could hide the evidence of fatigue from her weekend. For her body, he used a special preparation of a litre of Max Factor suntan cream, as base, with half a cup of ivory white and a little clown white.

On Wednesday, she finally shot the nude swimming-pool scene in which her character lures Dean Martin from Cyd Charisse's bed. Normally, an actress or her body double would wear a body stocking for a scene like this; no one expected her to do it naked. So when they saw her emerge from the water after slipping out of her bathing suit, the reaction was incredible. Everyone wanted to be on set. Weinstein called for security to bar the stage entrance. Dosed up on amphetamines for her fever and Demerol for her headaches, Marilyn was in the water for four hours while the shutters clicked and the cameras rolled. Like Pat Newcomb, Marilyn's press attaché, Cukor knew no one in their right mind could miss such an incredible publicity opportunity.

Most of the following day's filming was sacrificed to another photo-shoot. Cukor invited three photographers, William Woodfield, Lawrence Schiller and Jimmy Mitchell, on set and the pictures they took were immediately flashed all over the world. Fifty-two shots appeared in seventy magazines in thirty-two countries, grossing a total of $150,000. Marilyn had done her fair share of nude scenes as a starlet and subsequently appeared as naked as the censorship laws would allow in *Niagara*, *Bus Stop* and *The Misfits*. So this scene caused her hardly any anxiety. The opposite, if anything: she felt reborn in that pool, and not just because she had lost fifteen pounds in a matter of weeks. She always felt the same: she had no shame about her body, only about having to talk. Unbeknown to her, Natasha Lytess had written a poisonous article after they'd gone their separate ways in 1956, in which she'd described Marilyn's complete ease with her nudity as a sign of mental instability. 'Being naked seemed to soothe her,' Natasha wrote, 'almost hypnotise her.' She'd endlessly dissect her reflection sitting or standing in front of a full-length mirror, pouting, half closing her heavy-lidded eyes, totally absorbed by what she saw.

The obsession with mirrors had started when she was a child. She'd often be found standing stock-still in front of one, captivated by her likeness. As an adult, her friends and colleagues would find her incessantly scrutinising herself in a three-panel mirror, adjusting the fall of her dress, the curve of an eyebrow. It was virtually impossible for her to pass by a mirror without searching for herself in its surface. Truman Capote told of how one day he had seen her sitting for hours in front of her reflection. He had asked her what she was doing and she'd replied, 'I'm watching her.'

At the start of the fifties, Billie Holiday was singing one evening in a club in Los Angeles and Marilyn went along with her costume designer Billy Travilla. When he told her a copy of her nude calendar was hanging in the singer's makeshift dressing room, Marilyn rushed in and, without a glance or a word for Billie, stared, rapt, at the photos of herself. Billie threw the calendar in her face and chased her out, calling her a dumb bitch. And then in 1957, before moving into the apartment she lived in with Arthur Miller and kept as her New York *pied-à-terre* until her death, Marilyn had a good proportion of the walls covered with floor-to-ceiling mirrors.

But photographs have a precious advantage over mirrors: there's always someone behind them, a gaze, just as there's always someone in front, someone who can look at them besides you.

Rather than an inverted image, they give you an image of how other people – or one person – see you. With all the emphasis on photographs being machine-made, it's easy to forget the singular gaze that orchestrates them, the subjectivity that's always at work behind the lens. Mirrors divide, photographs unite. A few weeks before meeting Ralph Greenson, Marilyn had said to W. J. Weatherby, 'Sometimes it would be a big relief to be no longer famous. But we actors and actresses are such worriers, such – what is your word? – Narcissus types. I sit in front of the mirror for hours looking for signs of age. Yet I like old people: they have great qualities younger people don't have. I want to grow old without face lifts. They take the life out of the face, the character. I want to have the courage to be loyal to the face I've made. Sometimes I think it would be easier to avoid old age, to die young, but then you'd never complete your life, would you? You'd never wholly know yourself.'

Marilyn didn't live long enough to be undone by the passage of time, merely marked by its hand. But she tried hormone creams and 'youth' injections in the final months of her life. She even took to wearing gloves to hide the liver spots on her hands. By the end, there was something vaguely desperate about the uses to which she put her body in front of a camera. According to Eve Arnold, who had photographed her naked in 1960 and 1961, 'She had lost the contours of a young woman by then, but refused to acknowledge that her body was becoming mature . . . Her blindness to her physical change was becoming almost tragic.' Soon after the second shoot, Arnold discovered the negatives of her Marilyn nudes had vanished from her files.

Hollywood, Pico Boulevard, Fox Studios
31 May 1962

Marilyn disappeared for three days. 'This was perhaps the most mysterious weekend of Marilyn's life,' Henry Weinstein said afterwards. 'It was even more puzzling than the day of her death. Something terrible happened to her that weekend. It was deeply personal, so personal that it shook Marilyn's psyche. I saw it happen, and I blame myself for not immediately calling Dr Greenson and asking him to return.'

But after three days she came back. She came to, as one says after someone loses consciousness. She made it to work on 28 May for an eight-minute scene with Dean Martin, Cyd Charisse and Tom Tryon, who thought she looked like a piece of fine crystal about to shatter. She had only two words to say, 'Nick, darling.' Again and again she tried to get them right. Finally she began stuttering and Cukor flew into a rage. Marilyn ran off set, locked herself into her studio bungalow, and wrote on the mirror, in bright red lipstick, 'Frank, help me! Frank, please help me!' She had been trying to reach Sinatra all day. But the next day, to everyone's amazement, she raced through her scenes with a will, and worked all through the week.

The last images of Marilyn Monroe etched on celluloid on 31 May 1962 are virtually silent. Only thirty-five minutes in total of *Something's Got to Give* exist. They show a face of almost cruel beauty whose insomniac eyes bear a surprised, vaguely anxious expression. A woman in dire straits, who wears her floral dress, red on dazzling white, like a cry for help. She has been left for dead and now she has come home, and her sadness has that edge of violence common to all who have been rejected in this hard, mirror-like world. We see Marilyn acting out her life on Stage Fourteen at 20th Century Fox, but doing so as if she were already a ghost. Her hair is sheer white, like a brittle, glossy wig. She is her own double, Marilyn playing 'Marilyn', as if she wants to disappear into her image – or even further, into her image's reflection in the spectators' eyes, into the Technicolor blue of the swimming pool and the iridescent mists around the spotlights. Off camera, the director shouts, 'Cut!' The shot ends and Marilyn, who has been silent until then, listlessly repeats 'Cut' with the desolate, uncomplaining air of a child who has been interrupted in a game. She always hated the cry directors used to stop the cameras rolling, the antithesis to 'Action', the most common term in the lexicon of the studios and the heart.

The next day Marilyn would be thirty-six. It would be her last day of filming, the last time a camera would transform her into her image. Two months later, the director of her fate would call out 'Cut', and the thread and film of her life would be severed for ever. There would be no assistant director on hand to shout, 'Let's go again! One last take!'

Marilyn died a few hundred yards from 5454 Wilshire Boulevard, where her mother had been living when she was born. At the time, Gladys was working for the studios as an editor at Consolidated Film Industries, one of a host of laboratories that developed and printed the 'dailies', the unedited footage shown to producers, directors and company executives every morning of filming. Gladys worked six days a week, wearing white gloves to protect her hands from the negatives. She was a film-cutter, as editors were then known, cutting film where studio heads told her to and passing on the sections to her colleagues, who would recombine them for the final print.

Twenty-six years after Marilyn's death, on a beautiful August evening, five original videotapes containing the supposedly lost footage from Marilyn Monroe's last film were secretly removed from Fox's archives in Century City. Hidden in the car of a studio employee, they were driven straight to a building in Burbank. There, in front of a handpicked audience of a hundred and seventy people, they were projected onto an immense video screen. Unedited and without music, the footage opened on a clapperboard marked: 'REEL 17: *Something's Got to Give*, 14 May 1962'. Apart from some very brief scenes that had been included in a Fox documentary, every image from this last unfinished film had been shrouded in the utmost secrecy. Total silence fell when Marilyn appeared on the screen, a silence that lasted for the following forty-five minutes.

The film quality was blurry and, in certain places, faded, but its contents were overwhelming. Marilyn was dazzling. The editor had sequenced the footage with considerable skill, mingling excerpts and snatches of dialogue with comic scenes and ending on the eleven-minute night scene of Marilyn in the swimming pool: wide-eyed, her breasts just hidden under the water, wading to the edge of the pool with cheerfully awkward steps, and then, with a look to camera, pulling herself out and slipping on a blue-grey bathrobe. So many blues: the unreal blue of the water, the tender blue of the night, the fragile blue of her robe, the lost blue of her eyes.

The moment the last tape ended and the screen dissolved into glittering points of light, the audience burst into applause. The studio employees scooped up the tapes, without waiting to rewind them, and returned them to Fox's archives. Then they disappeared. Despite constant petitioning by Marilyn's admirers, the studio steadfastly denied the film's existence, saying that only ten minutes of it had ever been shot and that the footage had already been shown in a documentary entitled *Marilyn*, which 20th Century Fox had made in 1963.

In the spring of 1990, the tapes reappeared under strange circumstances. Henry Schipper, a young Fox news producer in Los Angeles, was combing the archives for material for a tribute to Marilyn when various clues put him on the track of *Something's Got to Give*. He was luckier, or more methodical, than previous researchers. Seated at his computer at Fox Entertainment News, ranging at will through one of the world's largest film cemeteries, he discovered that Fox's cameras had followed their favourite star everywhere, from her first screen test to her burial in Westwood Cemetery. But for a long time he couldn't find any trace of her final film. It was only after days of persistent searching that he found out that what he wanted – all the existing footage of *Something's Got to Give* – was a hundred metres below ground at the end of a tunnel in a salt mine in the centre of Kansas. At last the celluloid princess could be awakened from her loveless sleep. Realising he had got his hands on a crucial piece of the puzzle of Marilyn Monroe's life, Schipper took the reels to Fox's main projection room and stayed in there for two days, captivated by the rushes, amazed to find they were almost entirely intact and included footage of the director at work. The bulk of the material was Marilyn repeating scenes up to twenty times, making only the occasional mistake and never missing a line.

The heads of Fox had lied when they had declared the film to be untraceable and even erased from the company inventory. They had also claimed Marilyn was in a bad way throughout the shoot, pumped full of medication, so everyone thought her work on her last film couldn't be anything but a sad footnote to a brilliant career. The reality couldn't have been more different. Marilyn was on top form, turning in a performance easily on a par with the rest of her career. She was funny and heartbreaking, and every time she appeared, the screen exploded with light.

Beverly Hills, Roxbury Drive
31 May 1962

When the producers viewed the rushes of *Something's Got to Give*, they thought Marilyn was acting 'in a slow motion that was hypnotic'. There was talk of replacing her. Terribly agitated, Marilyn went to see Wexler on the evening of her penultimate day of shooting. Feeling under attack from all sides, she wasn't sure whether the threat was internal or external any more. George Cukor had been especially odious. Thirty takes for the same scene, and nothing in the can. 'Cut!' Marilyn shouted furiously. 'The same damn words I've been hearing for the past fifteen years: "Cut! Action! Take! One last take!" Don't movie people realise they're grabbing hold of *us*, the actors; they set us in motion like wind-up dolls, cut us to pieces, edit us back together . . . Movies are like sex: someone uses your body to act out fantasies that have nothing to do with you. And there isn't any of the tenderness you can get with sex that at least gives you a vague sense you exist, that you might just be a person, yourself. Neat, orderly cruelty always starts with other people.'

'Compromise!' said Wexler. 'Cukor is homosexual and he hates women – that's all true – but he's also a great filmmaker. Let him direct you.'

'No. I'm not going to put up with that sort of thing any longer. I'm not having anyone treat me brutally again. I signed my first contract with Fox in 1946 when I was twenty years old. Last winter, they sent me a telegram saying if I didn't make the last film in my contract, they'd hound me through the courts for the next ten years. I gave way in December. Now all I feel is contempt for the studio and everything it stands for. Just seeing "Fox" on a billboard makes me want to be sick.'

'Try to finish the picture. I understand Cukor: he's exasperated. I would be too. You have to get a grip.'

'I can't. Ralph left almost a month ago and nothing's gone right since. I'm thirty-six today. Cukor flew off the handle when he found out I was having a birthday party this afternoon. "Not on this set. Not now!" he shouted. But after we finished shooting, they gave me a birthday cake with July Fourth sparklers and two little figures of me, one with no clothes on and one in a bikini, and they tried to make a big show of it, wheeling it out on a trolley. Fox spent more than five thousand dollars on Elizabeth Taylor's birthday party on the set of *Cleopatra* in Rome, and this is all they could manage! The crew chipped in for the cake. Dean Martin supplied the champagne. Everyone sang "Happy Birthday". It's always the same little ritual, love trying to keep death at bay with endearments and kisses. But this time I was the one in danger. It felt like the cake was me, and I was being carried out on a stretcher.'

After a pause, she continued, 'Do you believe numbers mean things sometimes? I was born in 1926 and now it's 1962. Sixty-two is twenty-six backwards. Twenty-six is the number of years Jean Harlow lived. Thirty-six is the number of years I've lived, and the number of films she made. So either this is the last year of my life, or it's the year I'll be reunited with Norma Jeane, who was born in Los Angeles General Hospital at nine-thirty in the morning on June first, 1926 – the year Harlow died. Some days I'd like to live my life in reverse, you know, like a film being played backwards. Tell me something, Dr Wexler. What is it that makes the film rewind? Death or life? I'm afraid these might be my last days on set, my last sessions . . . You're not saying anything. You don't give a damn. You're just waiting for my hour to be up so I can pay you!'

She was silent for a long time. 'I've had no rest, I'm exhausted. Where do I go from here?' Then she abruptly got to her feet and left the room.

To hell, Wexler thought, without looking up.

Rome
1 June 1962

Bored, Ralph Greenson left the meeting with his Roman psycho-analytic colleagues that he had been stuck in all morning, and set off through Trastevere with no particular destination in mind. He stopped at a gift shop on Piazza Santa Maria and looked for a present for Marilyn among the toys. He wanted to send her a sign that would help her wait, a token on her birthday. Judging from what Wexler had told him, the chess piece had not been enough to allay her fears of abandonment. When the saleswoman asked him what he was looking for, he said he didn't really know.

'What age child?'

'Thirty-six . . . sorry . . . I mean, *three* to *six*. Between three and six years old.'

'A cuddly toy might be best,' the saleswoman suggested. Greenson searched through a mound of toys for a horse, some-thing with a family resemblance to the knight, and ended up settling for a little tiger, which he had wrapped. He asked if it could be sent to the States. 'I'm in a hurry, I'm afraid, and I'm sure you're more used to Customs and all the other formalities. I'll pay for postage, of course.'

The saleswoman obligingly handed Greenson a notepad so he could give her the address. With an attempt at levity, he wrote:

MM,
CURRENT OCCUPANT
12305 FIFTH HELENA DRIVE
BRENTWOOD
90049 3930 CA
USA
THE EARTH

He didn't give the sender's name or include a message. She would understand. In the end, Greenson thought, we're different species, she and I. Like the tiger and the whale, we're fated never really to meet. But which of us is the tiger and which the whale, I couldn't really say.

Marilyn rang her psychoanalyst's children very early on the morning of her last birthday and invited them over to celebrate. Joan and Danny spent the evening with her, drinking champagne out of plastic cups, sitting on unopened movers' cardboard boxes. As a present, they gave her a champagne glass with her name engraved inside. 'Now I'll know who I am when I'm drinking,' she said. A chessboard lay on the floor, the pieces in a jumble. The white knight was missing.

Two days later, Marilyn telephoned them again in tears and begged them to come round. She was in bed, naked, surrounded by pill bottles, wearing a black sleeping mask, with just a sheet over her. The Rodin statue was near her bed. It was the least erotic sight imaginable. She was desperate. She couldn't sleep – it was the middle of the afternoon. She was a waif, she said, she was ugly; people were only nice to her for what they could get from her. She had no one, she was no one. She talked about not having children. She said, 'It isn't worth living any more.' Joan and Daniel called Dr Engelberg, who arrived and swept the pill bottles into his black leather bag. Wexler was also summoned.

The next night, Marilyn went out in a black wig.

Hollywood, Pico Boulevard, Fox Studios
1 June 1962

Marilyn had met George Barris, the photographer, in New York in September 1954, when he was photographing *The Seven Year Itch*. In his first sight of her, she was leaning out of the window of a brownstone on East 61st, posing for a scene. He snapped a few photos of her, of that now-famous backside, before she glanced back at him and smiled.

'What sign are you?' he asked.

'Gemini. How about you?'

'Same. We should like the same things. What do you say to us doing a book together?'

'Why not? Let's do it some day. Don't stop, though. Go on taking my picture . . .'

Later, Barris was one of the photographers at the famous *Seven Year Itch* promotional shoot of a laughing Marilyn trying to push down her white dress as warm air billowed up from a subway vent. A clumsy edit of our desires and memories convinces us that this iconic image reveals more than just a flash of white underwear, although it may have been an altogether chaste affair, showing only Marilyn's thighs. As always, the image is not what we look at, it is what looks at us.

Marilyn was only too happy to strike up a rapport with the photographer in the hope that he'd dispense some of the magic of his profession, remind her of the way photographs provide a screen onto which one can project one's dreams. She always liked the similarity between the words *magic* and *image*. But they didn't get around to doing a book during her lifetime. For eight years she was busy making film after film and becoming an international movie star, and she forgot about their project until 1962, when she met up with him again on the set of *Something's Got to Give*. He had pitched a story to *Cosmopolitan*: could Marilyn, at thirty-six, continue to play sexy, beautiful young women? The editor reckoned it would make a cover.

When he walked onto Stage Fourteen, Barris spotted Marilyn right away and tapped her on the shoulder. 'Hey, I'm creeping up on you like the first time. Maybe you don't remember me, though.'

She turned around, smiled, and gave him a big hug, 'It's been a long time,' she said. 'What's the occasion? Have you come to photograph Miss Golden Dreams? What about our book? If we're going to do one, I'd like it to be more than just a picture book.'

'There can be text, sure. You should write it.'

'I will. I don't have such trouble with words, these days. They're almost friends. Something I always used to like about LA is that it's no names here. It's the city of the nameless. Getting around LA, numbers are what matter. If you don't want to be miles out on Wilshire, say, you'd better get the numbers in the address right. But naming things is important – I've come round to that. It depends who you tell, of course.'

'Well, talking of numbers,' he said, 'since today is June first,

I thought I'd fly out from New York to see my ol' friend – I said *ol'*, not *old*.'

She laughed as he hugged her again, and said, 'Happy-happy, and may you have only happy ones.'

Barris was telling her about the *Cosmopolitan* story when Cukor called her on set. Marilyn asked him to stick around – they could talk about the book and other stuff later. At five-thirty that Friday afternoon, Marilyn finished her scene. Someone shouted, 'Happy birthday, Marilyn!' One of the crew produced the cake. The sparklers threw off stars, the Dom Pérignon flowed. Barris thought it looked amazing, the light of the sparklers, the champagne bubbles, the tears running down her face, but he didn't take a picture.

Hollywood, Bel Air, Joanne Carson's house
August 1976

One summer day, almost fifteen years after Marilyn's death, Greenson heard Capote was in town to play an eccentric billionaire in the movie *Murder by Death*. He asked Joanne Carson, a mutual friend, to set up a meeting between them at her house, although he didn't tell her he wanted to talk about Marilyn's death. Carson obliged and, after effecting the introductions, tactfully left the two men alone.

'You knew Marilyn when she was still just an actress, before she became a myth,' Greenson launched in. 'I loved her, I'm sure you know that. You're an intelligent man. You know what *love* means in analysis, as well as out here, in what's called real life.'

'Are we talking about the same thing? I'm not so sure,' Capote said. 'Love seems to be a cure, as far as you analysts are concerned, whereas to me it's the actual sickness. There's something vaguely ludicrous about it, like a children's game where someone's playing at being someone else's mother—'

'Love is a bond,' Greenson said. 'Two people form an object relationship. They give, they receive . . .'

'Not two people,' Capote retorted. 'Two walking wounds. Two incomplete beings searching for something they'll never be able to find in another person. You know how to recognise that a relationship has changed from a sexual to a "loving" one? There are two signs, and they both relate to what's little and *en bas*, as the French say. The first is an undifferentiated intimacy, a regression to infancy in the Latin sense of *infans*: the one who does not speak, the vulnerable soul who is deprived of language, not that I should have to tell a psychoanalyst that. Hence lovers' private languages, their baby talk, pet names, teeny-weeny voices – cutesy little lovers with their cutesy little languages. The second sign that love has entered the picture is a sense of entitlement to the anal, as I'm sure you know, Mr Analyst: the licence to talk to a person about their digestion, their excretion, their shit.'

'But how do you distinguish between what we call "trans-ference love" and the other sort?' Greenson asked, as if he hadn't heard.

'You're incorrigible, you analysts!' Capote exclaimed, in his sexless, childlike falsetto. 'You refuse to admit that love doesn't justify anything, doesn't prove anything or anyone right or wrong, that it's all just a question of language. You're so busy justifying yourselves: *But I loved her*. So what? Your love was the murdering kind. That's all there is to it.'

As Greenson was leaving the Bel Air mansion, Capote whis-pered in his ear, 'It was *her* death, you know. Like my dumb film says, it was *Murder by Death*. Death was what killed her. She didn't kill herself. Neither did anyone else.'

As Capote turned away, he remembered a conversation he'd had with Marilyn when he'd gone to visit her in her house in Brentwood shortly before she died. He thought her beauty had had a completely different cast to it, and asked whether she'd lost weight.

'A few pounds,' Marilyn said. 'Fourteen or fifteen maybe, I don't know.'

'If you carry on like this,' Capote said, 'your soul will start showing through your skin.'

'Don't make fun of me. Who said that?'

'I did. No one quotes an author better than he does himself. How are you feeling, by the way? How is your soul?'

'It's out of the country for a while. Romi, my saviour, is at a conference in Europe, sitting at Freud's right hand.'

'This analysis will be the death of you, Marilyn. You've got to stop!'

Capote didn't like psychoanalysis and he loathed Hollywood. As for the Hollywood variant of psychoanalysis, he considered it worse than a fad: he thought it was a disease. 'Everyone in California is either in analysis, or an analyst, or an analyst in analysis,' he'd joke, whenever anyone tried to convince him to go to Couch Canyon. But he did in the end and, as ambivalent as ever, saw a male and female analyst simultaneously.

Capote's got it back to front, Greenson thought, as he drove back to Santa Monica. It's not analysis that gets everywhere in Hollywood, even the movies, it's the movies that take over everything, even analysis. People breathe, walk, talk – even shut off from each other in this goldfish bowl as if they're on set. They're constantly acting a part. Maybe Marilyn's analysis was scripted by some studio hack with half an hour to spare. Greenson had just read *My Story*, which had come out in 1971 as Marilyn's autobiography under her name, despite its having been compiled in the 1950s by Ben Hecht from conversations with her.

Maybe she was acting the part of Cecily after we stopped her playing it in the movie. Marilyn as Cecily: the quintessential hysteric with an Electra complex in a 1960s Hollywood version of analysis, complete with healed traumas, disinterred memories and a kindly, bearded, irresistible therapist. What about her death, though? What script did that come from? When he had read in *My Story*, 'I was the kind of girl they found dead in a hall bedroom with an empty bottle of sleeping pills in her hand,' he'd thought Marilyn had played her part to perfection on the night of 4 August 1962. Besides, hadn't she called her memoir *My Story*, rather than *My Life* or *Memoirs of an Actress*, as if at the peak of her glory she knew she was just filling in the gaps in someone else's script? It reminded him of the time on the set of *Something's Got to Give* when he had watched Cukor whisper to her her lines as she forgot the entire script.

That wasn't all, though, was it? he thought. He had played his part opposite her too. He had acted the role of the impossibly benevolent, far-from-objective analyst with skill and conviction. In the imaginations of Hollywood folk, Marilyn Monroe's death was a *film noir* all of its own:

The End of Miss Golden Dreams, A Motion Picture starring Marilyn Monroe and Romi Greenson

Synopsis: Hollywood, January 1960–August 1962
Death of a star. Monroe plays the part of Marilyn. The male lead, Romeo, a dark, hard, seductive figure she loves to death, who feeds her her last lines, is played by Ralph Greenson, her last analyst.

A case of transference love? Of fatal transference?

She gives love, but doesn't know who to. She dies, but no one knows of what. And when Romeo is accused of killing her, he does not even stop to wonder if he might have done so by loving her too much.

Westwood, Fifth Helena Drive
6 June 1962

Greenson had already visited Greece, Israel and Italy; now he was heading off to Switzerland. Marilyn didn't try to ring him directly, but instead wrote down a list of questions and got Eunice Murray to ask them over the phone. Greenson realised they were less important than the unspoken question, 'When are you coming back?', but he didn't ask Murray to put her on. Marilyn immediately embarked on a fervid bout of telephoning, ringing Lee Strasberg, Norman and Hedda Rosten, Ralph Roberts, Whitey Snyder and Pat Newcomb several times a day. They thought she sounded lost, searching for herself.

When Marilyn didn't appear on set the Monday after her thirty-sixth birthday, Peter G. Levathes, Fox's studio head, announced he was going to settle the Monroe problem. Next thing, Marilyn had arrived and declared herself not only ready but impatient to get back to work, even though she had been present on only twelve out of the shoot's thirty-four days. The following day, when she again didn't appear on set, Cukor dismissed the cast and crew and resolved to call off filming if she didn't turn up. Fox again threatened to revoke her contract, and Cukor started considering replacements: Kim Novak, Shirley MacLaine, Doris Day, maybe Lee Remick. Contacted by Mickey Rudin on Marilyn's behalf, Greenson promised to get back as quickly as possible, leaving his wife to follow him the next day.

Two days later, even though he had come off a seventeen-hour flight, he drove straight from the airport to Marilyn's house, where he found her in a coma – but alive. No one knows what they talked about when she came round, but the following day he took her to see a Beverly Hills plastic surgeon, Michael Gurdin, who had already done some work on Marilyn thirteen years earlier, to her nose and cheekbones. She was hoarse-voiced, her hair dirty and matted, make-up barely covering the bruising under her eyes. Her analyst said she had slipped in the shower. The doctor could see she was heavily medicated. She seemed especially concerned about a forthcoming photo shoot, asking if her nose was broken and how long it would take to fix if it were. When the X-rays showed no significant damage to the bones or cartilage, she threw her arms round Dr Greenson. Gurdin ruled out a fracture. She might have fallen, he said, but she also might have been hit: bruising to the nose can easily spread to the eyes.

Greenson rang Mickey Rudin at once and told him to let the studio know he had everything in hand. He was convinced she was emotionally and physically up to finishing the film on deadline.

He asked Eunice Murray not to mention the incident to the press or anyone from Fox, and informed the studio that, from now on, all artistic decisions involving Marilyn – shots, script alterations, costumes, everything – were to be discussed with him. At lunch at Fox the following day, Phil Feldman, the executive vice president of studio operations, told the analyst they were losing nine thousand dollars every day Marilyn didn't film, and asked Greenson to drive her to Century City personally.

'If she depends on you so heavily,' Feldman asked, 'what's going to happen to the picture if she chucks you?'

Greenson didn't answer, preferring to point out that he had managed to get her back on *The Misfits*' set after a week in hospital, and that she had been able to finish Huston's film. He thought he could do the same again now.

But that afternoon, a few minutes before the magistrates' court closed, Fox sued Marilyn for half a million dollars for breach of contract, and told the press she was no longer on the project. Greenson heard the news on the car radio on his way back from lunch. He rushed to Marilyn's house and gave her a tranquilliser shot.

Later that evening, a statement was put out that Lee Remick was going to replace Marilyn. Next morning, Dean Martin said he was pulling out of the film.

'I have the greatest respect for Miss Lee Remick and her talent, and for all the other actresses put forward for the role, but I signed up to make this film with Marilyn Monroe and I won't make it with anyone else.' He hadn't even wanted to make the film originally, he confessed, and had only agreed because Marilyn had set her heart on him being in it. Levathes' attempts to make him rethink were in vain.

Henry Weinstein would later say of Marilyn, 'Very few people experience terror. We all experience anxiety, unhappiness, heartbreaks, but that was sheer, primal terror.'

When he got back to Santa Monica that evening, despite the weight of exhaustion that had been building since his return from Europe, Greenson couldn't sleep. He went to bed, but when Hildi arrived home, two hours later, she found him in his armchair, holding Marilyn's X-rays up to his orange desk lamp. He started like a naughty child when she came in, then carried on solemnly examining the plates as if he were meditating. He scanned the patches of blurry white and fathomless black, searching not for lesions but for the secret trail of her beauty, winding through the strange densities and degrees of opacity. His mouth was open and shadowy as though he were about to speak.

Santa Monica, Franklin Street
11 *June* 1962

When he'd got back from Europe, Greenson had found a series of notes left by Marilyn, folded, ink-stained bits of paper, some of which she'd just pushed under the door without an envelope. One was particularly affecting: 'I keep coming back to the chessboard. I don't know why, but I keep thinking the game's down to its last moves. My whole life can be summed up by what those pieces can do. The way my body feels, the way I feel, what my acting's like, the power of a director I used to admire, sex, the scenes I've filmed, take after take after take: to me they're like moves on the sixty-four squares until it all ends with checkmate . . .' The note broke off. The psychoanalyst sank into a reverie. Struck by Marilyn's fascination with glass, mirrors and the chessboard's black and white squares, the thought came to him that they had never played the game of skill together.

'I'm devoted to you,' Greenson said, in a loud voice, almost a shout, as Marilyn sat down for her second session of the day at his practice – he'd insisted they meet there rather than at her house. 'I'll do anything I can to alleviate your suffering, you know that, but you simply have to finish this film. I gave them my word. The studio has agreed to renegotiate your contract into a million-dollar deal: half a million for this picture, plus a bonus if it's completed to the new schedule, and another half-million or more for a new musical. It's incredible. Fox is agreeing to revert to the Nunnally Johnson script you liked and, for good measure, to replace George Cukor with a director vetted by you. We've won.'

'I can't do it. And you can't help me either. Acting is not a problem I need to solve. It's the only solution I've got to my other problems. Being an actress isn't the cause of my panic, it's the only remedy I've got, and, I tell you, all the analysis in the world won't help now. I'm all the way down a dead end, like that house you made me buy.'

'All your life your basic problem has been rejection,' Greenson protested. 'But now the studio's not confirming your fantasy any more. And I want to free you of your fear of abandonment, or at least allow you to control it.'

'Every actor struggles with shyness more than anyone can imagine, you know. There is a censor inside us that says, "To what degree do we let go?" Like a child playing. I guess people think we just go out there and, you know, that's all we do. Just do it. But it's a real struggle. I'm one of the world's most self-conscious people. I really have to struggle. An actor is not a machine, no matter how much they want to say you are. Creativity has got to start with humanity, and when you're a human being, you feel, you suffer. You're gay, you're sick, you're nervous or whatever it is. Like any creative human being, I would like a bit more control so that it would be a little easier for me when the director says "Give me one tear, right now", to make a tear pop out. Once there were two tears because I thought, How dare he? You need anxiety, but now it's too much, it's like I'm under a black shroud. I can't break out of it.'

Her voice faded away. After a while, she broke the silence: 'It reminds me of a couple of films I made ten years ago. I've never had so many problems with parts. Michael Chekhov said when he coached me, 'Just thinking about the character, analysing it mentally, won't allow you to play it, to transform yourself into another person. Your rational mind will make you passive and distant. But if you develop your imaginary body, if you empty yourself and allow yourself to be possessed by the other person, your desires and feelings will allow you to act them out.' But that's just what I was afraid of: becoming another person.

'The anxiety's always been there, you know,' she said more fervently. 'I suffered agonies on *Clash by Night*, when I was starting out. I almost died of fear at the thought of dealing with Barbara Stanwyck and Fritz Lang – him most of all. He'd barred Natasha Lytess from the set and I couldn't act without having her close by. On the next one, *Don't Bother to Knock*, I threw up before every scene, like now. I had to play another baby-sitter, but she wasn't like me. She was a straight portrait of my mother, my crazy, impossible mother. I covered up my mother's existence back then. I'd tell people she was dead so I wouldn't have to tell them she was insane. That picture gave me the money to put her in a clinic. My movies have helped me survive, some of them have at least, and I guess playing a woman who couldn't look after a little girl helped me look after my mother in a way. It made me sick, having to relive all that stuff, though. They call it stage fright, but it wasn't for me, it was stage terror. The director was called Baker, like my mother. But don't tell Dr Freud that,' she said, with a stifled laugh. 'He'd despise me even more than Fritz Lang did. I was twenty-five and it was my first big part. After I'd read the script, I ran to Natasha's in the middle of the night literally shaking with fear. We worked together for two days and nights, optimistic one minute, the next in a total panic. I still remember what my character Nell said to Richard Widmark: "I'll be whatever you want me to be. I'll be yours. Haven't you ever felt that if you let somebody leave, you'll be lost, you won't know where to go because you haven't got anyone to put in their place?"'

Marilyn fell silent.

'Who do you belong to now?' asked Greenson.

'Whoever wants to have a piece of me. Men, producers, the public. So many people have taken a part of me and changed it, you know: Grace McKee my hair, Fred Karger my teeth, Johnny Hyde my nose and my cheeks, Ben Lyon my name . . . I loved it. You can't imagine how much I loved it. The greatest experience in my life was in the winter of 1954. It was during my Korean tour—'

'I've seen footage of it,' Greenson cut in. 'NBC showed it a few months ago. Can you say who you belong to?'

Marilyn was silent, remembering 'Marilyn' singing for seventeen thousand whistling, shouting soldiers without a trace of her usual terror. She'd started by visiting the wounded, then gone to the 45th Division and put on ten shows in sub-zero temperatures. It had snowed, but she wore only a figure-hugging, sleeveless, sparkling purple silk dress with no underwear. The GIs hadn't seen a woman for months. They went crazy, virtually devouring her limb from limb. To prevent a riot, she'd toned down a Gershwin song from 'do it again' to 'kiss me again'. She'd sung 'Diamonds Are A Girl's Best Friend' for those poor saps who were getting shot up for a pittance, then tried to make up for it with a cute dance. She knew they'd like that. Once she'd had to be whisked off stage in a helicopter. Two soldiers had held her by the legs as she'd hung out of the door, blowing kisses to the mass of men below, all yelling her name.

'Who do you belong to now?' the analyst asked again.

'Fear.'

'Fear of what? Being alone?'

'Alone? Some days I'm suffocated by a crew of forty people shouting the same thing at me over and over: "Take", "Cut", "First take, thirteenth take, twenty-fifth take"... I don't know, really. That word, "take" – I find it kind of terrifying and re-assuring at the same time. It's strange. It makes me feel there's somebody inside me they're taking, that at least I'm something. They take *me*, then they stop filming, but at least I was there in the viewfinder for a minute. At least I existed. Who do I belong to? My audience, the whole world, not because I'm talented or even beautiful, but because I've never belonged to anyone or anything. If that's the way it is, how can you not say yourself, "I belong to anyone who wants a piece of me"?'

'And do you belong anywhere?'

'I felt lost on the filming of *Don't Bother to Knock*. I had three addresses in as many months, two in West Hollywood, then a suite in the Bel Air Hotel in Stone Canyon, but nothing that made me feel I was at home. I was trying to become a good actress and a good person. But I didn't have you then . . . Sometimes I felt strong, but I had to go down very deep to find that feeling and it was hard bringing it up to the surface. Nothing's ever been easy. Nothing ever is easy, but it was less easy then than it is now. I couldn't talk about my past. It was too painful. I just wanted to forget.'

'To be able to forget something, you have to revisit it.'

'Relive it, you mean.'

'What did you want to relive at Kennedy's gala?'

'No, that wasn't it. I was honoured when they asked me to appear at the president's birthday celebrations in Madison Square Garden. There was a hush over the whole place when I came on to sing "Happy Birthday", like if I had been wearing a slip I would have thought it was showing, or something. I thought, Oh, my gosh, what if no sound comes out? A hush like that from the people warms me. It's sort of like an embrace. Then you think, By God, I'll sing this song if it's the last thing I ever do. And for all the people. Because I remember when I turned to the microphone I looked all the way up and back, and I thought, That's where I'd be, way up there under one of those rafters, close to the ceiling, after I paid my two dollars to come into the place.'

'Now you have to forget and start over. Go back to the film.'

'People have said I'm finished, that this is the end for me. You know, it might be a kind of relief to be finished. It's sort of like, I don't know, what kind of a yard dash you're running, but then you're at the finish line and you sort of see you've made it! But you never do. Cut! Let's go again! You always have to start all over again. Fucking Cukor. He can go fuck himself!'

Hollywood, Warner Bros Studios
December 1965

Fox had sunk two million into *Something's Got to Give*. 'The
poor dear has finally gone round the bend,' Cukor told a
columnist. 'The sad thing is, the little work we do have is no
good . . . I think she's finished.' But Cukor had an idea how to
get out of the stalemate – turn the whole débâcle into a tragi-
comedy. Marilyn, with her abusive demands and shameless
manipulation, would play the deranged actress. It would be a
classic Hollywood tale of beleaguered producers, interfering
psychoanalysts and a vampire acting coach who controls every
move the fragile star makes, ending in high melodrama. In the
last reel Marilyn would succumb to the death and madness she
was always in awe of, or at least gave the impression of being.

Cukor never got the chance to make this film about Marilyn
with her as the star, but two years after she died, he returned to
the subject of powerful female leads with portraits of women such
as the dancer Isadora Duncan and the silent movie star Tallulah
Bankhead. Remembering his travails on *Something's Got to Give*,
he imagined a movie about an actress losing her grip, in the style

of Billy Wilder's *Sunset Boulevard* or Mankiewicz's *All About Eve*. Like him, both directors had worked with Marilyn, and, in an act of sweet revenge on such hated rivals, he liked the idea of shooting a *noir* in Technicolor about Marilyn's final days. It would be his last, most beautiful film, which other studios besides Fox might go for, now Marilyn had become a myth. He even had a choice of titles: *Lost In the City of Angels*, or *A Star Dies*, a companion piece to his 1954 movie, *A Star Is Born*, in which Judy Garland played the troubled actress who was more interested in staying up all night than sweating it out under the lights on set all day. He envisaged it as a movie about the movie that could never be made. It would not only show the other side of the screen, the stupid, cruel inner workings of the studios, but also what lies behind a movie star's public face, the madness of someone desperately searching for an image of something she could actually embody.

He had no qualms in admitting it would also be his way of getting his revenge on her, because he had resented their altercations intensely. She had constantly changed scenes and lines during filming. Under Greenson's tireless supervision, the screenwriters had had to insert takes, change the order of scenes, put in new material. Paula Strasberg's involvement in every take of every scene drove him especially insane. As far as he was concerned, the Actors Studio's Method was pretentious nonsense and he firmly believed the director should retain all his traditional prerogatives. Whenever he had said 'Cut!' after a shot, Marilyn would turn to Paula – never him – to ask if it was all right. They'd go off into a corner and have an unbelievably intense discussion that would sometimes end in a favourable verdict, but more often in Marilyn saying, 'No, it's no good! Let's do another!' Dean Martin, meanwhile, would be off in some corner taking out his frustration on his golf clubs. Strasberg, Greenson, Henry Weinstein – how many people exactly did they think should be arguing over the final cut with him?

But he'd remained courteous throughout. If Marilyn said 'Let's do another' once too often, he'd just say 'Of course, darling', call out 'Last one, Marilyn', and do four or five takes without any film in the camera. He and his assistant, Gene Allen, would then watch the rushes in private and come out to find Marilyn waiting anxiously at the door. 'How was it?' she'd ask – Cukor once turned to Allen and whispered, 'Meaning: how was I?' – and he'd always reassure her with a charming smile, 'Splendid, Marilyn, splendid.' After the last day of shooting he said publicly, 'The studio has given in to her on everything. There's a certain ruthlessness about all of her actions. She pretended to be nice to me. I'm very sorry to see her this way, fighting ghosts. Even her lawyer, Mickey Rudin, can't take any more. She's had enough herself. I think this is the end of her career.'

Two years after her death, he realised that what he'd actually foreseen was the end of Marilyn rather than of her career. So now he wanted to re-create the incredible, involuntary force of her performances; her almost unbearable presence on screen in *Something's Got to Give*, despite her being so absent on set, even when she was physically there. It was completely hypnotic, the way she seemed to move across the screen in slow-motion, her eyes, which were what made her so beautiful, virtually expressionless. He'd put himself in the movie as the patient, brilliant director he'd found it so difficult to be in reality. It would be a comedy with tragic overtones. Maybe he should call it *The Only Thing That Counts Is What's On Screen*. He kept changing his mind, though, and in the end, when people started accusing Greenson of being in a conspiracy to murder Marilyn, he gave up. 'It's all too close to the bone,' he told Hedda Hopper, the Hollywood gossip columnist. 'There're too many powerful vested interests. And too much love swirling around.'

On the last day of his life, 24 January 1983, when he was talking to a friend, George Cukor mentioned *Something's Got to Give*: 'It was a dirty business,' he said. 'That was the worst rejection she ever had to take. When it came down to it, you know, she was just too innocent.'

New York, Eighth Avenue
Mid-June 1962

Within weeks of being fired, Marilyn was doing major interviews and photo-shoots with *Life*, *Vogue* and *Cosmopolitan*, counter-attacking with the only thing she had ever known how to exploit: her image. A photo of her naked in the swimming pool appeared on the cover of *Life* on 22 June. Whether you think of her as a glittering star or a faded rag doll in the last days of her life depends on whose impressions you listen to, the photographers or the journalists. Two decades later, the photographer Bert Stern described her in euphoric terms as strong and free: 'She had the power. She was the wind, that comet shape that Blake draws blowing around a sacred figure. She was the light, and the goddess, and the moon. The space and the dream, the mystery and the danger. But everything else all together too, including Hollywood, and the girl next door that every guy wants to marry.' The journalist Richard Meryman, however, who interviewed her for *Life*, was struck 'by how pasty her skin was – pasty and lifeless-looking. There was not much health in that skin. It wasn't white and it wasn't grey. It was a little bit coarse, lifeless. It looked like skin that had had make-up on it for a long, long time. She looked terrific, but when you really studied that face, it was kind of cardboardy. Her hair was lifeless, had no body to it, like hair that had been primped and heated and blown a thousand times.' A permanent, as they say. The only part of her that couldn't die because it was already dead.

Discouraged by the turn of events since he'd come back from Europe, Greenson wrote to a friend, Lucille Ostrow, that he felt his failure as a personal affront. To come to Marilyn's aid, he said plaintively, he had sacrificed not only his holidays, but also time in New York, when he was supposed to meet Leo Rosten. 'I've given up all my objectives and interests, and she is thrilled to be free of the film that was boring her. She's extremely well. Now I'm the one who's depressed, who feels alone and abandoned.' Greenson devoted every working hour to his 'favourite schizophrenic'. Everyone who'd worked on the movie was scathing, however. The screenwriter Walter Bernstein told anyone who'd listen that Greenson had wrapped Marilyn up in a cocoon: 'She has become an investment for him, and not just a financial one. He is not taking care of her; he's manufacturing her illness. It's become vital for him and various others that she be regarded as sick, dependent and at a loss. There is something sinister about this psychoanalyst who exerts an insane influence over her.'

On the Monday after she was fired, Marilyn left for New York. She saw nobody there, except W. J. Weatherby, whom she'd met up with now and then over the last two years. They had become close, if that was the word. She always appeared in disguise, wearing a headscarf, baggy blouse, loose trousers and no make-up. The journalist was not particularly susceptible to the narcissistic aspects of her beauty; he thought of himself as more interested in what lay behind the mask. He was particularly struck by a quality he tried to define by focusing on the word 'screen'. The image she projected of herself was a screen, he thought, an ecstatic refraction of certain inner qualities that masked a profound confusion.

They used to meet in a bar on Eighth Avenue, a joint filled with silent drinkers who liked a generous measure – not the kind of place you'd expect to run into a Hollywood movie star. Once, Weatherby chose a booth at the back in the shadows. After half an hour, he had begun to think she wasn't coming when he heard a woman's voice behind him, 'A dollar for your thoughts.'

'Not worth it,' he replied.

Marilyn had a glass in each hand. Her old pallor was overlaid with another layer, which made her more indecipherable.

'Here you go. Gin and tonic.'

'Great. We can go to another bar, though . . .'

'No, no, I like it. I'm not often taken to a *real* bar. It reminds of the one we drank in in Reno. Everyone's different in different places, though. I change anyway. I'm different in New York than I am Hollywood. I'm different here at this bar than at the studio. And it's the same with people. I'm different with Lee than with my secretary, and I'm different again with you. I realise that in interviews. The questions always demand certain answers and make you seem a certain kind of person. Often they tell me more about the interviewer than my answers do about me.'

'You seduce interviewers,' Weatherby said, with a disarming smile. 'You don't want them to get at the real you, but to fall in love with you and write love stories.'

'You think so?'

'Oh, yes. But don't you try to seduce every man you meet?' he joked. 'Don't you like to feel your power over them?'

'Sometimes I hate the effect I have on people. I get tired of the stupid attention, of working people up. It's not really a human thing. But it didn't happen with you. I like it better this way. I don't respect people who like you just because you're famous . . . I hope our little drink isn't going in that notebook.'

She reminded him of a child whistling or laughing in the dark. The more cheerful she tried to be, the more she felt the night draw in.

'Do you want another drink?' he asked.

'Sure. Have you read any good books recently?'

'*The Deer Park* by Norman Mailer. It might interest you. It's about Hollywood. I'll get you a copy.'

'Do you ever feel books are beyond you? I mean, that your mind can't handle them? Almost like they're in a foreign language, though the words are English. It makes me feel so dumb sometimes.'

'I wouldn't worry about it if I were you. You have sharper instincts than many intellectuals. You don't want to blunt your instincts just for the sake of second-hand knowledge. I'd rather be beautiful than wise.'

She frowned and looked away. He knew he'd made a mistake.

Not long after, they left and walked a few blocks up Eighth Avenue against the evening tide rushing towards the Port Authority Bus Terminal. He put her into a cab, then went back to their bar, sat down under a neon light that had been turned on in the meantime, opened his notebook and transcribed their conversation. He wondered if she was using him, if she was just being friendly or whether she thought there was something in their talks. He couldn't do anything for her career, he wasn't going to write about her, but still, he thought, the suspicion was there, as it was with everyone.

Two days later, they met up again as they'd planned. He thought she'd changed. She didn't look so youthful. Her face was gaunter, the cheekbones more angular, the lines showing through her clumsy make-up, as she probably realised. She was waiting for him this time and jumped up to give him a jaunty peck on the cheek. Weatherby froze involuntarily. She smelt of neglect, the shakes, too many tears.

'I nearly didn't come,' she said.

'I'm glad you did. How are you spending your time here?'

'Don't know. It's like being at the bottom of the pool, when you kick to try and come up to the surface. I feel like staying inside – away from people.'

'You got the blues?'

'Sort of . . .'

She carried on talking in a disjointed way. They ordered their drinks. She wanted a White Angel but the waiter didn't know what that was. They clinked their gin and tonics and wished each other good luck.

'They won't ever humiliate me,' she resumed. 'I know what it's like to feel a loser, that panic. I saw it in Betty Grable's eyes when the studio bosses ushered me into her dressing room to show I was taking over from her. I wouldn't do it. I walked away. They held it against me for a long time. I was very naïve back then. There was a whole period when I felt flattered if a man – any man – even took an interest in me! I believed too easily in people, and then I went on believing in them even after they disappointed me over and over again. I must have been very stupid in those days. I guess I'm capable of doing it again with someone, only he'd have to be someone more outstanding than a heel. I always paid the price, though, for everything I've ever done. There were times when I'd be with one of my husbands and I'd run into one of those Hollywood heels at a party and they'd paw me cheaply in front of everybody as if they were saying, *Oh, we had her.* I guess it's the classic situation of the ex-whore, though I was never a whore in the real sense. I was never kept; I always kept myself. But there was a period when I responded too much to flattery and slept around too much, thinking it would help my career, though I always liked the guy at the time. They were always so full of self-confidence and I had none at all and they made me feel better. But you don't get self-confidence that way.'

'Do you have plans after this film?'

'I once read the role of Blanche DuBois in *A Streetcar Named Desire.* I'd like to play that on Broadway when I'm older. I like the last line so much. You remember, Vivien Leigh in Kazan's film?'

He remembered. Deathly pale, driven mad by her impossible love.

'At the moment, I can't see myself saying on stage "Whoever you are, I've always depended on the kindness of strangers", but I know what she means. Friends and relatives can let you down. You can depend on them too much. But don't depend too much on strangers either, honey. Some strangers gave me a hard time when I was a kid.'

'I read once that you were raped as a child.'

'Don't let's talk about that. I'm tired of talking about that. I'm sorry I ever mentioned it to anyone.' Absentmindedly, she wiped the table with a paper napkin and then grinned at herself. 'The housewife. I enjoy housework. Takes my mind off things.'

After a series of silences punctuated by the odd remark, often obscure, Weatherby went to the bathroom. When he came back, he found a man standing by their table, trying to pick up the scruffy blonde who, he was convinced, was a prostitute off Eighth Avenue. Weatherby shouted at him and he meekly turned tail and went back to the bar.

'Our masks expose us, our roles kill us,' she said. 'I drag Marilyn Monroe around with me like an albatross. You know, I've been thinking of writing my will. Can't tell you why, but it's been on my mind. It's made me feel sort of gloomy. Anyway, you've got to get the most out of the moment. Let's make some mischief.'

'Do you want to dance on the bar?'

'We'd only be thrown out,' she said cheerily. 'This is a men's bar. Women have to lie low . . . You won't write anything of what I say to you, will you? Maybe I'll get married again myself. Only problem is, he's married right now. And he's famous, so we have to meet in secret.' Her lover was in politics in Washington, she added.

The following day, she sent a strange telegram to Bobby Kennedy, declining an invitation to dinner in Los Angeles.

ATTY GENERAL AND MRS ROBERT F. KENNEDY

1962 JUNE 13 PM
HICKORY HILL MCLEANVIR DEAR ATTORNEY
GENERAL AND MRS ROBERT KENNEDY: I WOULD
HAVE BEEN DELIGHTED TO HAVE ACCEPTED YOUR
INVITATION HONORING PAT AND PETER LAWFORD.
UNFORTUNATELY I AM INVOLVED IN A FREEDOM
RIDE PROTESTING THE LOSS OF THE MINORITY
RIGHTS BELONGING TO THE FEW REMAINING
EARTHBOUND STARS. AFTER ALL, ALL WE
DEMANDED WAS OUR RIGHT TO TWINKLE.
MARILYN MONROE

According to Peter Lawford, on Saturday, 4 August, the last day of her life, Marilyn said a terrible thing when she refused to come to a party at his house on the beach: 'What – so they can pass me round like a piece of meat? No thanks. I've had enough of that. I don't want to be used by anyone any more, Frank, Bobby, your brother-in-law – I can't even get through to him any more. Everyone uses me.'

'Please come,' Lawford begged. 'It will take you out of yourself.'

'No, I'm shattered. I've got no more answers for anyone. Do me a favour, though: tell the president I've been trying to call him. Say goodbye to him from me. Tell him I've done my bit.'

Her voice sank to a murmur and Lawford, unable to understand what she was saying, had to shout her name several times as if she was deaf. After a long, exhausted sigh, she said, 'Say "See you" to Pat and to the president and to you too, because you are a nice guy.'

Lawford could hear she wasn't crying wolf; he could feel her sinking. 'See you', he realised, doesn't necessarily mean 'Goodbye'. Sometimes it means, 'I'm doing my best. I'm trying to see you.'

Los Angeles, University of California
June 1966

As incompatible as they were inseparable, Marilyn and Ralph were losing one another, but not because they were going their separate ways. They were losing themselves in each other, like reversible figures on face cards, joined at the hip but staring off enigmatically in different directions. A fifty-five-year-old man and a woman trying to escape childhood, who met somewhere between daylight and memories, channelled words and remembered dreams, silence and tears. Love is always the remembrance of past love, desire is always the forgetting of other desires. Parallel worlds such as theirs always collide by accident and result in mutual checkmate.

In the past, images had reassured and protected her. Being photographed felt like a painless caress, a way of arousing desire so she could hide from the devastation of love. She'd always wanted to be desired so she wouldn't have to ask whether she was loved, but now passion had devastated love and even desire for her. Passion had made language turn in on itself, and her body had no way of anchoring it. When you love somebody you love their words, you visualise their presence. But Marilyn felt passion for Greenson; she waited for him, he overwhelmed her with his words and images. Susceptible as she was to losing herself, to being overwhelmed by the other, she loved him to the point of hallucination, the moment where the fulfilment of love no longer has anything to do with love, and its object is no longer a person. She didn't recognise him in his concrete, specific reality; instead he became a collection of signs, a towering abstraction, and this unreal creation was all that existed for her. Passion-fuelled love plays off madness, like co-stars in a movie. People have good reason to speak of *amour fou*. It homes in very close to madness before veering off at the last moment. When psychosis sets in, the love is bankrupt or dead. So it was inevitable that their parting would also be a question of passion, a confusion between the end of love and death itself.

After Marilyn's death, Greenson gave a talk at a symposium at UCLA entitled 'Sex Without Passion', in which, by implication, he also discussed its opposite: passion without sex. Convinced by Marilyn's sex life that desire and love were radically disconnected in her, he began with thoughts about women and sexual desire in general:

'Many women approaching their forties need sex and a sexual relationship to reassure themselves that they are still lovable and physically attractive people. But above all they need a sexual relationship to convince themselves they are lovable. Remember, a woman has one enormous advantage in the sexual act: she can perform it or let it be performed upon her without doing anything. She does not have to do anything in order to be able to give sexual satisfaction to someone. Women are able to use sex in non-sexual ways for non-sexual purposes. You see a great deal in recent years of people who engage in sexual activity without love and without passion. They use it for one or another reason, for conquest, or reassurance, for revenge or something of that order. Some women cannot allow themselves to feel directly, emotionally involved, with fantasies about the man with whom they are doing something as intimate as sex, and that is what sex is, a very intimate act. To be this intimately involved with someone means to them that he could hurt them, he could damage them, he could leave them. So they have to distance themselves from him and block out their fantasies.

'The interesting thing about the married men in their forties is that they admit they have less desire for sexual relations, but if you pursue this problem of frigidity in the male you will find that they are less interested in sex particularly with their wives . . . What is at the root of these special problems? . . . The man of forty-five or fifty can no longer kid himself that he has un-limited horizons for future opportunity for success. At forty-five he knows how close he is to making it or failing . . . At forty-five there does arise in the American male concern about his health, this has to do with the process of ageing . . . At forty-five if there should be some diminution of the erection, or in the capacity to maintain one, there does loom up in a man's mind the worry over possibly getting impotent.

'This fear of being found impotent might perhaps dissuade him from having intercourse, to avoid finding out about it. He may be using various rationalisations to avoid sex, or may use some kind of instrumentalities to help him with sex. I don't know how prevalent the use of various gadgets is to help along sexual practices, but I do not think it is localised to Beverly Hills or Hollywood alone. It seems to be quite frequent, at least in my practice, among some of the patients I know.

'Many men have a fear of promiscuity, partly out of the fear of impotence and partly in order to deny that impotence is a real consideration. They are not faithful because of a sense of morality, they remain moral because they are afraid of being a failure as a gadabout. They are true to their wives, or at least they remain unisexual or asexual, because they are afraid of not being able to compete with other men any more for a woman.'

Greenson's absence was another step in the process of Marilyn's destabilisation that his overbearing presence had set in train two years ago. Words like 'transport', 'rapture', 'exile' made her see that her distracted love of him was reducing her to a stray, a displaced person, like the woman in the painting in his Santa Monica office or the little girl she once was, whom Grace McKee had driven across town in her black 1940 American Bantam Hollywood. McKee hadn't told her where she was taking her until suddenly on El Centro Boulevard she saw a three-storey building. On the red-brick façade, she read 'LOS ANGELES ORPHANS HOME'.

To fall out of love is also to fall out of yourself, out of language. If you have been abandoned as a child, the ensuing vertigo, the sense of being pulled out of time, draws you back into the chaos of childhood. So Marilyn felt herself being reunited with the lonely child she once was, the child who wants to die.

Los Angeles, Hollywood Sign
June 1962

When was it? Late one night, Marilyn phoned André de Dienes and told him she couldn't sleep. She told him to come and take pictures of her, in a dark alley maybe; she said she'd pose sad and lonely. He threw his equipment into his car, and set out into the night. He lit her with the headlights, and took a series of pictures fraught with melodrama. He wondered if she was just acting, whatever that meant. Was she conscious that something tragic was going to happen? She'd grabbed life so firmly, she'd flung her arms round it so passionately, that she couldn't help embracing death in the process. Passion is a love unto death. Joined by passion, Greenson and Marilyn hadn't made love, so now all that was left to them was to make death, together or apart.

The following evening, as the pink haze in the LA sky deepened to crimson, Marilyn phoned Joan Greenson and said she wanted to go out for a drive – did she want to come? Joan picked her up in her convertible. Marilyn had on a maroon turtleneck and beige linen trousers and gave directions, her hair blowing in the wind, as Joan drove. At a set of lights a truck driver pulled up alongside them and asked her if she wanted to go out on a date. When she didn't answer, he yelled, 'Who do you think you are, for fuck's sake – Marilyn Monroe?'

Leaving Santa Monica Boulevard, they headed north up La Brea Avenue. Overhead, planes began their descent to LAX, like cumbersome birds returning to roost in the vast city, their landing lights flashing, the visceral backthrust of their jet engines merging with the steady roar of the evening traffic. They crossed Sunset by the Chinese Theater and headed up by Cahuenga, past the Hollywood Reservoir on the edge of the Hills. When they emerged from the maze of curving little streets that led to Griffith Park, Joan realised Marilyn was taking them to the Hollywood Sign. Soon she saw it rising hundreds of feet into the air like a giant subtitle on a shot of a steep, wooded hillside. 'HOLLYWOOD'. Nine letters, fifty feet high, thirty wide. They got out at its base. The night sky was matt blue and, in front of them, stretching as far as the sea, millions of points of light wavered like galaxies in the sky.

'Look at it pulsing in the night, like something out of the movies,' Marilyn said, gesturing at the city. 'Tormented souls wandering in the city of angels, suspended somewhere between Hell and Purgatory.'

Warning signs indicated a sheer drop that fell away within feet of where they were standing. From time to time a car passed, manoeuvring cautiously on the reddish sandy road. Joan said she felt scared.

'Don't worry,' Marilyn reassured her. 'You get some weird characters here, even coyotes sometimes, but nothing's ever happened when I've come here, except maybe I've thought of throwing myself into the pit. Romantic, eh? "MARILYN MONROE FOUND WITH HER SKULL SHATTERED AT

CITY LANDMARK. The Hollywood Sign, an advertising gimmick put up fifty years ago by the real-estate company Hollywoodland, was yesterday the site of a tragedy. Since the last four letters spelling 'land' fell down, the sign has become an icon for the movie industry and the city's three million inhabitants." Oh, except you can't get near it now. It used to be a favourite place for suicides, but now you've got to climb a tall fence if you want to end it all off this town's name.'

Los Angeles, Pinyon Canyon
Autumn 1970

In 1950 Joseph Mankiewicz had given Marilyn one of her first
major parts in *All About Eve*. He was known in Hollywood as
the analysts' filmmaker and the filmmakers' analyst. A trans-
planted easterner and son of European emigrants, like Greenson,
although German-Jewish rather than Russian-Jewish in his case,
he had had a similarly cultivated New York upbringing and
thought of California as a sort of exile, a 'cultural desert'. He
spent most of his time with the German-Jewish artists and
intellectuals who had fled Nazism. Hollywood was a city of
ivory towers and obscene wealth, as far as he was concerned,
a waste of sand and stupidity. He never got used to the abrupt
way night fell, the lack of transition, the way actions and objects
took precedence over thought and fantasy. Freud was the main
link between him and Greenson – virtually all Mankiewicz's
films have a silently reproachful portrait or statue lurking in
the shadows, undercutting the hero's life and achievements, and
in real life he had a portrait of Freud in his house to remind
him of humanity's irreparable flaws. He had turned to the

movie business after giving up his psychiatry studies as a young student.

Mankiewicz thought of cinema as an essentially verbal art. His motto was 'Pictures will talk'. He didn't like exteriors or films that revolved around actors' performances. He divided directors into two categories: the ones who manipulated images and the ones who manipulated meaning. He considered himself the latter, someone who turns to images only after conceiving of a film in terms of dialogue, and searches for truth through words rather than under an actor's skin. Despite his intensely intimate engagement with images in all his films, he had no time for spectacle. 'There's nothing to see in a film, any more than there is in a person,' he was fond of saying.

Psychoanalysis overtly inspired his directing technique. To prepare his actors, he'd encourage them to confide in him for months prior to filming, to talk about their childhood and relive their memories in order to break down their inhibitions. Just after the war, he saw the same analyst as Ralph Greenson, Otto Fenichel, one of the original Freudians, who died prematurely at the age of forty-eight in 1946. Years later, long after the summer of 1962, he rang Greenson and asked if they could meet. They had run into each other a few times at parties in the interim but they weren't close, or ever likely to be. He said that after the death of 'the sad blonde', as he called her, he needed to talk to the person who had treated her so he could find out 'everything about Marilyn'. He hadn't felt up to calling him immediately after her death, but now he felt that enough time had passed. They met in an anonymous diner on Sunset Boulevard.

'The situation was a simple one: Eve Harrington was about to turn into Margot Channing,' Greenson began, referring to the characters in *All About Eve*.

'That's not it,' replied the director. 'Marilyn wasn't the ambitious starlet devouring everything in her path, or the egocentric star who won't quit the stage. She was always Miss Caswell, the naïve beginner who understands the rules of the game, but refuses to checkmate anyone. When I chose her for the part, she was the loneliest person I had ever met. We filmed the exteriors in San Francisco, and for three weeks, or however long it was, we'd see her go off every day to eat on her own in a diner or somewhere. We always asked her to join us, and she'd always be happy to, but she never understood that we thought of her as one of us. She wasn't a solitary type, she was just profoundly alone.'

'Actors are always alone,' Greenson said. 'I've analysed my fair share so I think I have a working knowledge of the subject. They have a mass of parts and characters and ghosts in their heads, but on the outside they're completely alone. They need a script and a director to give meaning and shape to their inner worlds.'

'Yes, but Marilyn was very different from those actors who want to think aloud with their lines, who want to *express* themselves when all they need to do is make us hear the words that have been put in their mouth. I've never understood that strange process whereby a body and a voice, which is what an actor is, suddenly thinks it's a mind. For God's sake, when will the pianos realise they haven't written the concerto? Why does an actress suddenly think she's speaking *her* words, expressing *her* thoughts? Anyway, Marilyn never fell into that trap. She knew instinctively that wasn't right, and all her years of religious instruction in Strasberg's Method couldn't change that.'

Mankiewicz was starting to sound bitter, almost malicious. Clearly he needed to speak about the dead woman, even more than Greenson, who maintained a distracted, almost bored, silence.

'I'll tell you something,' Mankiewicz went on. 'When she projected an image of herself, she was trying to lose herself in it, to shrug off her real self like a piece of clothing in the hands of someone chasing her, like one of those heroines in the schlocky thrillers that were all the rage when I was starting out. She was constantly exposing her *self*, not just her body, to the public – to you, to me – in some terrible, deadly game. When I see her image on screen, it always seems like an over-exposed photograph, the light pouring off her face so you almost can't see it. Her Medusa face – it was a screen for us to project our desires on, but never to see behind, only we never realised that.'

'By the end, you know, she was more than just the sexual icon for which she was famous,' Greenson stated. 'To a certain degree – thanks to me, I think it's fair to say – she had learned how to start speaking for herself.'

'Right. How many sessions did it take you to discover that for Marilyn? I'll tell you a story. When we were filming *All About Eve*, I bumped into her one day in the Pickwick bookshop in Beverly Hills. She was often in there, leafing through the books and buying a few, although she'd hardly ever finish them. She read with the unmethodical voracity of anyone who's grown up in a house without books, who is ashamed at the vastness of what they'll never know. Anyway, next day on set, I saw she was reading Rilke. I complimented her on her choice and asked what drew her to him. "The terror," she said. "Rilke says beauty is nothing but the beginning of terror. I don't know if I really understand that, but I like the idea." A few days later, she gave me a book of Rilke's poetry. She loved giving presents, like someone who's never been given many. When I remember the strange, frozen look she sometimes had in her eyes, its denial of even the possibility of desire, I think of it as a reflection of terror.'

What a blowhard, Greenson thought. All his endless digressions! It's like one of his movies, a digression within a digression.

'As you may have suspected,' Mankiewicz suddenly said, 'I didn't really come here to speak to you about Marilyn. What interests me, as far as you two are concerned, is the power, the money, the recognition – what was the deal with them? Human relations always have their share of manipulation. We manipulate others and, in the end, we manipulate ourselves, like inveterate gamblers who play to lose, who want their own destruction. I'm fascinated by this drive in women. I wish there were more parts for actresses in general. You play with women, Dr Greenson, the way other people play backgammon or poker, and yet you think of yourself as a chess player.'

The analyst said nothing.

Mankiewicz got up abruptly and left the diner, as if he were breaking off with a lover who would never understand him. He decided to go for a walk before driving home. That evening, Los Angeles seemed to reveal itself for what it was more clearly than it had ever done before. The streets and avenues were lined with buildings in every conceivable architectural style – Mexican farms, Polynesian huts, Côte d'Azur villas, Egyptian or Japanese temples, Swiss chalets, Elizabethan thatched cottages – like something out of a giant prop house or bric-à-brac store. With its semblances of thoroughfares, its mocked-up houses, LA was a film set gesturing at a city. He could almost hear the director calling out 'Action' in a tired voice, as people passed each other, like actors between takes. It wasn't fake, because it wasn't even notionally concerned with the truth. All it was was a plausible backdrop for a scene in a movie set in Hollywood. A crime film, most likely. Flashing lights, cars with 'LAPD' on their panels, the camera zooming in on a low building halfway up a hillside and stopping on the word 'MOTEL', with one letter missing, picked out in scarlet neon against the blue night.

Mankiewicz thought of a line from *Suddenly Last Summer*: 'the moment death takes over the movie'. He had experienced that in August 1962, when death took over the film Marilyn starred in. Reaching the end of Vine Street he started to climb Pinyon Canyon, and dark silhouettes of palm trees began to materialise in the pale light, their sparse high branches gradually fading from mauve to black. They ran like a garland along the low hills, almost grotesquely beautiful. Even nature imitates the neon of a diner here, Mankiewicz thought. This town is just a mask the desert's invented for itself. I don't like exteriors. I'm not going to make movies any more.

Bel Air
Late June 1962

While he was working for *Vogue*, Bert Stern spent two nights at the Bel Air Hotel taking pictures of Marilyn. She was staying in a secluded bungalow, number ninety-six. Discarded liquor bottles, empty film cartons and pairs of shoes littered the bedroom floor, as his strobe lights flashed and an Everly Brothers record played in the background. On the second night they went on past midnight. Marilyn had been posing naked in bed for hours, drinking Dom Pérignon spiked with one-hundred-proof vodka. At one point she pulled back the sheet to show Stern her breasts and said, 'What do you reckon? Not bad for thirty-six.' He shot her leaning over the bed looking for a champagne bottle on the floor. It seemed unreal, a dream come true for someone like him, who, from the age of thirteen, had fantasised about finding a woman like this, who would do anything he desired.

Finally, she lay still under the sheets utterly passive and vulnerable. He sat down beside her. Her eyes were shut but her breathing was reassuringly regular. He kissed her and, despite hearing a vague 'No', slid his hand under the sheet and touched her. She didn't resist. He told himself she wanted to make love. But at the last moment he stopped. She opened her eyes a little. 'Where have you been so long?' she asked dreamily, then fell asleep. Stern was sure she wasn't talking to him.

Bert Stern's photos were published under the title 'Marilyn Monroe: The Complete Last Sitting'. He had brought ribbons, necklaces, veils, scarves and champagne glasses to the shoot, all manner of props to catch and reflect the light, but he was thrilled when Marilyn took far more of the initiative than he'd hoped, and acted as his partner rather than simply as an object for him to photograph. After the first two hours, which he spent suggesting shots from the catalogue of images in his head, she chose the scenarios she wanted and acted them out without words. From then on, they didn't talk; he, or rather they, took shots of *Marilyn*. Stern had photographed countless women, but she was exceptional. She entered into the process so completely that all he had to do was capture her on film.

He took 2,571 pictures, mainly nudes, some of them, the most beautiful, in black and white. All of them contain a secret, something masked that no one will ever uncover. The truth is never naked; it never emerges fully into the light. We see Marilyn draped in brightly coloured scarves with a corner between her teeth; in black woollen shawls and trashy necklaces; in evening dresses and chinchilla fur stoles with her hair up in a chignon; almost unrecognisable in a black wig, her arms dangling like those of a dazed child – and in every shot, she challenges the camera with an oblique, reserved look that seems to come from below or far away. Here I am, it says. It's me at last. Can you handle it? The most moving shots show her holding a towel over her left breast and rubbing it against her cheek, her head bent, like a child nuzzling its blanket. Her stomach is bare, revealing a big horizontal scar just above her hip. The photos are in black and white, and you can almost hear her singing 'That Old Black Magic', her song in *Bus Stop*, in her head.

She had copied out a sentence from Freud's *Civilisation and Its Discontents* in her diary: 'We are never so defenceless against suffering as when we love, never so helplessly unhappy as when we lose our loved object or its love.' In the margin she had added, 'Loving someone means giving them the power to kill you.'

'Sometimes,' Stern wrote later, 'when something is perfect in every last detail, it's not beautiful any more. It's overwhelming, terrifying. To get over this fear, we think no one could be this perfect, but Marilyn made you want her because of her imperfections and fragility, the sudden changes in her body and face from moment to moment and in different lighting. Her lips aren't perfect . . . so? That's what makes you want to kiss them.'

Santa Monica Beach
29 June–1 July 1962

Barris's *Cosmopolitan* photographs show no mottling of Marilyn's skin; neither do Bert Stern's for *Vogue* taken a week earlier. She had told Barris, 'I don't care about age. I like the view from up here. I can see the future opening up and it's mine as much as any woman's.' But when she sat in Stern's red Thunderbird outside Schwab's Drugstore and went over his photographs from the Bel Air Hotel, she took out a hairpin and scratched out every colour transparency that struck her as 'too Marilyn'. 'I was drunk and naked,' she told Greenson afterwards. 'But that's not what I minded. It was the schmaltzy music I could hear when I looked at them.'

Marilyn had a month to live. Greenson had no real idea what to do. He continued to confide in Anna Freud, who wrote to him on 2 July: 'Dear colleague and friend, I saw your patient has been remiss, late on set and even absent. I am surprised by what is happening to both of you. From what I understand from

Marianne Kris, she must have many good qualities but she is clearly far from being an ideal analytic patient.'

Marilyn talked to Joan Greenson a lot on the phone over the next few days, always seeming distracted. Joan was twenty-one, but Marilyn treated her as her little sister. She didn't want her to see naked photographs of her; she never talked about the men she slept with. 'She always presented herself to me as a virginal creature,' Joan said. But, in early 1962, Marilyn started mentioning the new man in her life. She didn't want to use his name, calling him 'the general' instead, which Joan supposed was a cover for John Kennedy. But when *Life* magazine published a profile of Attorney General Robert Kennedy and revealed that his colleagues in the Justice Department addressed him as 'the general', the penny dropped.

On 19 July, Marilyn invited Daniel and Joan over to celebrate Joan's birthday and thank them for being there for her while their father was away. In high spirits, she told Joan, 'You know, I could string together my life story out of the titles of songs I've sung in films. "Every Baby Needs A Da-Da-Daddy"; "Kiss"; "When Love Goes Wrong"; "Diamonds Are A Girl's Best Friend"; "Bye Bye Baby"; "After You Get What You Want, You Don't Want It"; "Heat Wave"; "Lazy"; "River Of No Return"; "I'm Gonna File My Claim"; "That Old Black Magic"; "I'm Through With Love"; "I Wanna Be Loved By You"; "Running Wild"; My Heart Belongs To Daddy"; "Incurably Romantic" . . . I don't sing in the movies any more, though, or at home. Why is that?'

Joan wondered whether 'Happy Birthday' counted.

The following day, Marilyn was admitted into the Cedars of Lebanon Hospital for a gynaecological operation. People speculated whether it was an abortion or a miscarriage. She gave her name at Reception as Zelda Zonk.

Santa Monica, Franklin Street
25 July 1962

The day Darryl Zanuck became president of Fox, Greenson saw Marilyn twice, first at his office and then at her house. Engelberg had already given her an injection of sedatives, and Greenson prescribed Nembutal on top of that. He had seen her every day since he'd got back from Europe. She phoned him constantly, sometimes at two or three or four in the morning, as well as regularly calling Bobby Kennedy.

Since he had started seeing her again, Greenson had felt Marilyn was getting better, even if she talked constantly about separation, absence and loneliness. His diagnosis might partly have been motivated by guilt, because he felt responsible for her being sacked by Fox while he was away. He might also have been trying to reassure himself that it would end at some point, that she would recover and free herself from him and he wouldn't be at her mercy seven days a week, twenty-four hours a day, a 'life prisoner', as he put it, of a method of treatment that he thought necessary for her but was gradually proving impossible for him. He realised that her anguish, her obsessive existential sense of waiting, wasn't directed at anyone real such as him, or even a nameless stranger. She was waiting for no one to respond to her waiting.

He sometimes wondered if she was only pretending to be better because she knew how much he wanted her to be better. She was an actress, after all. She could play the happy girl even with her doctor. Anything, just so long as she didn't lose him. At one session she said, 'I don't mind about dying. I know you'll call me afterwards.'

Greenson planned to go to New York the following month. His book was going slowly now Marilyn occupied most of his time and emotions. Anguish seemed to be the only way she could ensure another person would be there. Her distress had a night-marish quality. However much love, tenderness – greatness, even – it might contain, he knew it also had an inexorably destructive side. What if he did not want to be destroyed?

Lake Tahoe, Cal-Neva Lodge
28 and 29 July 1962

In the last thirty-five days of her life, Marilyn saw Greenson twenty-seven times and Engelberg twenty-four. Both gave her a series of sedative injections and 'youth shots', which they refrained from mentioning during the investigation after her death. Richard Meryman, the *Life* journalist who was the last person to interview her at the start of July, described her going into the kitchen at one point, where Engelberg gave her an injection, then returning in an almost electric state of animation.

She didn't go to New York again, but she was often out of town, and spent two weekends at the Cal-Neva Lodge, the casino resort reportedly owned jointly by Frank Sinatra and Sam Giancana, which Paul 'Skinny' D'Amato managed. Sinatra organised the first weekend, officially to celebrate her renegotiated contract with Fox – she planned to resume filming *Something's Got to Give* in the last week of August – with the added suggestion that they talk about a film project of his, which he thought would suit her. According to Ralph Roberts, she wasn't keen to go and only changed her mind when she heard Dean Martin was giving a show at the Lodge's Celebrity Room that weekend. Sinatra flew her up in his private plane, the *Christina*, a lavish affair with fitted carpets, carved wooden skirting boards, bar, piano and luxurious bathrooms with heated toilet seats, no less. She was given Bungalow Fifty-two, one of a group reserved for distinguished guests. Disguised in a black scarf and sunglasses, she spent most of the time in her room, and slept with the phone connected to the switchboard at her ear.

The second time she flew out to the California–Nevada border was the last weekend before her death. People saw her walking around like a ghost, in a kind of daze. She said unspeakable things to D'Amato. The occasion this time wasn't a celebration with friends, but a meeting with a cabal of sinister characters who didn't want her to have anything more to do with the Kennedys and were determined to make sure she kept her mouth shut. One evening, as fog shrouded the banks of Lake Tahoe, Marilyn was seen standing barefoot by the swimming pool, rocking back and forth, staring up at the hills. A few hours later she was found in a drug- and alcohol-induced coma. She was driven to Reno airport slumped in the back seat, like an unstrung marionette, and put on a plane. It was *The Misfits* all over again. She pleaded desperately for the twin-engine plane to land at Santa Monica, but the airport was closed for the night and they had to land at Los Angeles. She screamed that she wanted to go home. When her doctors and Eunice Murray picked her up, she was trembling with fear. She realised what the trip had been all about. 'Things happened that weekend that nobody's ever talked about,' Skinny D'Amato commented laconically afterwards.

A few days later, Sinatra is alleged to have brought photographer Billy Woodfield a roll of film to develop. In the darkroom, Woodfield supposedly exposed photographs of a drugged, unconscious Marilyn being sexually abused while Sinatra and Sam Giancana watched. Dean Martin was the only person to understand that the drugs and alcohol and her little-lost-girl routine were symptoms of a far worse problem. He told a journalist years afterwards that she had never been able to come to terms with the horror she had blundered into, the dark, seamy world of Sam Giancana, Johnny Rosselli and 'those spoilt Kennedy bastards', which lay beyond the land of dreams she shared with the audiences who paid to see her on screen. She had always desperately wanted to return to some sort of fairy-tale land, but in this one, there was no way of getting back. She knew things that no one would believe. Dean had realised she wasn't long for this world. 'If she hadn't kept her mouth shut, she wouldn't have needed drugs to get where she was going.' Marilyn had peered through the veil of her corrupted innocence, and the truth she'd seen had terrified her. But Dean didn't talk. And he wasn't the only one who knew the whole story about Monroe, the Kennedys and Sam Giancana, the grey thread of truth that ran through the glittering lies and fantasies of the city of angels.

One evening years later, when he was very drunk, Dean Martin said, 'Marilyn was only thirty-six when she died, but it was better that way. She didn't have to end up like June Allyson, who's just a voice on the radio these days. She does ads for Kimberly-Clark diapers for old men. She's still alive, if you can call it that.'

Santa Monica, Franklin Street
Late July 1962

'I've got to tell you something,' Marilyn said, as she arrived for her session. 'I read this line in Joseph Conrad that says more about me than any amount of analysis could. "It was written I should be loyal to the nightmare of my choice." It's sad, isn't it? But not all that sad. Beauty's never sad, but it is painful. I don't know why, but I've always associated beauty with cruelty.'

Following a train of thought that seemed to require no overt explanation, she moved on to the women in her life.

'Sometimes my relationships with women have been sexual, Doctor, sure, like with Natasha. But always dark and cruel, in a way. Always cold and distant.'

She fell silent, preferring to watch her memories rather than put them into words. The mould for the women she became close to was set by the first woman to play an important part in her professional life, Natasha Lytess, the drama teacher who took charge of her career in 1950. Like her, they were all intelligent, cultivated and manipulative. Marilyn would ask them what to do and who to be, but they'd never tell her. They preferred to be the invisible hands working the puppet's strings. She remembered a terrible scene in late 1950 at André de Dienes's house in the Hills. She and André were lying side by side on his living-room rug, listening transfixed to a version of *La Bohème*'s 'Mi chiamano Mimi' when the phone rang. 'A furious woman's asking for you,' André said. 'I think it's Natasha. I said I didn't know where you were. She's calling me a liar, screaming she knows you're here with me.' Marilyn began to cry. When André hung up, he told her off for being so stupid. Why had she let Natasha know where she was spending the afternoon? Marilyn rushed off to Natasha's in a state of high anxiety.

'Does this Natasha remind you of anyone?' Greenson asked.

'I don't know. No, wait, I do: you. Don't look like that . . . She reminds me of you because her parents were Russian, like yours. She was Jewish, like you; she was an intellectual, like you; she was about fifteen years older than me, like you; she was a failed actor, like you . . . She had just been fired by Columbia when I met her. It's funny, she taught me a job she couldn't do herself. A bit like analysts: you try to cure people of something you suffer from.'

'Which other women have you slept with?'

'Gone to bed with, Doctor, gone to bed. And slept with some-times without doing anything – that's how it's usually been. Gee, you know, when I was twenty, my mother and I slept in the same bed at my aunt Ana's for a few weeks when she came out of hospital in San Francisco . . . But, yes, I went to bed with Natasha. It always seemed like she had sharp edges. I felt hatred more than desire from her, and I suppose she did from me too, when I think about it. People said I was a lesbian. They love labels, don't they? It makes me laugh. Sex is never wrong if there's some love involved. But far too often people think it's like gymnastics, a mechanical exercise. If it was, they could just put machines in drugstores and people could make love without needing anyone else. That's what I think everyone's trying to make me into sometimes, a sex machine.'

'I was asking about other women. Have they been actresses? Joan Crawford, for instance?'

'Oh, yes, Crawford . . . Once. Only once. There was a cocktail party at her house, we felt good together. We went to Joan's bedroom and jumped on each other. Crawford had a gigantic orgasm and shrieked like a maniac. Next time I saw Crawford she wanted another round. I told her straight out I didn't much enjoy doing it with a woman. After I turned her down, she became spiteful. A year later, I was chosen to present one of the Oscars at the Academy's annual affair. I waited tremblingly for my turn to walk up to the platform and hand over the Oscar in my keeping. I prayed I wouldn't trip and fall and that my voice wouldn't disappear when I had to say my two lines. When my turn came I managed to reach the platform, say my piece, and return to my table without any mishap. Or so I thought until I read Joan Crawford's remarks in the morning papers. I haven't saved the clippings, but I have sort of remembered what she said. She said that Marilyn Monroe's vulgar performance at the Academy affair was a disgrace to all of Hollywood. The vulgarity, she said, consisted of my wearing a dress too tight for me and wriggling my rear when I walked up holding one of the holy Oscars in my hand. Bitch! She didn't think my rear was vulgar when we were in bed together.'

'Let's go back to Natasha. You told me one day she instantly fell in love with you. Since you associate her and me, do you think I've fallen in love with my patient?'

'You know what she told me just after we met? "I want to love you." I said, "You don't need to love me, Natasha. Just get me working." She kept badgering me with her hopeless passion like something out of Chekhov, all silent suffering and stifled tears. Love isn't something people are owed. It's not their due, is it, Doctor?'

'What was happening in your life when you met?'

'I needed someone to model myself on, not a lover. She tried to force her love on me when my aunt Ana died soon after we started working together. But there's always a silver lining when someone has a crush on you, I suppose, especially if you don't reciprocate it. We shared an apartment in the Sherry Netherlands Hotel, and all through the summer of 1949, Natasha introduced me to Proust, Woolf, Dostoyevsky . . . and Freud, *The Interpretation of Dreams*. Well, not all of it, just bits. Afterwards the Chekhov–Freud line, as I call it, was carried on by Michael Chekhov. I owe him everything. He said he was Chekhov's nephew. Everyone in Hollywood remembered him playing the old analyst who supervises Ingrid Bergman in Hitchcock's film . . . When I began lessons with him, I think it was the autumn of 1951, he said something I'll never forget, "You must try to think of your body as a musical instrument that expresses your ideas and your feelings; you must strive for complete harmony between body and psyche." What do you think, Romi? Isn't that what we're trying to do now? He wrote a book after that called *To the Actor: On the Technique of Acting*. It's been my bible, along with Freud. Why don't you write a book called *To the Psychoanalyst: On the Technique of Psychoanalysis*?'

'Let's go on with your relationships with women. Is there any significance in their being brunettes?'

'I don't know. Maybe when I'm with them, I can see what I'm not or what I used to be or what I might have been. The reason I dye my hair every two days is not just for my roles, you know, it's also so I'll never have to be the woman with reddish-brown hair I used to be again.'

'I sense a fear of homosexuality and, at the same time, a tendency to seek out situations where you will encounter it.'

'What would I know? When I started reading books about psychoanalysis and sexuality, I'd read words like "frigid", "rejected", "lesbian", and think I was every one of them. Some days I don't feel I'm anything and other days I wish I was dead. Then there's that other sad part I have to play: the beautiful woman.'

Just before Natasha Lytess died, she spoke about Marilyn: 'She was most definitely not a child. A child is naïve and open and trusting. But Marilyn was shrewd. I wish I had one-tenth of her ability for business, of her clever knack of promoting what was right for her and discarding what was not. My life and emotional well-being were in her hands entirely. I was the older one, the teacher, but she knew how deeply I felt, and she took advantage of it as only a young person and a beautiful person can. She said she always needed the other person more than they needed her. In fact it was the opposite.'

Santa Monica, Franklin Street
Early August 1962

One evening around eight o'clock, when Greenson was saying goodbye to his lost soul at the end of her session, she gave him a large envelope, saying, 'This is for you. Tell me what you think.' With a graceful gesture, she dropped it on the table by the couch as if she was shrugging off a piece of clothing. The envelope contained two tape recordings of her talking. 'I can't loosen up with you, Doctor,' she said. 'I need somewhere more private where I can be alone with myself. But I'm talking to you, even though you're not there – more than ever, in fact. These are the most private, most secret thoughts of Marilyn Monroe.'

The only record of these tapes is the transcript John Miner claimed to have made a week after she gave them to Greenson, which was published in the *Los Angeles Times* in August 2005.

*   *   *

REWIND
Ralph Greenson replays the tape Marilyn left for him at her last session. 'I have put my soul in you. Does that frighten you?' her voice says, in a whisper.

What can I give you? Not money. I know that from me that means nothing to you. Not my body. I know your professional ethics and faithfulness to your wonderful wife make that impossible. You know what Nunnally Johnson said? 'For Marilyn, sex is the simplest way to say thank you.' How I can say thank you to you, since my money isn't good with you? You have given me everything. Thanks to you, I am different, with myself and other people. Because of you I can now feel what I never felt before. So now I am a whole woman (pun intended – like Shakespeare). So now I have control – control of myself – control of my life. What I am going to give you is my idea that will revolutionise psychoanalysis.

Isn't it true that the key to analysis is free association? Marilyn Monroe associates. You, my doctor, by understanding and interpretation of what goes on in my mind, get to my unconscious, which makes it possible for you to treat my neuroses and for me to overcome them. But when you tell me to relax and say whatever I am thinking, I blank out and have nothing to say; that's what you and Dr Freud call resistance. So we talk about other things and I answer your questions as best I can. You are the only person in the world I have never told a lie to and never will.

Oh, yes, dreams. I know they are important. But you want me to free-associate about the dream elements. I have the same blanking out. More resistance for you and Dr Freud to complain about. I read his 'Introductory Lectures'. God, what a genius. He makes it so understandable. And he is so right. Didn't he say himself that Shakespeare and Dostoyevsky had a better understanding of psychology than all the scientists put together? Damn it's right, they do. Billy Wilder had me say in *Some Like It Hot*, 'I am no Professor Freud!' You remember, the scene where Tony Curtis was pretending that he had a block about sex and couldn't feel anything when I kissed him. He said he'd tried everything; he'd spent six months in Vienna with Professor Freud, flat on his back, but nothing doing. I kissed him three times, saying, 'I may not be Dr Freud, but could I take another crack at it?' Psychoanalysis is a fine thing, but love, the love you make with your mouth and hands and body, isn't a bad way of escaping death and the deep freeze either. Billy understood that.

You told me to read Molly Bloom's mental meanderings (I can use words, can't I?) to get a feeling for free association. It was when I did that that I got my great idea. As I read it something bothered me. Here is Joyce writing what a woman thinks to herself. Can he, does he really know her innermost thoughts? But after I read the whole book, I could better understand that Joyce is an artist who could penetrate the souls of people, male or female. It really doesn't matter that Joyce doesn't have breasts or other feminine attributes or never felt a menstrual cramp. Wait a minute. As you must have guessed, I am free-associating and you are going to hear a lot of bad language. Because of my respect for you, I've never been able to say the words I'm really thinking when we are in session. But now I am going to say whatever I think, no matter what it is. I can do that because of my idea, which, if you'll be patient, I'll tell you about. That's funny. I ask you to be patient, but I am your patient. Yet to be patient and to be a patient makes a kind of

Shakespearean sense, doesn't it? Back to Joyce. To me Leopold Bloom is a central character. He is the despised Irish Jew, married to an Irish Catholic woman . . . What is a Jew? . . . I couldn't tell if you're Jewish by looking at you. Same with women, you can't pick them from the outside. Is there even a woman inside a woman's body? . . . OK, my idea! To start with there is the doctor and the patient. I don't like the word, analysand. It makes it seem like treating a sick mind is different from treating a sick body. However, you and Dr Freud say the mind is part of the body. . . . Anyway, you are in his office and the doctor says, 'I want you to say whatever you are thinking, no matter what it is.' And you can't think of a damn thing. How many times after a session I would go home and cry because I thought it was my fault. While reading Molly's blathering, the IDEA came to me. Get a tape recorder. Put a tape in. Turn it on. Say whatever you are thinking like I am doing now. It's really easy. I'm lying on my bed wearing only a brassière. If I want to go to the refrig or the bathroom, push the stop button and begin again when I want to.

And I just free-associate. No problem. You get the idea, don't you? Patient can't do it in Doctor's office. Patient is at home with tape recorder. Patient free-associates sans difficulty. Patient sends tape to Doctor. After he listens to it, patient comes in for a session. He asks her questions about it, interprets it. Oh, yes, she can put her dreams on the tape too – right when she has them. You know how I would forget what I dreamed or even if I dreamed at all.

Dr Freud said dreams are the *via regia* to the unconscious and so I'll tell you my dreams on tape.

OK, Dr Greenson. You are the greatest psychiatrist in the world. You tell me. Has Marilyn Monroe invented an important way to make psychoanalysis work better? After you listen to my tapes and use them to treat me, you could publish a paper in a scientific journal. Wouldn't that be sensational? I don't want any credit. I don't want to be identified in your paper. It's my present to you. I'll never tell anybody about it. You will be the first to let your profession know how to lick resistance. Maybe you could patent the idea and license it to your colleagues. Ask Mickey. . . .

What I told you is true when I first became your patient. I had never had an orgasm. I well remember you said an orgasm happens in the mind, not the genitals.

It doesn't bother me, but this damn free association could drive somebody crazy. Oh, oh, crazy makes me think about my mother. I am not going to free-associate about her right now. Let me finish my thoughts about orgasms. You also said that a person in a coma or a paraplegic could not have an orgasm because genital stimulation did not reach the brain and that the contrary was possible, an orgasm could occur in the brain without any stimulation of the genitals. You said there was an obstacle in my mind that prevented me from having an orgasm; that it was something that happened early in my life about which I felt so guilty that I did not deserve to have the greatest pleasure there is; that it had to do with something sexual that was very wrong, but my getting pleasure from it caused my guilt. You said that when I did exactly what you told me to do I would have an orgasm, and that after I did it to myself and felt what it was, I would have orgasms with lovers. What a difference a word makes. You said I would, not I could.

Bless you, Doctor. What you say is gospel to me. What wasted years. Incidentally, if men weren't such idiots, and if there was an Oscar for best faker, I would have got it every year . . .

How can I describe to you, a man, what an orgasm feels like to a woman? I'll try. Think of a light fixture with a rheostat control. As you slowly turn it on, the bulb begins to get bright, then brighter and brighter and finally in a blinding flash is fully lit. As you turn it off it gradually becomes dimmer and at last goes out.

. . . I'll need you to keep me together for a year or more. I'll pay you to be your only patient.

Oh, I made you another present. I have thrown all my . . . pills in the toilet. Goodnight, Doctor.

Five years later Greenson published *The Technique and Practice of Psychoanalysis*. In the chapter entitled 'What Psychoanalysis Requires of the Psychoanalyst', he writes, 'It is often necessary to probe into the intimate details of the patient's sexual life or toilet habits, and many patients feel this to be very embarrassing . . . I point out the patient's sexual or hostile feelings to me straightforwardly; if he seems unduly upset by my intervention, however, I will try to indicate by my tone or in words that I am aware and have compassion for his predicament. I do not baby the patient, but I try to ascertain how much pain he can bear and still work productively.'

Hollywood, Sunset Boulevard
August 1962

The costume designer Billy Travilla had worked with Marilyn for years and dressed her for some of her best roles. They'd had a brief affair and she'd inscribed a copy of her nude calendar for him, 'Billy Dear, Please Dress Me Forever. I love you, Marilyn'. One evening, he was surprised to see her at La Scala restaurant on Sunset Boulevard, at a table with Pat Newcomb and Peter Lawford. He said hi but she turned away without replying. She was drunk, her eyes blank.

'Hey,' he said again. 'Marilyn, are you OK?'

'Who are you?' she said.

He knew, as he walked away, that she hadn't said it because she was embarrassed by the company she was keeping, but because, her voice thick, her hair in her eyes, she was asking herself the same question. He decided to write her a note but, as it turned out, he could have spared himself the effort. She died the following night.

* * *

At the start of August, Marilyn's last game with her psychoanalyst was playing itself out. The other candidates for the role of saviour had abdicated their posts. Strasberg was tired of her demands, Miller had remarried and was about to become a father, and DiMaggio desperately wanted them to get back together but was too eaten up by jealousy to be able to give her what she wanted. That left only Greenson, or Romi, as she sometimes now called him. On 3 August, she went to his house for an hour-and-a-half-long session on the couch. The date made her cry. She remembered the Doctor's Hospital on East End Avenue in New York, on 3 August five years earlier, where she had lost a child to a late abortion after an extra-uterine pregnancy. She thought about New York constantly. The torrid heat and humidity of that Friday echoed and intensified her anguish. She wanted to tear something – a veil, a skin, the chain of events that divided her from herself.

She had been telling Whitey Snyder and W. J. Weatherby for some time now that she wanted to leave Romi. What choice did she have? She'd never find herself otherwise. She'd be stuck without a husband, without friends, dependent on a man she could no longer think of as her saviour. On the afternoon of 3 August, Engelberg gave her an injection, and a prescription for Nembutal that doubled the dose Lee Siegel had prescribed her in the morning. She sent Eunice Murray out to the nearest drug-store on San Vicente Boulevard to get it. In the evening, despite a second session with Greenson at her home, and another injection just before he left, her distress grew more and more acute by the hour. She rang her old friend Norman Rosten and talked for half an hour, throwing a line out across time and space, as though she wanted to steep herself in a familiar voice, to lessen or mask the emptiness she felt. As soon as he heard the hard, strained note in her voice from the drugs, Rosten remembered what she'd said to him once at a party in Brooklyn Heights. She had been wearing a dress like the one at JFK's birthday gala, the material clinging to her like liquid, and sat on a windowsill, drinking and looking morosely down at the street below. He recognised her expression, although the cause of it was as unfathomable as ever, the sense she was unreachable, lost in some intimate daydream, prey to hard, black thoughts. After a long time, he went over and said, 'Hey, psst, come back!'

'I'm going to have trouble sleeping tonight,' she said. 'It happens now and then . . . It's a quick way down from here. Who'd know the difference if I went?'

Rosten, without knowing why, remembered a line of Rilke: 'Who, if I cried out, would hear me among the angels' hierarchies?' After a silence, he answered, 'I would, and all the people in the room who care. They'd hear the crash.'

She laughed. Then, giggling like children, they had made a pact. If either was about to jump or turn on the gas, he or she would call the other to be talked out of it. They joked about it in the way you can only when you're serious, and Rosten had had a presentiment that the phone would ring one day. He'd pick it up and hear her say, 'It's me. I'm on the window ledge.'

Santa Monica, Franklin Street
3 *August* 1962

That evening, after seeing off Marilyn, who was on her way to
La Scala, Ralph Greenson shut himself into his office, without
having had anything to eat, and released the pause button on
his tape recorder. 'I have to talk about Grace again, I can't see
any way round it,' Marilyn's voice murmured, above the tape
hiss.

> Grace McKee – that's what she was called when she and
> my mother met, which must have been two or three years
> before I was born. They were both working in the movies,
> so they shared a small two-bed apartment on Hyperion
> Avenue in what's now called Silver Lake, a run-down part
> of town not far from the studios. Grace had got my
> mother . . . it is awful the way my throat tightens up
> when I try to say 'mother' . . . my *mother* to dye her hair
> red. She was an archivist and my mother was a film-
> cutter. They were what used to be called 'good-time girls'.
> All they cared about was going out and drinking. They

had moved to different places by the time I was born, but they still cruised the bars together, and maybe they slept together, what do I know? I didn't live with my mother, she put me with the Bollenders when I was still very little. I've told you about that already, haven't I?: the poor orphan girl looking out the window at the glowing RKO Studios sign, imagining her mother inside, ruining her eyes peering at the stars' faces . . . On Sundays, hand in hand like teenage girls, they'd take me to Hollywood's picture palaces: huge, lavish Pantages Theater on the corner of Vine Street and Hollywood Boulevard, Grauman's Egyptian Theater, also on Hollywood Boulevard . . . That's where they had the première of *Asphalt Jungle*, my first real film. I couldn't go. I was sick. Oh, God, I was so sick! . . . The Chinese Theater a bit further west. When they didn't know what to do with me during the week, they'd send me with my ticket money to sit in those dark auditoria and stare up at the light and the faces they pored over all day at their editing tables. I loved being a little girl in the front row all alone in front of the big screen.

When I was nine years old – my mother had brought me to live with her about a year earlier – they got in a terrible fight. My mother attacked Grace with a knife. The police were called and Grace had my mother put in a psychiatric hospital. Grace became my legal guardian. I didn't live with her straight away, I was put in two more foster homes, but she came and got me in the end. She took me to the studios and the movies the whole time. She always said I'd be a star when I grew up.

One day, she drove me to an orphanage. I was getting on for ten. She had got married and she didn't have room for me in her place in Van Nuys. She paid for my board, and on Saturdays, she'd take me to lunch, then a movie. Sometimes she'd play dress-ups with me, and we'd go to a beauty parlour on Odessa Avenue. That's how I know so much about make-up. Grace thought Jean Harlow was the best. She used to tell me my middle name was because of her, but I knew it was spelled Jeane not Jean. But even so, Harlow was my idol as well. Grace dressed me all in white like her and powdered my face and gave me red lipstick. I was nearly a platinum blonde then, but I was only ten. It would have been odd, a little girl looking like a *femme fatale*. So I waited until I was twenty before changing my hair colour and my name. A week after my eleventh birthday, Grace took me out of the orphanage. But a few months later, when she realised her husband Doc – I'm sorry, that's what they called him – had abused me, she sent me to another 'mother', Ana Lower. She had a heart problem and neglected me, but I was very fond of her. For five years, I went back and forth between the two of them, totally confused, always having to do a double-take at school before I said who my mother was and where I lived. At Christmas – I think I was thirteen – Grace gave me my first portable gramophone, a Victrola. The wind-up spring was so stiff that the pitch would be off by the end of the record, but I loved listening to my favourite singers in the dark.

One day, Grace and her husband left California and she married me to the neighbours' son, James Dougherty. I was sixteen years old and I didn't want to go back to the orphanage. You asked me a long time ago what marriage meant to me. Here's one answer: 'A kind of painful, crazy friendship, with sexual privileges.' There, I've told you the story of my life, if that's the word for it. That will be all for today, as Dr Greenson used to say at the start. Night night, Doc!

Greenson pressed the pause button again. He never found out the rest of Grace's life story because when he resumed listening, after a few laps of the swimming pool, Marilyn had moved on to another subject.

I told you about the traumas I had filming *Don't Bother to Knock* ten years ago. There was something in the script I couldn't do. It was only talking to you that made me understand. I don't know if Baker and his screenwriter did it intentionally, but when Nell said 'I never wore nice dresses of my own at school', and that she'd been put in a mental institution in Oregon, it reminded me of my last visit to my mother. I have to tell you about that, even if it's painful. If you were here, you'd say, 'Especially if it's painful. If saying something doesn't come with a price, then there's no point saying it.'

She was living in Portland, Oregon, in a seedy hotel downtown. I wish I could forget the scene. I hadn't set eyes on my mother for six years. She'd left the San Francisco mental hospital a few months before. She wasn't eating, she wouldn't look at anyone. It was January, a rainy afternoon. I'd gone to see her with André de Dienes – I've already told you about him, my first lover, who I was crazy about when I was twenty. He had fitted out his Buick Roadmaster – he'd taken out the back seat and laid down a mattress, with blankets and lots of pillows, so I could sleep when I wanted on the long drives. I called it the cage. I was his prisoner, and I was happy.

My mother was sitting in the dark in a small, sad room on the top floor. I had brought her presents: perfume, a scarf, sweets and some photographs of me André had taken. She didn't react, just sat in her wicker chair, no 'thank you', no sign of pleasure. Her mouth set, no smile,

302

lipstick smeared over her lips. She didn't touch me. At one point, she put her head into her hands and bent down. I threw myself at her feet.

There was the sound of something like a nervy sob or laugh. Marilyn paused, then resumed in a more earnest tone:

I remember an earlier visit to San Francisco. Grace had taken me to see her. I must have been thirteen, or thereabouts. She didn't move then either. She just said at the end, 'I remember. You had such pretty little feet.' . . .
    If you were here, you'd ask me why I was silent for a moment then. It's because there was something I couldn't say straight away. When my mother looked up – I wish I could forget this – all she said was: 'I'd like to come and live with you, Norma Jeane.' Something in me snapped. I jumped up and said, 'Mom, we've got to go now, I'll see you soon.' I left my address and phone number on the table with the unopened presents and we headed south. I never got to see her again.

After another long silence during which Greenson could only hear the hiss and sigh of the tape, as if Marilyn had pushed the tape recorder away from her, she said,

It got dark after we left Portland and we stopped at somewhere called the Timberline Lodge Hotel, at the foot of Mt Hood, but it was full. We ended up down a narrow, winding road at another place called the Government Lodge. It was full of slot machines – even the johns had them. It was like one of those nightmares when you can't get where you're trying to go. It rained, then started to snow. I was very provocative with André that night, sexually I mean. He was sad, incredibly sad.

All he said to me was 'I didn't even think for a minute of taking pictures of you and your mother. I've never told anyone but my mother died when I was eleven. She threw herself down a well. It all seems a long way away now. I don't even know what country Transylvania is in, these days.'

It snowed all that night in the mountains in Oregon. It carried on the next day and the next night. We didn't leave our room. While I was doing my fingernails and toenails, I held out my hands towards André and showed him how the lines on my palm make a capital M. We compared our palms like kids. He told me that when he was a child in Transylvania, an old bell ringer had predicted that the letters MM would be very important later in his life. 'You know, Norma Jeane, at the time I was reading a strange old book and the man was worried that one page began "*Memento mori*".' I was fascinated and we spent a long time talking about the Ms on our palms. André laughed and said they didn't have anything to do with death. 'The opposite, they mean "Marry Me"!' he said. André also told me about going walking in the forest when he was a child and carving a double M in a tree. It's odd, Doctor, don't you think? That was only a few months before my initials became MM . . . We put our palms together. André took a photo of mine.

That night he made love to me. It felt like he was searching my body, desperately looking for something. I was in tears. He asked me why and I held him tight as if he was my child. I didn't know what to say. We had been travelling and taking pictures for a fortnight but this was the first time we made love. People use sex to win love, don't they, or at least to think they're loved or that they exist, or that they've lost themselves without becoming somebody else's, or that they've died but nobody's killed them? I often think I'm making love to the camera nowadays. It doesn't feel as good as with a man, but it doesn't hurt so much either. It's just someone's eyes owning your body.

Brentwood, Fifth Helena Drive
4 *August* 1962

When Arthur Miller opened the copy of *Life* magazine he'd
bought at a kiosk on East 57th Street and saw the photos of
Marilyn emerging naked from the swimming-pool, he couldn't
help thinking her defiant, wilful expression was forced, an attempt
to cover up what he called 'the wound of indignity'. He remembered returning to their Brooklyn apartment three years before
and finding her standing in a daze, without a stitch of clothing,
like a lost bird that had flown in through an open window. She
pushed her hair off her forehead and went to sit on the edge of
the bath, her eyes closed, her head bowed. He watched through
the open door as she slowly came back to herself and to him,
until finally she looked up and gave him a tender smile. She
shouldn't have to do these sorts of things any more, he thought.
There are other ways of getting through to people.

The interview Marilyn gave *Life* after being fired from
Something's Got to Give appeared the day before she died. In
it she comes across as calm, happy, confident. She talks about
going to Grauman's Chinese Theater as a child and putting her

feet in the movie star's footprints on the Walk of Fame outside. Uh-oh, she used to think, my foot's too big! I guess that's out. So it was a remarkable moment when she was memorialised there herself. It brought home to her that 'anything's possible, almost'.

To fans, the Hollywood Walk of Fame stretches down Hollywood Boulevard and Vine Street like a dazzling trail across a starlit sky, a triumphal procession through the history of movie-making. The star with Marilyn's name above the bronze camera is set in the reddish-brown concrete just outside the McDonald's at 6774 Hollywood Boulevard, not far from Grauman's Chinese Theater where she'd spent whole afternoons as a child, on her own or with Grace McKee, losing and finding herself in the darkness.

Just opposite, number 7000, is the Hollywood Roosevelt Hotel, which hosted the first Academy Awards dinner two years after it opened in 1927. Marilyn posed by its swimming pool when she was twenty-five, and often stayed there in the 1950s, in Suite 1200. The contempt her fame excited still came as a surprise back then: 'It stirs up envy, fame does,' she told Greenson. 'People you run into feel that, well, who is she? Who does she think she is, Marilyn Monroe? They feel fame gives them some kind of privilege to walk up to you and say anything to you, you know, of any kind of nature and it won't hurt your feelings. Like it's happening to your clothing. You're always running into people's unconscious.' In December 1985, soon after the Roosevelt's 1920s décor had undergone a dismal 1980s revamp, a woman on the hotel staff called Susan Leonard was cleaning a mirror in the manager's office when she saw a blonde woman in its reflection, coming towards her. She swung round but there was no one behind her. It took a while for the image to vanish. Later it transpired that the mirror used to hang on the wall in Suite 1200. Among other relics of Hollywood's golden age evoked by the hotel's themed rooms, you can now ask to see the 'haunted mirror'. It hangs in the low corridor by the elevators.

Late in the morning of Saturday, 4 August 1962, Agnes Flanagan, one of Marilyn's hairdressers and an old friend, paid an impromptu visit to Fifth Helena Drive. Shortly after she got there, she said that a delivery man appeared with a parcel. The packaging had been torn and clumsily mended with sticky tape. It seemed to have travelled all over the world. A smudged stamp indicated a date in Italian. Only three letters in the sender's details were legible: ROM. Roma? Romi? wondered Marilyn. A message from the past or the future? Love is always an anachronism. The signal reaches you after the source has ceased transmitting. Was the parcel in itself a message? She opened it and then went out to the swimming pool with its contents, a little stuffed tiger. She sat down with her feet in the water, hugging it in silence. Agnes thought she must be terribly depressed, although she didn't say anything. Not knowing what to do, Agnes eventually let herself out. Photographs of Marilyn's garden taken the following day show two stuffed animals by the swimming pool, one of which looks like the tiger.

She didn't mention the strange object to her analyst, who came over in the late afternoon. After asking Pat Newcomb to leave, Greenson talked to his patient for two hours, then suggested she go for a walk by the sea with Eunice. They walked a little way, but Marilyn couldn't keep her footing in the sand, so they came back and she carried on talking to Greenson until seven p.m. The telephone rang repeatedly, but Greenson wouldn't let Marilyn answer. He picked up once and curtly told a dumbfounded Ralph Roberts, 'She's not here,' before hanging up.

The Greensons were going out to dinner that evening, so at seven Greenson had to go home and change. He had only just arrived when Marilyn rang in a state of animation to pass on some good news about Joe DiMaggio's son. She asked him, almost as an aside, if he had taken her bottle of Nembutal. He said he hadn't, startled by the question because he thought she had been cutting down on her use of barbiturates recently. She didn't have any sleeping pills at her disposal as far as he knew, though, so he saw no reason to worry. In fact, Engelberg had prescribed her twenty-five capsules at her request the day before, enough to kill herself. He hadn't thought to tell Greenson.

Left alone, Marilyn stayed on the phone. At half past seven, she spoke to Peter Lawford. He thought she sounded terrible – drugs or alcohol, or both. He tried to warn her analyst but Greenson couldn't be reached, so he called his brother-in-law, Mickey Rudin. From this point on, accounts differ.

According to one version, the analyst and Rudin returned after dinner around midnight because Greenson, already in an edgy mood because he'd given up smoking, was concerned at the condition in which he'd left his patient. When they got there, Greenson went into her bedroom. It was a mess. The wooden bedside table was piled high with plastic pill bottles, none of them containing Nembutal, that jostled for space with a copy of Leo Rosten's novel, *Captain Newman, M.D.* Marilyn was in bed. She mumbled something incoherent and he decided to let her sleep. It didn't occur to him that her mention of Nembutal in her last call might have meant: I've got what I need to kill myself and I may use it. The novel on her bedside table had been placed face down so as not to lose her place. Greenson picked it up and read, 'The psychiatrist, full of compassion, learned that the young man he had cured of his trauma had died in combat. "Our job is to make the well," the doctor remarks, "well enough to go out and get killed."'

On the table there was also a letter she'd started to DiMaggio:

Dear Joe, if I can just make you happy, I will have succeeded in the largest and most difficult thing of all: to make someone completely happy. Your happiness means my happiness, and

Rudin, however, told it differently. He said that Greenson had called him around midnight. The analyst was waiting for him at Fifth Helena Drive and immediately said that Marilyn had died. There is also a third version of events, which says that Greenson neither heard from Marilyn nor saw her alive after their last phone call.

Night falls on the Pacific Coast. The Santa Ana, a hot, dry wind, sweeps through Los Angeles on its way to the ocean, bearing snatches of 'Dancing In The Dark', the Sinatra song Marilyn is playing at her home in Brentwood. Her house has thirty-inch-thick cement walls and wrought-iron bars on every window. The sturdy hand-worked doors and gates are the embodiment of solidity and protection, as the high stucco walls and soaring eucalyptus trees are of privacy. When she'd moved in, she had described her home as a fortress where she could feel safe from the world. But this evening it feels like a prison. She thinks of Fitzgerald's remark about Hollywood, city of 'thin partitions'.

She puts on Sinatra's 'Dancing In The Dark' again. *Dancing in the dark 'til the tune ends.* She remembers a night a few months earlier: they'd made love as if for the last time, hopelessly estranged and yet unable to let go of one another, like survivors of a shipwreck clinging to debris in a lurching sea. *We're dancing in the dark and it soon ends.* It was the first time they'd circled blindly around one another as they made love. *We're waltzing in the wonder of why we're here.* Usually he wanted the lights to be on. She loved the hungry, tender way he looked at her, the fact he could only orgasm if he saw desire in her eyes, the way he'd pull back at the last moment to take in her pellucid beauty. But it couldn't last. Dancers in the dark, their sad waltz had driven them apart and now all they had left was the night. *Time hurries by, we're here and we're gone.* Their time was up. All they had was the moment, the darkness, their sweat, their clutching hands; no image of the other, no words, just the music and their bodies. *Looking for the light of a new love, to brighten up the night.* She thought of Romeo. They'd also danced together in the dark, their bodies infinitely far apart but their hearts joined as if they had finally reached dry land. *And I have you love, and we can face the music together, dancing in the dark.*

On the other side of America, Norman Rosten was startled awake in the early-morning light of his New York apartment. He'd forgotten the cold stone balcony on East 57th Street, but as he heard the phone ringing, part of him sensed this was the call he had been steeling himself for ever since. Superficially, though, his conversation with Marilyn couldn't have been more cheerful and excited.

'Did you see the latest interview in *Life?*' she asked.

'You bet,' he said. 'It was great. Very brave and free. You talked as if you were someone who has nothing to lose.'

'There's always something to lose. But we have to start living, right?'

She talked about her house, which was almost finished. The tiles were in; the furnishings were finally on their way. 'It's Mexican, naturally,' she said, laughing. 'An imitation, of course. I can't wait for you to see the garden. It'll be so beautiful, all new shrubs. By the way, the film may still get made. And I've had offers from all over the world. Yes, some wonderful offers, but I'm not thinking about them yet.'

She barely paused for breath. There was something she was saying in code, a message between the lines he couldn't quite decipher.

'Let's all start to live before we get old,' she said. 'How are you really? How's Hedda? Are you sure everything's all right?

Listen, I have to hang up, got a long-distance call on the line. I'll speak to you on Monday. G'bye.'

Afterwards he thought she'd fooled him. She hadn't said she was on the verge of suicide – perhaps she didn't know yet. He and his wife were among the thirty-one mourners at Marilyn's funeral. The actress had left their daughter Patricia five thousand dollars to pay for her studies. When he got back to New York, he found a poem Marilyn had written for him.

I

I left my home of green rough wood,
A blue velvet couch.
I dream till now
A shiny dark bush
Just left of the door.

Down the walk
Clickity clack
As my doll in her carriage
Went over the cracks –
'We'll go far away.'

II

Don't cry my doll
Don't cry
I hold you and rock you to sleep
Hush hush I'm pretending now
I'm not your mother who died.

Brentwood, Fifth Helena Drive
Night of 4–5 August 1962

If this were *film noir*, it would open with a shot of the wind in
the eucalyptus trees. It has come off the Mojave Desert, travelling
over the salt lake beds strewn with crystals to blow in, soft and
warm, over Beverly Hills, Sunset Boulevard and Santa Monica.
Now it's passing Ventura Boulevard, gliding through Brentwood
on its way out to sea. It's a peaceful Saturday night, no different
from any other Saturday night in this part of LA.

Joan Greenson hears the phone ringing in her parents' bedroom
around three in the morning. Awake now, and feeling a little hungry,
she goes into the kitchen to raid the fridge. 'I asked Mom what
happened,' she recalled afterwards. 'She said there was a problem
over at Marilyn's, and I said "Oh", and went back to bed.'

Shortly before dawn, Sergeant Jack Clemmons is on duty as
watch commander at the police station on Purdue Street. The

phone rings. The caller identifies himself as Dr Hyman Engelberg. 'Marilyn Monroe has died. She's committed suicide.'

Thinking it could be a hoax, Clemmons asks, 'Who did you say this is?'

'I'm Dr Hyman Engelberg, Marilyn Monroe's physician. I'm at her residence. She's committed suicide.'

'I'll be right over.'

If this were *film noir*, a rewrite would put Greenson centre stage:

The screen goes momentarily black; a phone rings.

'West Los Angeles Police Department. Sergeant Clemmons speaking.'

'Marilyn Monroe has died of an overdose.'

'What?'

'Marilyn Monroe has died. She's committed suicide.'

'Who is this?'

'Her psychiatrist, Dr Greenson. This is not a hoax.'

Driving down San Vicente Boulevard, Clemmons radios for a back-up patrol car to meet him at 12305 Fifth Helena Drive. He speeds down the deserted streets to Carmelina Avenue, then turns into the short cul-de-sac. The address is at the end of the street. He goes into the house, enters a bedroom, and sees a body sprawled across a bed. A sheet is pulled up over its head, leaving visible only a shock of platinum-blonde hair. 'She was lying face down in what I call the soldier's position,' Clemmons said afterwards. 'Her face was in a pillow, her legs stretched out perfectly straight.' He immediately thinks she has been placed that way, with one hand close to the telephone and the cord under her body as she lies diagonally across the mattress.

*   *   *

A few weeks earlier in New York, Marilyn had told W. J. Weatherby, 'You know who I've always depended on? Not strangers, not friends – the telephone! That's my best friend . . . I love calling friends, especially late at night when I can't sleep.'

A distinguished-looking figure is sitting despondently by the bed, his head in his hands. He says he was the one who rang the police. Another man standing by the bedside table introduces himself as Dr Ralph Greenson, Marilyn Monroe's psychiatrist. He says she has committed suicide and points to the empty Nembutal bottle on the bedside table. 'She took the whole bottle. When I got here, I could see from many feet away that Marilyn was no longer living. There she was, lying face down on the bed, bare shoulders exposed, and as I got closer I could see the phone clutched fiercely in her right hand. I suppose she was trying to make a phone call before she was overwhelmed. It was just unbelievable, so simple and final and over.'

Sergeant Clemmons finds Dr Greenson's hypothesis odd. Why would she ring someone when Mrs Murray was in the house? Police Officer Robert E. Byron, who arrives on the scene later, notes in his report that Greenson had taken the telephone out of Marilyn's hand, no easy task once rigor mortis had set in. Studying the two doctors, Clemmons also notes that Dr Engelberg seems uncommunicative and that the psychiatrist, who does most of the talking, has a strange, defensive attitude. He seems to be challenging him to accuse him of something. Clemmons says afterwards he kept thinking, 'What the hell's wrong with this fellow? Because his attitude just didn't fit the situation. There was something wrong about the look in his eye.'

'Did you try to revive her?' he asks the psychiatrist.

'No, it was too late – we got here too late,' Greenson replies.

'Do you know when she took the pills?'

'No.'

Clemmons goes to ask Eunice Murray for her version of events.

'I knocked on the door,' Murray says, 'but Marilyn didn't answer, so I called her psychiatrist, Dr Greenson, who lives not far away. When he arrived, he also failed to get a response on knocking on the door, so he went outside and looked through the bedroom window. He saw Marilyn lying motionless on the bed, looking peculiar. He broke the window with a poker and climbed inside and came around and opened the door. He told me "We've lost her", and then he called Dr Engelberg.'

Returning to the bedroom, Sergeant Clemmons asks the doctors why they'd waited four hours before calling the police.

'We had to get permission from the studio publicity department before we could call anyone,' Greenson replies.

'The publicity department?' Clemmons repeats.

'Yes, the 20th Century Fox publicity department. Miss Monroe is making a film there.'

Clemmons subsequently tells several journalists, 'It was the most obvious murder I ever saw.'

If this were a film, a shot of the ambulance containing Marilyn's body under a white sheet would slowly fade out and be replaced by a black screen with 'THREE MONTHS EARLIER' in white letters. Then it would cut to the rushes, a clapperboard saying, 'SOMETHING'S GOT TO GIVE', and underneath, 'MARILYN, LAST TAKE'. The unedited footage that followed would look like images from a dream, almost too real, the lighting and grain possessing a strange, gruelling clarity that a camera wouldn't ordinarily be able to capture. Marilyn had been a tightrope-walker who was oblivious to the drop beneath her feet, but now she knew she could fall. She looked like a ghost. The ghost of the star of *Sunset Boulevard*, a blonde Norma Desmond.

Los Angeles County Coroner's office, the morgue
5 August 1962

Greenson never revealed much about the last time he saw Marilyn. In a phone conversation with the journalist Billy Woodfield, on the evening after the funeral, he said, 'Listen, I can't explain myself without revealing things I do not want to reveal. You can't draw a line and say, "I'll tell you that, but not that . . ." I cannot speak about it, because I cannot tell you the whole story . . . Ask Bobby Kennedy.' He did insist on one thing, though. He said she was asleep in the guest bedroom in the wing of her house rather than her own, as if she didn't feel at home. But he quickly added that she often slept there. When Woodfield asked him about the repeat prescriptions of chloral hydrate and the 'youth shots', Greenson said, 'Everyone makes mistakes. Including me.'

Speaking to Norman Rosten, he said, 'I received a call from Marilyn around four-thirty p.m. She seemed somewhat depressed and on large amounts of medication. I went over. She was furious with a friend who had slept fifteen hours the previous night whereas she'd slept terribly. After I'd spent approximately two hours and half with her, she seemed calmer.' Mickey Rudin remembered hearing the psychoanalyst exclaim on the night of Marilyn's death, 'Goddam it! Hy gave her a prescription I didn't know about!'

Rudin described Greenson as exhausted: 'He'd had enough; he'd spent the day with her. He wanted to at least have a peaceful Saturday evening and night.' Greenson also explained to an investigating officer that she had been extremely upset on the phone at not having a date that evening – the fact that the most beautiful woman in the world was alone. He thought she had died feeling rejected.

We know nothing directly from Greenson about the causes of his patient's death. This was a secret he carried to his grave. Remarks in letters to Marilyn's other analysts or comments he made in conversations, which were revealed thirty or more years later, are the only clue to his reactions. In a letter to Marianne Kris two weeks after Marilyn's death, he wrote, 'On Friday night, she had told the internist that I had said it was all right for her to take some Nembutal, and he had given it to her without checking with me, because he has been upset for his own personal reasons. He had just left his wife. On Saturday, however, I observed that she was somewhat drugged and guessed what drug she must have taken to be in the state.' He mentioned Marilyn's decision to stop therapy with him. 'She wanted to replace it with recordings of her thoughts. I realised I was starting to irritate her. She was often irritated if I was not absolutely and completely in agreement with her . . . She was angry with me. I told Marilyn we'd talk about it again, that she should call me on Sunday morning, and then I left. But that Sunday she was dead.'

The psychoanalyst was questioned at length, first by the police, who called him in two days later to the Justice Department to make a statement, then by the district attorney, who had commissioned a 'psychological autopsy', and finally by a collection of twelve experts called the Suicide Investigation Team. Robert Litman, one of two psychiatrists on this 'suicide team', was a former pupil of his. When he went to question Greenson, he found him terribly upset, and ended up acting more like a grief counsellor than a forensic investigator.

According to John Miner, before Greenson had left to go to the dinner, he had made arrangements for his patient to be given sedatives by enema because she had a physiological resistance to orally ingested medication. The chloral hydrate would help her sleep, and since Engelberg couldn't be reached to give her her usual injection, an enema seemed the most effective and the most familiar way of administering it. Greenson knew she had been having enemas for years because they had talked about it. In *The Technique and Practice of Psychoanalysis* he had even written that an analyst's interventions could be experienced as enemas, as pleasurable or as painfully intrusive.

Who gave her the enema? Greenson was in the habit of delegating the administering of drugs to others, so he might very well have entrusted it to Eunice Murray. Then again, he might never have actually left Fifth Helena that evening and so been present at her final procedure. For many years, he said he'd gone out to dinner with friends at a restaurant, but he never said who they were; neither did anyone come forward to corroborate his testimony. After his death in 1979, his family was never able to identify his dinner companions.

By his own account, Greenson behaved more like a doctor than an analyst in the last days and hours of Marilyn's life. He knew better than anyone that physical contact makes one less inclined to listen. The principle of omnipotence over the body that he would subsequently do his utmost to resist seems to have infected him, a fantasy of a root-and-branch analysis with inevitably fatal overtones. A few months later he would write, in *The Technique and Practice of Psychoanalysis*:

> What is a psychoanalyst? Answer: A Jewish doctor who can't stand the sight of blood! This joke does highlight certain important considerations. Freud addressed himself to the question of what motivates a person to devote himself to the profession of psychoanalysis and, although he personally disavowed them, he did single out two important early sources of the therapeutic attitude: 'My innate sadistic disposition was not a very strong one, so that I had no need to develop this as one of its derivatives. Nor did I ever play "the doctor game"; my infantile curiosity evidently chose other paths (1926b, p. 253)' . . . The urge to get inside the body or mind of another can be motivated by the longing for fusion and closeness as well as by destructive aims . . . The physician may be the sadistic father sexually torturing the victimised mother-patient, he may become the rescuer, or he may identify with the victim. Sometimes one finds that the physician is trying to act out a fantasy in which he does to his patient what he wanted his parent to do to him in childhood; this may be a variety of homosexuality and incest. Treating the sick may also be derived from the 'nursing' mother who alleviates pain by suckling the child . . . The psychoanalyst differs from all other medical therapists in that he has no bodily contact with the patient despite the high degree of verbal intimacy. He resembles the mother of bodily separation in this way rather than the mother of bodily intimacy.

In the years after Marilyn's death, Ralph Greenson offered repeatedly to be questioned by investigators in the hope that, if he were interviewed enough, the criticisms and accusations levelled at him would eventually be laid to rest. It was a vain hope. There are as many versions of what had happened as there were witnesses of wildly dissimilar degrees of plausibility, but the finger was frequently pointed at him. He was alleged to have killed Marilyn either inadvertently – an inappropriate prescription leading to a fatal cocktail of drugs – or intentionally, as part of a conspiracy. Left-wing, Jewish, a psychiatrist, he found himself accused of being a 'psychoanalytic murderer', a 'Zionist conspirator', who had been blackmailing his patient, and a 'Comintern agent', who had been spying on the President of the United States's mistress. Powerful and charming, he was portrayed as anything from a venal, syringe-wielding doctor on the Mafia's payroll to a lover in the throes of insane jealousy. Psychoanalyse the psychoanalyst! That was the name of the game. Even his relationship with his twin sister, Juliet, ostensibly the beloved, supported, deeply admired artist of the Greenschpoon family, became a sea of love–hate, which was then projected onto Marilyn in an act of massive counter-transference.

One witness said that Greenson often told his patients to keep journals between sessions, adding that he had disposed of Marilyn's red diary before the police arrived. Norman Jeffries, the odd-job man hired by Eunice Murray, said he saw Greenson with his own eyes trying to revive the actress with an intracardiac injection of adrenalin. Another account claimed the murder weapon was a six-inch needle driven into Marilyn's heart by a killer wearing latex surgeon's gloves, and who used such force the needle snapped on her sternum. Twenty years after the event, an ambulance driver named James Hall claimed that, when he was called to the scene, he saw Greenson injecting poison into his patient's chest. According to yet another version, one of the assassins sent by the Mafia- and CIA-affiliated Sam Giancana to kill Marilyn in order to compromise Robert Kennedy was nicknamed Needles.

Casting Greenson as an insane psychiatrist with a lethal penchant for injections reduces events to the plot of a B movie. It's also striking how similar it is to the *Los Angeles Times*'s account of Robert Walker's death eleven years earlier. The actor's arm was covered with blood from a struggle with the psychoanalyst who had given him the fatal injection, and after the paramedics had established Walker couldn't be revived, Dr Hacker had been seen wandering through the rain-sodden streets of Brentwood, in his shirt sleeves, completely lost.

Hollywood, Sunset Boulevard, Schwab's Drugstore
5 August 1962

On Sunday, 5 August, Marilyn had an appointment with the powerful Hollywood journalist Sidney Skolsky, who had an office above Schwab's Drugstore. Skolsky used to call her 'Miss Caswell' after her character in *All About Eve*, and she'd dress up to meet him like a *femme fatale* in black wig, long gloves and scarlet lipstick. Skolsky had known Jean Harlow personally, and Marilyn had been talking to him about doing a biopic of the original platinum blonde. She'd bought the rights to Harlow's biography in 1954 and they'd recently gone to see Harlow's mother to get her consent for a picture and to ask her questions about her daughter.

As time went by, Marilyn projected herself onto the dead actress with increasing intensity. Harlow was her mirror, her destiny, her love. When she posed naked for the photographer Tom Kelley in 1949, she knew she was imitating Harlow, who had done the same twenty years earlier for Edwin Hesser in Griffith Park. Similarly, at Madison Square Garden, she knew that Harlow had been invited by President Roosevelt to celebrate his birthday in 1937, a few months before her death, an invitation that caused her to leave the set of her last, unfinished film, *Personal Property*, and subsequently be ostracised by Hollywood. Marilyn began her career using her mother's name, then changed it, like her idol; Harlow had had an appalling relationship with her mother. Like Harlow, Marilyn's relationships with men invariably courted disaster. Marilyn liked Jean Harlow's attitude, the way, at the height of her glory, she'd said, 'I'd like to *become* an actress.' She even copied her 'Mmm', her murmur that could mean anything. Harlow had spoken the famous line 'Gentlemen prefer blondes' in a 1932 film, *Red-Headed Woman*, first looking at herself in a mirror, then to camera. She also appeared virtually naked in that film. Trying on a dress in a store, she positioned herself in front of a sunny window and asked, 'Can you see through this?' Off-camera a store clerk said, 'I'm afraid you can, Miss Lillian.' Back came the triumphant reply: 'I'll wear it.' When she was filming *The Misfits*, Marilyn was very aware that Clark Gable had made five films with Harlow, especially when he held her in his arms. He told her that on the last picture he'd made with Harlow, he'd felt he was kissing a ghost. And when Marilyn put her hands in the wet cement on Hollywood Boulevard on 26 June 1953, she felt as if she was reaching down into the past. Jean Harlow's handprints, dated 29 September 1935, were next to hers. She had been nine years old when her mother and Grace had shown her the spot in front of the Chinese Theater. 'I know I'll die young like Jean Harlow,' Marilyn would often say, with a strange glint in her eye.

Skolsky was no stranger to depressions, and a heavy user of prescription drugs himself, hence the scurrilous gossip that he spent his days over a drugstore for ease of access. That Sunday, he waited and waited for Marilyn to show, but it wasn't until he, and the rest of the world, read in the paper that Marilyn had died that he realised *The Jean Harlow Story* would never be made. Instead, Harlow's story had been re-enacted by the woman who, after dreaming of Harlow's life, had lived out her dream to its conclusion.

Paris, Hôtel Lancaster – New York City
5 August 1962

Billy Wilder was on a plane between New York and Paris on 5 August 1962 when the news of Marilyn Monroe's death broke. When the plane landed, he was surrounded by a crush of reporters shouting questions:

'What do you think of Marilyn?'

'How do you explain her?'

'What did you mean when you said she had a terrifying flesh impact, that she both loved and feared the camera?'

'Is she a good actress?'

'Do you think she cracked up because she couldn't manage her role in her new film?'

The director asked what she'd done now.

She hadn't done anything, they said.

Wilder wondered why they were all at the airport, what was so urgent, but nonetheless he came down very hard on her: 'She can be the most malicious woman in Hollywood. She's plastic, a beautiful DuPont creation, with a chest of granite and a brain like Gruyère, full of holes.'

When he arrived at his hotel, Wilder saw the headline in the afternoon papers: 'EXTRA: MARILYN MONROE IS DEAD!'

For Chrissakes, he thought. Those shits – why didn't they have the good taste to tell me? 'This is ridiculous, you know, because you ventilate your heart, and you say certain things that you would not have said if they had told me she was dead. Marilyn didn't deserve that. You get wonderful loonies in this world, like Monroe. And then they go and lie down on the psychoanalyst's couch and come out all doomy and uptight. It would have been better for her not to try and walk straight. She had two left feet, that was her charm.'

Years later, on a soaking afternoon in the summer of 1998 as El Niño blanketed California in rain, the ninety-one-year-old Billy Wilder gave an interview in his austere office down a small street in Beverly Hills. The interviewer asked him what he had thought of her death.

'It's just so odd, you know, that she should have died at the moment of the greatest brouhaha in her life. Namely the thing with Kennedy. She was screwing Kennedy . . . she was screwing *everybody*. He was too. I've had an idea for a picture about him for ages. He's on his way to the Century City Hotel, where he had a suite, and an Air Force One helicopter comes and lands on the roof. Cut to girls in different rooms in the hotel. They all go and turn on the shower, all hoping they'll be chosen, you see. A few weeks before she died, she went to New York, and she sang her interpretation of "Happy Birthday" . . . the Strasberg one. And then she killed herself. She always seemed unsure of herself to me, terrified of who she was, even the way she walked. I found myself wanting to be her analyst not her lover, which was a surprise. I probably couldn't have helped her any more than anyone else, but oh, she would have been so pretty on the couch.'

Billy Wilder had a love–hate relationship with Marilyn, and

for a long time after her death, he thought of her as the modern incarnation of the archetypal actress's refusal to grow old. He toyed with the idea of doing an update in colour of his black and white masterpiece, *Sunset Boulevard*, another portrait of an actress who clings to her image because that's the only way she knows to ward off insanity and death. He never made it, though, apparently because of the effect seeing *Something's Got to Give* had had on him. But at the end of his career, in 1978, he still did something along those lines: he made a stunning film about an old, reclusive actress on a Greek island, which he called *Fedora*.

Gainesville, Florida, Collins Court Old Age Home
5 August 1962

A little old woman walks along a sidewalk splashed with sunshine in a small town in Florida. Gladys Baker doesn't remember the time she worked in the film business, the daughter she had – she has no memories of anything. When a psychiatrist at Rockhaven Sanitarium, where she is hospitalised, told her that her daughter had died, she didn't react. She doesn't remember the girl called Norma Jeane; she doesn't know who Marilyn Monroe is. It only registers a year later. On a dark night she escapes by making a rope out of her sheets. She arrives in the Los Angeles suburbs clutching a Bible and a Christian Science textbook under her arm. A Baptist minister finds her in his church and talks to her before Rockhaven Sanitarium staff come to pick her up. 'Marilyn is gone,' she says. Not Norma Jeane, the minister is very clear about that. 'They told me when it happened. People need to know that I never wanted her to become an actress. All her career did was hurt her.'

* * *

At birth, Norma Jeane was registered under her mother's ex-husband's name. The certificate reads either 'Mortensen' or 'Mortenson', it's difficult to tell which. She adopted her stage name, which she was known by when she died and under which she achieved immortality, at the age of twenty, but she kept her official name until seven years before her death. Just two of the names that echo fatefully down the corridors of her life. From Mortenson to Greenson, from Catherine, Greenson's mother, to Marilyn – a love story links them, like a tape played again and again. Norma Jeane's father could have been one of the lovers her mother took in 1925 after separating from her second husband. The likeliest candidate is Raymond Guthrie, a film developer at RKO, who was in love with her for a few months. Gladys called her daughter after a wonderful actress of the time, Norma Talmadge.

Norma Jeane called André de Dienes one afternoon in the summer of 1946 and told him to come over to her apartment – she had important news. As he remembers it, when he got there, she burst out, 'Guess what? I have a new name!' She wrote out her new name for him: MARILYN MONROE. He thought there was something almost preternaturally beautiful about the way she drew the capital Ms.

In her last complete film, *The Misfits*, Marilyn literally played the role of her life, embodying Marilyn Monroe on screen in all her misfit glory. In her last days, however, she started to live her life as though she were in a role, one moment playing Miss Caswell in *All About Eve*, a graduate of the Copacabana school of drama saddened by growing older, the next a nameless woman in a nameless *noir* with a working title such as *Blonde, DOA*.

Beverly Hills
5 *August 1962*

At 12.05 a.m. Sergeant Franklin is in his squad car, driving down Roxbury Drive. Just as he takes Olympic Boulevard, a Mercedes passes him at top speed heading for the San Bernardino Freeway. Franklin figures it's going about one-twenty, and notices that its lights aren't on. He clamps on his flashing light and sets off in pursuit. The car accelerates, weaving between lanes. The driver seems to be trying to escape something, as if he's fleeing the scene of a crime. Franklin turns on the siren and the car finally stops near the Pico Country Club. When he looks through the front window, he sees the familiar face of Peter Lawford, drunk and frightened and haggard.

'Sorry,' Lawford stammers. 'I've got to take someone to the airport.'

'You're going the wrong way. You should be heading west, not east.' Franklin shines his torch on the other occupants of the car. The passenger in the front seat is a middle-aged man wearing a tweed jacket and a white shirt.

'He's a doctor,' Lawford said. 'He's coming with us to the airport.'

Later, Franklin would recognise the man as Dr Ralph Greenson. 'When I saw the news footage of the funeral, I knew Greenson was the man in the car.' But at the time, Greenson didn't say a word. Franklin shone his torch on a third man in the back. The beam of light picked out the United States Attorney General, Robert Kennedy, his eyes half closed, his shirt torn.

Sunday morning. The police question the neighbours. Witnesses report noises in the night: a helicopter, broken glass, shouts, a woman's voice yelling 'Murderers!' In the dust of Arizona, a year earlier, Marilyn had shouted 'Murderers, liars! I hate you!' in *The Misfits*: She'd shouted it at the men trying to lasso the mustangs as if they were pieces of meat rather than wild animals.

Looking in from the terrace, a shattered window reveals a bare-walled bedroom in an unremarkable Mexican-style hacienda. Inside is a naked woman, who looks far too white. The sheets form pockets of shade around her body, like flecks of foam on a breaking wave. A man stands frozen for a moment, then silently climbs in. He loosens the fingers clamped round the telephone and puts the receiver back on the base next to the bed. The woman's mouth is half open. It was always open. He had never seen it shut in any photograph. Her eyes . . . He doesn't see her eyes. He knows they're closed. He wants them to be, their blue, fleeting gaze, which he had never been able to fathom, especially when he most needed to – he wants that blue to be at peace. The woman is Marilyn Monroe, the man Ralph Greenson. He is her psychoanalyst, but he can't even look at her. The light has consumed her, drowned her in white. Her body has become a blinding pool of light, an extinguished star that still shines. To be the first to see a woman dead, Greenson thinks, is a victory as bitter as being the first to see her naked.

After the body has been stretchered out and taken off to the morgue in a noiseless ambulance, Greenson leaves the house and notices a plaque in the paving stones by Marilyn's front door that he's never seen before. It is inscribed with the Latin motto *Cursum perficio*: 'I've finished my race.' This is something St Paul says to Timothy in the New Testament, he learns later, but that morning, as her body goes off for an autopsy, he smiles and thinks that she may not have finished her race, but he has.

The autopsy is conducted at Los Angeles County Coroner's mortuary at ten-thirty a.m., on 5 August. Her body is brought over from the morgue, where the staff have refused huge sums to allow people to photograph the most famous corpse in the world. Bids went up to ten thousand dollars, and Marilyn's body had to be taken out of the refrigerator and hidden in a broom cupboard. The coroner's team proves more amenable. On Sunday evening, after the autopsy is over, compartment number thirty-three is opened and Leigh Wiener, a *Life* photographer, takes pictures of Marilyn's eviscerated body. Dying is, among other things, a process whereby one is turned into an object, merchandise, a piece of meat like the wild horses. For one last time, Marilyn was reduced to the thing she had desperately wanted not to be any more: an image. Arthur Miller would later write, 'The encounter between an individual pathology and the insatiable appetite of a capitalist culture of consumption. How is one to understand this mystery? This obscenity?'

Beverly Hills, Roxbury Drive
7 *August 1962*

Greenson hadn't even waited to sit in the chair facing Wexler before he asked, 'Do you want to hear her tapes? Her last sessions. Her last solo.'

Wexler groaned. Greenson was entrusting him with Marilyn's voice the way you tell a stranger in a bar a secret so you won't have to think about it any more.

'When she gave me the tapes to listen to,' Greenson went on, 'she said, "I have absolute confidence and trust you will never reveal to a living soul what I say to you." As she was leaving, she asked me to erase them after I'd listened to them. But I couldn't. I feel shattered. I don't know what I'll do with them, but I'm going to transcribe them at least.'

It was her voice more than what she said that prevented Greenson erasing the tapes. He always liked to think of himself as a provider of meaning, but her voice reduced him to a helpless member of the audience. He gave the tapes to his colleague to listen to in private. He said they could talk about them afterwards, if he wanted.

Wexler played the first tape and started when he heard:

> I went to Joan Crawford's. She asked me to wait while she gave her daughter an enema. The little one yelled she didn't want one, or at least not the way she gave them. Crawford was so furious she was going to hit her. I offered to do it myself. I gave the little angel an enema so gently it made her burst out laughing. Joan gave me a sour look and said, 'I do not think one needs to spoil the children.' I got the impression she could be cruel towards her daughter . . . Doctor, I want you to help me get rid of Murray. While she was giving me an enema last night I was thinking to myself, Lady, even though you're very good at this, you've got to go. I began remembering a little bit about the enemas I had as a child. They were what you and Dr Freud call repressed memories. I'll work on it and give you another tape.

Marilyn moved on to a different subject on the second tape.

> I stood naked in front of my full-length mirrors for a long time yesterday. I was all made-up with my hair done. What did I see? My breasts are beginning to sag a bit . . . My waist isn't bad. My ass is what it should be, the best there is. Legs, knees and ankles still shapely. And my feet are not too big. OK, Marilyn, you have it all there.

Vienna, 19 Berggasse
1933

One night, as he was trying to get to sleep, Greenson was visited by an unnerving, long-buried memory. It was of one of the Master's gatherings of his disciples, where Freud had discussed ways to achieve closure in transference. He had used a strange term, 'dissolution', and explained that transference could create emotional bonds similar to those that analysts experienced in their private lives. In these cases, the analysts could only detach themselves from the patient by forming another attachment – to another person or to another aspect of the patient. 'As long as one is alive and experiencing desire,' Freud had said, 'all one will ever do is exchange one hold for another, substitute one influence for another.' To dispel any lingering illusions on the part of his disciples, he had added, 'To think these are the product of error in any way only leads one to make a succession of further errors.'

For the purposes of illustration Freud, as he often did, had taken an example from literature, in this case the fairy tale *Hans in Luck*. He had left the room for a second and returned with a book from the shelves in his consulting room. Quickly finding his place, he began reading in a husky voice. The low light in the waiting room, Freud's tired voice, the painfully slow way he read – all these gave the story a tragic dimension that might, Greenson thought afterwards, have been unwarranted.

The story was straightforward, as simple as fortune itself, a parabola that rose and fell in a swift, pre-ordained curve. After working hard for his master for seven years, Hans finally decided he needed to go home and see his poor mother again, so he asked for his wages. Grateful for his work, his master paid him with a lump of silver as big as his head. The only problem was that the silver was very hard to carry. So, at the first opportunity Hans exchanged it for a horse. But that was problematic too, for different reasons, so he exchanged the horse for a cow, then the cow for a pig, then the pig for a goose, then the goose for a scissor-grinder's wheel, and finally ended up with a heavy stone. After a while, tired and thirsty, he stopped at a well, rested the stone on the edge and bent down to drink. But, as he did so, his shoulder nudged the stone and it fell down the well. Mightily relieved, Hans then set off with a light heart, his troubles at an end, and walked on till he reached his mother's house.

'This is what I wanted you to understand,' Freud had concluded, shutting the book. 'As far as sexual drives are concerned, we can only end up with permutations and displacements, never with complete renunciation or an overcoming or resolution of the complex, the ultimate mystery. That is sexuality, a permanent exchange in which every drive and act inevitably provokes a succession of other drives and acts.' This might not be word for word what Freud had said that evening, but it was the gist Greenson remembered, the moral being: everything has a price in transference, just as it does in love.

That evening in Vienna, Greenson had felt emboldened to ask Freud what he thought the transferential exchange revolved around.

'Sexuality, always sexuality,' Freud had replied. 'After forty years of practice I still find what I did when I started: the scenes our patients introduce us to are invariably sexual. As are the traumatisms they involve us in, or play out before our eyes. If somebody transfers his infantile complexes onto us, it is wrong to assume that means he has shed them. He has retained a part of them, the affect, in a different form, the transference. He has changed dress, or skin. He has sloughed off a layer and given it to the analyst. So it is a delicate matter, the attempt to bring transference to an end, since this could simply mean the end of the subject who speaks to us. God forbid that he should now go forth naked and without a skin. As in *Hans in Luck,* our therapeutic gains are always the result of an exchange. The last term of the exchange only disappears into the well when the patient dies.' After saying this, Freud fell silent for a while, then bade the trainee analysts farewell with icily punctilious courtesy.

As he lay there in the dark remembering this conversation, Greenson found himself thinking Freud had been mistaken – that people exchange throughout their lives not only desires and objects, but also identities, whether simultaneous or successive, identities that are not simply sexual but also familial and social. He examined the fairy tale for insights that might help him understand what had happened between Marilyn and him. Was the question of sex less central to analysis and transference than Hans's constant need to exchange what he has, the quest to free oneself of earthly burdens and return to one's original state? Greenson was struck by the fact that Hans was going back to his mother's house. He was returning to where he was born in order to die.

He saw himself and his patient facing one another, talking like awkward actors, 'dancing in the dark', as Marilyn would sometimes sing under her breath when she found it hard to put something into words. All their sessions had been like acts in a play, a comedy of errors in which they were the stars. Transference defined everything on stage: her memories, stories and dreams; the costumes she wore to re-enact her experiences, the costumes she gave him to wear for his part in her inner theatre; the lines she delivered in the tragedy she had written; the time he spent waiting backstage, like a clothes rail on which she hung her discarded costumes at every scene change.

But now the comedy was over, the curtain had fallen, and the enigma of her self was intact. Greenson went over it all. Her identity: the layers she constantly sloughed off in a permanent cycle, revealing herself only to mask herself again. Her theatrical transference, her excessive displays of love towards him. Her passion for being naked. Her tremulous, exiled image that always seemed about to lose its balance on screen. The way, in life as well as in the movies, she seemed to tread an invisible line between the rawest reality and the purest fantasy. He saw it all again and it made no sense. He hadn't tried to strip her of her identities, to estrange her from the characters she brought with her – it was her choice – and he was right not to have tried to, he thought. Love is a skin. Being loved protects us from the coldness of the world. Identity is the onion you must be careful not to peel. Because when you remove the last layer of skin, what have you got left?

Beverly Hills, Roxbury Drive
8 August 1962

Wexler was becoming increasingly exhausted by his colleague's anguished, obsessive need to make him watch the film of Marilyn's last weeks. Greenson spoke in a halting, disjointed way, coughing constantly, as if he were an actor reciting lines from a script he hadn't really learned.

'Her last year. I should tell you about her last year. She had come to me because she couldn't take any more. I put all my effort, all my language, into supporting her. Of course I saw a warning in *Something's Got to Give*, but I didn't want to listen.'

'I know you didn't,' said Wexler. 'She was in agony when you left for Europe. You underestimated the schizophrenic element of her condition. In the brief time I saw her, I was struck by the fact she often spoke about herself in the third person: "Marilyn would do that . . . She wouldn't say this . . . She would play that scene like this . . ." I pointed this habit out to her and asked if she heard a voice in her head saying "she". She looked at me in surprise and said, "Don't you? I don't hear just one. It's more like a crowd."'

*　　*　　*

When he returned the tapes to Greenson, Wexler was unsure whether to draw his colleague's attention to an obvious but seemingly overlooked aspect of his and Marilyn's *folie à deux*. Eventually he decided to speak his mind even if it jeopardised their friendship.

'You know as well as anyone,' he began, 'that massive acts of transference are always addressed to the mother and that the couch speeds up regression. In a way, by dying, Marilyn has now rejoined her mother. She has shed the final veil, like a luckless Hans losing his final possession down the well . . .'

'Well,' Greenson started to agree, 'that was precisely why I didn't let her lie on the couch for most of our analysis – so she wouldn't regress. She was ready by the end, though. Those tapes were a method we developed for her to talk without seeing who she was talking to. But I don't think I was playing a maternal role there.'

'Hence your decision to grow a beard. You wanted to reassure her and yourself that you were a father rather than a mother.'

'No. I was just copying Freud.'

'All you ever do is deny things,' Wexler snapped. 'You're constantly saying, no, I wasn't her mother, no, I didn't think of myself as her mother. But you know from Freud that when someone says "This is not about my mother", that's exactly when you're dealing with the mother. Do you want me to spell it out for you? You couldn't take each other any more. You left her physically, but you couldn't leave her emotionally. She wanted to leave you, but you couldn't let her go. Let's face it. The loss you felt was that of an abandoned child.'

Greenson stared at his colleague with a look of hatred, but didn't say anything. Wexler decided not to push it any further.

Greenson never stopped thinking of himself as a father to Marilyn. On 20 August 1962, he wrote to Marianne Kris: 'I was her therapist, the good father who would not disappoint her and

341

who would bring her insights, and if not insights, just kindness. I had become the most important person in her life, [but] I also felt guilty that I put a burden on my own family. But there was something very lovable about this girl and we all cared about her and she could be delightful.' He probably never acknowledged that his approach took him into areas far removed from Freudian theory, where, instead of father, life, love and desire, the signature themes were mother, homosexuality, excrement and death. With the freedom allowed by transference, Marilyn said unthinkable things on her tapes in the voice of someone who can't pretend to be a nice little girl in love with Daddy any more. Raw things, dark things. Dark like her mother's hair and death; dark like the clothes of Paula Strasberg, 'the Black Baroness', or Joan Crawford in *Johnny Guitar*; dark like Eunice Murray's uniform; dark like shit or a dirty child. Dirtiness is sexless, like love, and, for Marilyn, these two states coalesced in the pure passivity of the enema.

What if the only way Marilyn could escape Greenson was by dying? Wexler wondered. And if the only way he could possess her was by killing her? When he listened to the tapes, Wexler felt he knew that the truth that had played itself out between them was that you can kill someone by caring about them too much. He couldn't say this to his colleague, but the piece of music Greenson had wanted to play, a 'transference in father major', as it were, had mutated imperceptibly into 'compassion for suffering in mother minor'. At first Greenson had decided not to give her any injections himself, obviously because it seemed too phallic an act to him, but then he'd changed his mind and, towards the end of her life, had often given her tranquilliser shots. And, at the same time, in leaving Engelberg to take care of the prescriptions and Eunice Murray the enemas, he had also imperceptibly assumed the place of the mother in Marilyn's love for him, and also in his love for Marilyn.

*　　*　　*

By the time *The Technique and Practice of Psychoanalysis* came out, relations between the two colleagues had cooled. So Wexler smiled indulgently when he read Ralph Greenson, MD, declare, 'It is the doctor who has the right to explore the naked body and who has no fear or disgust of blood, mucus, vomit, urine, or faeces [Freud, 1926b, p. 206]. He is the rescuer from pain and panic, the establisher of order from chaos; emergency functions performed by the mother in the first years of life. In addition, the physician inflicts pain, cuts and pierces the flesh and intrudes into every opening in the body. He is reminiscent of the mother of bodily intimacy as well as the representative of the sadomasochistic fantasies involving both parents.'

Westwood Memorial Park Cemetery, Glendon Avenue
August 1984 and August 1962

An August morning in 1984. Truman Capote is being laid to rest in the centrepiece of a nondescript cemetery, a decrepit pink mausoleum approached by a tree-lined avenue. A pianist discreetly plays airs from *House of Flowers*, the Harold Arlen musical for which he wrote the libretto, as cameras roll at the entrance to the funerary chapel. The atmosphere is one of furtive animation, the etiolated bustle of old, ferociously social acquaintances meeting up after a long absence. People hug and whisper stagily amid a rustle of linen suits. Trembling lips air-kiss an array of wrinkled or silicon-smooth cheeks. Feet shift unsteadily on the gravel. Eyes blink behind tinted bifocals as past conquests heave into view. The fading stars of the 1950s and 1960s embrace with frozen smiles; the Californian sun, affairs, stimulants and the passage of time have all taken their toll. And as they semaphore to one another, their slender fingers waving on fragile wrists, the surrounding high-rises plunge the cemetery's ill-kept lawns into the shade.

*   *   *

The same cemetery, twenty-two years earlier. It is one in the afternoon on 8 August 1962, when the Reverend A. J. Soldan conducts Marilyn Monroe's remains to the funerary chapel. 'How beautiful the Creator made her,' he preaches. Marilyn had asked for Judy Garland's song 'Somewhere Over The Rainbow' from *The Wizard of Oz* to be played. The tape recording sounds muffled and scratchy, a long way away. The service begins with a halting rendition of Tchaikovsky's Sixth Symphony on the organ, and then psalms. Carl Sandburg has been asked by DiMaggio to give the address but he is too ill to attend, so Lee Strasberg speaks instead. The click and whirr of cameras from every news organisation in the world drowns him out. The occasion doesn't offer much in the way of a spectacle, though. Only close relations have been invited. Westwood may be nearby, but it is no Hollywood. Joe DiMaggio, who planned everything, insisted that no one from the business could attend: no producers, no studio directors, no actors, no screenwriters. He is determined to play the part of Marilyn's bodyguard, which she had given him ten years earlier when they met, to the bitter end. She asked him to guard her body so she wouldn't come to grief on it herself.

Marilyn would have been glad to see Romi there, grim-faced but dry-eyed, supported by Hildi and Joan, who, with their black veils and shining tears, add pathos to the scene. 'There were hundreds of reporters and photographers,' Joan Greenson said afterwards. 'At first, we weren't allowed to enter the chapel, because the undertaker said "the family" was with the deceased. What family? If she'd had a family, we wouldn't have been there.'

Daniel Greenson is in tears. He had always thought of Marilyn Monroe as a ghost, really. He remembers talking to her about politics three months earlier in Santa Monica, trying to bring her round to his militant position. He remembers how she put on a black wig and went out apartment-hunting with him when he decided to move out of his parents' place. He remembers seeing her, wearing the same disguise, sitting at the back of the crowded auditorium in Beverly Hills High School, avidly following one of his father's lectures. He remembers the last time he saw the woman they are now laying to rest. It was an evening in June. He had given Marilyn a goodbye kiss; he was going out, she was peeling potatoes.

This is the day that Daniel Greenson, who is studying medicine, decides to become a psychoanalyst – not in order to follow in his father's footsteps, but to understand what he had been a witness to: the game of hide-and-seek the actress and her psychoanalyst had seemed to play blindfolded, their verbal hand-to-hand, or soul-to-soul, combat. In time, his life and work would bring home to him that one can never know the truth about a person, whether one is their son or their psychoanalyst. But he now realises that the truth always hides in words, in the brief notes slipped under a door or the remarks whispered in a distracted ear in a cemetery avenue, which, like bodies dying if they are not touched, leave no trace unless they are recorded.

Last take, last scene. The bronze coffin with a champagne-coloured satin lining is open. Marilyn, in a Pucci green dress and a matching green chiffon scarf with a bouquet of pink roses in her arms, is ready for her final role. Her team has been busy: Marjorie Pelcher, her dresser, has worked up her outfit; Agnes Flanagan, her hairdresser, has seen to her hair; Whitey Snyder has plied his magic; even her old hairdresser, Pearl Porterfield, has reported for duty and now casts a knowing eye over the results. When the body was embalmed, cushion ticking was needed to compensate for the damage done to Marilyn's breasts by the autopsy. Her hair is in terrible condition and Agnes Flanagan ends up using a wig based on her screen image. The credits for this production would have to make special mention of the faithful Whitey (whose nickname came from his skill at mixing whites without the result looking like plaster or snow). Years earlier, he had jokingly promised Marilyn that he would make her up for the last time, make sure nobody else art-designed her final look. More recently, she had given him a jewel from Tiffany's as a token of her affection: a clip brooch mounted on a gold coin with an inscription, which he never revealed. 'This is for you, my dear Whitey,' she had said, 'while I'm still warm.' He was Fox's head of make-up, and had created the look of all the stars of the day: Betty Grable, Gene Tierney, Linda Darnell. Destiny had come full circle when he had done Marilyn's make-up for *Something's Got to Give*. Now he has to drink a whole bottle of gin before he can make her up for the last time.

A short line of men and women dressed in black is silhouetted against an almost white sky. The coffin slowly makes its way past the crypts of two of her transient mothers, Ana Lower and Grace McKee Goddard. Her crypt is sealed. If she could see the footage of her funeral, she would have one last surprise: of all her lovers and husbands, only one has come – Joe DiMaggio. Three times a week for the next twenty years, he will lay flowers at her plaque, just as he had promised her he would. She had made him repeat his promise; she had wanted to know he'd be as faithful as William Powell was after Jean Harlow's death.

It is a sad, hollow ceremony, thoughtful but futile, like a passer-by picking up a toy that's fallen out of a pushchair and carefully putting it on a wall, even though he knows nobody will come for it. Everyone tries to give a meaning to it, but it feels like an image that can be neither articulated nor erased. 'You know where our poor idol is buried?' George Cukor said later. 'The cemetery entrance has a car dealership and a bank on either side; she lies between Wilshire Boulevard and Westwood Boulevard, surrounded by traffic.'

Capote is buried in the same cemetery a few feet away. A friend of Marilyn's murmurs into the distracted ear of one of the mourners, 'He loved her, you know, as much as he could love any woman. Nineteen fifty-four in New York: that was their time.

347

They used to go dancing in a club that shut down, the El Morocco on East 54th Street.' There's a photograph of them: two bodies moving on a narrow, slightly raised dance floor that floats like a black circle in a ring of blinding lights. They were already out of it when they'd got to the club. She kicked off her shoes so as not to tower over him and they danced themselves into exhaustion. A tiny man in a pin-striped suit, dark tie and tortoiseshell glasses clinging to a radiant blonde, as if he's shifting a grandfather clock. She isn't looking at her partner but out at the smoke-filled room. He isn't looking at anything, his whole body rigid either with shame and sadness, or perhaps joy.

The musician Artie Shaw stands to give the address. In a low voice, he says, 'Truman died of a surfeit of everything, of an excess of life, of living too intensely. Yet in the last few years it seemed as if he were ready to give it all up. And in time, what will remain won't be his celebrity or his dealings with celebrities, but his work. That is what he wanted us to remember. Truman, your music will play in our ears long after we have forgotten the names of the figures who inspired it. Say hello to your friend Marilyn, who you never took in your arms and who loved you more than most of the men she slept with. Your plaques are now separated by three walls bearing the inscriptions: "TENDERNESS", "DEVOTION", "PEACE". Those are what you gave one another and what life begrudged you so bitterly. Tell her that your friends have come to spend a moment with their beloved vanished stars, that we will remember her, Marilyn, the white queen without a castle, and that we will never remember her so well as in your words. Now, in both your shadows, our memories turn to your splendid account of her. Truman, the truest of writers, you knew better than anyone how to balance reality and truth in your novels. Goodbye, Truman, may you have a long, peaceful death.'

The last of the mourners disperse. Turning away from the headstones of Natalie Wood and Darryl F. Zanuck, they return to their cars by way of the north-east corner of the cemetery so they can pay their respects to the plaque that reads 'MARILYN MONROE'. So many graves, so many names. Years later, Dean Martin, Jack Lemmon and Billy Wilder will also be buried – if that is the word for a bronze coffin slid into a niche in a breeze-block wall – alongside Marilyn in Westwood Memorial Park.

And in the distance, the overhanging hills with the white letters spelling out 'HOLLYWOOD' are already hazy in the smog.

Beverly Hills, Milton 'Mickey' Rudin's law firm
6 August 1962

Mickey Rudin had negotiated Marilyn's last contract for *Something's Got to Give*. When he arrived at the death scene, he accompanied her body to the nearby mortuary, then rang Joe DiMaggio to ask him to help organise the funeral.

Among the invoices Rudin had to pay on the estate's behalf was a final one from Ralph Greenson for $1,450 for sessions in July and the first four days of August, and another from 20th Century Fox for a coffee pot, which the commissary had provided for her last birthday.

Marilyn Monroe's estate was estimated at $92,781. Her last will divided the money equally between her mother, her half-sister and friends, and left various objects to a value of $3,200 to Lee Strasberg. As far as licensing rights and royalties were concerned, the principal beneficiary was the Anna Freud Centre in London, an institute 'dedicated to the emotional well-being of children'. Marilyn had left a sizeable legacy to her former analyst in New York, Marianne Kris, 'so that she can continue her work in the psychiatric institutions and groups of her choice'. Kris had in turn chosen the Hampstead Clinic in London, a decision that Elisabeth Young-Bruehl, Anna Freud's biographer, explains by saying, 'Marilyn Monroe's bequest came to the Hampstead Clinic while the clinic was adjusting to the tremendously influential work that Anna Freud had undertaken outside it – work in which the plight of children, like the young Marilyn Monroe, who had been bounced from one foster home to another, was central.' Another patient of Marianne Kris, Jackie Kennedy, also bequeathed ten thousand dollars to Anna Freud's institute, probably on her analyst's recommendation.

Marilyn's financial bequests, her transference onto whoever was the beloved analyst at the time, and her numerous sexual relationships, form a strange nexus around her death and her will. Yet her relations with successive analysts had deteriorated so badly that one is entitled to ask whether she would have left her money to the same people if she had had time to alter her last wishes. She had made it clear in the last months of her life that she was intending to rewrite her will, and had arranged to meet Mickey Rudin to discuss this on Tuesday, 7 August. She died three days before. This meant that every screen appearance of the woman whom the Freudian establishment had refused to let play a patient of Sigmund Freud benefited an institution that bears the name of Freud's daughter.

Since the actress's death, the broadcast rights for her films and songs have brought in approximately $1.5 million a year, more than Marilyn earned in her life. Hundreds of brands have paid for the right to use her image for publicity or marketing purposes. Besides posters and T-shirts, Marilyn's face and body are reproduced everywhere – even on schoolbooks, venetian blinds, tights, billiard cues and cake moulds.

From the day she died, everything she owned became a cult object. Hyman Engelberg said he had hundreds of calls from women claiming that if they had known she was in such dire straits they would have tried to help her. She had not only been an object of desire to men, he realised, but also a lost girl with whom many women empathised profoundly.

In December 1999, the possessions she'd left to Strasberg were sold for $13.4 million at Christie's in New York. Everything she'd touched had become a fetish. The wool cardigan from Saks, which she wore at the end of June 1962 in Barris's photographs on Santa Monica beach, went for $167,500; the backless dress from *Let's Make Love* for more than $52,900. The designer Tommy Hilfiger paid a fortune for two pairs of jeans from *The Misfits*. Bidding on the Jean Louis muslin sheath dress encrusted with tiny rhinestones she'd worn for seven minutes at Madison Square Garden went up to almost a million dollars. Her books, many of them with handwritten marginalia, were auctioned as a single lot for six hundred thousand. One lot consisted of a scrap of paper with 'He doesn't love me' scribbled on it – a remark that could have applied to plenty of men in her lifetime but virtually none today. Two other notes were auctioned, one of which read, 'If I have to commit suicide, I must go through with it.' The other, folded inside a book, was a poem:

> People say I am lucky to be alive.
> It's hard to believe.
> Everything hurts so much.

A couple of years after Marilyn's death, two screenwriters, David L. Wolper and Terry Sanders, began researching a film about her, *The Legend of Marilyn Monroe*. They got in touch with Doc Goddard, the widowed husband of Grace McKee. He refused to be interviewed on film, but he did tell them the whereabouts of the white piano that had been bought by Gladys Baker for her daughter, sold for $235 to pay for her hospitalisation when

Marilyn was nine years old and subsequently bought back as soon as Marilyn could afford it. It was in J. Santini & Bros Fireproof Warehouse somewhere in New Jersey. They shot it from below, like the sledge Rosebud in *Citizen Kane*, and added a voiceover: 'This white piano was the child she never had.' As the camera zoomed in, there was no escaping the fact that the piano wasn't originally white but had been repainted, probably for a 1930s musical comedy. It was as artificial as Marilyn's blonde hair, as the screen separating life from the movies, and psycho-analysis from madness in Hollywood. At Christie's, it found a new buyer, the singer Mariah Carey, and fetched $662,500 this time.

The gift shops along Sunset Boulevard still sell maps of Hollywood with Marilyn's address included among those of living movie stars. Shots of the outside of her house were used in a biopic in 1980 called *Marilyn: The Secret History*, with Catherine Hicks playing her. The director David Lynch, who for a long time planned to make a film of the last months of her life, owns a relic of sorts of her: a piece of the fabric on which she is supposed to have posed for the famous nude calendar that Tom Kelley shot, possibly the inspiration for his film *Blue Velvet*.

All these objects sealed off behind glass, the iconic possessions that have become part of collective memory, the images suspended like freeze-frames in a perpetual state of mourning – they are the relics of a myth, these days. Her words are more complicated. Thousands of pages must have been written about her life: novels, essays, biographies, investigations, confessionals of every stripe. Only the people who really loved her – Joe DiMaggio, Ralph Roberts, Whitey Snyder – haven't put pen to paper. When Joseph Mankiewicz, by then retired, came across W. J. Weatherby's *Conversations with Marilyn*, in the mid-1970s, he was shocked that no one had asked Weatherby why he had waited fifteen years to gather together his memories and make them into a book. Why was he only now describing in detail what she had said, her gestures, clothes and facial expressions, using notes he'd made in the last two years of her life? In his preface, Weatherby said he wanted to strip away the 'mental makeup' she hid behind and reveal the 'true Marilyn'. Mankiewicz hated people using psychology to justify self-interest. Saying you're doing something for love when you're doing it for money, that's real prostitution.

The range of motives for people's public actions tends to be limited to either love, hatred, self-interest, honour, money or revenge . . . Often it's only a variant of one thing: the need to disguise what one is because one is afraid one might be nothing. Sexual anxiety is nothing compared to status anxiety, the fear of not being recognised by the society in which one lives. Mankiewicz thought this was true of Marilyn. It was also true of her psychoanalyst, of her biographers, of everyone who's written or made films about her in the hope that a little of the stardust from her comet-like progress through the 1960s would rub off on them. But they shouldn't talk about love, he thought. They're selling her just as much as they're selling themselves.

The truth is that, while there may be hundreds of books about this woman and her death, the documents themselves have disappeared or been buried with her. The recordings of her voice have been lost or erased. Thousands of hours of her speaking were captured by microphones all over her house. The tapes were hidden or destroyed after being processed by the public bodies or private individuals who commissioned the surveillance. The two centres of power, political and psychoanalytical, that dominated the last months of Marilyn's life tried to erase everything to do with her in their archives. As for Fox, the studio that said her last movie could be a new beginning and offered her a glittering new contract, they gave instructions that everything related to her final film should be buried in the files.

Santa Monica, Franklin Street
August 1962–November 1979

The death of his patient had a devastating effect on Ralph Greenson, although when he talked about love and grief in regard to her, it was open to question whether he was in fact referring to *amour-propre* and social death. 'Marilyn's death was extremely painful to him,' his widow would later say. 'Not just that it was so public, which was terrible in itself, but that Marilyn, he felt, was doing much better. He knew he hadn't quite brought her through, but she was better – and then to lose her, that was quite painful.' Dr Greenson's patients were surprised to see him grow a beard again. When a producer asked him why, he said he wanted to be someone else. Showing no inclination to go into therapy himself, he started practising child therapy. His colleagues noticed he wasn't the fighter he used to be; the beard was his way of turning himself into an elder statesman. 'He had lost a lot of the old fire,' a member of the Psychoanalytic Institute said. 'He still worked after that but he turned in on himself. He became a little strange ...' Photographs reveal a palpable physical and emotional decline. 'He wanted to reinvent himself but ended up becoming a completely different person,' another of his colleagues said.

A week after Marilyn died, he went to New York at his wife's instigation to be analysed by Max Schur. The friendship between the two analysts dated from their medical studies in Bern and Vienna. Their first session lasted hours, but Schur reassured him that he would soon be over the worst.

Initially unable to think or write, Greenson gradually realised that a kind of thin, almost transparent, veil of depression had settled over him. He began a memoir of his life, which he entitled *My Father, the Doctor*.

Marilyn Monroe was all I knew. She only used her original name, Norma Jeane, twice in our sessions, when we first met and just before I left for Europe. She never used Mortenson, her family name, nor did she say why she had chosen her mother's maiden name as her stage name. I didn't make the connection with my need always to be on stage. Don't I treat my patients and give my talks and write my articles under an assumed name?

Romeo! As if. 'Romeo the psychoanalyst'. However much he loved Shakespeare, my father didn't have to call us Romeo and Juliet. I don't know if Marilyn was thinking of it at the time, but on the last tape she gave me, she said, 'I'll take a year of day and night study of Shakespeare with Lee Strasberg. I'll pay him to work only with me. He said I could do Shakespeare. I'll make him prove it. That will give me the basics Olivier wanted. Then I'll go to Olivier for the help he promised. And I'll pay whatever he wants. Then I'll produce and act in the Marilyn Monroe Shakespeare Film Festival, which will put his major plays on film. I'll need you to keep me together for a year or more. I'll pay you to be your only patient. I've read all of Shakespeare and practised a lot of lines.

I won't have to worry about the scripts. I'll have the greatest scriptwriter who ever lived working for me and I don't have to pay him. Oh, Monroe will have her hand in. I am going to do Juliet first. Don't laugh. What with what make-up, costume and camera can do, my acting will create a Juliet who is fourteen, an innocent virgin, but whose budding womanhood is fantastically sexy.' As for Greenschpoon, that felt too Brooklyn Jewish. But I didn't renounce my father's name. Changing it was really to do with giving up medicine. My father remained a general practitioner all his life and I suppose I always tried to show the same concern for my patients as he did. But what's the good of writing about that?

Like Marilyn and Inger Stevens, the actress Janice Rule had taken Lee Strasberg's classes at the Actors Studio and was one of Greenson's patients. In the weeks after Marilyn's death, she thought he seemed shattered. He told her he felt 'crucified' by the press. During one session, he said something she found very moving: 'There is no way in my lifetime I will ever be able to answer any of this. I only worry how it will affect you as a patient.'

Suffering from heart problems that caused him to be frequently hospitalised, Greenson found his last years hard. Rule saw him near the end. Greenson had always urged her to vent her emotions during analysis. She often used foul language in their sessions, so much so that one day he'd said to her, 'I just have to tell you that it's hard for me to put that face together with what comes out of your mouth!' They met up again when he was old and ill and had just had his third pacemaker fitted. He suffered aphasia and it infuriated him when he couldn't express himself. He said to her, 'You taught me that "fuck" is a very good word. When I could finally speak, that is the first word I said.'

Greenson fought off physical and intellectual collapse for four years. One patient, shocked by how much weight he'd lost, his shortness of breath, said, 'You don't look like an analyst.'

He lifted his shirt and showed her the scar from his pacemaker surgery. 'We're just as mortal as everyone else.'

Fate toys with Marilyn's life story. Like a demented editor taking revenge on a director, it randomly joins the sequences, linking contradictory takes and juxtaposing scenes with divergent meanings. On the editing table it rewinds the thirty months Romi and Marilyn spent self-destructively entangled in each other's madness. The dénouement reverses everything that has come before. Marilyn exists only through her voice and words. The only trace of the last hours of her life is the tapes she made for her analyst and the phone-taps ordered by the Kennedys, or their enemies, and carried out, depending on whose version you believe, by Fred Otash for the CIA or Bernard Spindel for the FBI. The private detectives steal her words, as her image has been stolen for the previous thirty-six years. The reel we're left with, after Fate has edited it, shows Greenson as a man whom words haven't been able to justify. His tapes have been erased by time, and he has disappeared beneath the surface of the images that remain of him.

Maresfield Gardens
1962–82

In one respect, Greenson reacted to his depression fairly quickly, drawing closer to the Freudian establishment and resuming his work on analytic theory. He saw fewer patients and immersed himself in teaching and writing, focusing primarily on the subject that had fascinated him for the previous three years, 'the working alliance' between patient and analyst. He studied failed analyses, the indications and contraindications for psychoanalytic treatment in severe cases, patients who were unsuited to analysis or who exhibited abrupt changes in pathologies, and mounted a stirring defence of the therapeutic alliance as a means of resolving stalemates in transference.

At the urging of his editor, soon after Marilyn's death he set about finishing *The Technique and Practice of Psychoanalysis*. It was to be his only book. In the preface, he pays tribute to his father and mentions the name he was born with. 'The transmission of knowledge can be an attempt to overcome a depressive state,' he says, in a line he wrote before meeting Marilyn. Books are often the children of grief. He might not have wept publicly for Marilyn, despite often referring to his sorrow and to his sense that he was in mourning for her, but his book is a five hundred-page lament couched in the form of advice to débutant and seasoned analysts. A lament is always directed primarily at oneself, just as criticism of the failings and weaknesses of others is always a sign of an inner struggle. In his work, therefore, Greenson treats with extreme punctiliousness subjects such as 'The Weekend Is A Desertion', 'The Real Relationship Between Patient And Analyst' and 'What Psychoanalysis Requires of the Psychoanalyst'. His handbook lists in painstaking detail everything an analyst should not do with a patient – a summation, in other words, of everything he had done with Marilyn during her thirty months of analysis.

For a while, Greenson used episodes from her analysis to illustrate his lectures at UCLA, and made a point of emphasising the appropriateness of all his clinical decisions. Two years after his patient's death, he gave a lecture at UCLA entitled 'Drugs in the Psychotherapeutic Situation', in which he said, 'Psychiatrists and physicians must be willing to become emotionally involved with their patients if they hope to establish a reliable therapeutic relationship.' Defending himself in the *Medical Tribune* on 24 October 1973, he said he had done 'what he thought best, particularly after other methods of treatment apparently hadn't touched her one iota'. He defended his policy of making her a member of his household, negotiating with the studios on her behalf and, in general, taking such an active role in the decisions she made about her life. He said he had had a precise aim. He had thought his method was the only possible one for that specific woman, but he had failed: she had died. He never used the word 'suicide'.

Greenson more or less stopped seeing patients in the mid-1970s, and gave up teaching. But he continued writing articles, which were collected and published in 1993 under the title, *Loving, Hating and Living Well*. He never got over his infatuation with

Hollywood, and would often suggest ideas for movies to Leo Rosten, which Rosten always found absurd and unfilmable. He counted the friends he'd lost and the colleagues who'd died. Once, on his way back from a funeral, he told his wife, 'We have to learn to live better. I mean, take more intense pleasure in those close to us, remain curious and active, and work, keep on working.'

He described his attitude to death in a short article. 'I am an analyst by profession, but also a Jew, and that is why I cannot renounce some promise of an afterlife.' The following year, although he was finding it harder to lecture, he spoke about 'the Sexual Revolution' in a talk at San Diego University called 'Beyond Sexual Satisfaction?'.

On 18 August 1978, he wrote a final, unpublished, article entitled 'Special Problems in Psychotherapy With the Rich and Famous'. Without mentioning Marilyn by name, he wrote of a famous, beautiful, thirty-four-year-old actress who came to see him because of her lack of self-esteem.

> Rich and famous people think that if a course of therapy
> lasts too long they are the victims of a confidence trick.
> They want the therapist to be their friend. They even want
> their wife and children to become members of the
> therapist's family. These patients are seductive. They need
> their therapist twenty-four hours a day, they're insatiable.
> They can also drop you at any moment and treat you as
> they have been treated by their parents or servants. You are
> in their employ and can be fired at any moment.

He gave his last talk to the Southern California Institute of Psychoanalysis on 6 October 1978 on the subject of: 'People lacking family'.

*　　*　　*

When the death of his famous patient threw him into disarray, the Freudian establishment were quick to rally round. Anna Freud immediately sent her condolences.

> I am terribly sorry about Marilyn Monroe. I know exactly how you feel because I had exactly the same thing happen with a patient of mine who took cyanide two days before I came back from America a few years ago. One goes over and over in one's head to find out where one could have done better and it leaves one with a terrible sense of being defeated. But, you know, I think in these cases we are really defeated by something which is stronger than we are and for which analysis, with all its powers, is too weak a weapon.

Greenson answered by return of post.

> Santa Monica, 20 August
>
> My dear Anna,
>
> It was so kind of you to write such an understanding letter. It was a terrible blow in many ways. She was my patient and I took care of her. She was so pathetic and had had such a terrible life. I had hopes for her and we thought we were making progress. Now she is dead and I realise that all my knowledge, desire and determination weren't enough. I was more to her than an attentive therapist, but I don't know what – perhaps a brother in arms in some obscure battle. Maybe I should have seen I was also an enemy to her, as she was to me. The 'working alliance' has its limits. It was not my fault, but I was still the last man who let this strange, unhappy woman down. God knows I tried, but I could not overcome all the destructive forces that her past experiences and present way of life exposed her to. Sometimes I think this world

wanted her to die, or at least many of the people in it, particularly those who put on a show of distress when she died. It makes me furious, but mainly I feel sadness and disappointment. It is a blow to my pride but also to the profession of which I am considered a leading representative. I will need time to get over it and I know that when the feeling goes it will leave a scar. Good friends have written me very kind letters and that has helped. It hurts to remember, but it is only by going over it that one day I will be able to forget . . .

A few months later, Greenson took up his pen again: 'I have to reassure my friends and enemies. I am still functioning!'

Anna replied, 'Marianne Kris spoke to me about Marilyn Monroe and her experiences with her a great deal over the summer. I don't think anyone could have kept her in this life.'

Three years later, Greenson wrote another letter, which he didn't send:

Santa Monica, September

My dearest Anna Freud,

I've finished my book. It is the only way I have of escaping death. I had a strange thought . . . Anyway, judge for yourself. Writing, it seems to me, is essentially a matter of surrendering to the child within us. The same need drives me to make my marks on a page as drives a neglected child to scream. But what is it?

Your devoted,

Ralph Greenson

He continued to correspond with Anna Freud until his death, and she played the role of supervising analyst in the aftermath of Marilyn. He seemed to combat his feelings of guilt by appealing to destiny, that of his patient and that of any course of analysis. An unfinished letter was found in his papers:

Santa Monica
    Dear Anna, my respected friend,
    You're right. One's fate is written. Names, letters, phrases are engraved on our forgetful memories rather than on tombstones. I am struck by the recurring patterns in my patient's life. Do you know what I learnt recently? Marilyn's adoptive mother, without whom she would never have become the star we knew, was an alcoholic and a drug-user as well. Grace McKee died in September 1953 of an alcohol and barbiturate overdose. She was buried in Westwood Memorial Park, where we laid Marilyn to rest. But Marilyn did not attend her funeral.

In 1965, Greenson and Anna Freud's relationship assumed a more formal dimension when he became an official fundraiser in LA for the Hampstead Clinic, which was short of consulting-room space. The principal American donor, Lita Annenberg Hazen, was so generous that when Freud's house at 14 Maresfield Gardens came on the market, the Hampstead Clinic was able to buy it. The house was finished in February 1968 after work by the architect Ernst Freud, Anna Freud's favourite older brother, whom Greenson was treating with sedative injections for his dreadful migraines. When his last analyst Max Schur died in 1969, Greenson again turned to Anna Freud. She replied, 'I agree that mourning is a terrible task, surely the most difficult of all. And it is only made bearable by the moments, which you also describe so well, when one feels fleetingly that the lost person has entered into one and that there is a gain somewhere which denies death.' In the same letter, she referred to his request to call her by her first name:

I am willing to call you Romi, and you can call me Anna, under one condition: that you promise not to rage against fate, God (?), and the world when my time comes to disappear. My father used to call that 'not to kick'. One kicks against fate, but as you describe it, one only hurts oneself, and through hurting oneself, those who are nearest to one. I would not like to think that someday I shall give you such a cause.

Ralph Greenson and Anna Freud subsequently exchanged letters about a documentary on the Hampstead Clinic that Greenson thought was necessary for fundraising. Anna and her companion, Dorothy Burlingham-Tiffany, ended up agreeing to appear in the film. They thought it very good, and held out great hopes for it. Greenson, however, was to die before he could show it in California as he had planned. In the last letter she wrote to him, in November 1978, Anna asked, 'What will happen to psychoanalysis in the future? And where will its backbone be when our generation is gone?'

Greenson died on 24 November 1979. Anna, who had lost Dorothy just five days earlier, wrote to Hildi, 'You ask who's coming with me on holiday. The answer is simple: I'm going alone, since I do not believe in replacement partners. I am trying to learn how to be alone outside my work.' Hildi answered that she felt on the threshold of solitude too. 'I feel that terrible *homesickness* for all the marvellous years, including the many times when all four of us were together.'

At a memorial service, Anna gave the eulogy on behalf of the Freudian establishment. 'We are raising new generations of psychoanalysts all over the world. Nevertheless, we have not yet discovered the secret of how to raise the real followers or people like Romi Greenson, namely, men and women who make use of psychoanalysis to its very limits: for the understanding of them-selves; of their fellow beings; for communication with the world at large; in short, for a way of living.' On behalf of the Los Angeles Psychoanalytic Society, Albert Solnit lauded 'Captain Greenson, MD': 'He was a clinical scientist and a romantic in the classical sense. He loved life in all of its forms and expressions: musical, poetic, artistic and athletic. He showed constant concern for those who struggle to achieve, those who fail, those who life puts at risk, those who suffer and go without.'

A year later, Marianne Kris died in London at Anna's house in Freud's widow Martha's room. Anna herself was eighty years old 'with a silly heart'. 'It's as if I'm trying to be next, having heart problems straight after Marianne's death,' she wrote to Hildi Greenson. She was to die in 1982.

New York
January 1964

In Arthur Miller's play *After the Fall*, first directed in 1964 by
Elia Kazan in New York, the husband Quentin says to the wife
Maggie, who is clearly modelled on Marilyn, 'A suicide kills two
people. That's what it's for.' During his session the day after
seeing a performance of the play, Ralph Greenson said to Max
Schur, 'Miller has his highly autobiographical character say, "You
don't want my love, you want my destruction." It wasn't hard
to think that about Marilyn.'

'Would you say it was love you felt for her?' Schur asked.

'I loved her and I didn't love her. I didn't love her as an adult. I
loved her as a child, or someone sick, for her fallibilities, her fears.
But her fear also frightened me: it was bigger than her, it was
somewhere she could hide, and I thought I could accommodate it,
contain it, make it go away.'

'OK,' Schur said. 'Shall we stop there?'

Greenson had gone into analysis in New York partly to help

him resolve his mourning for Marilyn, and partly to get away from Hollywood, to rediscover a space of words and language – to forget the movies, at least for a while. When he thought about their years together, he said to himself that Los Angeles had ended up catching Marilyn and killing the New York side of her, killing the Marilyn who'd fled Hollywood one day to become someone else, the Marilyn who'd given a press conference upon arriving in New York City on 'the new Monroe'. By the end of the 1970s, as far as movies were concerned, Manhattan had conquered Hollywood anyway. New York was the only place where Greenson could finally lay claim to the phrase he had repeated to Sergeant Clemmons as the Schaefer ambulance men took her body away: 'We lost her.' He often said that to Schur, without specifying who he meant by 'we'.

During the ensuing sessions, he wondered what had brought him to this psychoanalyst. Schur had been Freud's doctor during his final years in Vienna and afterwards in London. Was he seeking some sort of rapprochement with Freud after his unorthodox treatment of Marilyn? No doubt he and Schur also identified with one another in a way. Schur had been a doctor more than an analyst. But Greenson had also been drawn to him for a more unconscious reason. He only realised this after Schur had died, and once *Freud: Living and Dying*, the book Schur had hardly had time to complete, was published in 1972. Greenson saw his choice of fourth analyst as a repetition.

When the press started to insinuate that he had killed his patient with an injection to the heart, Greenson read the passage where Schur described giving Freud the morphine injection that had released him from the burdens of his suffering and this life:

On the following day, 21 September, while I was sitting at

his bedside, Freud took my hand and said to me: 'My dear Schur, you certainly remember our first talk. You promised me then not to forsake me when my time comes. Now it's nothing but torture and makes no sense any more.'

I indicated that I had not forgotten my promise. He sighed with relief, held my hand for a moment longer, and said, 'I thank you,' and after a moment of hesitation he added: 'Tell Anna about this.' All this was said without a trace of emotionality or self-pity, and with full consciousness.

I informed Anna of our conversation, as Freud had asked. When he was again in agony, I gave him a hypodermic of two centigrams of morphine. He soon felt relief and fell into a peaceful sleep. The expression of pain and suffering was gone. I repeated this dose after about twelve hours. Freud was obviously so close to the end of his reserves that he lapsed into a coma and did not wake up again. He died at 3 a.m. on 23 September 1939.

Greenson remained in analysis with Max Schur for seven years, although not on a regular basis.

Santa Monica, Franklin Street
8 *August* 1962

When they heard Marilyn Monroe was dead, most people's first assumption was that she had been murdered. The questions about the part her last analyst had played began immediately: insinuations that he had abetted a crime or even perpetrated it. As the years passed, Greenson was portrayed in ever-darker shades. He mutated into a sort of Dr Mabuse, manipulating his patient to the point of madness and death, while Eunice became the reincarnation of Mrs Danvers, the housekeeper who terrorises the second Mrs de Winter in *Rebecca*. It is true that the accusations of murder (whether out of jealousy, or on the orders of the Kennedys or the Mafia, or as part of a Communist conspiracy) receded over time and were never supported by anything but the most dubious testimony. But the scenario of Greenson killing his patient through medical negligence was plausible – and tenacious.

John Miner was desperate to understand what had happened. One of Greenson's versions of events, which implied that Marilyn had been murdered, exonerated him of any guilt for not having been able to prevent his patient's death. But the other version, suicide, could equally well have hidden genuine guilt on his part if he had been privy to a murder. What had killed her? A lethal combination of Nembutal and chloral hydrate, or of analysis and lovers' passion? The essential question for Miner was whether Greenson had set the scene for a suicide, then covered up the traces of an unnatural death. This wouldn't necessarily prove his complicity in murder, unless complicity begins when one covers up a crime, as Freud wrote in one of his last articles, often quoted by Greenson in the UCLA lectures Miner attended. But why would Greenson have done that? Did Marilyn's death reflect a political imperative or a subversive movement, or was it simply the logical conclusion of psychoanalysis's failure to save the movie star?

Miner rang Greenson – there were questions he needed to ask. He wanted to hear the whole story.

'What story?' Greenson replied. 'You know there's never just one story. There's only ever different stories combined into a narrative. I'm not going to tell you the story of the last years or hours of Marilyn's life, or even the story of my experiences. Nor will I expect you to believe everything I tell you is true, just that it's necessary. You'll hear her voice on the tapes – and mine, if I can add anything, but really they speak for themselves. Anyway, come over. I'll look forward to reliving it all with you, the most beautiful and terrible years of my life. Come at five, after the funeral.'

Miner didn't waste any time when he got to Greenson's house. He barely waited to sit down before asking, 'Why did you say "Marilyn Monroe has committed suicide" at first?'

'I didn't when I called the police. I said "Marilyn Monroe has died from an overdose", which didn't mean someone else couldn't have given her the drugs. It was only then that I said she'd taken her life . . . or her death, maybe. Still, why would I say that? They wouldn't have understood that it's possible to want to die because you're disgusted by death rather than life – the bitter death that makes you drink to forget, that hides in the panic attacks that make you nauseous. We'll never know the truth about what happened because suicide and murder are only mutually exclusive hypotheses when you're dealing with conscious acts and motives. In the unconscious, suicide is virtually always a form of murder, and murder can sometimes be a form of suicide. Marilyn told me once, "I am not afraid of dying. That happened a long time ago." I said, "Everyone is afraid of death because it's the unknown." And, of course, a belief in paradise and immortality is a form of consolation for this fear that we all experience to differing degrees. And, of course, I accept that if one is desperate and in agony, one can avail oneself of this consolation. But I absolutely reject the proposition that one can live any sort of good life by relying on a notion of immortality. We're all afraid of death, but the only decent way to confront it is to live well. Someone who has lived well, who has had a good, rich life, can face death. He fears it, of course, but he goes to meet it and he dies honourably. Yes, it's true, I do think the only immortality we can hope for is to live on in the memories of others.'

'Who are you talking about now? Who are you talking to?' Miner interrupted, dumbfounded by Greenson's lecture.

At the time of Miner's questioning, Greenson had fifteen years ahead of him in which to remember Marilyn and to confront his own mortality. At a UCLA extension division programme entitled 'Violent Death' in October 1971, he gave a lecture called 'The Dread and Love of Death'. 'It is my contention,' he said, 'that one of the keys to understanding man's contradictory reactions and behaviour to death stems from that fact that he is fascinated by death. To be fascinated means that one is ensnared and capti-vated and robbed of one's good judgement because one is flooded by a variety of contrary feelings and impulses, which cannot be disentangled or integrated because some of these reactions are conscious and others unconscious. Death mobilises dread, loathing and hate, but it may also be appealing, glorious and irresistible.' He quoted Freud – 'It is indeed impossible to imagine our own death; and whenever we attempt to do so we can perceive that we are in fact still present as spectators' – then explained that the reason the most popular films are full of images of death is precisely because it is inconceivable. Concluding his introduc-tory remarks, he noted 'that man is also able to kill himself, an act which is far more widespread and frequent than we ever dreamed of'. Marilyn had said to Greenson one day, 'Killing oneself is something that belongs to us. A privilege, not a sin or a crime. A right, even if it doesn't entitle one to anything.' Later he had found out about a note she had written to Natasha Lytess before attempting to commit suicide with an overdose of Nembutal in 1950, in which she left her the only thing of value she possessed – a fur stole. She'd also tried to kill herself during the filming of *Some Like It Hot* in 1959. Two years later he was convinced he personally had rescued her during the filming of *The Misfits*.

Quoting e. e. cummings, who died the same year as Marilyn – 'dying is fine) but Death/?o/baby' – Greenson contrasted the process of dying with the state of death. He spoke of a patient who had tried to kill himself to avoid dying and suggested that a fear of dying can co-exist with a desire to be dead. He mentioned another patient who had made him promise that, if she was fatally ill, either he or a doctor she was also fond of would sit by her bedside, even if she was totally unconscious, until they were absolutely certain of her being dead. He didn't cite Marilyn by name, but she might well have been who he was thinking of, because she also considered death essentially as another form of solitude, although possibly a little harder and longer than the one she was used to. She had played chess with death all her life, and in the end she had lost.

Ralph Greenson always sought to justify the role he had played in Marilyn's life and death. In Vienna in the summer of 1971, he met Paul Moor, an international journalist and musician. They talked mainly about music, but also about Marilyn a little. 'Her prime need,' Greenson assured him, 'was the warmth and affection our family could give her. She had never experienced it as a child, and her fame made it impossible when she was older.' Soon afterwards, he said on German television, 'The most beautiful people can believe they are desired, but never that they are loved.'

Santa Monica, Franklin Street
8 August 1962

Night fell as John Miner continued to question Greenson.

'You just have to tell me the facts, Doctor,' he said. 'I'll do the interpreting, if that's all right.'

'I'll tell you what I've already told the police countless times,' Greenson said. 'On Saturday I went to see my patient at one or so in the afternoon, and then returned to conduct my afternoon sessions from five to seven in the evening. At twelve-thirty Eunice Murray called, as I had asked her to do if there was ever a problem. I picked the phone up after a few rings and heard her say "Come, it's very urgent." I told her I'd be there in a quarter of an hour. The bedroom was locked but I could see a light under the door. I went back outside to see in through a window, which was also locked, and took a dishcloth and broke the glass. There were no bars, so I put my hand through, unlatched the window and climbed into the room. Marilyn was lying face down, naked, on the blue bed sheets. She still had the phone, "her best friend", in her right hand. Then I opened the door and let Mrs Murray in.'

A couple of things gave Miner pause. Greenson couldn't have seen a light under the door because the bedroom carpet was too thick for any to filter through. The door couldn't have been locked either: Marilyn wouldn't have stood for it after her incarceration in Payne Whitney. He guessed Greenson had been too dazed to remember the details accurately, or maybe he had simply dispensed with whatever wouldn't work in a script. The unnerving gleam of light, the locked door, the shadowy terrace, the heroically smashed window, the pool's blue light catching on the splinters of glass: none of it was necessary as far as her death was concerned, but it made for a good exterior night shot. Which didn't mean Greenson had something to hide, only that he had something to show. John Miner decided not to pull him up on the inaccuracies in his story.

Greenson fell silent, letting the scene play itself out in his mind. I broke the window as she said she had when she was hospitalised in New York. Why did she throw that chair? To get out of the room or into herself, to pass through the mirror? Why did I break the garden window? Finally to see the woman who had killed me with her death and whose body I could never really look at? Did I want to join her on the other side? What about our chess-board? Where's that now she's dead?

Haunted by his black and white memories, Greenson visualised the glass chessboard. If I were to tell the story of what really happened, I'd call it *Marilyn: Living and Dying*, like Schur, or *The Marilyn Defence*, like Nabokov. It wouldn't be a true story, the course of a single life followed from birth to death. It would be more like a chaotic set of points of force. A chess problem revealing how the pieces had moved on a board. A web of actions, reactions, manoeuvres, failings, mistakes, betrayals, selfishness and an unattainable forgiveness, all overseen by an improbable god. And the truth of it would lie in the silences between the words.

Riled by Greenson's remorseful silence, Miner asked, 'Why did you meet the toxicologist R. J. Abernethy before he drew up his report on August thirteenth and try to steer him towards the suicide theory?'

'She didn't want to die. She had too many plans. Only the hopeless make an effective job of killing themselves.'

'What about the journal that's meant to have disappeared in the clean-up after her body was taken to the morgue?'

'The red diary. Red like me and my crypto-Communist friends. It'll look more realistic in the script. The colour of spilled blood. It works better in Technicolor.'

'If I asked you "Who killed Marilyn Monroe?", what would your answer be?'

'I don't know. Psychoanalysis must have played a part. It didn't kill her, as the anti-Freudians and anti-Semites say, but it didn't help her survive either.'

Greenson had nothing more to add, although Miner waited, but a note probably dating from late summer 1978 was found in his papers after his death:

> I'll never write 'The MM Case'. I don't have the words.
> It's like in those movies when the images on screen are too
> powerful and suddenly I can't hear a word anyone's
> saying.
>   My God, the way you can delude yourself! Self-analysis
> – what a chimera. I was blamed, and I blame myself, for
> taking Marilyn into our household and making her a
> virtual member of the family. Did I kill her? Or did
> psychoanalysis, as people are starting to say? When they
> say it was the hold my family had over her that killed her,

they don't see that maybe it was my other family that was the problem: Freud and Co.

I want to understand the kinship ties, the lines of descent in the family I unwittingly made Marilyn a part of; she didn't have a clue herself of course. Are the sins of the fathers really visited on their children? How many generations does it go on for?

I'll try to describe the psychoanalytic family we were both ensnared in, but I've got to do it as a chart. I need plans and diagrams to see it all – maybe it's my scientific training, or maybe I need to explore the territory between us, visualise the space of ideas and actions around us. Some things you can only understand when you have a visual image of them.

Marilyn didn't know anything about my psychoanalytic or my private life, but it may still have left its mark on her. All her other analysts were close to Anna Freud. In her imagination, and ours, she was one of us, a member of the family of European Jewish exiles in California. Even the house I got her to buy so she could feel at home for once was next to Hanna Fenichel's, the widow of my second analyst. But this is the strangest connection: Anna Freud told me that when Joseph Kennedy was the American ambassador in London, he arranged for Marianne Kris to emigrate to the States in 1940. Marianne was Marilyn's analyst, Marilyn was JFK's mistress, then Marianne became Jackie's analyst.

I feel dizzy. I'm going to have to stop.

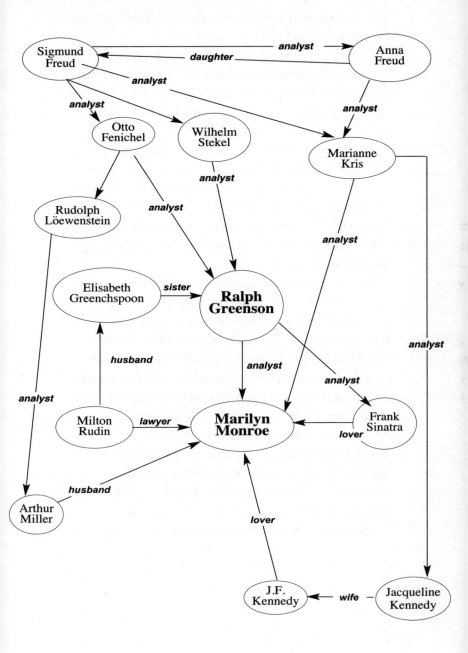

Beverly Hills, Roxbury Drive
November 1978

'Milton, do you mind reading what I've written about our leading lady?'

'You won't be able to say anything about her. You're the last person who could; you're still caught up in the whole thing. Don't think you can step out of the story somehow and uncover the truth of it. It was a whole galaxy of affects and interests and people and relationships. You were both prisoners of psychoanalysis.'

'You don't need to remind me of all the connections. I've mapped out the settings and actors. You don't know the half of it. Look at this . . .'

'That's an odd expression. An analyst would say "Listen to this." Anyway . . .'

'All right, listen, if you'd rather, and don't interrupt. Marilyn was analysed by Marianne Kris, who had previously been analysed by Anna Freud, who also briefly analysed Marilyn. Anna Freud had been analysed by her father, who had also been Marianne Kris, Otto Fenichel and Wilhelm Stekel's analyst. The last two were my analysts, so I'm Freud's grandson twice over. Fenichel was Rudolf Löwenstein's analyst, who was Arthur Miller's analyst, Marilyn's third husband. I was Frank Sinatra's analyst, her lover. This is the milieu Marilyn was analysed in—'

'It's not a milieu,' Wexler interrupted, 'it's a structure. Which means that these are not just sociological coincidences. They are incestuous, psychological ties that make up a system – a web, a network, whatever you want to call it – within which Marilyn's psychological experiences and analyses ran their course. And when your patient died, the system exploded. I've thought a lot about that photo that was taken on the *Manitou* four days after her funeral. JFK's on the yacht with his brother-in-law Peter Lawford, his sister Patricia Kennedy, who was Marilyn's great friend, and Pat Newcomb, who did her press and was with her on the last morning of her life. If you look at those rows of white teeth and actors' smiles under the star-spangled banner, various things become clear. First: you're not in the photo. Second: you could have taken it, because you're the link between everyone in the photo. Third: a tragedy was always going to part what Marilyn had joined. Death was always going to disperse that galaxy.'

This was the last thing Wexler said to Greenson. Over the following months, Greenson stopped seeing or talking to his colleagues, not that he could have explained why.

Neither analyst was in a position to be objective about 'the Marilyn case'. Like all analytic case studies, it was essentially a fictional construct, a spiral of conflicting interpretations, a trail followed in every conceivable direction. Not one of its facts, even now, is set in stone. Perhaps more information will come to light that will shuffle the cards once again and fragment the narrative into a myriad of vignettes, opinions and uncertainties. It is, after all, a legend. A story is only true if someone believes it, and it changes at every telling. A case study is not a novel that says what happened: it is, among other things, an analyst's fictional self-representation. You can't fully detach the analyst's life from the patient's, and what is said in public bears no relation to how the particular lives intertwined in private. Even when some degree of the private becomes public, you still don't get any closer to the truth. What is known simply changes to incorporate these new elements and thereby create a new version of the legend. No one will ever know anything about what really happened. Psychoanalysis doesn't reveal the truth about the people who experience it. It just gives them a version of who and what they are that they can live with, and says how things might have happened.

Los Angeles, Hillside Memorial Park Cemetery
November 1979

Taking a seat opposite the journalist he'd commissioned to co-write his memoirs, Wexler slowly began telling his life story.

'Before I cross the final threshold . . . I'm eighty now, for goodness' sake . . . I'm going to take a look in the rear-view mirror at all the strange, confused, pathetic things that went on in "the Marilyn years". You've no idea what analysis was like in Hollywood in those days. The directors were on our couches, and we were writing scripts for them. Freud thought you could read his case histories like novels. Romi – Ralph Greenson – wanted his case histories to be like movies he'd directed. I preferred having someone tell me their story and turn it into a script there and then – with a little bit of direction, naturally. But of course I owe Romi a huge debt. He introduced me to the whole show-business crowd. We'd go for brunch on Sundays at the writer and producer Dore Schary's house, where LA's starriest would gather. Romi and I hit it off straight away and we decided to share offices. We worked together, we compared cases, we co-authored articles. When Romi went on vacation, I'd fill in for him.'

'What was he like?'

'I'll get to that. I've often wanted to make a picture about a movie-stars' analyst, in the Hollywood I knew when the Psychoanalytic Society was after me. I don't know if the public would go for something like that these days, let alone a producer. A picture? Who's in it? Who's it for? Who cares? But if I did make it, I'd open with an aerial shot of a sea of umbrellas and a bald head in the middle. That was me, yesterday, as the heavens opened, saying goodbye to the friend I'd lost. Actually we'd lost each other a long time ago. It didn't happen yesterday.

'Romeo's funeral at the Hollywood Forever Cemetery on Santa Monica Boulevard was a farce, like all funerals. I took a bitter delight in replaying all the old scenes in my mind and trying to remember the last time we saw each other . . . No, don't worry, it's my age, it's not tears. I'm legally blind. Clinically, my vision is nil. A blind psychoanalyst is simply taking the Oedipus complex to its logical conclusion, after all. You can't imagine how little I miss my sight. I don't watch movies any more, I remember them.

'Anyway, as I was saying, if I made a film about yesterday's ceremony, it would go: "NOVEMBER 1979" in bold. General shot of cemetery, then cut to a wide shot of a funeral plaque: "RALPH GREENSON", and a voiceover of an old man saying, "They called me Romi. I wanted to be laid to rest in the graveyard of the stars. As for her – well, she's in Westwood Memorial Park. I've never gone back to her plaque. I don't have a handprint in the cement on Hollywood Boulevard or a bronze star on the Walk of Fame. I'm a low-level star, not one of those ones you see for centuries after they've burned out."'

Milton Wexler had said his farewells to Ralph Greenson in the rain and fog the previous day. Concerned about appearances, images and symbols to the last, Greenson had wanted his remains to rest in Hillside Memorial Park mausoleum, surrounded by movie celebrities. When Wexler saw the urn containing Romi's ashes in its niche in the wall, he felt too intense a mixture of hatred and tenderness to comprehend that he'd lost someone he loved. He decided that the only thing you can do when a friend dies is hate him, resent him for abandoning you and think of all the mean things you couldn't say when he was alive.

Poor Romi, he thought, as he left the mausoleum where Greenson resided behind a black marble slab, he didn't understand much about this profession. His colleagues didn't really understand him either. The homage given by Robert Stoller echoed in Wexler's mind:

Anyone can sense the power of that love in the many papers and books he published – especially his great *The Technique and Practice of Psychoanalysis*, and the collected papers in *Explorations in Psychoanalysis*. And when we read them, from the very first to the very last – with their original, mischievous, gentle, provocative, outrageous, erudite, funny, empathic, warm, forceful, inquisitive, steadfast, modest, abrasive, exhibitionistic, shy, and brave parts – then even a stranger is at least grazed by Greenson's presence.

For he could only think and write by pouring himself out, searching for the sources of mental life in the living, sentient experience. Only from that bountiful though mysterious well did he then – later, carefully, with roots in the realities of the quickened analytic treatment – turn to theory . . . Then a catastrophe struck. Immediately following a routine pacemaker replacement, Greenson's heart threw an embolus, instantly shutting down his most joyous aspect, the capacity to communicate with words. For some months, he could not talk, write, or read, and – most awful – he lost a priceless essence: he had stopped dreaming. So he found the therapists, the will, and the vigour and put himself back together: he learned to talk, to write, to read. One morning, on awakening, he remembered he had dreamed. With that, he could return to his delight – clinical work – and to its gift: his thinking and writing on the nature of psychoanalysis. Though speech never returned quite to normal, he again, with a quiet bravery (a counterpoint to his flamboyance when the issues were small), gave presentations, discussed others' papers, and participated on panels. But he was forced to give way, step by step. His heart could no longer support him. Finally there was nothing left. Work and Love. Greenson's life suggests a small addendum: when one's life is well lived, work is love.

'A labour of love. Maybe,' Wexler resumed, as the cogs of the journalist's tape recorder spun. 'Analysis is that in a way . . . in many ways. But you always wonder: who does the analyst stand for in the transference? And also, in the counter-transference, who does the analyst take himself for? The patient's father, mother, child? Romi wasn't a meek and mild humanist. In a way, he was the opposite of Stoller's portrait of him yesterday. He didn't practise the talking cure – his was a cure by drama, tragedy. He was a violent soul, a tiger that liked to trap its prey, a wolf that cried too obviously for anyone to believe him. He often said a strange thing: "Nothing is harder than to make people believe something you really feel." He didn't believe in anything except his capacity to make others believe. Nothing was sacred for him, not analysis, or psychiatry, or psychology, or ordinary social relationships. He questioned everything, dared everything. His contempt for rules and limits was what made him attractive. He was an actor, always on stage, always rewriting his part. A gambler. That's what I would have said at his grave if I'd been asked to speak.'

'What about his analysis of Marilyn Monroe?'

'A word that often cropped up recently in his conversation was "affliction". He talked about his adaptation of Fitzgerald's *Tender Is The Night*. Two people who destroy one another, analyst and patient. The truth is, he didn't understand what happened between the two of them. Perhaps he had been too much of a doctor, a man of the body, to be able to listen to Marilyn's suffering without wanting to cure it at any cost. And too much of an actor also to be an analyst through and through. But there was something else, I think. There's a conflict between words and images in all of us. Maybe, in the end, Marilyn was freed from the necessity of just being an image while images ended up overpowering Romi. He'd have liked to make movies, been an *auteur*, an artist. But he didn't ever dare. He gave his opinions from the wings, whispering suggestions about dialogue, composition, shots, adaptations. It got on scriptwriters' and directors' nerves, but they had no choice. They had to accept the good doctor's interventions if they wanted his patient to be the subject, or rather the object, of their images. Images brought Romi to his knees. Then at the end, as you know, words abandoned him too. Fate is cruel: it gave him silence, and it has given me darkness. The word and the dream, the twin shores on which analysis founders, have summoned us at the end of our lives. The images took him, and all I have left is the sound of voices. Write that down. It's good, isn't it?'

'Shall we move on to her now?' the journalist suggested abruptly. 'You treated her too for a while, I believe.'

Wexler fell silent, then drew a deep breath. 'I am the survivor of an ugly story, like all stories that are made up of dreams and money, power and death. Poor Romi! He would have loved to play the lead role as the love interest, or at least a supporting one. He didn't realise he was going to be merely an extra in Marilyn's life. With a lot of screen time, sure: the last person to talk to her while she was alive, and the first, as far as anyone knows, to see her dead. Supporting role's unfair, though: he was already a star on the lecture circuit before he started analysing her, and his couch was a must for any aspiring member of the movie élite. But Marilyn's death broke him. He survived, but he was never the same again. There was a secret of some kind between them, a kind of pact whereby each said to the other, "I won't die so long as I'm under your spell."'

The day after Greenson died, his son entrusted Milton Wexler with the task of sorting through his papers and giving whatever he saw fit to UCLA's psychiatry department. Wexler spent days, with an assistant, going through them. In a file of carefully collated article drafts and random notes from some of the thousands of sessions Greenson had conducted with patients, they found this note, which his colleague seemed to have drafted before a police examination.

> It was in January 1960 that Marilyn Monroe first came to consult me. She told me I was her fourth analyst, but her first 'male analyst'. I didn't know I would be the last (I don't count Milton Wexler who stepped in for a few weeks in the spring of 1962). She was in such a fragile physical and psychological state that I knew it would be touch and go and

The rest was missing.

Wexler remembered Greenson's habit of comparing analysis with chess. One day, seeing Wexler obviously bored by his talk of opening gambits, pincer movements and so on, Greenson had burst out, 'But Freud's the one who compares analysis to chess. Shall I read you what he says?'

388

He had rushed out to his office and come back moments later holding a crumpled sheet of paper containing quotations he'd clearly copied from an article. Almost as if he were declaiming verse, he read, "'Anyone who tries to learn the noble game of chess from books will soon discover that only the openings and end-games admit of an exhaustive systematic presentation and that the infinite variety of moves which develop after the opening defy any such description. This gap in instruction can only be filled by a diligent study of games fought out by masters. The rules which can be laid down for the practice of psycho-analytical treatment are subject to similar limitations. Sigmund Freud, 1913.'" Greenson spoke in a state of wild elation, almost on the verge of tears.

He carried on reading as Wexler watched, stunned. "'For it is really too sad that in life it should be as it is in chess, where one false move may force us to resign the game for lost, but with the difference that we can start no second game, no rematch. Sigmund Freud, 1915.'"

Wexler wasn't listening. He marched out of the office and slammed the door.

Sitting there in front of that chaotic mass of papers, after more years than he cared to count, Milton Wexler shook himself out of his reverie and began thinking things he hadn't been able to articulate while Marilyn was alive or when he talked to Greenson. He thought about the game of chess and saw the knight's dashing progress, leaping over squares, advancing on two axes, vertical and horizontal, always landing on a different-coloured square from the one he'd set off from. He thought about the black queen, Marilyn's implacable awareness of the horror of life, and her mother. Marilyn had mirrored her mother's search for sexual perfection, her knack of catching men, then jettisoning them when they'd served their purpose, her fear of ageing, the difference between who she was and what she saw in the mirror. Like her mother, Marilyn might have panicked at the prospect of becoming less desirable, the possible fate of any woman who becomes a mother. Greenson hadn't seen the parallels between her role in *Something's Got to Give* and her experiences, the brutal echoes of Gladys Baker's unhappy, unforgettable life. The return of the lost mother, one of the few scenes Marilyn had filmed after her analyst had gone to Europe, was a replay of the moment in her childhood when she had seen her mother, whom she thought was dead, emerge from the mental institution. Perhaps, Wexler thought, becoming a mother had tipped Gladys Baker over into madness, and perhaps not becoming a mother at the age of thirty-six yet having to play one had done the same to Marilyn Monroe. A mother whom her children did not recognise and who would not reveal herself to them. She was said to have become pregnant during filming, not known who the father was, and to have had an abortion after being fired. But, then, so many things were said about her.

There'd been no winner in the game of chess between the movie star and her analyst. Who had killed Marilyn? Not Romi, thought Wexler. Too much of a coward. Who, then? Norma Jeane, as some people said, or her mother, Gladys? Marilyn's story begins with a pane of glass through which the little Norma Jeane is watching her mother coming to visit the adoptive family she has left her with. Then a mirror, in which Gladys examines her own beauty, while the little girl who does not know who she's named after watches her mother looking at herself. And so the story unfolds, glass pieces moving across a glass chessboard from a fairy tale, like Snow White and her stepmother.

From the start the white queen (a queen only in her dreams at first) struggles with the black queen (whose dark madness is still to come, but all the images she has seen in negative have already taken their toll). Is that why she wanted to be a platinum blonde, so she is not like Snow White, with her pale skin, cherry-red lips, black eyebrows and hair? She has no choice anyway. She grows inexorably into a young woman who's terrified when the glass eye of the camera does not desire her, and panic-stricken when it does. Her only resource is to project herself onto the screen, the mirror for her dreams. In fairy tales, what kills the daughter's beauty? The stepmother with the poisoned comb, the apple of sin, which brings knowledge and sexuality when she is older, work and suffering. Who won, the white queen or the black? Marilyn had written in her notebook: 'White is passivity, the passivity of the person who is looked at, who's trapped. Black is the pupil of the eye, the screen when the movie ends, the heart of the man who leaves you.'

Shaking himself, Wexler thought back to when Romi was dying. He had muttered incomprehensibly the last time he'd seen him – Wexler had only caught the occasional word: 'Not the white queen . . . two black knights . . . diagonal . . . bishop . . .'

Santa Monica, Franklin Street
8 *August 1962*

Rather than being angry at Miner's insistent questioning, Greenson appeared nauseous, sad, defeated. Without a word, he turned on the first tape.

> Ever since you let me be in your home and meet your
> family, I've thought about how it would be if I were your
> daughter instead of your patient. I know you couldn't do
> it while I'm your patient, but after you cure me, maybe
> you could adopt me. Then I'd have the father I've always
> wanted and your wife whom I adore would be my mother,
> and your children, brothers and sisters. No, Doctor, I
> won't push it. But it's beautiful to think about it. I guess
> you can tell I'm crying. I'll stop now for a little bit . . .

Miner saw that the psychoanalyst's face was covered with tears and suggested they stop the tape. Greenson shrugged.

'You were very close to her, Doctor. How do you feel about her death?'

'You don't understand. You can't understand that she set me free and condemned me in all perpetuity. I lost her just as she almost reached me. Language was stirring in her. At last, she was talking to me, after almost three years. She was looking life in the face, she wasn't staring back at the dark road behind her . . .'

'What will stay with you about her?'

'Not her image, I tell you, not that vision that made me look away and hurt as only real beauty can. Not her image, no – her voice. That melancholic, ghostly voice singing "Happy birthday, Mr President. . ." I heard it again yesterday on TV – it was on every channel. You know, we work only with the voice in psychoanalysis. It is no coincidence Freud came up with this strange system that splits the patient's body in two. On the one hand, there's the patient's image, his mass, the way he occupies space, and on the other, there's his voice, which we listen to and which leaves its mark in time all the more effectively because there's no image. Analysis is a little like silent movies, where scenes followed the intertitles on a black background. Words bring things into being. It is no coincidence either that I was so sceptical about movies that claimed to portray psychoanalysis, to let people see the invisible work of words. No coincidence – Fate arranges things so well – that the traces Freud left are either images without words, hours of silent celluloid, or talks recorded for radio.' Greenson grew vehement: 'And it's no coincidence that Marilyn Monroe recorded the tapes you just listened to in darkness, at night, and didn't say those things in our sessions when I could see her. Marilyn knew that reality lies in a voice when it breaks loose from images. One day, she said to me, "You don't need to use your voice in a special way. If you think of something sexual, your voice naturally follows suit." She had two voices in fact, the one in her movies – studied, tamed, a wayward murmur or sigh, like someone waking up from a dream – and the one she used off-screen, calmer and clearer. In her sessions, she switched between the two, but she had stopped using her actress's voice towards the end. Even in her last film, she was using her off-screen voice more.'

Greenson made an effort to compose himself, then continued his monologue. 'There was a struggle going on in her from the start between her voice and her skin. She thought her skin was the only thing that could speak, by being seen or touched or bruised. I don't know . . . I don't know what happened, and this may shock you, but I think she was really getting better at the end, I think she was starting to talk ... Still, I'm boring you with my stories. I'll leave you with her, with her voice, without any images to get in the way. Listen to the tapes as many times as you want. I'm going back to my patients. Take notes if you think it'll be useful, but don't take the tapes out of this room.'

Miner settled down in an armchair facing the picture window that was golden in the setting sun. Finally there was no possibility of seeing Marilyn. Now he could hear truths about her without complicating them by looking at her beauty, as everyone always did. He decided he was going to play that last tape again; he was never going to stop playing it. He pressed REWIND.

Downtown Los Angeles, West 1st Street
April 2006

Forger Backwright is alone in front of his computer in the *Los Angeles Times* building. Every light on every floor is on. After listening to John Miner's recording again, he decides to publish the contents of Marilyn's last sessions without raising any doubts as to the veracity of the former deputy coroner's transcriptions. He figures he doesn't need to explain the real reason Miner had broken his promise to Greenson – that it wasn't because he wanted to salvage his reputation but because he was in financial trouble. He won't let on that the old man had struck a hard bargain, or that personally he is sceptical of what Marilyn is reported to have said in her last sessions, especially the light, hopeful note in everything she had confided to her psychoanalyst. He won't dwell on how uncannily her words echo what Dr Greenson himself had repeatedly said and written. By implying that she was killed, the tapes not only say – between the words, as it were – that she hasn't committed suicide, but also that he hasn't killed her. It isn't the radiantly optimistic portrait of Marilyn that gives Backwright pause so much as the representation of

Greenson as wholly indifferent to money: the faithful husband, committed analyst and attentive father to the lost little girl he had helped.

Forger Backwright isn't convinced about who Marilyn was either. He replays the film he's managed to download after searching for it for ages on BitTorrent: Marilyn in a black slip doing dirty things in the flickering light of a raddled piece of celluloid. It's strange, he thinks. If it is her, if this pornographic sequence really shows Marilyn Monroe when she was still only Norma Jeane Mortenson, then she looks older in this piece of film, when she hasn't turned twenty, than she does naked fifteen years later in the last take of *Something's Got to Give*. Film's skin is like a person's: it grows slack, overwhelmed by time. Death has already touched these old images, but they are markedly less eloquent about sex and its weight of unhappiness than any words might have been. Staring at them, his mind full of the tapes he has just listened to and the thousands of pages he has read about her final years, Backwright feels like a film editor trying to construct a story with a beginning and an end out of scraps that make no sense. He knows the truth lies only in the contradictions between these different takes, the fragments of dialogue, the punchlines that didn't make it into the final movie, the jump cuts and jerky camera movements.

The morning edition has been put to bed, and the journalist isn't working any more, although he's still here in front of his screen, in the middle of the night. Backwright has decided to keep his questions to himself for now, and to give them the only form that can come close to a semblance of truth. He thinks of the novel he began eight months earlier, after studying the memories and recordings John Miner had either relayed or invented. He'll finish it now. Replay the whole murky story. He

isn't sure about the title: 'MARILYN'S LAST SESSIONS'? He'll
see. He brings the first page of the manuscript up on the screen
and starts to read:

> *Los Angeles, Downtown, West 1st Street*
> *August 2005*
>
> *Rewind the tape. Rerun the story. Replay Marilyn's last*
> *session. The end: that's always where a story starts.*

Forger Backwright adds 'REWIND' as the title.

Further Reading

Like most people who have written about Marilyn Monroe, the author has not had access to private sources of letters and documents concerning the two main protagonists of this book.

At the Department of Special Collections at the University of California at Los Angeles, the letters between Ralph Greenson and Marilyn Monroe's previous analysts are not available to the general public. At the library of the Los Angeles Psychoanalytic Society, everything related to Monroe's analysis is inaccessible.

The dialogue attributed to Marilyn Monroe is attested by different sources, including biographies and interviews. The contents of the tapes Dr Greenson is alleged to have had in his possession are quoted from their transcripts in *Victim, The Secret Tapes of Marilyn Monroe*, by Matthew Smith, and the 5 August 2005 edition of the *Los Angeles Times*.

The clinical and theoretical statements made by Dr Greenson are drawn from his published works and his archives at UCLA. Donald Spoto, Marilyn Monroe's biographer, was able to consult them and they are quoted from the American edition of his biography. The same is true of the long letter sent by Monroe to Dr Greenson in February 1961.

Billy Wilder's recollections come from Cameron Crowe's collection of interviews.

The dialogue, reported speech and letters are either invented or quoted from the articles and books contained in the following bibliography:

Arnold, Eve, *Marilyn Monroe*, Harry N. Abrams, 1987

Barris, George, *Marilyn, Her Life in Her Own Words*, Citadel Press, 1995

Berthelsen, Detlev, *Alltag bei Familie Freud; Die Erinnerungen der Paula Fichtl*, Hoffman & Campe, 1987

Brown, Peter Harry, and Patte B. Barham, *Marilyn, The Last Take*, Signet, 1992

Capote, Truman, *Music for Chameleons*, Random House, 1980

Churchwell, Sarah, *The Many Lives of Marilyn Monroe*, Granta Books, 2005

Crowe, Cameron, *Conversations with Billy Wilder*, Faber and Faber, 1995

Dienes, André de, *Marilyn mon amour*, St Martin's Press, 1985

—, *Marilyn*, Taschen, 2004

Farber, Stephen, and Mark Green, *Hollywood on the Couch*, William Morrow and Company, 1993

Freeman, Lucy, *Why Norma Jeane Killed Marilyn Monroe*, Hastings House, 1993

Greenson, Ralph, *The Technique and Practice of Psychoanalysis*, International Universities Press, 1967

—, *Explorations in Psychoanalysis*, International Universities Press, 1978

—, *On Loving, Hating and Living Well*, International Universities Press, 1993

Leaming, Barbara, *Marilyn Monroe*, Weidenfeld & Nicolson, 1998

Mailer, Norman, *Marilyn, Biography of Marilyn Monroe*, Coronet, 1974

Mecacci, Luciano, *Freudian Slips: The Casualties of Psychoanalysis from the Wolf Man to Marilyn Monroe*, Vagabond Voices, 2009

Monroe, Marilyn, *My Story*, Stein and Day, 1974

Oates, Joyce Carol, *Blonde*, Fourth Estate, 2000

Rosten, Norman, *Marilyn: A Very Personal Story*, Usborne, 1974

Sartre, Jean-Paul, *The Freud Scenario*, Verso, 1985

Schur, Max, *Freud: Living and Dying*, Chatto & Windus, 1972

Smith, Matthew, *Victim, The Secret Tapes of Marilyn Monroe*, Century, 2003

Spoto, Donald, *Marilyn Monroe, The Biography*, Chatto & Windus, 1993

Summers, Anthony, *Goddess: The Secret Lives of Marilyn Monroe*, Gollancz, 1985

Victor, Adam, *The Marilyn Encyclopedia*, The Overlook Press, 1999

Vitacco-Robles, Gary, *Cursum Perficio, Marilyn Monroe's Brentwood Hacienda, The Story of Her Final Months*, Writers Club Press, 2000

Weatherby, W. J., *Conversations with Marilyn*, Paragon House, 1976

Wexler, Milton, *A Look Through the Rear-view Mirror*, Xlibris Corporation, 2002

Wolfe, Donald H., *The Assassination of Marilyn Monroe*, Sphere, 1999

Young-Bruehl, Elisabeth, *Anna Freud*, Summit Books, 1988

Zolotow, Maurice, *Marilyn Monroe*, W. H. Allen, 1961

Permissions Acknowledgements

The publisher gratefully thanks the following organisations and individuals:

OneWest Publishing/Taschen for the use of excerpts from *Marilyn* by Andre de Dienes.

The Truman Capote Literary Trust for the use of excerpts from *Breakfast at Tiffany's* and *Music for Chameleons* by Truman Capote.

Warner Chappell Music for the use of lyrics from 'Dancing in the Dark' by Frank Sinatra.

W.W. Norton for the use of lines from 'Dying is Fine' by ee cummings.

Dr Daniel Greenson for the use of all published and archival material relating to Dr Ralph Greenson.

Personal Acknowledgements

All my gratitude goes to Martine Saada, without whom this book would never have come to be.